The Night Watch

ALSO BY SARAH WATERS
FROM CLIPPER LARGE PRINT

Affinity
Tipping the Velvet

The Night Watch

Sarah Waters

W F HOWES LTD

This large print edition published in 2006 by
W F Howes Ltd
Unit 4, Rearsby Business Park, Gaddesby Lane,
Rearsby, Leicester LE7 4YH

1 3 5 7 9 10 8 6 4 2

First published in the United Kingdom in 2006
by Virago Books

A CIP catalogue record for this book is available
from the British Library

ISBN 1 84632 414 9

Typeset by Palimpsest Book Production Limited,
Polmont, Stirlingshire
Printed and bound in Great Britain
by Antony Rowe Ltd, Chippenham, Wilts.

To Lucy Vaughan

1947

CHAPTER 1

*S*o *this*, said Kay to herself, *is the sort of person you've become: a person whose clocks and wrist-watches have stopped, and who tells the time, instead, by the particular kind of cripple arriving at her landlord's door.*

For she was standing at her open window, in a collarless shirt and a pair of greyish underpants, smoking a cigarette and watching the coming and going of Mr Leonard's patients. Punctually, they came – so punctually, she really could tell the time by them: the woman with the crooked back, on Mondays at ten; the wounded soldier, on Thursdays at eleven. On Tuesdays at one an elderly man came, with a fey-looking boy to help him: Kay enjoyed watching for them. She liked to see them making their slow way up the street: the man neat and dark-suited as an undertaker, the boy patient, serious, handsome – like an allegory of youth and age, she thought, as done by Stanley Spencer or some finicky modern painter like that. After them there came a woman with her son, a little lame boy in spectacles; after that, an elderly Indian lady with rheumatics. The little lame boy would sometimes stand scuffing up moss and dirt from the broken path to the house with his great boot, while his mother spoke with Mr Leonard in the hall. Once, recently, he'd looked up and seen Kay watching; and she'd heard him making a fuss on the stairs, then, about going on his own to the lavatory.

'Is it them angels on the door?' she had heard his mother say. 'Good heavens, they're only pictures! A great boy like you!'

Kay guessed it wasn't Mr Leonard's lurid Edwardian angels that frightened him, but the thought of encountering her. He must have supposed she haunted the attic floor like a ghost or a lunatic.

He was right, in a way. For sometimes she walked restlessly about, just as lunatics were said to. And other times she'd sit still, for hours at a time – stiller than a shadow, because she'd watch the shadows creeping across the rug. And then it seemed to her that she really might be a ghost, that she might be becoming part of the faded fabric of the house, dissolving into the gloom which gathered, like dust, in its crazy angles.

A train ran by, two streets away, heading into Clapham Junction; she felt the thrill and shudder of it in the sill beneath her arms. The bulb in a lamp behind her shoulder sprang into life, flick-ered for a second like an irritated eye, and then went out. The clinker in the fireplace – a brutal little fireplace; this had been a room for a servant, once – gently collapsed. Kay took a final draw on her cigarette, then pinched out the flame of it between her forefinger and thumb.

She had been standing at her window for more than an hour. It was a Tuesday: she'd seen a snub-nosed man with a wasted arm arrive, and had been waiting, in a vague kind of way, for the Stanley Spencer couple. But now she'd decided to give up on them. She'd decided to go out. The day was fine, after all: a day in the middle of a warm September, the third September after the war. She went through to the room, next to this one, that she used as a bedroom, and began to get changed.

The room was dim. Some of the window-glass had been lost, and Mr Leonard had replaced it with lino. The bed was high, with a balding candlewick bedspread: the sort of bed which turned your thoughts, not pleasantly, to the many people who must, over the years, have slept on it, made love on it, been born on it, died on it, thrashed around on it in fevers. It gave off a slightly sour scent, like the feet of worn stockings. But Kay was used to that, and didn't notice. The room was nothing to her but a place in which to sleep or to lie sleepless. The walls were empty, feature-less, just as they had been when she'd moved in. She'd never hung up a picture or put out books; she had no pictures or books; she didn't have much of anything. Only, in one of the corners, had she fixed up a length of wire; and on this, on wooden hangers, she kept her clothes.

The clothes, at least, were very neat. She picked

her way through them now and found a pair of nicely darned socks, and some tailored slacks. She changed her shirt to a cleaner one, a shirt with a soft white collar she could leave open at the throat, as a woman might.

But her shoes were men's shoes; she spent a minute polishing them up. And she put silver links in her cuffs, then combed her short brown hair with brushes, making it neat with a touch of grease. People seeing her pass in the street, not looking at her closely, often mistook her for a good-looking youth. She was regularly called 'young man', and even 'son', by elderly ladies. But if anyone gazed properly into her face, they saw at once the marks of age there, saw the white threads in her hair; and in fact she would be thirty-seven on her next birthday.

When she went downstairs she stepped as carefully as she could, so as not to disturb Mr Leonard; but it was hard to be soft-footed, because of the creaking and popping of the stairs. She went to the lavatory, then spent a couple of minutes in the bathroom, washing her face, brushing her teeth. Her face was lit up rather greenishly, because ivy smothered the window. The water knocked and spluttered in the pipes. The geyser had a spanner hanging beside it, for sometimes the water stuck completely – and then you had to bang the pipes about a bit to make it fire.

The room beside the bathroom was Mr Leonard's treatment-room, and Kay could hear, above the sound of the toothbrush in her own mouth and the splash of water in the basin, his passionate monotone, as he worked on the snub-nosed man with the wasted arm. When she let herself out of the bathroom and went softly past his door, the monotone grew louder. It was like the throb of some machine.

'Eric,' she caught, 'you must *hmm-hmm*. How can *buzz-buzz* when *hmm-buzz* whole again?'

She stepped very stealthily down the stairs, opened the unlatched front door, and stood for a moment on the step – almost hesitating, now. The whiteness of the sky made her blink. The day seemed limp, suddenly: not fine so much as dried out, exhausted. She thought she could feel dust, settling already on her lips, her lashes, in the corners of her eyes. But she wouldn't turn back. She had, as it were, her own brushed hair to live up to; her polished shoes, her cuff-links. She went down the steps and started to walk. She stepped like a person who knew exactly where they were going, and why they were going there – though the fact was, she had nothing to do, and no one to visit, no one to see. Her day was a blank, like all of her days. She might have been inventing the ground she walked on, laboriously, with every step.

She headed west, through well-swept, devastated streets, towards Wandsworth.

'No sign of Colonel Barker today, Uncle Horace,' said Duncan, looking up at the attic windows as he and Mr Mundy drew closer to the house.

7

He was rather sorry. He liked to see Mr Leonard's lodger. He liked the bold cut of her hair, her mannish clothes, her sharp, distinguished-looking profile. He thought she might once have been a lady pilot, a sergeant in the WAAF, something like that: one of those women, in other words, who'd charged about so happily during the war, and then got left over. 'Colonel Barker' was Mr Mundy's name for her. He liked to see her standing there, too. At Duncan's words he looked up, and nodded; but then he put down his head again and moved on, too out of breath to speak.

He and Duncan had come all the way to Lavender Hill from White City. They had to come slowly, getting buses, stopping to rest; it took almost the whole day to get here and home again afterwards. Duncan had Tuesday as his regular day off, and made the hours up on a Saturday. They were very good about it, at the factory where he worked. 'That boy's devoted to his uncle!' he'd heard them say, many times. They didn't know that Mr Mundy wasn't actually his uncle. They had no idea what kind of treatment he received from Mr Leonard; probably they thought he went to a hospital. Duncan let them think what they liked.

He led Mr Mundy into the shadow of the crooked house. The house always looked at its most alarming, he thought, when looming over you like this. For it was the last surviving building in what had once, before the war, been a long terrace; it still had the scars, on either side, where it had been attached to its neighbours, the zig-zag of phantom staircases and the dints of absent hearths. What held it up, Duncan couldn't imagine; he'd never quite been able to shake off the feeling, as he let himself and Mr Mundy into the hall, that he'd one day close the door a shade too hard and the whole place would come tumbling down around them.

So he closed the door softly; and after that the house seemed more ordinary. The hall was dim and rather hushed; there were hard-backed chairs set all the way around it, a coatless coat-rack, and two or three pallid-looking plants; the floor was a pattern of white-and-black tiles, some of which had got lost, exposing the grey cement beneath. The shade of the light was a lovely rose-coloured porcelain shell – meant for a gas-lamp, probably, but now fitted up with a bulb in a bakelite socket and a fraying brown flex.

Duncan noticed flaws and features like this; it was one of the pleasures of life for him. The earlier they arrived at the house, the more he liked it, for that gave him time to help Mr Mundy to a chair and then wander quietly around the hall, looking everything over. He admired the finely turned banisters, and the stair-rods with their tarnished brass ends. He liked the discoloured ivory knob on a cupboard door; and the paint on the skirting-boards, which had been combed to look like wood.

9

But at the back of the passage that led to the basement was a bamboo table, set out with tawdry ornaments; and amongst the plaster dogs and cats, the paperweights and majolica vases, was his favourite thing of all: an old lustre bowl, very beautiful, with a design of serpents and fruits. Mr Leonard kept dusty walnuts in it, with a pair of iron nutcrackers on the top, and Duncan never approached the bowl without feeling, as if in the fibres of his bones, the fatal little concussion that would occur if some careless person were to take the nutcrackers up and let them slip against the china.

The walnuts sat in the bowl today just as usual, however, the layer of dust upon them woolly, undisturbed; and Duncan had time, too, to look quite closely at a couple of pictures hanging crookedly on the wall – for everything hung crookedly, in this house. They turned out to be rather commonplace, with very ordinary Oxford frames. But that gave him a sense of pleasure, too – a different sort of pleasure – the pleasure he got from looking at a moderately handsome thing and thinking, *You're not mine, and I don't have to want you!*

When there was movement in the room upstairs, he stepped nimbly back to Mr Mundy's side. A door had opened on the landing, and he heard voices: it was Mr Leonard, seeing out the young man who always had the hour before them. Duncan liked seeing this man, almost as much as

10

he liked seeing Colonel Barker and the lustre bowl; for the man was cheery. He might be a sailor. 'All right, mates?' he said today, giving Duncan a bit of a wink. He asked what the weather was doing now, and enquired after Mr Mundy's arthritis – all the while removing a cigarette from its packet, then putting it to his mouth, taking out a box of matches and striking a light: all perfectly easily and naturally with one hand, while the other, undeveloped arm hung at his side.

Why did he come, Duncan always wondered, when he could get along so well just as he was? He thought that perhaps the young man wanted a sweetheart; for of course, the arm was something a girl might object to.

The young man tucked the box of matches back into his pocket and went on his way. Mr Leonard led Duncan and Mr Mundy upstairs – going slowly, of course; letting Mr Mundy set the pace.

'Blinking nuisance,' said Mr Mundy. 'What can you do with me? Put me on the scrap-heap.'

'Now, now!' said Mr Leonard.

He and Duncan helped Mr Mundy into the treatment-room. They lowered him into another hard-backed chair, took his jacket from him, made sure he was comfortable. Mr Leonard got out a black notebook and looked briefly inside it; then he sat facing Mr Mundy in a stiff chair of his own. Duncan went to the window and sat on a low sort of padded box that was there, with Mr Mundy's jacket in his lap. The window had a bitter-smelling

11

net curtain across it, slightly sagging from a wire. The walls of the room were done in lincrusta, painted a glossy chocolate brown.

Mr Leonard rubbed his hands together. 'So,' he said. 'How are we, since I saw you last?'

Mr Mundy ducked his head. 'Not too bright,' he said.

'The idea of pains, still?'

'Can't seem to shake them off at all.'

'But you've had no resort to false remedies of any kind?'

Mr Mundy moved his head again, uneasily. 'Well,' he admitted after a second, 'perhaps a little aspirin.'

Mr Leonard drew in his chin and looked at Mr Mundy as if to say: *Dear, dear.* 'Now, you know very well, don't you,' he said, 'what a person is like, who employs false remedies and spiritual treatment at the same time? He is like an ass pulled by two masters; he moves nowhere. You do know this, don't you?'

'It's only,' said Mr Mundy, 'so awfully sore—'

'Soreness!' said Mr Leonard, with a mixture of amusement and great contempt. He shook his chair. 'Is this chair sore, because it must support my weight? Why not, since the wood from which it is made is as material as the bone and muscle of your leg, which you say hurts from bearing *your* weight? It is because nobody believes that a chair *may* hurt. If you will only not believe in the hurt of your leg, that leg will become as negligible to you as wood is. Don't you know this?'

'Yes,' said Mr Mundy meekly.

'Yes,' repeated Mr Leonard. 'Now, let us make a start.'

Duncan sat very still. It was necessary to be very still and quiet through all of the session, but particularly now, while Mr Leonard was gathering his thoughts, gathering his strength, concentrating his mind so that he might be ready to take on the false idea of Mr Mundy's arthritis. He did this by slightly putting back his head and looking with great intensity, not at Mr Mundy, but at a picture he had hung over the mantelpiece, of a soft-eyed woman in a high-necked Victorian gown, whom Duncan knew to be the founder of Christian Science, Mrs Mary Baker Eddy. On the black frame of the picture someone – possibly Mr Leonard himself – had written a phrase, not very handily, in enamel paint. The phrase was: *Ever Stand Porter at the Gate of Thought.*

The words made Duncan want to laugh, every time: not because he found them especially comical, but simply because to laugh, just now, would be so dreadful; and he always, at this point, began to grow panicked at the thought of having to sit so silently, for so long: he felt he would be bound to make some sound, some movement – leap up, start shrieking, throw a fit . . . But it was too late. Mr Leonard had changed his pose – had leant forward and fixed Mr Mundy with his gaze.

13

And when he spoke again, he spoke in a whisper, intently, with a tremendous sense of urgency and belief.

'Dear Horace,' he said, 'you must listen to me. All that you think about your arthritis is untrue. You have no arthritis. You have no pain. You are not subject to those thoughts and opinions, which have illness and pain as a law and condition of matter . . . Dear Horace, listen. You have no fear. No memory frightens you. No memory makes you think misfortune will come to you again. You have nothing to fear, dear Horace. Love is with you. Love fills and surrounds you . . .'

The words went on and on – like a rain of gentle blows from a stern lover. It was impossible, Duncan thought – forgetting, now, his desire to laugh – not to want to surrender yourself to the passion of them; impossible not to want to be impressed, moved, persuaded. He thought of the young man with the wasted arm; he imagined the man sitting where Mr Mundy was now, being told, 'Love fills you', being told, 'You must not fear', and willing and willing his arm to lengthen, to flesh itself out. Could such a thing happen? Duncan wanted, for Mr Mundy's sake, and the young man's sake, to think that it could. He wanted it more than anything.

He looked at Mr Mundy. Soon after the start of the treatment he had closed his eyes; now, as the whispers went on, he began, very gently, to cry. The tears flowed thinly down his cheeks, they gathered at his throat and wet his collar. He made no attempt to catch them, but sat with his hands loosely in his lap, his neat, blunt fingers now and then twitching; and every so often he drew in his breath and let it out again in a great shuddering sigh.

'Dear Horace,' Mr Leonard was insisting, 'no mind has any power over you. I deny the power of thoughts of disorder over you. Disorder does not exist. I affirm the power of harmony over you, over every organ of you: the arms of you; the legs of you; the eyes and ears of you; the liver and kidneys of you; the heart and brain and stomach and loins of you. Those organs are perfect. Horace, hear me . . .'

He kept it up for forty-five minutes; then sat back, quite untired. Mr Mundy got out his hand-kerchief at last and blew his nose and wiped his face. But his tears had already dried; he stood without help, and seemed to walk a little easier, and be a little lighter in his mind. Duncan took him his jacket. Mr Leonard rose and stretched, had a sip of water from a glass. When Mr Mundy paid him, he took the money with an air of great apology.

'And tonight, of course,' he said, 'I shall include you in my evening benediction. You'll be ready for that? Shall we say, half-past nine?' For he had many patients, Duncan knew, whom he never saw: patients who sent him money, and whom he worked on from a distance, or by letter and telephone.

He shook Duncan's hand. His palm was dry, his

fingers soft and smooth as a girl's. He smiled, but his look was inward-seeming, like a mole's. He might, at that moment, have been blind.

And how awkward for him, Duncan thought suddenly, *if he were!*

The idea made him want to laugh again. When he and Mr Mundy were back on the path in front of the house, he did laugh; and Mr Mundy picked up his hilarity and began to laugh too. It was a sort of nervous reaction, to the room, the stillness, the barrage of gentle words. They caught one another's eye, as they left the shadow of the crooked house and walked towards Lavender Hill, and laughed like children.

'I shan't want a flighty sort of woman,' the man was saying. 'I had enough of that sort of thing with my last girl, I don't mind telling you.'

Helen said, 'We always advise our clients to keep as open a mind as possible, at this stage of things.'

The man said, 'Hmm. And an open wallet, too, I dare say.'

He wore a dark blue demob suit, already shiny at the elbows and the cuffs, and his face was sallow with a tired tropical tan. His hair was combed with fantastic neatness, the parting straight and white as a scar; but the oil had little crumbs of scurf caught in it, which kept drawing Helen's eye.

'I dated a WAAF once,' he was saying bitterly now. 'Every time we passed a jeweller's she'd just happen to turn her ankle—'

Helen drew out another sheet. 'What about this lady here? Let's see. Enjoys dressmaking and trips to the cinema.'

The man leant to look at the photograph and at once sat back, shaking his head. 'I don't care for girls in spectacles.'

'Now, remember my advice about the open mind?'

'I don't want to sound harsh,' he said, giving a quick glance at Helen's own rather sensible brown outfit. 'But a girl in spectacles – well, she's let herself down already. You've got to ask yourself what's going to go next.'

They went on like this for another twenty minutes; eventually, from the file of fifteen women that Helen had initially drawn up, they'd put together a list of five.

The man was disappointed, but hid his dismay in a show of aggression. 'So, what happens now?' he asked, pulling at his shiny cuffs. 'This lot are shown my ugly face, I suppose, and have to say whether or not they like the look of it. I can see already how that will turn out. Perhaps I should have had myself photographed with a five-pound note behind my ear.'

Helen imagined him at home that morning, choosing a tie, sponging his jacket, straightening and restraightening the parting in his hair.

She saw him down the stairs to the street. When she went back up to the waiting-room she looked at Viv, her colleague, and blew out her cheeks.

Viv said, 'Like that, was he? I did wonder. He

17

wouldn't do for our lady from Forest Hill, I suppose?'

'He's after someone younger.'

'Aren't they all?' Viv stifled a yawn. On the desk before her was a diary. She patted her mouth, looking over the page. 'We've no one, now,' she said, 'for nearly half an hour. Let's have a cup of tea, shall we?'

'Oh, let's,' said Helen.

They moved about more briskly, suddenly, than they ever did when dealing with clients. Viv opened the lowest drawer of a filing cabinet and brought out a neat little electric kettle and a teapot. Helen took the kettle down to the lavatory on the landing and filled it at the sink. She set it on the floor, plugged it into a socket in the skirting-board, then stood waiting. It took about three minutes to boil. The paper above the socket was rising, where steam had struck it in the past. She smoothed it down, as she did every day; it lay flat for a moment, then slowly curled back up.

The bureau was in two rooms above a wig-maker's, in a street behind Bond Street station. Helen saw the clients, individually, in the room at the front; Viv sat at her desk in the waiting-room, greeting them as they came in. There was a mismatched sofa and chairs, where people could sit when they came early. A Christmas cactus in a pot sent out occasional startling blooms. A low table held nearly current copies of *Lilliput* and *Reader's Digest*.

Helen had worked here since just after the end of the war; she'd taken it on as a temporary thing – something light-hearted, a contrast to her old job in a Damage Assistance department in Marylebone Town Hall. The routines were straightforward enough; she tried to do her best for the clients, and genuinely wished them well; but it was sometimes hard to remain encouraging. People came to look for new loves, but often – or so it seemed to her – only really wanted to talk about the loves that they had lost. Recently, of course, business had been booming. Servicemen, returning from overseas, found wives and girl-friends transformed out of all recognition. They came into the bureau still looking stunned. Women complained about their ex-husbands. 'He wanted me to stay in all the time.' 'He told me he didn't care for my friends.' 'We went back to the hotel we spent our honeymoon in, but it wasn't the same.'

The water boiled. Helen made the tea at Viv's desk and took the cups into the lavatory; Viv was in there already, and had raised the window. At the back of their building there was a fire-escape: if they climbed out they could reach a rusting metal platform with a low rail. The platform shud-dered as they moved about on it, the ladder heaving against its bolts; but the spot was a sun-trap, and they made straight for it whenever they had the chance. They could hear the ring of the street-door and telephone from there; and, like

19

hurdlers, had perfected a way of getting over the sill of the window with great speed and efficiency.

At this time of day the sun fell rather obliquely, but the bricks and metal it had been striking all morning still held its heat. The air was pearly with petrol fumes. From Oxford Street there came the steady grumble of traffic, and the *tap-tap* of workmen fixing roofs.

Viv and Helen sat down and carefully eased off their shoes, stretching out their legs – tucking in their skirts, in case the men from the wig-maker's should happen to come out and glance upwards – and working and turning their stockinged feet. Their stockings were darned at the toes and the heels. Their shoes were scuffed; everybody's were. Helen got out a packet of cigarettes and Viv said, 'It's my turn.'

'It doesn't matter.'

'I'll owe you, then.'

They shared a match. Viv put back her head and sighed out smoke. Then she looked at her watch.

'God! There's ten minutes gone already. Why does time never go so quickly when we've got the clients in?'

'They must work on the clocks,' said Helen. 'Like magnets.'

'I think they must. Just as they suck away at the life of you and me – suck, suck, suck, like great big fleas . . . Honestly, if you'd told me, when I was sixteen, that I should end up working in a place like this – well, I don't know what I would have thought. It wasn't what I had in mind at all. I wanted to be a solicitor's secretary . . .'

The words dissolved into another yawn – as if Viv hadn't the energy, even, to be bitter. She patted at her mouth with one of her slim, pale, pretty ringless hands.

She was five or six years younger than Helen, who was thirty-two. Her features were dark, and still vivid with youth; her hair was a rich brownish-black. Right now it lay bunched behind her head against the warm brick wall, like a velvet cushion.

Helen envied Viv her hair. Her own hair was light – or, as she thought of it, colourless; and it did that unforgivable thing – grew absolutely straight. She wore it waved, and the constant perming dried it out and made it brittle. She'd had it waved very recently: she could catch the faint stink of the chemicals every time she turned her head.

She thought over what Viv had said, about wanting to be a solicitor's secretary. She said, 'When I was young, I wanted to be a stable-girl.'

'A stable-girl?'

'You know, with horses, ponies. I'd never ridden a horse in my life. But I'd read something or other, I suppose, in a girl's annual or somewhere. I used to go trotting up and down the street, making clopping noises with my tongue.' She remembered the thrill of it, very clearly, and had an urge to get up, now, and try cantering up and down the fire-escape. 'My horse was called Fleet. He was

21

very fast and very muscular.' She drew on her cigarette, then added in a lower tone, 'God knows what Freud would say about it.'

She and Viv laughed, flushing slightly.

Viv said, 'When I was really young I wanted to be a nurse. Seeing my mother in the hospital put me off that, though . . . My brother wanted to be a magician.' Her gaze grew distant; she started to smile. 'I always remember. My sister and I made him a cloak, from an old curtain. We dyed it black – but of course, we didn't know what we were doing, we were only kids; it came out looking terrible. We told him it was a specially magic one. And then my father got him one of those boxes of magic tricks, for his birthday. I bet it cost a fortune, too! He got everything he wanted, my brother; he was absolutely ruined. He was the sort of kid who, every time you took him into a shop, he'd want something. My auntie used to say, "You could take Duncan into a wool shop, and he'd come out wanting a ball of wool."'

She sipped her tea, laughing again. 'He was a lovely kid, really. My dad gave him that box, and he couldn't believe it. He spent hours reading the book, trying to work the tricks out; but in the end, you know, he put it all away. So we said, "What's the matter? Didn't you like the box after all?" And he said, Well, it was all right; but he'd thought it was going to show him how to do *real* magic, and it was just tricks.' She bit her lip, and shook her head. 'Just tricks! Poor little thing. He was only about eight.'

Helen smiled. 'It must have been nice, having a baby brother. My brother and I were too close in age; we just used to quarrel. Once he tied one of my plaits to the handle of a door, and slammed it.' She touched her scalp. 'It hurt like hell. I wanted to kill him! I believe I would have, if I'd known how. I do think children would make the most perfect little murderers, don't you?'

Viv nodded – but a little vaguely, this time. She smoked her cigarette; and they sat together, for a minute or two, in silence.

There's that curtain come down, thought Helen; for she was used to Viv doing this: giving little confidences, sharing memories – then drawing back suddenly, as though she had given away too much. They had worked together for almost a year, but what Helen knew about Viv's home life she'd had to put together from bits and pieces, scraps that Viv had let drop. She knew, for example, that her background was a very ordinary one; that her mother had died, ages ago; that she lived with her father in south London, cooking his dinners when she went home from work at night, and doing his laundry. She wasn't married or engaged – which seemed odd to Helen, for such a good-looking girl. She never spoke of having lost a lover to the war, but there was something – something disappointed about her, Helen thought. A sort of greyness. A layer of grief, as fine as ash, just beneath the surface.

But it was her brother, this Duncan, who was the biggest mystery. He had some queerness or scandal attached to him – Helen had never been able to work out what. He didn't live at home, with Viv and their father; he lived with an uncle or something like that. And though he was apparently quite healthy, he worked – she'd gathered – in an odd kind of factory, for invalids and charity cases. Viv always spoke about him in a very particular way; she often said, for example, 'Poor Duncan,' just as she had a minute ago. But the tone could have an edge of annoyance to it, too, depending on her mood: 'Oh, *he's* all right.' 'He hasn't got a clue.' 'He's in a world of his own, he is.' And then, down would come that curtain.

Helen had a respect for curtains like that, however; having one or two things in her own life that she preferred to keep in darkness . . .

She drank more of her tea, then opened up her handbag and brought out a piece of knitting. She'd got into the habit, during the war, of knitting socks and scarves for soldiers; now, every month, she sent off a parcel of various lumpy, muddy-coloured items to the Red Cross. Currently she was working on a child's balaclava. The wool was second-hand, with strange kinks; it was hot work for summer; but the turns in the pattern were absorbing. She moved her finger and thumb rapidly along the needle, counting stitches under her breath.

Viv opened her own bag. She got out a magazine and began to leaf through it.

'Want your Stars?' she asked Helen, after a while. And, when Helen nodded: 'Here we are, then. *Pisces, the Fish: Caution is the best course today. Others may not be sympathetic to your plans.* That's your gentleman from Harrow, earlier on. Where's mine? *Virgo, the Maiden: Look out for unexpected visitors.* – That makes it sound like I'm going to get nits! *Scarlet brings luck.*' She made a face. 'It's only a woman in some office somewhere, isn't it? I'd like her job.' She turned another couple of pages, then held the magazine over. 'How about that for a hair-do?'

Helen was counting stitches again. 'Sixteen, seventeen,' she said, and glanced at the picture. 'Not bad. I shouldn't like to have to set and reset it every time, though.'

Viv yawned again. 'Well, that's one thing I do have: time.'

They spent a few more minutes looking over the fashions, then glanced at their watches, and sighed. Helen made a mark on her paper pattern and rolled her knitting up. They pulled on their shoes, dusted down their skirts, climbed back over the window-sill. Viv rinsed out the cups. She got out her powder and lipstick and moved to the mirror.

'Better freshen up the old war-paint, I suppose,' she said.

Helen briefly tidied her own face, then went slowly back up into the waiting-room. She straightened the pile of *Lilliputs*, put away the tea things

25

and the kettle. She looked through the diary on Viv's desk – turning the pages, reading the names. *Mr Symes, Mr Blake, Miss Taylor, Miss Heap* . . . She could guess already at the various disappointments that had prompted them to call: the jilts, the betrayals, the rankling suspicions, the deadnesses of heart.

The thought made her restless. How horrible work was, really! Even with Viv to make it bearable, how awful it was to be here, while everything that was important to you, everything that was real, had meaning, was somewhere else, out of reach . . .

She went into her office and looked at the telephone on her desk. She oughtn't to call at this sort of time in the day, for Julia hated to be interrupted when she was working. But now that she'd thought of it, the idea took hold: a little thrill of impatience ran through her, she found herself physically almost twitching, wanting to pick the receiver up.

Oh, bugger it, she thought. She snatched up the telephone and dialled her own number. It rang once, twice – and then came Julia's voice.

'Hello?'

'Julia,' said Helen quietly. 'It's only me.'

'Helen! I thought you were my mother. She's already called twice today. Before her I had the Exchange, some sort of problem with the line. Before *that* there was a man at the door, selling meat!'

'What sort of meat?'

'I didn't enquire. Cat meat, probably.'

'Poor Julia. Have you managed any writing at all?'

'Well, a little.'

'Killed anybody off?'

'I have, as it happens.'

'Have you?' Helen settled the receiver more comfortably against her ear. 'Who? Mrs Rattigan?'

'No, Mrs Rattigan's had a reprieve. It was Nurse Malone. A spear through the heart.'

'A spear? In Hampshire?'

'One of the Colonel's African trophies.'

'Ha! That will teach him. Was it awfully grisly?'

'Awfully.'

'Lots of blood?'

'Buckets of it. And what about you? Been putting out the banns?'

Helen yawned. 'Not much, no.'

She had nothing to say, really. She had just wanted to hear Julia's voice. There was one of those noisy telephone silences, full of the tinny electric muddle of other people's conversations in the wire. Then Julia spoke again, more briskly.

'Look here, Helen. I'm afraid I'll have to ring off. Ursula said she'd call.'

'Oh,' said Helen, suddenly cautious. 'Ursula Waring? Did she?'

'Just some tiresome thing about the broadcast, I expect.'

'Yes. Well, all right.'

'I'll see you later.'

'Yes, of course. Goodbye, Julia.'

'Goodbye.'

Puffs of air; and then the line went dead as Julia put the telephone down. Helen spent a moment with the receiver still at her ear, listening to the faint, gusty echo that was all that remained of the severed connection.

Then she heard Viv coming out of the lavatory, and quickly and softly set the receiver back in its cradle.

'How's Julia?' Viv thought to ask, as she and Helen were going around the office at the end of that day, emptying the ashtrays, gathering their things. 'Has she finished her book?'

'Not quite,' said Helen, without looking up.

'I saw her last book the other day. What's it called? *The Dark Eyes of—*?'

'*The Bright Eyes,*' said Helen, '*of Danger.*'

'That's right. *The Bright Eyes of Danger.* I saw it in a shop on Saturday; and moved it right to the front of the shelf. A woman started looking at it, too, after that.'

Helen smiled. 'You ought to get a commission. I'll make sure to tell Julia.'

'Don't you dare!' The idea was embarrassing. 'She's doing ever so well though, isn't she?'

'She is,' said Helen. She was shrugging on her coat. She seemed to hesitate, and then went on, 'You know, there's a write-up on her in the *Radio*

Times this week. Her book's going to be on *Armchair Detective.*'

'Is it?' said Viv. 'You ought to have told me. The *Radio Times*! I shall have to buy one on my way home.'

'It's only a brief thing,' said Helen. 'There's— There's a nice little photo, though.'

She didn't seem as excited about it, somehow, as she ought to have been. Perhaps she was just used to the idea. It seemed an incredible thing to Viv, to have a friend who wrote books, had her picture in a paper like the *Radio Times*, where so many people would see it.

They switched off the lights and went downstairs, and Helen locked the door. They stood for a minute, as they usually did, looking in at the wigs in the wig-maker's window, deciding which wigs they would buy if they had to, and laughing at the rest. Then they walked together as far as the corner of Oxford Street – yawning as they said goodbye, and making comical faces at the thought of having to come back tomorrow and do another day, all over again.

Viv went slowly after that, almost dawdling: gazing into the windows of shops; wanting the worst of the going-home rush to be over before she tried to catch a train. Usually she took a bus, for the long journey home to Streatham. Tonight, however, was a Tuesday night; and on Tuesdays she took the Tube and went to White City, to have tea with her brother. But she hated the Underground: hated the

29

press of people, the smells, the smuts, the sudden warm gusts of air. At Marble Arch, instead of going down into the station, she went into the park, and walked along the path beside the pavement. The park looked lovely with the late, low sun above it, the shadows long, cool-seeming, bluish. She stood at the fountains and watched the play of the water; she even sat on a bench for a minute.

A girl with a baby came and sat beside her – sighing as she sat, glad of the rest. She had on a headscarf left over from the war, decorated with faded tanks and spitfires. The baby was asleep, but must have been dreaming: he was moving his face – now frowning, now amazed – as if he were trying out all the expressions he would need, Viv thought, when he was grown up.

She finally went down into the Underground at Lancaster Gate; she only had five stops, then, to Wood Lane. Mr Mundy's house was a ten-minute walk from the station, round the back of the dog-track. When races were on you could hear the crowds – a funny sound: loud, almost frightening, it seemed to surge after you down the streets like great waves of invisible water. Tonight the track was quiet. The streets had children in them – three of them balanced on one old bicycle, weaving about, raising dust.

Mr Mundy's gate was fastened with a fussy little latch, which somehow reminded Viv of Mr Mundy himself. His front door had panels of glass in it. She stood at them now, and lightly tapped, and, after a moment, a figure appeared in the hall beyond. It came slowly, with a limp. Viv put on a smile – and imagined Mr Mundy, on his side, doing the same.

'Hello, Vivien. How are you, dear?'

'Hello, Mr Mundy. I'm all right. How are you?'

She moved forward, wiping her feet on the bit of coconut-matting on the floor.

'Can't complain,' said Mr Mundy.

The hall was narrow, and there was a moment's awkwardness, every time, as he made room for her to pass him. She went to the bottom of the stairs and stood beside the umbrella-stand, unbuttoning her coat. It always took her a minute or two to get used to the dimness. She looked around, blinking. 'My brother about, is he?'

Mr Mundy closed the door. 'He's in the parlour. Go on in, dear.'

But Duncan had already heard them talking. He called out, 'Is that Vivien? V, come and see me in here! I can't get up.'

'He's pinned to the floor,' said Mr Mundy, smiling.

'Come and see!' called Duncan again.

She pushed at the parlour door and went inside. Duncan was lying on his stomach on the hearth-rug with an open book before him, and in the small of his back sat Mr Mundy's little tabby cat. The cat was working its two front legs as if kneading dough, flexing and retracting its toes and claws, purring ecstatically. Catching sight of Viv, it narrowed its eyes and worked faster.

31

Duncan laughed. 'What do you think? She's giving me a massage.'

Viv felt Mr Mundy at her shoulder. He had come to watch, and to laugh along with Duncan. His laugh was light, and dry – an old man's chuckle. There was nothing to do but laugh too. She said, 'You're barmy.'

Duncan began to lift himself up, as if about to start physical jerks. 'I'm training her.'

'What for?'

'The circus.'

'She'll snag your shirt.'

'I don't mind. Watch.'

The cat worked on as if demented while Duncan raised himself higher. He began to straighten up. He tried to do it in such a way that the cat could keep her place on his back – even, could walk right up his body. All the time he tried it, he kept laughing. Mr Mundy called encouragement. At last, though, the cat had had enough, and sprang to the floor. Duncan brushed at his trousers.

'Sometimes,' he said to Viv, 'she gets on my shoulders. I walk about – don't I, Uncle Horace? – with her draped around my neck. Quite like your collar, in fact.'

Viv had a little false-fur collar on her coat. He came and touched it. She said, 'She's snagged your shirt after all.'

He twisted to look. 'It's only a shirt. I don't have to be smart like you. Doesn't Viv look smart, Uncle Horace? A smart lady secretary.'

He gave her one of his charming smiles, then let her hug him and kiss his cheek. His clothes had a faintly perfumed smell – that, she knew, was from the candle factory – but beneath the scent he smelt like a boy; and when she lifted her hands to him his shoulders seemed ridiculously narrow and full of slender bones. She thought of the story she'd told Helen that afternoon, about the box of magic tricks; and remembered him vividly, again, when he was little – how he used to come into her and Pamela's bed, and lie between them. She could still feel his thin arms and legs, and his forehead, which would get hot, the dark hair sticking to it, fine as silk . . . She wished for a moment that they were all children again. It still seemed extraordinary to her, that everything had turned out the way it had.

She took off her coat and her hat, and they sat down. Mr Mundy had gone back out to the kitchen. There came the sounds of him, after a minute, preparing tea.

'I ought to go and give a hand,' she said. She said this every time she came. And Duncan always answered, as he did now, 'He prefers it on his own. He'll start up singing in a minute. He had his treatment this afternoon; he's a little bit better. Anyway, I'll do the washing-up. Tell me how you are.'

They exchanged their little pieces of news.

'Dad sends his love,' she said.

'Does he?' He wasn't interested. He'd only been

seated for a moment, but now he got up excitedly and brought something down to her from a shelf. 'Look at this,' he said. It was a little copperish jug, with a dent in its side. 'I got it on Sunday, for three and six. The man asked seven shillings, and I knocked him down. I think it must be eighteenth-century. Imagine ladies, V, taking tea, pouring cream from this! It would have been silvered then, of course. Do you see where the plating's come off?' He showed her the traces of silver at the join of the handle. 'Isn't it lovely? Three and six! That bit of damage is nothing. I could knock that out if I wanted.'

He turned the jug in his hands, delighted with it. It looked like a piece of rubbish to Viv. But he had some new object to show her every time she came: a broken cup, a chipped enamel box, a cushion of napless velvet. She could never help thinking of the mouths that had touched the china, the grubby hands and sweating heads that had rubbed the cushions bald. Mr Mundy's house, itself, rather gave her the creeps: an old person's house, it was, its little rooms crowded with great dark furniture, its walls swarming with pictures. On the mantelpiece were flowers of wax and pieces of coral under spotted glass domes. The lamps were gas ones still, with fish-tail flames. There were yellow, exhausted photographs: of Mr Mundy as a slim young man; another of him as a boy, with his sister and mother, his mother in a stiff black dress, like Queen Victoria. It was all dead, dead, dead; and yet here was Duncan, with his quick dark eyes, his clear boy's laugh, quite at home amongst it all.

She picked up her bag. 'I've brought you something.'

It was a tin of ham. He saw it and said, 'I say!' He said it in the affectionate, faintly teasing way he'd said *smart lady secretary*, before; and when Mr Mundy came limping in with the tea tray, he held the tin up extravagantly.

'Look here, Uncle Horace! Look what Viv has brought us.'

There was corned beef on the tray, already. She had brought that last time. Mr Mundy said, 'By golly, we are well set up now, aren't we?'

They pulled out the leaves of the table and put out the plates and cups, the tomato sandwiches, the lettuce-hearts and cream crackers. They drew up their chairs, shook out their napkins, and began to help themselves to the food.

'How is your father, Vivien?' Mr Mundy asked politely. 'And your sister? How's that fat little chap?' He meant Pamela's baby, Graham. 'Such a fat little chap, isn't he? Fat as butter! Quite like the kids you used to see about when I was a boy. Seemed to go out of fashion.'

He was opening the tin of ham as he spoke: turning its key over and over with his great, blunt fingers, producing a line of exposed meat like a thin pink wound. Viv saw Duncan watching; she saw him blink and look away. He said, as if with

35

a show of brightness, 'Are there fashions in babies, then, like in skirts?'

'I'll tell you one thing,' said Mr Mundy, shaking out the ham, scooping out the jelly. 'What you never used to see, that was wheeled perambulators. You saw a wheeled perambulator round here, that was something marvellous. That was what you used to call top-drawer. We used to cart my cousins about in a wagon meant for coal. Kids walked sooner then, though. Kids earned their living in those days.'

'Were you ever sent up a chimney, Uncle Horace?' asked Duncan.

'A chimney?' Mr Mundy blinked.

'By a great big brute of a man, setting fire to your toes to make you go faster?'

'Get away with you!'

They laughed. The empty ham tin was set aside. Mr Mundy took out his handkerchief and blew his nose – blew it short and hard like a trumpet – then shook the handkerchief back into its folds and put it neatly back in his pocket. His sandwiches and lettuce-hearts he cut into fussy little pieces before he ate them. When Viv left the lid of the mustard-pot up, he tipped it down. But the slivers of meat and jelly that were left on his plate at the end of the meal he held to the cat: he let her lick them from his hand – lick all about his knuckles and nails.

When the cat had finished, she mewed for more. Her mew was thin, high-pitched.

'She sounds like pins,' said Duncan.

'Pins?'

'I feel as though she's pricking me.'

Mr Mundy didn't understand. He reached to touch the cat's head. 'She'll scratch you, mind, when her dander's up. Won't you, Catty?'

There was cake to be eaten, after that; but as soon as the cake was finished, Mr Mundy and Duncan got up and cleared the cups and plates away. Viv sat there rather tensely, watching them carrying things about; soon they went out to the kitchen together and left her alone. The doors in the house were heavy and cut off sound; the room seemed quiet and dreadfully airless, the gas-lamps hissing, a grandfather clock in the corner giving a steady *tick-tick*. It sounded laboured, she thought – as though its works had got stiff, like Mr Mundy's; or else, as if it felt weighted down by the old-fashioned atmosphere, like her. She checked the face of it against her wrist-watch. Twenty to eight . . . How slowly the time ran here. As slowly as at work. How unfair it was! For she knew that later – when she would want it – it would seem to rush.

Tonight, at least, there was a distraction. Mr Mundy came in and sat down in his armchair beside the fire, as he always did after dinner; Duncan, however, wanted Viv to cut his hair. They went out to the kitchen. He put down newspaper on the floor, and set a chair in the middle. He filled a bowl with warm water, and tucked a towel into the collar of his shirt.

37

Viv dipped a comb in the water, wet his hair, and started cutting. She used a pair of old dress-making scissors; God knows what Mr Mundy was doing with those. Probably he did his own sewing, she wouldn't put it past him. The newspaper crackled under her shoes as she moved about.

'Not too short,' said Duncan, hearing her clip.

She turned his head. 'Keep still.'

'You did it too short last time.'

'I'll do it how I do it. There is such a thing as a barber's, you know.'

'I don't like the barber's. I always think he's going to cut me up and put me in a pie.'

'Don't be silly. Why would he want to do that?'

'Don't you think I'd make a nice pie?'

'There's not enough meat on you.'

'He'd make a sandwich of me, then. Or he'd put me in one of those little tins. And then—' He turned and caught her eye, looking mischievous.

She straightened his head again. 'It'll end up crooked.'

'It doesn't matter, there's no one to see. Only Len, at the factory. I haven't got any admirers. I'm not like you—'

'Will you shut up?'

He laughed. 'Uncle Horace can't hear. He wouldn't mind, even if he could. He doesn't trouble over things like that.'

She stopped cutting and put the point of the scissors to his shoulder. 'You haven't told him, Duncan?'

'Of course I haven't.'

'Don't you, ever!'

'Cross my heart.' He licked his finger, touched his chest; looked up at her, still smiling.

She wouldn't smile back. 'It isn't a thing to joke about.'

'If you can't joke about it, why do you do it?'

'If Dad should hear—'

'You're always thinking about Dad.'

'Well, somebody has to.'

'It's your life, isn't it?'

'Is it? I wonder, sometimes.'

She cut on in silence – unsettled, but wanting to say more; almost hoping that he'd keep teasing her, for she had no one else to talk to; he was the only person she'd told . . . But she left it too long; he got distracted, tilting his head to look at the damp black locks on the newspaper under his chair. They'd fallen as curls, but as they dried they were separating into individual strands and growing fluffy. She saw him grimace.

'Isn't it queer,' he said, 'how nice one's hair is when it's on one's head; and how gruesome it becomes, the instant it's cut off. You ought to take one of those curls, V, and put it in a locket. That's what a proper sister would do.'

She straightened his head again, less gently than before. 'I'll proper sister you in a minute, if you don't keep still.'

He put on a silly Cockney voice. '*I was proper sistered!*'

39

That made them laugh. When she'd finished cutting he moved the chair aside and opened the back door. She got her cigarettes, and they sat together on the step, gazing out, smoking and chatting. He told her about his visit to Mr Leonard's; about the buses he and Mr Mundy had had to take, their little adventures . . . The sky was like water with blue ink in it, the darkness sinking, stars appearing one by one. The moon was a slim and perfect crescent, almost new. The little cat appeared, and wound herself around their legs, then threw herself on to her back and writhed, ecstatic again.

Then Mr Mundy came out from the parlour – came out to see what they were doing, Viv supposed; had perhaps heard them laughing, through the window. He saw Duncan's hair and said, 'My word! That's a bit better, now, than the cuts you used to get from Mr Sweet!'

Duncan got up and started tidying the kitchen. He made a parcel of the paper and the hair. 'Mr Sweet,' he said, 'used to nip you with his scissors, just for fun.' He rubbed his neck. 'They said he took a man's ear off once!'

'That was all talk,' said Mr Mundy comfortably. 'Prison talk: that's all that was.'

'Well, that's what a man told me.'

They quarrelled about it for another minute or two; Viv had the feeling they were almost doing it on purpose – showing off, in some funny way, because she was there. If only Mr Mundy hadn't come out! He couldn't leave Duncan alone for a minute. She'd liked it, sitting on the step, watching the sky get darker. But she couldn't bear it when they started talking so airily about prison, all of that; it set her teeth on edge. The closeness and the fondness she'd felt for Duncan a moment before began to recede. She thought of her father. She found herself thinking in her father's voice. Duncan moved gracefully across the kitchen and she looked at his neat dark head, his slender neck, his face that was handsome as a girl's, and she said to herself almost bitterly: *All he put us through, look, and there's not a bloody mark on him!*

She had to go back into the parlour and finish her cigarette there, on her own.

But there wasn't any point in getting worked up about it. It would wear her out, just as it had worn out her father. And she had other things to think about. Duncan made more tea, and they listened to a programme on the wireless; and at quarter-past nine she put her coat on. She left at the same time every week. Duncan and Mr Mundy stood at the front door to watch her go, like an old married couple.

'You don't want your brother to walk you to the station?' Mr Mundy would ask her; and Duncan would answer before she could, in a negligent sort of way, 'Oh, she's all right. Aren't you, Viv?'

But tonight he kissed her, too, as if aware that he'd annoyed her. 'Thanks for the haircut,' he said quietly. 'Thanks for the ham. I was only teasing, before.'

41

She looked back twice as she went off, and they were still there, watching; the next time she looked, the door was closed. She imagined Mr Mundy with his hand on Duncan's shoulder; she pictured them going slowly back into the parlour – Duncan to one armchair, Mr Mundy to the other. She felt again the airless, flannel-like atmosphere of the house on her skin, and walked more briskly – growing excited, suddenly; liking the chill of the evening air and the crispness of the sound of her heels on the pavement.

Walking quickly, however, meant that she arrived too soon at the station. She had to stand about in the ticket-hall while trains came and went, feeling horribly exposed in the harsh, dead light. A boy tried to catch her eye. 'Hey, Beauty,' he kept saying. He kept going past her, singing. To put herself out of his way she went to the bookstall; and it was only as she was looking over the rack of magazines that she remembered what Helen had said, that afternoon, about the *Radio Times*. She took down a copy and opened it up, and almost at once found an article headed:

DANGEROUS GLANCES

URSULA WARING introduces Julia Standing's thrilling new novel *The Bright Eyes of Danger*, featured on 'Armchair Detective' at 10.10 on Friday evening (Light Prog.).

The article was several columns long, and gave an account of the novel in very glowing terms. Above it was a photograph of Julia herself: her face tilted, her eyes downcast, her hands raised and pressed together at the side of her jaw.

Viv looked at the photo with a touch of dislike: for she'd met Julia once, in the street outside the office, and had not taken to her. She'd seemed too clever – shaking Viv's hand when Helen introduced them, but not saying, 'How do you do?' or 'Pleased to meet you', or anything like that; saying coolly instead, as if she'd known Viv for years: 'Successful day? Have you got heaps of people married?' 'More fool them if we have,' Viv had answered; and at that she'd laughed, as if at a joke of her own, and said, 'Yes, indeed . . .' Her voice was very well-to-do, and yet she'd talked slangily: 'louse up your plans', 'go dotty'. What Helen, who was so nice, saw in her to like so much, Viv couldn't imagine. But then, that was their own business. Viv closed her mind to it.

She put the magazine back in the rack and moved away. There was no sign, now, of the boy who'd sung at her. The clock showed two minutes to half-past ten. She went across the ticket-hall – not towards the platforms, but back to the station entrance. She stood close to a pillar, looking out into the street: drawing her coat more tightly around her because, with so much standing about, she'd got chilled.

A moment later a car drew slowly up to the kerb;

43

it came to a stop a few yards on, away from the worst glare of the station. She could see its driver as it passed, dipping his head, trying to spot her. He looked anxious, handsome, hopeless: she found herself feeling towards him much of what she'd felt towards Duncan, earlier on; the same mix of love and exasperation. But there was still that edge of excitement there, too: it rose again now, and grew sharper. She glanced up and down the street, then more or less ran to the passenger door. Reggie leant across and opened it; and as she climbed inside he reached for her face, and kissed her.

Back at Lavender Hill, Kay was walking. She'd been walking, more or less, all afternoon and evening. She'd walked in a great, rough sort of circle, from Wandsworth Bridge up to Kensington, across to Chiswick, over the river to Mortlake and Putney, and now she was heading back to Mr Leonard's; she was two or three streets from home. In the last few minutes she'd fallen into step, and into conversation, with a fair-haired girl. The girl, however, wasn't much good.

'I wonder you can go so fast, in heels so high,' Kay was saying.

'One gets into the habit, I suppose,' the girl answered carelessly. 'There's not much to it. You'd be surprised.' She wasn't looking at Kay, she was looking ahead, along the street. She was meeting a friend, she said.

44

'I've heard it's as good an exercise,' Kay persisted, 'as riding a horse. That it's good for the shape of the legs.'

'I couldn't really say.'

'Well, perhaps your boyfriend could.'

'I might ask him.'

'I wonder he hasn't told you so already.'

The girl laughed. 'Like to wonder, don't you?'

'It makes one think, looking at you, that's all.'

'Does it?'

The girl turned to Kay and met her gaze for a second – frowning, not understanding, not understanding at all . . . Then, 'There's my friend!' she said, and she raised her arm to another girl across the street. She went on faster, to the edge of the kerb, looked quickly to left and to right, then ran across the road. Her high-heeled shoes were pale at the instep; they showed, Kay thought, like the whitish flashes of fur you saw on the behinds of hopping rabbits.

She hadn't said 'Goodbye', 'So long', or anything like that; and she didn't, now, look back. She had forgotten Kay already. She took the other girl's arm, and they turned down a street and were lost.

CHAPTER 2

'Where's your best girl?' Len asked Duncan across the bench, at the candle factory at Shepherd's Bush. He meant Mrs Alexander, the factory's owner. 'She's late today. Have you had a tiff?'

Duncan smiled and shook his head, as if to say, *Don't be silly*.

But Len ignored him. He nudged the woman who sat next to him and said, 'Duncan and Mrs Alexander have had a row. Mrs Alexander caught Duncan making eyes at another girl!'

'Duncan's a real heart-breaker,' said the woman good-humouredly.

Duncan shook his head again, and got on with his work.

It was a Saturday morning. There were twelve of them at the bench, and they were all making night lights, threading wicks and metal sustainers into little stubs of wax, then putting the stubs in flame-proof cases ready for the packers. In the centre of the bench there ran a belt, which carried the finished lights away to a waiting cart. The belt moved with a trundling sound and a regular squeak – not very noisily but, when combined with the hiss and clatter from the candle-making machines in the other half of the room, just noisily enough so that, if you wanted to speak to your neighbour, you had to raise your voice a little louder than was really comfortable. Duncan found it easier to smile and gesture. Often he'd go for hours without speaking at all.

Len, on the other hand, could not be silent. Getting no fun out of Duncan now, he started to gather up spare bits of wax; Duncan watched him begin to press them all together, moulding and shaping them into what emerged, in another minute, as the figure of a woman. He worked quite cleverly – frowning in concentration, his brow coming down and his lower lip jutting. The figure grew smoother and rounder in his hands. He gave it oversized breasts and hips, and waving hair. He showed it to Duncan first, saying, 'It's Mrs Alexander!' Then he changed his mind. He called down the bench to one of the girls: 'Winnie! This is you, look!' He held the figure out and made it walk and wiggle its hips.

Winnie screamed. She was a girl with a deformity of the face, a squashed-in nose and a pinched-up mouth, and a pinched-up nasal voice to match. 'Look what he's done!' she said to her friends. The other girls saw and started laughing.

Len added more wax to the figure, to its breasts and bottom. He made it move more mincingly. '*Oh, baby! Oh, baby!*' he said, in a silly feminine way. Then, 'That's how you go,' he called to

47

Winnie, 'when you're with Mr Champion!' Mr Champion was the factory foreman, a mild-mannered man whom the girls rather terrorised. 'That's how you go. I heard you! And this is what Mr Champion does.' He held the figure in the crook of his arm and passionately kissed it; finally he put his fingernail to the fork of its legs and pretended to tickle it.

Winnie screamed again. Len went on tickling the little figure, and laughing, until one of the older women told him sharply to stop. His laugh, then, became more of a snigger. He gave Duncan a wink. 'She wishes it was her, that's all,' he said, too low for the woman to catch. He pressed the wax figure back into formlessness and threw it into the scrap-cart.

He was always boasting privately to Duncan about girls. It was all he ever talked about. 'I could have that Winnie Mason if I wanted to,' he'd said, more than once. 'What do you think it would be like, though, kissing her mouth? I think it'd be like kissing a dog's arse.' He claimed he often took girls into Holland Park and made love to them there at night. He described it all, with tremendous grimaces and winks. He always talked to Duncan as if he, Len, were the older of the two. He was only sixteen. He had a freckled brown gypsy face, and a pink, plump, satiny mouth. When he smiled, his teeth looked very white and even inside that mouth, against the tan and speckle of his cheek.

Now he sat with his hands behind his head,

rocking on the two back legs of his stool. He looked lazily around the Candle Room, going from one thing to another in search of some kind of distraction. After a minute he moved forward as if excited. He called down the bench: 'Here's Mrs A, look, coming in. She's got two blokes with her!'

Still working at the night lights, the women turned their heads to see. They were grateful for any sort of break in the day's routine. The week before, a pigeon had got into the building and they had gone round the room shrieking, for almost an hour – making the most of the excitement. Now a couple of them actually stood up, to get a better look at the men with Mrs Alexander.

Duncan watched them peer until their curiosity became irresistible. He turned on his stool to look too. He saw Mrs Alexander heading for the biggest of the candle-making machines, leading a tall, fair-haired man, and one who was shorter and darker. The fair-haired man stood with his back to Duncan, nodding. Every so often he made notes in a little book. The other man had a camera: he wasn't interested in how the machine worked; he kept moving about, looking for the best shot of it and the man who ran it. He took a picture, and then another. The camera flashed like bombs.

'Time and Motion,' said Len authoritatively. 'I bet they're Time and— Look out, they're coming!'

He sat forward again, took up a stub of wax and a length of wick and started to fit them together with an air of tremendous industry and concentration. The girls all down the bench fell silent, and worked on as nimbly as before. But when they saw the photographer coming, well ahead of Mrs Alexander and the other man, they began to lift their heads, boldly, one by one. The photographer was lighting a cigarette, his camera swinging from his shoulder on its strap.

Winnie called to him, 'Aren't you going to take our picture?'

The photographer looked her over. He looked at the girls who sat beside her, one of whom had a burnt face and hands, shiny with scars, another of whom was almost blind. 'All right,' he said. He waited for them to draw together and smile, then held up his camera and put his eye to it. But he only pretended to release the shutter. He pressed the button half-way and made a clicking sound with his tongue.

The girls complained. 'The bulb didn't flash!'

The photographer said, 'It flashed all right. It's a special, invisible one. It's an X-ray kind. It sees through clothes.'

This was so obviously something he had come up with to flatter plain girls who pestered him to take their picture, Duncan was almost embarrassed. But Winnie herself, and the other girls, all shrieked with laughter. Even the older women laughed. They were still laughing when Mrs Alexander came over with the fair-haired man.

'Well, ladies,' she said indulgently, in her well-bred Edwardian voice, 'what's all this?'

The girls tittered. 'Nothing, Mrs Alexander.' Then the photographer must have winked or made some gesture, because they all burst out laughing again.

Mrs Alexander waited, but could see at last that she wasn't going to be let in on the joke. She turned her attention, instead, to Duncan. 'How are you, Duncan?'

Duncan wiped his hands on his apron and got slowly to his feet. He was well known, throughout the factory, as one of Mrs Alexander's favourites. People would say to each other, in his hearing, 'Mrs Alexander's going to leave Duncan all her money! You'd better be nice to Duncan Pearce, he's going to be your boss one day!' Sometimes he made the most of it, hamming it up, raising a laugh. But he always felt a sort of pressure when Mrs Alexander singled him out; and he felt that pressure even more today, because she had brought her visitors with her, and was very obviously about to introduce him to them as if he were her 'star worker'.

She turned her head, looking for the fair-haired man, who was still putting notes in his book about the candle-making machine. She reached, and just touched his arm. 'May I show you—?' Along the bench, the girls had stopped tittering and were all looking up, expectant. The man drew nearer and raised his head. 'Here's our little night-light department,' Mrs Alexander said to him. 'Perhaps Duncan could explain the process to you? Duncan, this is—'

The man, however, had stopped in his tracks and was gazing at Duncan as if he couldn't believe his eyes. He started grinning. 'Pearce!' he said, before Mrs Alexander could go on. And then, at Duncan's blank stare: 'Don't you know me?'

Duncan looked properly into his face; and recognised him at last. He was a man named Fraser – Robert Fraser. He had once been Duncan's cell-mate in prison.

Duncan was too stunned, for a moment, even to speak. He'd felt, in an instant, plunged right back into the world of their old hall: the smells of it, the muddled, echoey sounds of it, the grinding misery and fear and boredom . . . His face grew chill, then very warm. He was aware of everyone watching, and felt caught out – caught out by Fraser on the one hand, and by Mrs Alexander, and Len and the girls, on the other.

Fraser, however, had started laughing. He looked as though he felt the oddness of the situation just as Duncan did; but he seemed able to pass it off as a tremendous joke. 'We've met before!' he said, to Mrs Alexander. 'We knew each other – well,' he caught Duncan's eye, 'years ago.'

Mrs Alexander looked, Duncan thought, almost put out. Fraser didn't notice. He was still grinning into Duncan's face. He held out his hand, quite formally; but with his other hand he grabbed hold of Duncan's shoulder and playfully shook him. 'You look exactly the same!' he said.

'You don't,' managed Duncan at last.

For Fraser had grown up. When Duncan had last seen him he'd been twenty-two: lean and white and angular, with a rash of spots on his jaw. Now he must be almost twenty-five – a little older than Duncan himself, in other words, but he was as different from Duncan as it was possible to imagine: broad-shouldered, where Duncan was slender; tanned, and madly healthy-looking and fit. He was dressed in corduroy trousers, an open-necked shirt, and a brown tweed jacket with leather patches on the sleeves. He carried a satchel like a hiker's bag, with the strap across his chest. His fair hair was long – Duncan, of course, had only ever seen him with it cropped – and quite ungreased: every so often, because of the vigour of his gestures, a lock of it would tumble over his brow, and he kept putting up a hand to smooth it back. His hands were as suntanned as his face. His nails were cut bluntly, but shone as if polished.

He looked so grown-up and confident, and so at home in his ordinary clothes, that Duncan, on top of everything else, was suddenly shy of him. In his nervousness he almost laughed; and Mrs Alexander, seeing him smile, smiled too.

'Mr Fraser,' she said, 'has come to write about you, Duncan.'

But at that, he must have looked startled. Fraser said quickly, 'I'm putting together a piece on the factory, that's all, for one of the picture weeklies. That's what I'm doing just now; things like that.

53

Mrs Alexander has been kind enough to show me around. I had no idea—'

For the first time, his grin faltered. He seemed to realise at last what he was doing at Duncan's bench; and what Duncan was. 'I had no idea,' he finished, 'of finding you here. How long have you been here?'

'Duncan's been with us for almost three years,' said Mrs Alexander, when Duncan hesitated.

Fraser nodded, taking that in.

'He's one of our ablest workers. – Duncan, since you and Mr Fraser are such old friends, why don't you show him what your job entails? Mr Fraser, perhaps your man could take a photograph?'

Fraser looked round, rather vaguely, and the photographer stepped forward. He moved about, lifting the camera to his eye again, squaring up the shot as, reluctantly, Duncan picked up one of the little stubs of wax and began explaining to Fraser about the wicks, the metal sustainers, the flame-proof cups. He did it badly. When the flash of the camera went he blinked and, for a second, lost the thread of what he was saying. Meanwhile Fraser nodded and smiled, struggling to hear, and gazing with a fixed, preoccupied interest at every new thing that was pointed out to him; once or twice putting back that lock of ungreased hair from before his brow. 'I see how it goes,' he said, and, 'Yes, I've got it. Of course.'

It only took a minute to explain. Duncan put the night light he had made on to the shuffling belt in the middle of the bench, and it was carried off to the cart at the end of it. 'That's all it is,' he said.

Mrs Alexander moved forward. She had been hovering, all this time, and had the slightly disappointed air of a parent who'd seen their child making a mess of its lines in the school play. But, 'There,' she said, as if in satisfaction. 'Quite a simple process. And every one of our little night lights, you see, has to be put together by hand. I suppose you couldn't guess at how many you've assembled in your time here, Duncan?'

'Not really,' answered Duncan.

'No . . . Still, you're keeping well, I hope? And how's' – she'd thought of a way to save the situation – 'how's the collection?' She turned to Fraser. 'I expect you know, Mr Fraser, that Duncan is a great collector of antiques?'

Fraser, looking partly self-conscious and partly amused, admitted that he didn't know this. 'Oh!' said Mrs Alexander with great enthusiasm, 'Oh, but it's quite a hobby of his! All the handsome things he turns up! I call him the scourge of the dealers. What's your latest find, Duncan?'

Duncan saw that there was no way out of it. He told her, in a rather stilted way, about the cream-jug he'd shown Viv at Mr Mundy's earlier that week.

Mrs Alexander widened her eyes. Apart from the fact that her voice was raised to combat the din and clatter of the factory floor, she might have been at a tea-party.

'Three and six, you say? I shall have to tell my

friend Miss Martin. Antique silver's her great passion, she'll be mad with envy. You must bring the little jug in, Duncan, and show me. Will you do that?'

'Yes,' said Duncan. 'If you like.'

'Yes, do. – And how, by the way, is your uncle? Duncan takes great care, Mr Fraser, of his uncle—'

Duncan heard this, and gave a twitch, took a step, almost in panic. Mrs Alexander saw the expression on his face and misinterpreted it. 'There,' she laughed, patting his shoulder, 'I'm embarrassing you. I'll leave you to your night lights.' She nodded down the bench. 'Len, how are you? Everything all right, Winnie? Mabel, you've spoken to Mr Greening about your chair? Good girl.' She touched Fraser's arm again. 'Would you care to follow me, now, to the Packing Room, Mr Fraser?'

Fraser said he would, in just a moment. 'I'd like to make a note of something here first,' he said. He waited for her to move off, then began to scribble something in his book. He came close to Duncan again as he did it, saying, in an apologetic way, 'I have to go, Pearce, as you can see. But, look here. Here's my address.' He ripped the page out and handed it over. 'You'll give me a call? Some time this week? Will you?'

'If you like,' said Duncan again.

Fraser grinned at him. 'Good man. We can talk properly then. I want to know everything you've been doing.' He moved off, as if reluctantly. 'Everything!'

Duncan lowered his head, to draw out his stool. When he looked up again, Fraser, the photographer, and Mrs Alexander were just going out of the door that took them through to the next building.

The girls started laughing again the moment the door was closed. Winnie called down, in her squashed-up voice: 'What's he given you, Duncan? Is it his address? I'll give you five bob for it!'

'I'll give you six!' said the girl beside her.

She and another girl got up and tried to grab the paper from him. He fought them off, beginning to laugh – relieved that they'd chosen to take the whole thing in this sort of spirit and not another. Len said, about Fraser, 'See how he browned up to you, Duncan? He's heard you're in line for promotion. Where d'you know him from?'

Duncan was still fending off the girls, and didn't answer. By the time they'd finished teasing him and moved on to something else, the scrap of paper with Fraser's address on it had got crumpled almost to a ball. He put it into his apron pocket: he put it right at the bottom of the pocket so that it shouldn't fall out, but for the next hour or so he kept slipping his hand to it, slyly, as if to reassure himself that it was still there. What he really wanted to do was take it out and have a proper look at it; he didn't want to do that, though, with so many people about. At last he could bear it no longer. When Mr Champion came round, he asked permission to go to the lavatory. He went into one of the stalls, and locked the door; and took the paper from his pocket and smoothed it out.

He felt much more excited doing this than he'd felt when talking to Fraser face to face; he'd been too self-conscious then, but now the fact of Fraser's having turned up, and having been so friendly – having gone to the trouble of writing down his address, of saying, 'You'll give me a call? Will you?' – seemed wonderful. The address was a Fulham one, and not very far away. Duncan looked at it and began to imagine how it would be if he went round there – say, one evening. He pictured himself making the journey. He thought of the particular clothes he'd wear – not the clothes he was wearing now, which smelt of stearine and scent, but a nice pair of trousers he had, and an open-necked shirt, and a smart jacket. He imagined how he'd be with Fraser when Fraser opened his door. 'Hello, Fraser,' he'd say, nonchalantly; and Fraser would cry, in amazement and admiration: 'Pearce! You look like a proper man at last, now you've left that wretched factory!' 'Oh, the factory,' Duncan would answer, with a wave of his hand. 'I only go there as a favour to Mrs Alexander . . .'

He went on daydreaming like this for five or ten minutes – playing the same scene over and over, of himself arriving at Fraser's door; unable, quite, to imagine what would happen once Fraser had asked him in. He went on doing it, even though he had no intention, actually, of ever going to Fraser's house; even while a part of him was saying, *Fraser won't want to see you really. He gave you his address for politeness' sake. He's the sort of person who gets madly pleased over little things, for a minute, and then forgets all about them . . .*

He heard the swing of the wash-room door, and Mr Champion's voice: 'All right in there, Duncan?'

'Yes, Mr Champion!' he called; and pulled the chain.

He looked again at the paper in his hand. He didn't know what to do with it now. Finally he tore it into little pieces and added them to the swirling water in the lavatory.

'Must you wriggle so, darling?' Julia was saying.

Helen moved a shoulder. She said fretfully, 'It's these taps. This one's freezing; the other nearly burns your ear off.'

They were lying together in the bath. They did this every Saturday morning; they took it in turns who had the smooth end, and this week it was Julia's turn. She was lying with her arms stretched out, her head put back, her eyes closed; she had tied up her hair in a handkerchief but a few strands had fallen and, as the water slopped over them, they moulded themselves to her jaw and throat. Frowning, she tucked them back up behind her ear.

Helen moved again, then found an almost comfortable position and grew still, enjoying at last the lovely creep of the warm water into her armpits, her groin – all the creases and sockets of her flesh. She put her hands flat upon the water's surface, testing its resistance, feeling its skin. 'Look at our legs all mixed up,' she said softly.

She and Julia always spoke quietly when they were taking their bath. They shared the bathroom with the family who lived in the basement of their house; they all had regular bath-times, so there was not much danger of being caught out; but the tiles on the walls seemed to magnify sound, and Julia had the idea that their voices, the splashing, the rub of their limbs in the tub, might be heard in the rooms downstairs.

'Look how dark your skin is, compared to mine,' Helen went on. 'Really, you're as swarthy as a Greek.'

'The water makes me seem darker, I suppose,' answered Julia.

'It doesn't make *me* seem dark,' said Helen. She prodded the pink and yellowish flesh of her own stomach. 'It makes me look like pressed meat.'

Julia opened her eyes and gazed briefly at Helen's thighs. 'You look like a girl in a painting by Ingres,' she said comfortably.

She was full of ambiguous compliments like this. 'You look like a woman in a Soviet mural,' she had said recently, when Helen had returned from a shopping trip with two bulging string bags; and

Helen had pictured muscles, a square jaw, a shadowy lip. Now she thought of *odalisques* with spreading bottoms. She put a hand to Julia's leg. The leg was rough with little hairs, interesting to the palm; the shin was slender and pleasant to grip. On the bone of the ankle a single vein stood out, swollen with heat. She studied it, pressed it, and saw it yield; she thought of the blood gushing inside it, and gave a little shudder. She slid her hand from Julia's ankle to her foot, and began to rub it. Julia smiled. 'That's nice.'

Julia's feet were broad and unhandsome – an Englishwoman's feet, Helen thought, and the only really unlovely part of Julia's whole body; and she held them in a special sort of regard, for that reason. She tugged slowly, now, at the toes, then worked her fingers between them; she put her palm against them and gently pressed them back. Julia sighed with pleasure. A strand of her hair had fallen again, and again clung to her throat – dark, flat and lustrous as a piece of seaweed, or a lock from a mermaid's head. Why, Helen wondered, were the mermaids' heads that you saw in books and films always coloured gold? She was sure that a real mermaid would certainly be dark, like Julia. A real mermaid would be strange, alarming – nothing like an actress or a glamour-girl at all.

'I'm glad you've got feet, Julia, rather than a tail,' she said, working with her thumb at the arch of Julia's foot.

'Are you, darling? So am I.'

61

'Your breasts would look handsome, though, in a brassière made of shells.' She smiled. She'd remembered a joke. 'What,' she asked Julia, 'did the brassière say to the hat?'

Julia thought about it. 'I don't know. What?'

'"You go on ahead, and I'll give these two a lift."'

They laughed – not so much at the joke, as at the silliness of Helen's having told it. Julia still had her head put back: her laughter, caught in her throat, was bubbling, childish, nice – not at all like her conventional 'society' laugh, which always struck Helen as rather brittle. She put a hand across her mouth to stifle the sound. Her stomach quivered as she shook, her navel narrowing.

'Your navel's winking at me,' said Helen, still laughing. 'It looks awfully saucy. The Saucy Navel: that sounds like a seaside pub, doesn't it?' She moved her legs, yawning. She was rather tired, now, of stroking Julia's foot; she let it fall. 'Do you love me, Julia?' she whispered, as she changed her pose.

Julia closed her eyes again. 'Of course I do,' she said.

They lay for a time, then, not speaking. The water-pipes creaked, cooling down. From some hidden part of the plumbing there came a steady *drip-drip*. In the basement there were thumps, as the man who lived there walked heavily from room to room; soon they heard him shouting at his wife or his daughter: *'No, you great daft bitch!'*

Julia tutted. 'That revolting man.' Then she opened her eyes and, 'Helen,' she cried softly, 'how can you?' For Helen had tilted her head over the side of the bath and was trying to listen. She waved her hand for Julia to be silent. '*Work it up your arse!*' they heard the man say: a phrase he liked, and used often. Next came the gnat-like whining that was all that ever reached them of his wife's replies.

'Really, Helen,' said Julia, disapprovingly. Helen moved meekly back into the bath-tub. Sometimes, if the shouting started up and she was alone, she'd go so far as to kneel on the carpet, draw back her hair, put her ear to the floor. '*You'll end up like those fucking eunuchs upstairs!*' she had heard the man shout one day, by doing this. She'd never told Julia.

Today he grumbled on for a minute or two, then gave it up. A door was slammed. The things that Helen and Julia had brought down to the bath-room – the scissors and tweezers, the safety-razor in its case – gave a jump.

It was half-past eleven. They planned an idle sort of day, with books and a picnic, in Regent's Park; they lived quite near it, in one of the streets just to the east of the Edgware Road. Helen lay a little longer, until the water began to cool; then she sat up and washed herself – turning awkwardly around, so that Julia could soap her back and rinse it; and doing the same for Julia herself, when Julia had turned. But when she'd risen and stepped out of the tub Julia sank back down again, stretching out into the extra space and smiling like a cat.

Helen studied her for a second, then bent and kissed her – liking the look and the feel of Julia's slick, warm, soap-scented mouth.

She put on her dressing-gown and opened the door – listening first, to be sure there was no one in the hall. Then she ran lightly towards the stairs. Their sitting-room was on this floor, beside the bathroom. Their kitchen and bedroom were one floor up.

She had just finished dressing, and was combing her hair at the bedroom mirror, when Julia joined her: Helen watched her through the glass, carelessly dusting herself with talcum powder, then tugging the handkerchief from her head and going naked about the room, picking out knickers, stockings, suspenders and a bra. Her towel she added to a pile of garments on the cushions that made a little window-seat; almost at once it slid to the floor, taking a sock and a petticoat with it.

The window-seat was one of the things that had attracted them to the house when they'd first viewed it. 'We'll be able to sit there together in the long summer evenings,' they had said. Now Helen looked at the mess of clothes which obscured the sill; she looked at the unmade bed; and then at the cups and mugs, and the piles of read and unread books, which lay on every surface. She said, 'This room's impossible. Here we are, two middle-aged women and we live like sluts. I can't believe it. When I was young, and used to think about the house I'd have when I was grown up, I always pictured it as terribly neat and tidy – just like my mother's. I always imagined that neat houses came to one, like – I don't know.'

'Like wisdom teeth?'

'Yes,' said Helen, 'just like that.' She passed her sleeve across the surface of the mirror; it came away grey with dust.

Other people of their age and class, of course, had chars. They couldn't do that, because of the business of sharing a bed. There was another little room on the floor above this, which got presented to neighbours and visitors as 'Helen's room'; it had an old-fashioned divan in it, and a severe Victorian wardrobe where they kept their overcoats and jerseys and wellington boots. But it would be too much fuss, they thought, to have to pretend to a daily woman that Helen slept there every single night; they'd be sure to forget. And weren't char-ladies, anyway, awfully knowing about that sort of thing? Now that Julia's books were doing so well they had to be more careful than ever.

Julia came to the mirror. She had put on a creased dark linen dress and run her fingers roughly through her hair; but she could step out of any kind of chaos, Helen thought, and look, as she did now, absurdly well groomed and handsome. She moved closer to the glass, to dash on lipstick. Her mouth was a full, rather crowded one. But she had one of those faces, so regular and even, it was exactly the same in reflection as it was in life. Helen's face, by contrast, looked rather queer and lopsided when studied in a mirror. *You look like a lovely onion*, Julia had told her once.

They finished putting on their make-up, then went out to the kitchen to gather food. They found bread, lettuce, apples, a nub of cheese, and two bottles of beer. Helen dug out an old madras square they'd used as a dust-sheet when decorating; they put it all in a canvas bag, then added their books, their purses and keys. Julia ran upstairs to her study for her cigarettes and matches. Helen stood at the kitchen window, looking out into the backyard. She could just see the bad-tempered man, moving and stooping. He kept table-rabbits down there, in a little home-made hutch: he was giving them water or food, or perhaps checking the plumpness of them. It always bothered her, imagining them all crushed together like that. She moved away, and shouldered the bag. The bottles clinked against the keys. 'Julia,' she called, 'are you ready?'

They went down, and out to the street.

Their house was part of an early nineteenth-century terrace, facing a garden. The terrace was white – that London white, more properly a streaked and greyish yellow; the grooves and sockets of its stucco façade had been darkened by fogs, by soot, and – more recently – by brick-dust. The houses all had great front doors and porches – must once, in fact, have been grand residences: home, perhaps, to minor Regency strumpets, girls called Fanny, Sophia, Skittles. Julia and Helen liked to imagine them tripping down the steps in their Empire-line dresses and soft-soled shoes, taking their mounts, going riding in Rotten Row.

In miserable weather the discoloured stucco could look dreary. Today the street was filled with light, and the house fronts seemed bleached as bones against the blue of the sky. London looked all right, Helen thought. The pavements were dusty – but dusty in the way, say, that a cat's coat is dusty, when it has lain for hours in the sun. Doors were open, sashes raised. The cars were so few that, as Helen and Julia walked, they could make out the cries of individual children, the mutter of radios, the ringing of telephones in empty rooms. And as they drew closer to Baker Street they began to hear music from the Regent's Park Band, a faint sort of *clash* and *parp-parp-parp* – swelling and sinking on impalpable gusts of air, like washing on a line.

Julia caught Helen's wrist, grew childish, pretending to tug. 'Come on! Come quick! We'll miss the parade!' Her fingers moved against Helen's palm, then slid away. 'It makes one feel like that, doesn't it? What tune is it, d'you think?'

They slowed their steps and listened more carefully. Helen shook her head. 'I can't imagine. Something modern and discordant?'

'Surely not.'

The music rose. 'Quick!' said Julia again. They smiled, grown-up; but walked on, faster than before. They went into the park at Clarence Gate, then followed the path beside the boating lake.

They approached the bandstand and the music grew louder and less ragged. They walked further, and the tune revealed itself at last.

'Oh!' said Helen, and they laughed; for it was only 'Yes! We Have No Bananas'.

They left the path and found a spot they liked the look of, half in sunlight, half in shade. The ground was hard, the grass very yellow. Helen put down the bag and unpacked the cloth; they spread it out and kicked off their shoes, then laid out the food. The beer was still cold from the frigidaire, the bottles sliding deliciously in Helen's warm hand. But she went back to the bag and, after a moment's searching, looked up.

'We forgot a bottle-opener, Julia.'

Julia closed her eyes. 'Hell. I'm dying for a drink, as well. What can we do?' She took a bottle and started picking at its lid. 'Don't you know some terribly bright way of getting the tops off?'

'With my teeth, do you mean?'

'You were in the Brownies, weren't you?'

'Well they rather jibbed, you know, at Pale Ale, in my pack.'

They turned the bottles in their hands.

'Look, it's hopeless,' said Helen at last. She looked around. 'There are boys over there. Run and ask them if they have a knife or something.'

'I can't!'

'Go on. All boys have knives.'

'You do it.'

'I carried the bag. Go on, Julia.'

'God,' said Julia. She rose, not graciously, took up the bottles, one in each hand, and began to walk across the grass to a group of lounging youths. She walked stiffly, rather bowed, perhaps only self-conscious, but Helen saw her, for a second, as a stranger might: saw how handsome she was, but also how grown-up, how almost matronly; for you could catch in her something of the angular, wide-hipped, narrow-breasted figure she'd have in earnest in ten years' time. The youths, by contrast, were practically schoolboys. They put up their hands to their eyes, against the sun, when they saw her coming; they rose lazily from their places, reached into their pockets; one held a bottle against his stomach as he worked with something at the top. Julia stood with folded arms, more self-conscious than ever, smiling unnaturally; when she came back with the opened bottles her face and throat were pink.

'They only used keys, after all,' she said. 'We might have done that.'

'We'll know next time.'

'They told me to "take it easy, missus".'

'Never mind,' said Helen.

They had brought china cups to drink from. The beer foamed madly to the curving porcelain lips. Beneath the froth it was chill, bitter, marvellous. Helen closed her eyes, savouring the heat of the sun on her face; liking the reckless, holidayish feel of drinking beer in so public a place. But she hid the bottles, too, in a fold of the canvas bag.

'Suppose one of my clients should see me?'

'Oh, bugger your clients,' said Julia.

They turned to the food they'd brought, broke the bread, made little slices of the cheese. Julia stretched out with the bunched-up canvas bag behind her head as a pillow. Helen lay flat and closed her eyes. The band had started on another tune. She knew the words to it, and began quietly to sing.

'There's something about a soldier! Something about a soldier! Something about a soldier that is fine! – fine! – fine!'

Somewhere a baby was crying from a pram; she heard it stumbling over its breath. A dog was barking, as its owner teased it with a stick. From the boating lake there came the creak and splash of oars, the larking about of boys and girls; and from the streets at the edges of the park, of course, came the steady snarl of motors. Concentrating, she seemed to hear the scene in all its individual parts: as if each might have been recorded separately, then put with the others to make a slightly artificial whole: 'A September Afternoon, Regent's Park'.

Then a couple of teenage girls walked past. They had a newspaper, and were talking over one of the cases in it. 'Mustn't it be awful to be strangled?' Helen heard one of them say. 'Should you rather be strangled, or have an atomic bomb fall on you? They say at least with an atomic bomb it's quick . . .'

70

Their voices faded, drowned out by another gust of music.

'There's something about his bearing! Something in what he's wearing! Something about his buttons all a-shine! – shine! – shine!'

Helen opened her eyes and gazed into the luminous blue of the sky. Was it crazy, she wondered, to be as grateful as she felt now, for moments like this, in a world that had atomic bombs in it – and concentration camps, and gas chambers? People were still tearing each other into pieces. There was still murder, starvation, unrest, in Poland, Palestine, India – God knew where else. Britain itself was sliding into bankruptcy and decay. Was it a kind of idiocy or selfishness, to want to be able to give yourself over to trifles: to the parp of the Regent's Park Band; to the sun on your face, the prickle of grass beneath your heels, the movement of cloudy beer in your veins, the secret closeness of your lover? Or were those trifles all you had? Oughtn't you, precisely, to preserve them? To make little crystal drops of them, that you could keep, like charms on a bracelet, to tell against danger when next it came?

She moved her hand, thinking this – just touched her knuckles to Julia's thigh, where no one could see.

'Isn't this lovely, Julia?' she said quietly. 'Why don't we come here all the time? The summer's nearly over now, and what have we done with it? We might have come here every evening.'

'We'll do that next year,' answered Julia.

71

'We will,' said Helen. 'We'll remember, and do it then. Won't we? Julia?'

But Julia wasn't listening now. She had raised her head to talk to Helen, and her attention had been caught by something else. She was looking across the park. She lifted a hand to shade her eyes and, as Helen watched, her gaze grew fixed and she started to smile. She said, 'I think that's— Yes, it is. How funny!' She raised the hand higher, and waved. '*Ursula!*' she called – so loudly, the word jarred against Helen's ear. 'Over here!'

Helen propped herself up and peered in the direction in which Julia was waving. She saw a slim, smart-looking woman making her way across the grass towards them, beginning to laugh.

'Good Lord,' the woman said, as she drew closer. 'Fancy seeing you, Julia!'

Julia had got to her feet and was brushing down her linen dress. She was laughing too. She said, 'Where are you off to?'

'I've been lunching with a friend,' said the woman, 'up at St John's Wood. I'm on my way to Broadcasting House. We don't have time for picnics and so on, at the BBC. What a charming spread you've made here, though! Perfectly bucolic!'

She looked at Helen. Her eyes were dark, slightly mischievous.

Julia turned, made introductions. 'This is Ursula Waring, Helen. Ursula, this is Helen Giniver—'

'Helen, of course!' said Ursula. 'Now, you won't mind my calling you Helen? I've heard such a lot about you. No need to look nervous! It was all of it good.'

She leant to shake Helen's hand, and Helen half rose, to meet it. She felt at a disadvantage, sitting down while Julia and Ursula were standing up; but she was very conscious, too, of her Saturday-morning appearance – of her blouse, which she'd once unpicked and refashioned in an attempt at 'make-do and mend', and her old tweed skirt, rather seated at the back. Ursula, by contrast, looked neat, moneyed, tailored. Her hair was put up in a chic, rather masculine little hat. Her leather gloves were soft and unscuffed, and her low-heeled shoes had flat fringed tongues to them – the kind of shoes you expected to see on a golf-course, or a Scottish highland, somewhere expensively hearty like that. She was not at all as Helen had pictured her from the things that Julia had said about her over the past few weeks. Julia had made her sound older and almost dowdy. Why would Julia have done that?

'You caught the broadcast last night?' Ursula was saying.

'Of course,' said Julia.

'Rather good, wasn't it? Did you think so, Helen? I think we did awfully well. And wasn't it tremendous, seeing Julia's face in the middle of the *Radio Times*!'

'Oh, it was rotten,' said Julia, before Helen could answer. 'That picture's so frightfully Catholic! I look like I'm about to be bound to a wheel, or have my eyes put out!'

73

'Nonsense!'

They laughed together. Then Julia said, 'Look here, Ursula. Why don't you join us?'

Ursula shook her head. 'I know if I sit, I simply shan't want to get up. I shall be sick with envy, though, thinking about you all day. It's just too disgustingly clever of you both. But of course, you live so very near. And such a charming house, too!' She spoke to Helen again. 'I said to Julia, one would never know such a place existed, so close to the Edgware Road.'

'You've seen it?' asked Helen in surprise.

'Oh, just for a moment—'

Julia said, 'Ursula called round, one day last week. Surely I told you, Helen?'

'I must have forgotten.'

'I wanted to take a peek,' said Ursula, 'at Julia's study. It's always so fascinating, I think, seeing where writers do their work. Though I'm not sure whether I really envy you, Helen. I don't know how I'd feel, having my friend scribbling away over my head, working out the best way to despatch her next victim – by poison, or the rope!'

She said the word 'friend', Helen thought, in a special sort of way – as if to say: *We understand one another, of course.* As if to say, in fact: *We're all 'friends' together.* She had taken off her gloves, to bring out a silver cigarette-case from her pocket; and as she opened the case up Helen saw her short manicured nails, and the discreet little signet ring on the smallest finger of her left hand.

74

She held the cigarettes out. Helen shook her head. Julia, however, moved forward, and she and Ursula spent a moment fussing with a lighter – for a breeze had risen and kept blowing out the flame.

They spoke further about *Armchair Detective* and the *Radio Times*; about the BBC and Ursula's job there. Then, 'Well, my dears,' said Ursula, when her cigarette was finished, 'I must be off. It's been so nice. You must both come over, some time, to Clapham. You must come for supper – or, better still, I could put together a bit of a party.' Her gaze grew mischievous again. 'We could make it an all-girl thing. What do you say?'

'But of course, we'd love to,' said Julia, when Helen said nothing.

Ursula beamed. 'That's settled, then. I'll let you know.' She took Julia's hand and playfully shook it. 'I've one or two friends who would be thrilled to meet you, Julia. They're such fans!' She started putting on her gloves, and turned to Helen again. 'Goodbye, Helen. It's been so nice to meet you properly.'

'Well,' said Julia, as she sat back down. She was watching Ursula making her quick, smart way across the park in the direction of Portland Place.

'Yes,' said Helen, rather thinly.

'Amusing, isn't she?'

'I suppose so. Of course, she's more your class than mine.'

Julia looked round, laughing. 'What's that supposed to mean?'

'She's a bit hearty, is all I meant . . . When did you take her to the house?'

'Just last week. I told you, Helen.'

'Did you?'

'You don't think I did it in secret?'

'No,' said Helen quickly. 'No.'

'It was only for a minute.'

'She's not how I imagined. I thought you told me she was married.'

'She is married. Her husband's a barrister. They live apart.'

'I didn't know she was – well,' Helen lowered her voice, 'like us.'

Julia shrugged. 'I don't know what she is, really. A bit of an oddity, I think. Still, that party might be fun.'

Helen looked at her. 'You wouldn't want to go, really?'

'Yes, why not?'

'I thought you were just being polite. "An all-girl thing." You know what that means.' She looked down, her colour rising slightly. 'Anyone might be there.'

Julia didn't answer for a moment. When she spoke, she sounded impatient or annoyed. 'Well, what if they are? It won't kill us. It might even be fun. Imagine that!'

'It'll certainly be fun for Ursula Waring, anyway,' said Helen, before she could stop herself.

'Having you there, like some sort of prize pig—'

Julia was watching her. She said coldly, 'What's the matter with you?' And then, when Helen wouldn't answer: 'It's not—- Oh, no.' She began to laugh. 'Not really, Helen? Not because of *Ursula*?'

Helen moved away. 'No,' she said; and she lay back down, with a sharp, graceless movement. She put her arm across her eyes, to keep off the sun and Julia's gaze. After a moment she felt Julia lie down, too. She must have reached into the bag and brought out her book: Helen heard her leafing through its pages, looking for her place.

But what Helen could see, in the shifting blood-coloured depths of her own eyelids, was Ursula Waring's mischievous dark gaze. She saw the way that Ursula and Julia had stood together, lighting their cigarettes. She saw again Ursula playfully shaking Julia's hand. Then she thought back. She remembered how keen Julia had been to get to the park – *Come on! Come quick!* – her fingers slipping away from Helen's in her impatience. Was it Ursula she'd wanted to see? Was it? Had they arranged the whole thing?

Her heart beat faster. Ten minutes before she had been lying just like this, enjoying the familiar, secret nearness of Julia's limbs. She'd wanted to hold on to that moment, make a crystal bead of it. Now the bead felt shattered. For what was Julia to her, after all? She couldn't lean to her and kiss her. What could she do, to say to the world that

77

Julia was hers? What did she have, to keep Julia faithful? She had only herself: her pressed-meat thighs, her onion face . . .

These thoughts raged through her like a darkness in her blood, while Julia read on; while the band played a final *parp-parp-parp*, then put its instruments away; while the sun crept slowly over the sky, and shadows extended themselves across the yellow ground. But at last the miserable panic subsided. The darkness shrank, folded itself up. She said to herself, *What an idiot you are! Julia loves you. It's only this beast in you she hates, this ridiculous monster—*

She moved her wrist again, so that it just touched Julia's thigh. Julia kept still for a moment, then moved her own wrist, to meet it. She put down her book and propped herself up. She took up an apple and a knife. She peeled the apple in one long strip, then cut the fruit into quarters and handed two of them to Helen. They ate together, watching the running about of dogs and children, as they had before.

Then they caught each other's gaze. Julia said, with a hint of coolness still, 'All over, now?'

Helen coloured. 'Yes, Julia.'

Julia smiled. When she'd finished eating the apple she lay back down, and picked up her book again; and Helen watched her as she read. Her eyes were moving from word to word, but apart from that her face was still, closed, blemishless as wax.

★   ★   ★

78

'You look like a film-star,' said Reggie, as Viv got into his car. He made a show of looking her over. 'Can I have your autograph?'

'Just get going, will you?' she said. She'd been standing in the sun, waiting for him, for half an hour. They moved together and briefly kissed. He let down the handbrake and the car moved off.

She was wearing a light cotton dress and a plum-coloured cardigan, and sunglasses with pale plastic frames; instead of a hat she had a white silk scarf, which she'd tied in a knot beneath her chin. The scarf and the sunglasses looked striking against the dark of her hair and the red of her lipstick. She straightened her skirt, making herself comfortable; then wound down her window and sat with her elbow on the sill, her face in the draught – like a girl in an American picture, just as Reggie had said. Slowing the car for a traffic-light, he put his hand on her thigh and murmured admiringly, 'Oh, if the boys in Hendon could only see me now!'

But of course, he kept well away from north London. He'd picked her up at Waterloo and, having crossed the river and got to the Strand, he headed east. They had places they liked, an hour from the city: villages in Middlesex and Kent, where there were pubs and tea-rooms; little beaches on the coast. Today they were motoring out towards Chelmsford; they were just going to drive, until they found a pretty spot. They had hours together: all afternoon. She'd told her father she was going on a picnic with a girlfriend. She'd stood at one end of the kitchen table the night before, making sandwiches, while he'd sat at the other fixing rubber soles to his shoes.

They wove through the City and Whitechapel; when they started on a wider, smoother road Reggie put the car in a higher gear and moved his hand back to her thigh. He found the line of her suspender, and began to follow it; her dress being thin, she could feel the pressure of his touch – his thumb and palm and moving finger – as vividly as if she'd been naked.

But her mood was wrong, somehow. She said, 'Don't,' and caught his hand.

He gave a groan like a man in torment and pretended to fight against her grip. 'What a teaser you are! Can I stop the car? It's that, you know, or run it off the road.'

He didn't stop the car. He speeded up. The streets grew clearer. Billboards appeared at the side of the road, advertising *Players, Please!* and *Wrigley's, 'Jiffy' Dyes* and *Vim*. She sat more loosely, watching the peeling back of the city – the blitzed Victorian high streets giving way to red Edwardian villas, the villas giving way to neat little houses like so many bowler-hatted clerks, the little houses becoming bungalows and prefabs. It was like hurtling backwards through time – except that the bungalows and prefabs turned into open green fields, and after that, she thought, if you narrowed your eyes and didn't look at things like telegraph poles or aeroplanes in the sky, you could have been in any time, or no time at all.

They passed a pub, and Reggie worked his mouth as if thirsty. He'd laid out his jacket on the back seat, but got her to reach into its pocket and bring out a little flask of Scotch. She watched him lifting it to his mouth. His lips were soft and smooth; his chin and throat were freshly shaved, but already dark with dots of stubble. He drank clumsily, concentrating on the road. Once the whisky ran from the corner of his mouth and he had to catch it with the back of his swarthy hand.

'Look at you,' she said, half playfully, half crossly. 'You're dribbling.'

He said, 'I'm drooling. It's from sitting next to you.'

She made a face at the idea. They drove on more or less in silence. He kept to the main road for almost an hour, but then, coming to an unsigned junction, followed the quietest-looking route; and after that they took the lanes which caught their fancy. London, suddenly, became almost un-imaginable – the hardness and dryness and dirt of it. The hedges that bordered the lanes were high and moist and, though it was autumn, still filled with colour: sometimes Reggie drew close to the side to let another driver pass, and flowers shook their petals through the window into Viv's lap. Once a white butterfly came into the car and spread out its papery, powdery wings on the curve of the seat beside her shoulder.

Her mood began to lift. They started to point out little things to each other – old-fashioned churches, quaint-looking cottages. They remembered a day, years before, when they had come into the country and stopped at a cottage and spoken to its owner, and he'd taken them for a married couple and asked them into his parlour and given them glasses of milk. Reggie said now, as he slowed the car before a little house the colour of creamy French cheese, 'There's space at the back, look, for pigs and chickens. I can see you, Viv, chucking out the swill. I can see you picking apples in an orchard. You could make me apple pies, and bloody great suet puddings.'

'You'd get fat,' she said, smiling, poking his stomach.

He dodged away from her. 'It wouldn't matter. You're supposed to be fat, aren't you, in the country?' He kept an eye on the road, but dipped his head to look at the upstairs window. He lowered his voice. 'I bet there's the hell of a feather mattress in the room up there.'

'Is that all you think about?'

'It is, when you're around. – Oops.'

He swerved, to avoid the hedge; then put his foot down again.

They began to look about for a place to stop the car and eat their lunch, and took a track that led between fields towards a wood. The track seemed well maintained at first; the further they drove, however, the rougher and narrower it grew.

The car bumped about, getting whipped by brambles, and long grass swept and crackled underneath it like rushing water beneath a boat. Viv bounced on the seat, laughing. Reggie frowned, leaning forward, tugging at the steering-wheel. 'If we meet someone coming the other way, we're buggered,' he said. And she knew he was thinking about what would happen if they were to have an accident, smash up the car, get stuck . . .

But the track dipped and turned and they found themselves, all at once, in a lush green clearing beside a stream, breathtakingly pretty. Reggie put on the brake and turned off the engine; they sat for a moment, amazed and awed by the quiet of the place. Even after they'd opened the doors and begun to climb out they hesitated, feeling like intruders: for all they could hear was the tumbling of the stream, the calling of birds, the shushing of leaves.

'It sure as hell ain't Piccadilly,' said Reggie, getting out at last.

'It's lovely,' said Viv.

They spoke almost in murmurs. They stretched their arms and legs, then walked across the grass to the edge of the stream. When they gazed along the bank they could see, half hidden in the trees, an old stone building with shattered windows and a broken roof.

'That's a mill,' said Reggie, moving towards it, catching hold of Viv's hand. 'Can you see the shaft of the wheel? This must have been a proper river once.'

She pulled him back. 'Someone might be there.'

But no one was there. The house had been abandoned years before. Grass grew through the gaps between its flagstones. Pigeons fluttered in its beams, and its floors were covered with bird droppings and broken slate and glass. Somebody, at some point, had cleared a space and made a fire; there were cans and bottles, and filthy messages on the walls. The cans were rusty, the bottles silvery with age.

'Tramps,' said Reggie. 'Tramps, or deserters. And courting couples.' They went back to the stream. 'I bet this is a regular Lovers' Lane.'

She gave him a pinch. 'Trust you to find it, then.'

He still had hold of her hand. He lifted her fingers to his lips, looking coy, pretending modesty. 'What can I say? Some men are gifted like that, that's all.'

They were talking, now, in normal voices, had lost their sense of awe and caution and begun to feel as though the place was theirs: that it had been waiting, picturesquely, just for them to come and claim it. They followed the stream in the other direction and found a bridge. They stood on the hump of it, smoking cigarettes; Reggie put his arm around her waist and rested his hand on her backside, moving his thumb, making her dress and her petticoat slide against the silk of her knickers.

They threw the ends of their cigarettes into the stream and watched them race. Then Reggie peered more closely at the water.

'There's fish in there,' he said. 'Big sods, look at

that!' He went down to the side of the stream, took off his wrist-watch and dipped in his hand. 'I can feel them nibbling!' He was as excited as a boy. 'They're like a bunch of girls, all kissing! They think my hand's a man-fish. They think their luck's in!'

'They think you're lunch,' Viv called back. 'They'll have one of your fingers if you're not careful.'

He leered. 'That's like a girl, too.'

'The sort of girls you know, maybe.'

He rose and shook water at her. She laughed and ran away. The water struck the lenses of her sunglasses and when she wiped them, the lenses smeared.

'Now look what you've done!'

They went back to the car for their picnic, leaving the car's doors open. Reggie got out a tartan rug from the boot and they spread it on the grass. He brought out a bottle of gin and orange, too, and a couple of beakers – one pink, one green. The beakers were meant for children, Viv knew: they were rough against the lip where they'd been bitten and thrown about. But she was used to that sort of thing; there was simply no point minding. The gin and orange had become warm in the car: she swallowed, and felt the glow of it almost at once, loosening her up. She unwrapped the sandwiches. Reggie ate his in great, quick bites, swallowing the bread before he'd chewed it, then biting again; talking with the food still on his tongue.

'This is that Canadian ham, isn't it? It's not too bad after all.'

He'd pulled at his tie, undone the button of his shirt. The sun was on him, making him frown, showing up the creases in his forehead and beside his nose. He was thirty-six, but had recently, Viv thought, begun to look a little older. His face was sallow – that was the Italian blood in him – and his hazel eyes were still very handsome, but he was losing his hair – losing it not neatly, in a round little patch; it was thinning all over, his scalp here and there showing luminously through. His teeth, which were straight and very even, and which Viv remembered as having once been dazzlingly white, were turning yellow. The flesh of his throat was getting loose; there were folds in the skin in front of his ears. *He looks like his father*, she thought, watching him chew. He'd shown her a picture once. *He could be forty, at least.*

Then he caught her eye, and gave her a wink; and something of her old, pure affection for him flared up in her heart. When they'd finished their sandwiches he drew her to him and they lay on the rug, he on his back with his arm around her, she with her cheek in the firm, warm hollow between his shoulder and his chest. Now and then she raised herself a little to sip, awkwardly, at her drink; finally she swallowed it all in a gulp and let the empty beaker fall. He rubbed his face against her head, his rough chin plucking at her hair.

She looked into the sky. Her view of it was framed

by branches, by the restless tips of trees. The branches were thick with leaves still, but the leaves were ruddy, or golden, or the greenish-yellow of army uniforms. The sky itself was perfectly cloudless: blue as the bluest skies of summer.

'What bird is that?' she asked, pointing.

'That? That's a vulture.'

She gave him a nudge. 'What is it, really?'

He shaded his eyes. 'It's a kestrel. See how it hovers? It's waiting to dive. It's after a mouse.'

'Poor mouse.'

'There he goes!' He lifted his head, the muscles in his chest and throat growing tight beneath her cheek. The bird had swooped, but now rose again with empty claws. He lay back down. 'He's lost it.'

'Good.'

'It's only another sort of lunch. He's entitled to his bit of lunch, isn't he?'

'It's cruel.'

He laughed. 'I'd no idea you were so tender-hearted. – Look, now he's trying again.'

They watched the bird for a minute, marvelling together at the buoyancy of it, its graceful swoops and soars. Then Viv took off her sunglasses, to see it more clearly; and Reggie looked, not at the kestrel, but at her.

'That's better,' he said. 'It was like talking to a blind girl, before.'

She settled back on the rug and closed her eyes. 'You're used to them, of course.'

'Ha ha.'

He was still for a moment, then reached across her and picked something up. After a second she felt a tickling on her face, and brushed her cheek, thinking a fly had settled on it. But it was him: he had a long blade of grass and was stroking her with the tip of it. She closed her eyes again and let him do it. He followed the lines of her brow and her nose, the curve above her mouth; he worked the grass across her temples.

'You've changed your hair, haven't you?' he said.

'I got it cut, ages ago. – You're tickling me.'

He moved the blade of grass more firmly. 'How's that?'

'That's better.'

'I like it.'

'Like what?'

'Your hair.'

'Do you? It's all right.'

'It suits you . . . Open your eyes, Viv.'

She opened them, briefly, then screwed them up again. 'The sun's too bright.'

He raised his hand – held it a foot away from her face, to make a shade. 'Open them now,' he said.

'What for?'

'I want to look into your eyes.'

She laughed. 'Why?'

'I just do.'

'They're the same as they were the last time you looked into them.'

'That's what you think. Women's eyes are never the same. You're like cats, the lot of you.'

He tickled her face until she did as he asked and opened her eyes again. But she opened them wide, being silly.

'Not like that,' he said. So she looked at him properly. 'That's better.' His expression was soft. 'You've got lovely eyes. You've got beautiful eyes. Your eyes were the first thing I noticed about you.'

'I thought it was my legs you noticed first.'

'Your legs, too.'

He held her gaze, then threw the blade of grass away and leant and kissed her. He did it slowly, parting her lips with his own, pushing gently into her mouth. He tasted of the ham, still; the ham and the gin and orange. She supposed she must taste of it too. As the kiss went on, a speck of something – meat, or bread – came between their tongues, and he broke away to pick it from his mouth. But when he came back to her, he kissed her harder; and began to lean more heavily against her. He ran his hand down her body, from her cheek to her hip; then he stroked upwards again and cupped her breast. His hand was hot, and gripped her hard, almost painfully. When he drew it away and began to pluck instead at the buttons at the front of her dress, she stopped his fingers and lifted her head.

'Someone might come, Reg.'

'There's nobody about,' he said, 'for miles!'

She looked at his hand, still tugging at the buttons. 'Don't. You'll crease it.'

89

'Undo it for me, then.'

'All right. Wait.'

She looked around, conscious that anyone could be watching, hidden in the shadows of the trees. The sun was bright as a spotlight, the piece of ground they were lying on flat and quite un- obscured. The only sounds, however, were those of the stream, the birds, the restless leaves. She unfastened two of the buttons on her dress; then, after a moment, two more. Reggie drew the bodice back, exposing her bra; he put his mouth to the silk of it, feeling for her nipple, drawing at her breast. She moved about under his touch. But the queer thing was, she'd wanted him more, before, in the car in the middle of Stepney; she'd wanted him more while they were standing on that bridge. He kept his mouth fixed hard to her breast, and moved his hand back down her body to her thigh. When he caught hold of her skirt and began to push it up, she stopped his fingers again, and again said, 'Someone might see.'

He moved away, wiped his mouth. He tugged at the rug. 'I'll put this over us.'

'They could still see.'

'Jesus, Viv, I'm at that point where a troupe of girl-guides could go past and it wouldn't put me off! I swear, I'm bursting. I've been bursting for you all day.'

She didn't think he had been. For all his talk, for all his nonsense – here, and in the car – she didn't think he had been; and she wanted it less than ever now. He pulled up the rug and tucked it around her, then put his arm beneath it and tried to reach between her legs again. But she kept her thighs closed; and when he looked at her she shook her head – let him think what he liked. She said, 'Let me—' and moved her own hand to the buttons of his trousers, easing them open one by one, then sliding inside.

He groaned at the feel of her bare fingers. He twitched against her palm. He said, 'Oh, Viv. Christ, Viv.'

The seams of his underpants were taut against her wrist and made her clumsy; after a moment he reached and brought himself right out, then put his hand loosely around hers. He kept the hand there as she was doing it, and had his eyes shut tight the whole time; in the end she felt he might as well be doing it himself. The tartan rug went up and down over their fists. Two or three times she lifted her head and looked around, still anxious.

And she remembered, as she did it, other times, from years before, when he'd been in the army. They'd had to meet in hotel rooms – grubby rooms, but the grubbiness hadn't mattered. Being together was what had mattered. Pushing against each other's bodies, each other's skin and muscle and breath. That was what bursting for somebody meant. It wasn't this. It wasn't jokes about feather beds and Lovers' Lanes.

At the very last second he closed her hand, to

make a sort of trap for the spunk. Then he lay back, flushed and sweating and laughing. She held on to him a little longer before she drew her fingers away. He raised his head, the flesh of his throat bunching up. He was worried for his trousers.

'Got it all?'

'I think so.'

'Careful.'

'I am being careful.'

'Good girl.'

He tucked himself away, then fastened up his buttons. She looked around for a handkerchief, something like that; and finally wiped her hand on the grass.

He watched her do it, approvingly. 'That's good for the ground,' he said. He was full of life now. 'That'll make a tree grow. That'll make a tree, and a knickerless girl will one day come and climb it; and she'll get in the club, by me.' He held out his arms. 'Come here and give me a kiss, you beautiful creature!'

The simplicity of him, she thought, was quite amazing. But it had always been his faults and frailties that she'd loved most. She'd wasted her life on his weaknesses – his apologies, his promises . . . She moved back into his embrace. He lit another cigarette and they lay and smoked it together, gazing up again into the trees. The kestrel had vanished; they didn't know if it had caught its mouse or gone after another. The blue of the sky seemed to have thinned.

It was September – the end of September – and not summer: presently she gave a shiver, getting cold. He rubbed her arms, but soon they sat up, drank the last of the gin and orange, then stood and brushed down their clothes. He turned the cuffs of his trousers inside out, to shake the grass from them. He borrowed her handkerchief, and wiped her lipstick and powder from his mouth. He walked a little way off, and turned his back, and had a pee.

When he came back she said, 'Stay here'; and she went herself to a clump of bushes, drew up her skirt, pushed down her knickers and got into a squat. 'Watch out for nettles!' he called after her; but he called it vaguely, he didn't see where she had gone and couldn't see her once she'd stooped. She watched him bending at the car's wing-mirror, combing his hair. She watched him rinsing out the beakers in the stream. Then she looked at her hand. The spunk on her fingers had dried as fine as pretty lace; she rubbed at it, and it became plain white flakes that drifted to the ground and were lost.

He had to be home by seven o'clock, and it was already half-past four. They strolled to the little bridge again, and stood looking down into the water. They wandered back to the ruined mill; he picked up a piece of broken glass and cut their initials into the plaster, alongside the dirty messages. *RN, VP,* and a heart with an arrow.

But when he'd thrown the glass away, he looked at his watch.

'Better get going, I suppose.'

They went back to the car. She shook out the rug, and he folded it up and put it away, with the beakers, in the boot. Where the rug had been there was a square of flattened grass. It seemed a shame, in so lovely a place: she went over it, kicking the grass back up.

The car had been sitting in the sun all this time. She climbed in, and almost burnt her leg on the hot leather seat. Reggie got in beside her and gave her his handkerchief – spread it out beneath the crook of her knees, to keep her from burning.

When he had done it, he bent forward and kissed her thigh. She touched his head: the dark, oiled curls; the white scalp showing palely through. She looked at the lush green clearing again and said softly, 'I wish we could stay here.'

He let his head drop until it was resting in her lap. 'So do I,' he said. The words were muffled. He twisted round, to meet her gaze. 'You know— You know I hate it, don't you? You know, if I could have done it differently—? All of it, I mean.'

She nodded. There was nothing to say that they hadn't said before. He kept his head in her lap a moment longer, then kissed her thigh again and straightened up. He turned the key, and the engine rumbled into life. It seemed horribly loud, in the silence – just as the silence had seemed weird and wrong to them when they'd first arrived.

He turned the car, drove slowly back up the bumping track, and rejoined the road they'd come out on; they went past the cheese-coloured cottage without slowing down, then picked up the main road to London. The traffic was much heavier now. People were coming back, like them, from afternoons out. The speeding cars were noisy. The sun was in front of them, making them squint: every so often they'd make a turn, or pass through trees, and lose it for a minute; then it would reappear, bigger than before, pink and swollen and low in the sky.

The sun, and the warmth, and perhaps the gin that she had drunk, made Viv feel dozy. She put her head against Reggie's shoulder and closed her eyes. He rubbed his cheek against her hair again, sometimes turning his head to kiss her. They sang together, sleepily, old-fashioned songs – 'I Can't Give You Anything But Love', and 'Bye Bye Blackbird'.

> *Make my bed and light the light,*
> *I'll arrive late tonight.*
> *Blackbird, bye bye.*

When they reached the outskirts of London, she yawned and reluctantly straightened up. She got out her compact and powdered her face, redid her lipstick. The traffic seemed worse than ever, suddenly. Reggie tried a different route, through Poplar and Shadwell, but that was bad too. Finally they got caught in a jam at Tower Hill. She saw him looking at his watch, and said, 'Let me out here.' But he kept saying, 'Just give it a second.' He hated to give way to other drivers. 'If that little twerp in front would just – Christ! It's blokes like him who—'

The car moved forward. Then they got in another jam on Fleet Street, going into the Strand. He looked for a way to get out of it, but the side-streets were blocked by drivers with the same idea. He beat his fingers on the steering-wheel, saying, 'Damn, damn.' He looked at his watch again.

Viv sat tensely, catching his mood, shrinking down a little in her seat in case someone should spot her; but thinking of the place in the woods still, not wanting to give it up yet: the mill, the stream and bridge, the hush of it. *It ain't Piccadilly* . . . Reggie had brushed out the car before they'd started back, getting out all the petals and bits of grass that had been shaken in from the hedges. He'd nudged at the butterfly with his fingers until it had quivered and fluttered away.

She turned her head and looked into the lighted windows of shops, at the boxes of mocked-up chocolates and fruits, at the perfume bottles and liquor bottles – the same kind of coloured water doing, probably, for 'Nights of Parma' and 'Irish Malt'. The car inched forward. They drew near a cinema, the Tivoli. There were people outside it, queuing for tickets, and she gazed rather wistfully across them, at the girls and their boyfriends, the husbands and wives. The cinema had coloured lights on it, and the lights seemed to shine more luridly, more luminously, for shining in the twilight rather than the dark. She saw odd little disconnected details: the glint of an earring, the gleam of a man's hair, the sparkle of crystal in the paving-stones.

Then Reggie braked and tooted his horn. Someone had sauntered across the road in front of him and moved casually on. He threw up his hands. 'Don't mind me, mister, will you? Jesus Christ!' He followed the sauntering figure with his gaze, looking disgusted; but then his face changed. The figure, in stepping on to the pavement, must have given something away. Reggie started to laugh. 'My mistake,' he said, nudging Viv. 'What do you think of that? It's not a mister, it's a miss.'

Viv turned to look – and saw Kay, in a jacket and trousers. She was drawing a cigarette from a case and, with a stylish, idle gesture, tapping it lightly against the silver before raising it to her lips.

'What the hell's the matter?' asked Reggie in amazement.

For Viv had cried out. Her stomach had contracted as if she'd been struck in it. She put up a hand to hide her face and, ducking further down in her seat, said to Reggie with awful urgency: 'Go on. Drive on!'

He gaped at her. 'What's the matter?'

'Just drive on, can't you? Please!'

'Drive on? Have you gone barmy?'

The way ahead was still jammed with cars. Viv

moved about as if tormented. She looked back, towards Fleet Street. She said desperately, 'Go that way, can't you?'

'Which way?'

'The way we came.'

'The way we came? Are you—?' But now she'd actually grabbed the steering-wheel. 'Jesus!' said Reggie, pushing her hand away. 'All right. All right!' He looked over his shoulder and began, laboriously, to turn the car. The car behind gave a blast of its horn. The drivers heading for Ludgate Circus gazed at him as if he was a lunatic. He worked the gears, sweating and cursing, and slowly edged the car round.

Viv kept her head down; but looked back once. Kay had joined the line of people outside the cinema: she was holding a lighter to her cigarette, and the flame of it, springing up, through the twilight, lit her fingers and her face. *Hush, Vivien*, Viv remembered her saying. The memory was stark, after all this time – stark and terrible – the grip of her hand, the closeness of her mouth. *Vivien, hush.*

'Thank God for that!' said Reggie, when they were inching forwards again in the other direction. 'Talk about not drawing attention to ourselves. What on earth was all that for? Are you all right?'

She didn't answer. She'd felt the grinding of the gears, the lurching forwards and backwards of the car, in what seemed to be all her muscles and bones. She folded her arms across herself, as if to hold herself together.

'What is it?' asked Reggie.

'I saw someone I knew,' she said at last; 'that's all.'

'Someone you knew? Who was it?'

'Just someone.'

'Just someone. Well, I expect they got a bloody good look at you and me, too. Hell, Viv.'

He went grumbling on. She didn't listen. He stopped the car at last in some street near Blackfriars Bridge; she said she'd take a bus from there, and he didn't argue. He pulled up in a quiet-looking spot, and drew her to him so that they could kiss; afterwards he borrowed her handkerchief again and wiped his mouth. He wiped the sweat from his fore-head, too, and, 'What a trip!' he said – as if the afternoon had been some sort of disaster; as if he'd forgotten, already, the stream and the ruined mill, the initials on the wall. She didn't care. The feel of his hand on her arm, of his lips against her mouth, was suddenly frightful. She wanted to get home, be on her own, away from him.

As she opened her door he reached for her again. He'd put his hand into a pocket in the dashboard and was bringing something out. It turned out to be two tins of meat: one beef, and one pork.

She was so distracted, she started to take them. She opened her bag to put them away. But then something seemed to give way inside her, and she was suddenly furious. She pushed them back at him. 'I don't want them!' she said. 'Take them— Give them to your wife!'

The tins fell, and bounced from the seat. 'Viv!' said Reggie, astonished, hurt. 'Don't be like that! What have I done? What the hell's the matter? Viv!'

She got out, closed the door, and walked away. He leant across the seat and wound down the window, still calling her name – still saying, in amazement, 'What's the matter? What have I done? What—?' Then his voice began to grow hard – not so much, she thought, with anger, as with simple weariness. 'What the hell have I done, now?'

She didn't look back. She turned a corner, and the words faded. After that he must have started the engine again and driven off. She joined a queue at a bus-stop, and waited ten minutes for a bus; and he didn't come after her.

When she got home, she found the flat full of people. Her sister Pamela had come round, with her husband, Howard, and their three little boys. They'd come to bring Viv's father some tea. Pamela had warmed it up on the stove, and the narrow kitchen was stuffy and hot. There was washing draped on the laundry rack, hoisted up but dangling almost to the floor; Pamela must have done that, too. The wireless was on full-blast. Howard was sitting on the kitchen table. The two eldest boys were charging about, and Viv's father had the baby in his lap.

'Nice day?' asked Pamela. She was drying her hands, working the towel into the creases between her fingers. She looked Viv over. 'You've caught the sun. All right for some.'

Viv went to the sink and peered into her father's shaving mirror. Her face was pink and white, blotchy. She drew forward her hair. 'It was hot,' she said. 'Hello, Dad.'

'All right, love? How was your picnic?'

'It was OK. How's things, Howard?'

'All right, Viv. Doing our best, aren't we? How d'you like this weather? I tell you—'

Howard could never stop talking. The two boys were the same. They had things to show her: noisy little pop-guns; they put in the corks and fired them off. Her father followed the words on everybody's mouths – nodding, smiling, moving his own lips slightly; for he was awfully deaf. The baby was struggling in his arms, reaching for the pop-guns, wanting to get down. When Viv drew close her father held him out to her, glad to give him up. 'He wants you, love.'

But she shook her head. 'He's too big, that one. He weighs a ton.'

'Give him here,' said Pamela. 'Maurice— Howard, don't just bloody well sit there!'

The racket was terrible. Viv said she was going to go and take her shoes and stockings off. She went into her bedroom and closed the door.

For a second she just stood, not knowing what to do with herself – thinking that she might start crying, be ill . . . But she couldn't start crying with her dad and her sister in the other room. She sat on the bed, then lay down with her hands on her stomach; lying down, however, made her feel worse. She sat up again. She got to her feet. She couldn't shake off the shock of it, the upset of it.

Hush, Vivien.

She took a step; then tilted her head, hearing a noise above the muffled din of the radio, thinking it might be Pamela or one of the boys, in the hall. But the noise turned out to be nothing. She stood undecided, for almost a minute, biting her hand.

Then she went quickly to her wardrobe and drew back its door.

The wardrobe was filled with bits of rubbish. There were some of Duncan's old school-clothes there, hanging up beside her dresses; there were even two or three ancient frocks of her mother's, which her father had never wanted to throw away. Above the rail was a shelf, where she kept her sweaters. Behind the sweaters were photograph albums, old autograph books, old diaries, things like that.

She tilted her head, listening again for footsteps in the hall; then she reached into the shadows behind the albums and brought out a little tobacco tin. She brought it out as naturally as if she reached for it every day, when in fact she'd placed it there three years before and hadn't looked at it since. She'd pressed the lid down very tightly then, and now the joints in her wrists and fingers felt weak. She had to get a coin, and prise away at it with that. And when the lid was loosened she hesitated again – still listening out, anxiously, in case someone should come.

Then she drew the lid off.

Inside the tin was a small parcel of cloth. Inside the parcel of cloth was a ring: a plain gold ring, quite aged, and marked with dents and little scratches. She took it up, held it for a second in the palm of her hand; then slipped it on her finger and covered her eyes.

At ten to six, when the men who ran the candle-making machines turned off the pumps, the sudden silence in the factory made your ears ring. It was like coming out of water. The girls at Duncan's bench took it as a signal to start getting ready to go home: they got out their lipsticks and their compacts and things like that. The older women started rolling cigarettes. Len took a comb from his trouser pocket and ran it through his hair. He wore his hair a bit spivvily, swept back behind his ears. When he put the comb away he caught Duncan's eye, and leant forward.

'Have a guess what I'll be doing tonight,' he said, with a glance down the bench. He lowered his voice. 'I'm taking a girl to Wimbledon Common. She's stacked like this.' He gestured with his hands, then rolled his eyes and gave a whistle. 'Oh, mama! She's seventeen. She's got a sister, too. The sister's a looker, but got less up top. What do you think? You doing anything tonight?'

'Tonight?' said Duncan.

'Want to come along? The sister's a heart-throb, I'm telling you. What kind do you like? I know loads of girls. Big ones, little ones. I could fix you up, like that!' Len snapped his fingers.

Duncan didn't know what to say. He tried to picture a crowd of girls. But each one was like the little figure of wax that Len had made earlier, with curves and juts and waving hair, and a rough blank face. He shook his head, beginning to smile.

Len looked disgusted. 'You're missing out, I swear to God. This girl's a stunner. She's got a bloke, but he's in the army. She's used to doing it regular and she's feeling the pinch. I tell you, if the sister wasn't so friendly I'd be after her myself—'

He went on like that until the factory whistle sounded; then, 'Well, it's your funeral,' he said, getting to his feet. 'You think of me, that's all, at ten o'clock tonight!' He gave Duncan a wink of his brown gypsy eye, then hurried away – lurching a little from side to side, like a stout old lady; for his left leg was short, and fused at the knee.

The girls and the women went off quickly, too. They called goodbye as they went: 'Ta ta, Duncan!' 'So long, love!' 'See you Monday, Duncan!'

Duncan nodded. He couldn't bear the mood of the factory at this time of the day – the forced, wild jollity, the dash for the exit. Saturday nights were worst of all. Some people actually ran, to be first out through the gates. The men who had cycles made a sort of race of it: the yard, for ten or fifteen minutes, was like a sink with its plug pulled. He always found a reason to linger or dawdle. Tonight he got a broom, and swept up the parings of wax and the cuttings of wick from the floor beneath his stool. Then he walked very slowly to the locker-room and got his jacket; he visited the lavatory and combed his hair. When he went outside he'd taken so long, the yard was almost deserted: he stood for a moment on the step, getting used to the feel of space and the change of temperature. The Candle Room was kept cool because of the wax, but the evening was warm. The sun was sinking in the sky, and he had a vague, unhappy sense that time had passed – real time, proper time, not factory time – and he had missed out on it.

He had just put down his head and started to make his way across the yard when he heard his name called: 'Pearce! Hi, Pearce!' He looked up – his heart giving a thump inside his chest, because he'd already recognised the voice, but couldn't believe it. Robert Fraser was there, at the gate. He looked as though he'd just come running up. He was hatless, as Duncan was. His face was pink, and he was smoothing back his hair.

Duncan quickened his pace and went over to him. His heart was still lurching about. He said, 'What are you doing here? Have you been here all afternoon?'

'I came back,' said Fraser breathlessly. 'I thought I'd missed you! I heard the whistle go when I was still three streets away. You don't mind? After I'd gone this morning I thought how crazy it was, that you were here and— Well. Do you have an hour? I thought we could go for a drink. I know a pub, right on the river.'

'A pub?' said Duncan.

Fraser laughed, seeing his expression. 'Yes. Why not?'

Duncan hadn't been to a pub in ages, and the thought of going inside one now, with Fraser – of sitting at a table at Fraser's side, drinking beer, like a regular chap – was tremendously exciting, but alarming too. He was thinking, as well, of Mr Mundy, who would be waiting for him at home. He pictured the table set for tea: the knives and forks put neatly out, the salt and pepper, the mustard already mixed in its pot . . .

Fraser must have seen the look of indecision in his face. He said, as if disappointed, 'You've got other plans. Well, never mind. It was just a chance. Which way are you going? I could walk with you—'

'No,' said Duncan quickly. 'It's all right. If it's just for an hour—'

Fraser clapped him on the arm. 'Good man!'

He led Duncan south, towards Shepherd's Bush Green: the opposite direction to the one that Duncan would normally have taken. He walked loosely, easily, with his hands in his pockets and his shoulders back, and now and then he jerked his head to keep the hair out of his eyes. His hair seemed very fair with the evening sunlight on it; his face was still pink and lightly sweating. When they'd picked their way through the worst of the traffic he got out a handkerchief and wiped his forehead and the back of his neck, saying, 'I need a drink! I need several drinks, in fact. I've been out at Ealing since two o'clock, putting together a humorous piece on pig farming. My photographer spent more than an hour trying to coax a whimsical expression out of a sow. I tell you, Pearce, the next time I see a pig it had better be on a plate and have sage and onion coming out of its ears.'

He kept talking as they walked. He told Duncan about some of the other writing jobs he'd recently been sent on: a beautiful-baby competition; a haunted house. Duncan listened just closely enough to be able to nod and laugh when he was meant to. The rest of the time he was looking Fraser over, getting used to the amazing sight of him on a street, in ordinary clothes. But Fraser must have been doing something similar, for after a while he stopped talking and caught Duncan's eye, looking almost rueful.

'This is bloody queer, isn't it? I keep expecting Chase or Garnish to appear and start barking at us. "Keep in!" "Fall Back!" "Stand to your doors!" I saw Eric Wainwright last year. You remember him? He saw me, too, I know he did – but cut me dead. He was in Piccadilly, with some awful tart of a girl. I ran into that prig Dennis Watling, too, a couple of months ago, at a political meeting. He was going on about prison at the top of his voice – as if he'd spent twelve years there, instead of twelve months. I think he was sorry to see me turn up. I think he thought I stole his thunder.'

They were passing through Hammersmith now, crossing cheerless residential streets; soon, however, at Fraser's direction, they made a turn. The feel of the area began to change. The houses were replaced, here and there, by bigger buildings, warehouses and works; the air smelt sourer, dark and vinegary. The dirt surface of the road fell away, exposing cobbles, and the cobbles were slippery, as if with grease. Duncan didn't know this area at all. Fraser stepped on, in his confident way, and he had to hurry to keep up. He suddenly felt almost nervous. *What on earth am I doing here?* he thought. He looked at Fraser and saw a stranger. The preposterous idea came to him that Fraser might be mad; that he might have lured Duncan here and be meaning to kill him. He didn't know why Fraser would want to do such a thing, but his mind ran on with the idea, extravagantly. He pictured his own body, strangled or stabbed. He wondered who might find it. He thought of his father and Viv being visited by policemen; being told that he had been found in this queer place, and never knowing why.

Then all at once they turned again and emerged from shadow, and were at the river. Here was the pub that Fraser had been making for: a wooden, wonderfully quaint-looking building that made Duncan think, at once, of Dickens, of *Oliver Twist*. He was enchanted with it. He forgot all his anxiety about being stabbed or strangled. He stopped, put his hand on Fraser's arm, and said, 'But, it's lovely!'

'You think so?' said Fraser, grinning at him again. 'I thought you'd like it. The beer's not bad, either. Come on.' He led Duncan through the narrow, crooked little doorway.

Inside, the place was not quite so charming as its exterior promised; it had been done up like an ordinary public bar, and there were nonsensical things on the walls, horse-brasses and warming-pans and bellows. It was also, already, at half-past six, rather crowded. Fraser pushed his way to the bar and bought a four-pint jug of beer. He gestured to doors at the back of the room, which opened on a pier, overlooking the river; but the pier was busier, even, than the bar. He and Duncan turned around and made their way back through the crush of people and went out again to the street. There was a set of river-stairs there. Fraser stood at the top and looked over. There was plenty of room, he said, down on the beach. 'The tide's right out. It's perfect. Come on.'

They climbed down the steps, going carefully because of the jug of beer and the glasses. The beach was muddy, but the mud had had the afternoon sun on it and was more or less dry. Fraser found a spot at the base of the wall: he took off his jacket and spread it out, and the two of them sat on it, side by side, their shoulders almost touching. The wall was warm, and tarnished from the Thames: you could see very clearly the line, about six feet up, where the greenish stain of the water gave way to the grey of permanently exposed stone. But the tide, at the moment, was low; the river looked narrow – absurdly narrow, as if you could very easily just nip across, on tiptoe, from this side to the other. Duncan screwed up his eyes, making the view grow blurry; imagining for a moment the water rushing in, swallowing him up. The wall was warm against his back, and he could just feel the nudging of Fraser's arm against his own, as Fraser undid his cuffs and rolled up his sleeves.

Fraser poured out beer. 'Here's yours,' he said, lifting his glass. He drained it in three or four gulps, then wiped his mouth. 'Christ! That's better, isn't it?' He poured out more, and drank again.

Then he put his hand into his pocket and drew out a pipe and a pouch of tobacco. As Duncan watched, he began the business of filling the pipe up – teasing out strands of tobacco with his long brown fingers, then thumbing them firmly into the bowl. He caught Duncan's eye, and smiled. 'A bit different to the old days, eh? It's the first thing I bought when I got out.' He put the stem of the pipe to his mouth, then struck a match and held the flame of it to the bowl; his throat tightened as he sucked, and his cheeks went in and out, in and out – like the sides, Duncan thought, of a hot-water bottle; or, if you wanted to be more romantic about it, like a Spanish wineskin. He watched the bluish smoke rise up from Fraser's mouth and be snatched away by breezes.

For a while they just sat, drinking their beer – shading their eyes to look at the sun, which seemed fantastically pink and swollen in the late summer sky. The heat of it brought out the stink of the river and the beach, but it was hard to mind that in a place like this; there was too much glamour to the scene. Duncan thought of sailors, smugglers, lightermen, jolly jack tars . . . Fraser laughed. 'Look at those lads,' he said.

A group of boys had appeared, further along the beach. They had taken off their shirts, their shoes and socks, rolled up their trousers, and were running to the water. They ran in that shrinking, girlish way that even grown-up men must run across pointed stones; and when they reached the river they began to splash and lark about. They were young – much younger than Duncan and Fraser, perhaps fourteen or fifteen. Their hands and feet were too big for their bodies, which were all very slender and slight. They looked as though they had too much life in them, that the life was rushing about inside them, giving them awkward angles and tilts.

The people drinking out on the pier at the back of the pub had seen the boys too, and started to call encouragement. The boys began to splash mud instead of water; one fell right in, and emerged quite black, like a thing of clay – like some weird sort of mannequin, meant to be paraded about the streets. He waded further out, then plunged head first into the water and came up clean again, shaking the river from his hair.

Fraser laughed and leant forward. He put his hand to his mouth and cheered, like the people on the pier. He seemed as full of life as the boys themselves, his bare lower arms very tanned, his long hair bouncing about his brow.

After a minute he sat back, smiling. He drew on his pipe again, then struck another match and held it to the bowl, cradling the flame. But he looked at Duncan as he did it, from beneath his slightly lowered brows; and as soon as the tobacco was properly relit and the match shaken out, he took the pipe from his lips and said, 'Wasn't it odd, my running into you at the factory like that?'

Duncan's heart sank. He didn't answer. Fraser went on, 'I've been thinking about it all day. It's just, not at all the sort of place I'd have expected to find you working.'

'Isn't it?' said Duncan, lifting his glass.

'Of course it isn't! Doing work like that, amongst people like that? The place is only one step up from a charity, isn't it? How can you stand it?'

'Everybody else there stands it. Why shouldn't I?'

'You really don't mind it?'

Duncan thought it over. 'I don't like the smells much,' he said at last. 'They seep into your clothes. And sometimes you get a headache, from all the noise; or your eyes go funny, because of the belt.'

Fraser frowned. 'That wasn't what I meant, exactly,' he said.

Duncan knew that it wasn't what he'd meant. But he lifted a shoulder, and went on in the same light tone, 'It's easy work. It's not so different from sewing canvas, actually. And it lets you think of other things. I like that.'

Fraser still looked baffled. 'You wouldn't rather do something a little more – well – a little more inspiring?'

That made Duncan snort. 'It doesn't matter what I'd *rather*. Can't you just imagine the look on the face of the DPA man, if I'd said I'd *rather* this or I'd *rather* that? I'm lucky to have any job at all; even a pretend one. It was different for you. If you were like me – if you had my sort of past, I mean—' He couldn't be bothered. He began to pick at the surface of the beach: at the stones and bits of broken china, the oyster shells and bones. 'I don't want to talk about it,' he said, when he saw Fraser still waiting. 'It's boring. Tell me, instead, what you've been doing.'

'I want to know about you, first.'

'There's nothing to know. You know it all, already!' He smiled. 'I mean it. Tell me where you've been. You wrote me a letter, once, from a train.'

'Did I?'

'Yes. Just after you'd got out. Don't you remember? Of course, they wouldn't let me keep it; I read it, though, about fifty times. Your hand-writing was all over the place, and the paper had a mark on it – you said it was onion-juice.'

'Onion-juice!' said Fraser thoughtfully. 'Yes, now I remember. A woman on the train had an onion, and it was the first any of us had seen in about

113

three years. Someone got out a knife and we cut it up and ate it raw. It was glorious!' He laughed, and drank more of his beer, his Adam's apple leaping like a fish in his throat.

The train, he said, must have been the one he'd taken to Scotland; he'd been at a sort of logging-camp up there, with other COs, right until the end of the war. 'I came down to London after that,' he said, 'and got some work with a refugee charity – sorting out people who'd just got over here, finding them houses, getting their children into schools.' He shook his head, thinking about it. 'The things I heard would make your hair curl, Pearce. Stories of people who'd lost everything. Russians, Poles, Jews; stories of the camps— I couldn't believe it. What you've read in the papers is nothing, nothing at all . . . I did it for a year. That was as long as I could stand it. Any more of it, and I think I would have finished up wanting to blow my own brains out!'

He smiled – then realised what he'd said, caught Duncan's eye, and blushed; and at once started talking again, to cover the blunder up. He'd been at the charity, he said, until the previous autumn; then he'd started to try his hand at journalism, with a view to writing for political magazines. A friend of his had got him the 'hack job' he was doing now; he was sticking with it in the hope that something more serious would come along. He'd been involved with a girl, for a month or two, but it hadn't worked out – he coloured again as he told Duncan that. She'd been one of the other people, he said, at the charity for refugees.

He spoke seriously, fluently, like a commentator on the radio. His well-bred accent was very marked, and once or twice Duncan found himself almost wincing, knowing that the accent must be carrying across the beach, reaching the ears of other drinkers. He began to look at Fraser and, as he had before, to see him as a stranger. He couldn't imagine the life that Fraser had had, in the logging-camp in Scotland and then in London, with a girl; he could only really picture him, still, as he'd used to see him every day, in the small chill cell at Wormwood Scrubs, with the coarse prison blanket over his shoulders, mopping up his cocoa with his breakfast bread, or standing at the window, his lean white face lit up by moonlight or by coloured flares in the sky.

He gazed down into his glass, then became aware that Fraser had fallen silent and was watching him.

'I know what you're thinking,' Fraser said, when he looked up. He'd lowered his voice, and seemed self-conscious. 'You're wondering how it was for me, working with those refugees, listening to the stories I had to hear – knowing other men had fought while I'd done nothing.' He threw a stone, so that it bounced across the beach. 'It made me sick, if you want to know. Sick with myself – not because I'd objected; but because objection hadn't been enough. Sick because I hadn't tried harder, hadn't tried to find other ways – and hadn't made

115

other people try to find them with me – earlier in the war. Sick, for being healthy. Sick, simply, for being alive.' He blushed again, and looked away. He said, more quietly than ever, 'I thought of you, as it happens.'

'Me!'

'I remembered – well, things you'd said.'

Duncan gazed down into his glass again. 'I thought you'd forgotten all about me.'

Fraser moved forward. 'Don't be an ass! My time's been taken up, that's all. Hasn't yours been?'

Duncan didn't answer. Fraser waited, then turned away as if irritated. He drank more of his beer, then went back to fiddling with his pipe, sucking at the stem, making his cheeks like wine-skins again.

He's wishing he'd never asked me here, thought Duncan, prising at a stone. *He's wondering why he did. He's working out how soon he can get rid of me.* He thought again of Mr Mundy, waiting at home, with the tea ready; looking at the clock; perhaps opening the front door to gaze anxiously down the street . . .

He became aware, once again, that Fraser was watching him. He looked round, and their gazes met. Fraser smiled and said, 'I'd forgotten how inscrutable you can be, Pearce. I'm used to fellows, I suppose, who do nothing but talk.'

'I'm sorry,' said Duncan. 'We can go, if you like.'

'For God's sake, I didn't mean that! I just—Well, won't you tell me anything about yourself? I've been going on like a lunatic, while you've hardly said a word. Don't you— Don't you trust me?'

'Trust you!' said Duncan. 'It isn't that. It's nothing like that. There's nothing to tell, that's all.'

'You've tried that once. It won't wash, Pearce! Come on.'

'There's nothing to say!'

'There must be something. I don't even know where you live! Where *do* you live? Up near that factory of yours?'

Duncan moved uncomfortably. 'Yes.'

'In a house? In rooms?'

'Well,' said Duncan. He moved again; but could see no way out of it . . . 'In a house,' he admitted, after a moment, 'up in White City.'

Fraser stared, just as Duncan had known he would. 'White City? You're joking! So close to the Scrubs? I wonder you can stand it! Fulham was near enough for me, I don't mind telling you. White City . . .' He shook his head, unable to believe it. 'But, why there? Your family—' He was thinking back. 'They used to live in – where was it? Streatham?'

'Oh,' said Duncan automatically, 'I don't live with *them*.'

'You don't? Why not? They've looked after you all right, haven't they? You've sisters, haven't you? One in particular— What was her name? Valerie? Viv!' He pulled at his hair. 'God, it's all coming back. She used to visit. She was good to you. She

117

was better to you than my bloody sister was to me, anyway! Isn't she good to you, still?'

'It isn't her,' said Duncan. 'It's the others. We never got on, even before—Well, you know. When I got out it was worse than ever. My oldest sister's husband hates my guts. I heard him talking about me once, to one of his friends. He called me— He called me Little Lord Fauntleroy. He calls me Mary Pickford, too. – Don't laugh!' But he began to laugh, himself.

'I'm sorry,' said Fraser, still smiling. 'He sounds like a regular charmer.'

'He's the sort of person, that's all, who can't bear it when people are different to him. They're all like that. But Viv isn't. She understands – well, that things aren't perfect. That people aren't perfect. She—' He hesitated.

'She what?' asked Fraser.

They were recapturing some of their old closeness. Duncan lowered his voice. 'Well, she's seeing some man.' He glanced around. 'A married man. It's been going on for ages. I never knew, when I was inside.'

Fraser looked thoughtful. 'I see.'

'Don't look like that! She isn't a—Well, she isn't a tart, or whatever you're thinking.'

'I'm sure she isn't. Still, I'm sorry to hear it, somehow. I remember her; I remember liking the look of her. And these things, you know, hardly ever turn out well, especially for the woman.'

Duncan shrugged. 'It's their business, isn't it? What does "turning out well" mean? Do you mean, being married? If they were married they'd probably hate each other.'

'Perhaps. But, what's the man like? What kind of bloke is he? Have you met him?'

Duncan had forgotten this way Fraser had, of catching hold of a subject and niggling away at it, just for the pleasure of thinking it through. He said, more reluctantly, 'He's some sort of salesman, that's all I know. He gets her tins of meat. He gets her loads, all the time. She can't take them home, my dad would wonder. She gives them to me and Uncle Horace—'

He stopped, in confusion and embarrassment at what he'd just said. Fraser didn't notice; he latched on to Duncan's words instead.

'Your uncle,' he said. 'That's right, Mrs Alexander mentioned him, at the factory. She said what a wonderful nephew you are, or something like that.' He smiled. 'So your family isn't quite so bad as you paint it, after all . . . Well, I'd like to meet your uncle, Pearce. I'd like to meet Viv, too. I'd certainly like to see where you live. Will you let me come and visit you, some other time? For we— Well, there's nothing to stop us from being friends again, is there? Now that we've hooked up together like this?'

Duncan nodded; but didn't trust himself to speak. He finished the beer that was in his glass, then turned his head, imagining the look that he knew would appear on Fraser's face, if he was ever to go home with Duncan and see Mr Mundy there.

He went back to picking at the litter of things on the beach. Soon his eye was drawn by something in particular, and he levered it up. It turned out, as he'd thought, to be the stem and part of the bowl of an old clay pipe. He showed it to Fraser, then started picking the mud from it with a piece of wire. Partly to change the subject he said, as he did it, 'There might have been a man here, three hundred years ago, smoking tobacco just like you. Isn't that a funny thought?'

Fraser smiled. 'Isn't it?'

Duncan held the pipe up and studied it. 'I wonder what that man's name was. Doesn't it torment you, that we'll never know? I wonder where he lived and what he was like. He didn't know, did he, that his pipe would be found by people like us, in 1947?'

'Perhaps he was lucky not to be able to imagine 1947.'

'Maybe someone will find *your* pipe, three hundred years from now.'

'Not a chance of it!' said Fraser. 'I'd lay a thousand pounds to a penny that my little pipe, and everything else, will be burnt to cinders by then.' He finished his beer, and got to his feet.

'Where are you going?' Duncan asked him.

'To get more beer.'

'It's my turn.'

'It doesn't matter. I drank most of this jug. I need the lavatory, too.'

'Shall I come with you?'

'To the lavatory?'

'To the bar!'

Fraser laughed. 'No, stay here. Someone will take our place. I won't be long.'

He'd started to move off across the beach as he was speaking, beating idly with the empty jug against his thigh. Duncan watched him climb the water-stairs and disappear over the top.

The pub, it was true, was more crowded than before. People had brought their drinks out, as Fraser and Duncan had, to the street and the beach; a few men and women were sitting or perching on the wall above Duncan's head. He hadn't realised, before, that they were there. He didn't like to think that they were looking down at him, or might have been listening to the things he had been saying . . .

He put the piece of clay pipe in his pocket; then gazed out at the river. The tide was turning, and the surface of the water seemed to tussle with itself, like snakes. The boys who'd been splashing about in the mud had all sat down at the edge of the shore; now they rose and came back up the beach, driven in by the tide. They looked younger than ever. They were grinning, but also shivering, like dogs. They walked more wincingly, too: Duncan imagined the soles of their feet having softened in the water, getting cut by stones and shells. He tried to stop himself looking at them as they climbed the water-stairs; he had a sudden horror of seeing a boy's white foot with blood on it.

He lowered his head, and started picking at the beach again. He found a comb with broken teeth. He prised up a shard of china from a cup, its dainty handle still attached.

And then – he didn't know why; it might have been that someone spoke his name, and the words reached his ears through some freak lull in the sounds of voices, laughter, water – he turned his head towards the pier again, and his gaze met that of a bald-headed man who was sitting with a woman at one of its tables. Duncan knew the man at once. He came from Streatham; he lived in a street close to the one in which Duncan had grown up. But now, instead of nodding to Duncan, instead of smiling or lifting his hand, the bald-headed man said something to the woman he was with, something like, 'Yes, that's him all right'; and the two of them stared at Duncan, with an extraordinary mixture of malevolence, avidity and blankness.

Duncan quickly looked away. When he glanced back, and found the man and woman still watching, he changed his pose – turned his head, moved his legs, shifted his weight to his other shoulder. He was still horribly aware of being observed, being discussed, sized up, disliked. *Look at him*, he imagined the man and woman saying. *He thinks he's all right, he does. He thinks he's just like you and me.* For he tried to picture himself as he must appear to them; and he saw himself, without Fraser beside him, as a kind of oddity or fraud. He turned his head again, more slyly – and yes, there they were, still watching him: they were lifting drinks and cigarettes, looking at him now with the empty yet bullying expressions of people who have settled down for a night at the cinema . . . He closed his eyes. Someone above him gave a raucous laugh. It seemed to him that the laughter could only be directed at him – that, one by one, the drinkers outside the pub were nudging their neighbours, nodding and smiling, spreading the story that Pearce was here – Duncan Pearce was here, drinking beer on the beach, just as if he had as perfect a right to do it as anybody else!

If only Fraser would come! How long had it been, since he'd gone off with the jug? Duncan wasn't sure. It seemed like ages. He'd probably got talking to someone, some ordinary man. He was probably flirting with the barmaid. And suppose, for some reason, he never came back? How would Duncan get home? He wasn't sure he could remember the way. His mind was getting blank or dark – he tried to concentrate, and it was just as though he was blindfolded and putting out his foot, and could feel soft ground, crumbling away . . . Now he began really to panic. He opened his eyes and looked down at his hands, for he'd once heard a doctor say that looking at your own hands, when you were frightened, could make you feel calmer. But he'd grown too conscious of himself: his hands seemed odd to him, like a stranger's. His whole body felt queer and wrong: he was aware all at once of his heart, his lungs; it began to seem to him that if he were to draw his attention away from those organs for a single instant, they'd fail. He sat on the beach with his eyes shut tight, sweating and almost panting under the frightful burden of having to breathe, press blood through his veins, keep the muscles in his arms and legs from flying into a spasm.

In what might have been five minutes more – or what might easily have been ten or even twenty – Fraser came back. Duncan heard the sound of the full jug being set down on the stones, then felt the touch of Fraser's thigh against his own as Fraser sat.

'It's crazy in there,' he was saying. 'It's like a scrum. I— What's the matter?'

Duncan couldn't answer. He opened his eyes and tried to smile. But even the muscles of his face were against him: he felt his mouth twist, and must have looked ghastly. Fraser said again, more urgently, 'What is it, Pearce?'

'It's nothing,' said Duncan at last.

'Nothing? You look like absolute hell. Here.' He passed Duncan his handkerchief. 'Wipe your face, you're sweating. Is that better?'

'Yes, a bit.'

'You're trembling like a leaf! What's it all about?'

Duncan shook his head. He said unsteadily, 'It'll sound stupid.' His tongue was sticking to his mouth.

'I don't care about that.'

'It's just, there's a man over there—'

Fraser turned to look. 'What man? Where?'

'Don't let him see you! He's over there, on the pier. A man from Streatham. A bald-headed man. He's been looking at me, him and his girl. He – he knows all about me.'

'What do you mean? That you've – been inside?'

Duncan shook his head again. 'Not just that. About why I was in there. About me and – and Alec—'

He couldn't go on. Fraser watched him a little longer, then turned and gazed again at the figures on the pier. Duncan wondered what the man would do when he saw Fraser looking. He imagined him making some awful gesture – or simply nodding at Fraser and smiling.

But after a moment, Fraser turned back. He said gently, 'There's no one looking, Pearce.'

'There must be,' said Duncan. 'Are you sure?'

'Quite sure. No one's looking at all. See for yourself.'

Duncan hesitated, then put his hand across his eyes and peered between his fingers. And it was true. The man and the woman had disappeared and a quite different couple were sitting at their table. This man had sandy-coloured hair; he was pouring crumbs into his mouth from a bag of crisps. The woman was yawning: patting at her lips with a plump white hand. The rest of the drinkers were talking amongst themselves, or gazing back into the bar, or out at the water – gazing anywhere, in fact, but at Duncan.

Duncan let out his breath, and his shoulders sank. He didn't know what to think now. For all he knew, he might have imagined the whole thing. He didn't care. His panic had drained him, emptied him out. He wiped his face again and said shakily, wretchedly, 'I ought to go home.'

'In a minute,' said Fraser. 'Drink some of this beer, first.'

'All right. But you'll – you'll have to pour it.'

Fraser lifted the jug and filled their glasses. Duncan took a gulp, and then another. He had to hold his glass with two hands, to keep it from spilling. In time, however, he began to feel calmer. He wiped his mouth and glanced at Fraser.

'I suppose you must think me a bit of a fool.'

'Don't talk tripe! Don't you remember—?'

Duncan spoke over his words. 'I'm not used, you see, to going about like this, on my own. I'm not like you.'

Fraser shook his head, as if annoyed or exasperated. He looked at Duncan, then looked away. He shifted his pose, drank more of his beer. Finally he said, very awkwardly, 'I wish, Pearce, that I'd kept in touch with you. I wish I'd written, more than I did. I— I let you down. I see that now, and I'm sorry. I let you down badly. But that year, in the Scrubs: once I'd got out, it seemed – I don't know – it seemed like a dream.' He met Duncan's gaze, his eyelids fluttering. 'Do you understand me? It seemed like someone else's life, not mine. It was just as though I'd been plucked right out of time, then dropped back in it, and had to take up where I left off.'

Duncan nodded. He said slowly, 'It wasn't like that, for me. When I came out, everything was different. Everything was changed. I'd always known it would be, and it was. People said, "You'll do all right." But I knew I never would.'

They sat without speaking, as if both exhausted. Fraser got out his matches and his pipe. And now the flame showed brightly, the day was darkening. He rolled down his sleeves and fastened his cuffs, and Duncan felt him shiver.

They watched the movement of the river. The surface of the water, in just a few minutes, had lost its hectic, restless look. The shore had narrowed further already, the water creeping forwards as if, like a cat's rough tongue, it was wearing the land away with every stroke and lap. Then a tug went rapidly by, and made waves: they rushed and were sucked back, then rushed again; then wore themselves out and ran more feebly.

Fraser threw a stone. He said, 'How does Arnold have it? *The eternal note of sadness* – is it? And *the* something *naked shingles of the world* . . .' He passed his hand over his face, laughing at himself. 'Christ, Pearce, the moment I start quoting poetry, we're done for! Come on.' He levered himself up. 'Forget the beer, and let's go. I'll walk you home. Right to the door. And you can introduce me to your – Uncle Horace, was it?'

Duncan thought of Mr Mundy, pacing the parlour, coming limping to answer their ring. But he hadn't the energy, now, for fear or embarrassment or anything like that. He got to his feet, and followed Fraser up the water-stairs; and they started off together, northwards, towards White City, through the steadily darkening streets.

CHAPTER 3

'Don't you know the war's over?' the man behind the counter in a baker's shop asked Kay.

He said it because of her trousers and hair, trying to be funny; but she had heard this sort of thing a thousand times, and it was hard to smile. When he caught her accent, anyway, his manner changed. He handed over the bag, saying, 'There you are, madam.' But he must have given some sort of look behind her back because, as she went out, the other customers laughed.

She was used to that, too. She tucked the bag under her arm and put her hands in her trouser pockets. The best thing to do was brazen it out, throw back your head, walk with a swagger, make a 'character' of yourself. It was tiring, sometimes, when you hadn't the energy for it; that's all.

Today, as it happened, her spirits were rather high. The idea had come to her, that morning, to pay a visit to a friend. She'd walked from Lavender Hill to Bayswater, and was now heading up the Harrow Road. Her friend Mickey worked in a garage there, as an attendant on the pumps.

Kay could see her in the forecourt of the garage as she drew closer: Mickey had set up a canvas chair, and was lounging in it reading a book. Her legs were spread out, for she was dressed, not exactly mannishly, as Kay was, but like a boy-mechanic, in dungarees and boots. Her hair was fair, the colour and texture of dirty rope; it was sticking up as if she had just got out of bed. As Kay watched, she licked a finger and turned a page. She didn't hear Kay coming, and Kay walked towards her with a queer sort of stirring in her heart. It was simply the pleasure of seeing a friend, after seeing, for weeks at a time, only strangers; that's all it was. But for a second Kay thought the feeling was going to expand up into her throat and make her cry. She imagined how ridiculous she'd look to Mickey, turning up out of the blue like this, in tears. And she thought seriously of giving the whole thing up – slipping away before Mickey should see her.

Then the feeling shrank back down again.

'Hello, Mickey,' she called blandly.

Mickey looked up, saw Kay, and laughed with pleasure. She laughed all the time, in an unforced, natural sort of way that people found awfully winning. Her voice was a throaty one, with a permanent cough in it. She smoked too much. 'Hey!' she said.

'What's the book?'

Mickey showed the cover. She read the books that people left in their cars, when they brought their cars to the garage to be fixed. This one was a paperback copy of Wells's *The Invisible Man*. Kay took it, and smiled. 'I read that,' she said, 'when I was young. Have you got to the bit where he makes the cat invisible, except for its eyes?'

'Yes, isn't it funny?' Mickey was rubbing her greasy palm on her dungarees, so that she could take Kay's hand. She was so small and slender, her hand was not much bigger than a child's. She tilted her head, half-closed one eye. She looked like the Artful Dodger. She said, 'I'd just about given up on you, I haven't seen you in so long! How are you keeping?'

'I thought it might be your lunch-break. Do you get a lunch-break? I brought you some buns.'

'Buns!' said Mickey, taking the bag and looking inside it. Her blue eyes widened. 'Jam ones!'

'With genuine saccharine.'

A car drew in. 'Hang on,' said Mickey. She put the buns down and went to speak to the driver and, after a second, began the business of filling up the car's tank. Kay took her place in the canvas chair, lifting the book and opening it at random.

'But you begin to realise now,' said the Invisible Man, 'the full disadvantage of my condition. I had no shelter – no covering – to get clothing was to forgo all my advantage, to make of myself a strange and terrible thing. I was fasting; for to eat, to fill myself with unassimilated matter, would be to become grotesquely visible again.'

131

'I never thought of that,' said Kemp.

Meanwhile, the pump had sprung into life and begun to throb and whine and click, and the smell of petrol, which had been faint before, grew heady. Kay put the book down and looked at Mickey. She was standing rather nonchalantly, one hand on the roof of the car, the other tense about the trigger of the petrol-gun, her eyes on the dial on the face of the machine. She was not quite handsome, but carried herself with a certain style; and it was extraordinary how many girls – even normal girls – could be intrigued and impressed by a pose like this.

The driver of this car, however, was a man. Mickey tapped the last few drops of petrol from the gun, screwed on the cap of his tank, took his coupons; and came sauntering back to Kay, pulling a face.

'No tip?' said Kay.

'He gave me threepence, and told me to buy a lipstick with it. His motor was rubbish, too. Wait here, will you? I'll talk to Sandy.'

She disappeared into the garage. When she came back a few minutes later she had taken off her dungarees to reveal ordinary blue slacks and a funny little Aertex shirt, full of creases and stains. She had washed her face and combed her hair. 'He's given me forty-five minutes. Shall we go to the boat?'

'Do we have time?' asked Kay.

'I think so.'

They went, as quickly as they could, down a couple of side-streets until they reached the

132

Regent's Canal. A hundred yards along the tow-path there was a line of houseboats and barges. Mickey had lived here since before the start of the war. It was quite a little village. There were warehouses and boatyards all about it, but the residents were artists and writers as well as real bargees – all rather self-consciously 'interesting' and 'picturesque', Kay sometimes thought them; all rather overpleased with the figures they knew they cut to the people who lived in ordinary flats and houses. Still, perhaps that was fair enough. Mickey's boat – *Irene* – was a stubby little barge with a pointed prow, which always made Kay think of a clog. Its hull was tarred, and patched alarmingly. Every morning Mickey had to spend twenty minutes or more thrusting and drawing on the handle of a horrid little pump. Her WC was a bucket, set up behind a canvas screen. In winter the contents of the bucket could turn to ice.

But the interior of the boat was very charming. The walls were panelled with varnished wood, and Mickey had made shelves for ornaments and books. The lights were Tilly lamps, and candles in coloured shades. The galley kitchen was like a giant version of a child's pencil-box, with secret drawers and sliding panels. The plates and cups were kept in their places with bars and straps. Everything was fastened as if against the swell of a high sea; in fact, the roll of the surface of the canal was quite gentle, and only disconcerting if you were unused to it or had forgotten what to expect.

Kay always stooped a little when she stood in Mickey's boat. If she straightened, the top of her head just brushed the ceiling. Mickey herself moved about with perfect ease and comfort – sliding back some of the panels in the galley to bring out tea, a teapot, two enamel mugs. 'I can't boil the water,' she said – the stove had gone out, and they hadn't time to relight it – 'but I'll get some from the girl next door.'

She went off with the teapot in her hand, and Kay sat down. The boat rocked, bumping hollowly against the bank, as a series of barges went by. She heard the voices of men, unnervingly clear: '—*up Dalston way. I swear to God! Going up and down, like a ruddy great monkey on a*—'

Mickey returned with the water, and set out tin plates. Kay picked up her bun, then put it down again. She took out her cigarettes instead – but paused, with the lighter in her hand. She gestured to the stains on Mickey's shirt.

'I suppose it's all right to smoke around you? After all that prancing about, I mean, with the petrol-gun. You won't go up in a whoosh of flame or anything?'

'Not if you're careful,' said Mickey, laughing.

'Well, thank goodness for that. For I should hate it, you know, if you did.' She held the cigarettes out. 'Care for a tickler?'

Mickey took one. Kay lit it for her, then lit her own. Behind her head was a sliding window: she pushed it open, to draw off the smoke.

'How are things at Sandy's?' she asked, turning back.

Mickey shrugged. She was only at the garage, really, because it was one of the few places a woman could work and wear trousers. She had to have some sort of job: she didn't, like Kay, have a wealthy family behind her, an income of her own. She'd begun to think, she told Kay now, of trying for a post as a chauffeur. She liked the idea of driving again, and of getting out of London.

They talked this over while they smoked. Mickey ate her bun, then opened the bag and ate another. Kay, however, left her own bun sitting in front of her, untasted; and Mickey said at last, 'Aren't you going to eat that?'

'Why? Do you want it?'

'That's not what I meant.'

'I've already eaten.'

'I bet you have. I know your meals. Tea and tobacco.'

'And gin, if I'm lucky!'

Mickey laughed again. The laugh became a cough. But, 'Eat it up,' she said, wiping her mouth. 'Go on. You're still too thin.'

'So what?' said Kay. 'Everybody's thin, aren't they? I'm in fashion, that's all.'

Actually the greasy, saccharine look of the bun had made her start to feel almost queasy; but now, for Mickey's sake, she picked the thing up and began to nibble at it. The sensation of the dough on her

135

tongue and in her throat was horrible; but Mickey watched until she'd eaten it all.

'All right now, matron?'

'Not bad,' said Mickey, narrowing her eye, looking like the Artful Dodger again. 'Next time, I'll buy you a dinner.'

'You want to feed me up.'

'Why not? We could make a night of it, get a bit of a crowd together.'

Kay pretended to shudder. 'I'd be the skeleton at the feast. Besides' – she tossed her head like a debutante – 'I'm awfully busy these days. I go out all the time.'

'You go to funny places.'

'I go to the cinema,' said Kay; 'there's nothing funny about that. Sometimes I sit through the films twice over. Sometimes I go in half-way through, and watch the second half first. I almost prefer them that way – people's pasts, you know, being so much more interesting than their futures. Or perhaps that's just me . . . But you can get up to all sorts at the movies; you take my word for it. You can even—'

'Even what?'

Kay hesitated. *Even get up a woman,* she'd been going to say, crudely; for one night recently at the cinema she'd got talking to a tipsy girl, and had finished by leading the girl into an empty lavatory and kissing her and feeling her up. The thing had been rather savagely done; she felt ashamed, thinking of it now. 'Even nothing,' she said flatly, at last. 'Even nothing . . . Anyway, you could always come and visit me.'

'At Mr Leonard's?' Mickey made a face. 'He gives me the creeps.'

'He's all right. He's a miracle worker. One of his patients told me. He cured her shingles. He could fix your chest.'

Mickey drew back, coughing again. 'No fear!'

'You dear butch thing,' said Kay. 'He wouldn't actually have to look at it. You just sit in a chair and he whispers at you.'

'He sounds bloody depraved. You've been there too long; you can't tell how weird it is any more. And what about that house? When's it going to fall down?'

'It's on its way,' said Kay, 'believe me. When the wind gets up, I can feel it swaying. I can feel it groaning. It's like being at sea. I think it's only thanks to Mr Leonard that it stays up at all. I think he keeps the place standing through sheer force of mind.'

Mickey smiled. But she was looking into Kay's face, and her gaze had grown serious. And when her smile had faded she said, in a different sort of voice, 'How much longer are you going to stay there, Kay?'

'Till the day it collapses, I hope!'

'I mean it,' said Mickey. She hesitated, as if thinking something over. Then, 'Listen,' she said, leaning forward. 'Why don't you come and live here with me?'

'Live here?' said Kay, surprised. 'On the *Quaint Irene*?' She glanced around. 'She's not much bigger than a shoe-box. That's all right for a little powder-monkey like you.'

'Just for a while,' said Mickey. 'If I get that driving job, I'd be away on overnights.'

'What about the rest of the time? Say you brought a girl back?'

'We could work something out.'

'Hang up a blanket? I might as well be back at boarding-school! Besides, I couldn't leave Lavender Hill. You don't know what it means to me. I'd miss Mr Leonard. I'd miss the little boy with his great big boot. I'd miss the Stanley Spencer couple! I've grown attached to the old place.'

'I know you have,' said Mickey. She said it in a way that meant: *That's what bothers me.*

Kay looked away. She'd been talking lightly all this time, putting on an act, trying to hide the fact that, as before, real emotion was rising up in her, making her embarrassed and afraid. For here, she thought, was Mickey, on about a pound a week, ready to share it – just like that, at the drop of a hat, through simple kindness. And here was Kay herself, with money unspent, and with absolutely nothing wrong with her, living like a cripple, like a rat.

She moved forward and picked up her tea. She found, to her horror, that her hands were shaking. She didn't want to put the mug back down and draw attention to the tremor; she lifted it higher, and tried to meet it with her mouth. But the tremor

138

grew worse. Tea spilled; she saw it stain one of Mickey's cushions. Abruptly, she set the mug down again and tried to mop up the worst of it with her handkerchief.

She caught Mickey's eye as she was doing it; and her shoulders sank. She leant forward, putting her elbows on her knees, her face in her hands.

'Look at me, Mickey!' she said. 'Look at the creature I've become! Did we really do those things we did? – you and I, when the war was on? Sometimes I can't bring myself to get out of bed in the mornings. We carried stretchers, for God's sake! I remember lifting' – she spread her hands – 'I remember lifting the torso of a child . . . What the hell happened to me, Mickey?'

'You know what happened,' Mickey said softly.

Kay sat back and turned away, in disgust at herself. 'It's no more than happened to thousands of us. Who didn't lose someone, or something? I could walk on any street in London, stretch out my arm, touch a woman or a man who lost a lover, a child, a friend. But I— I can't get over it, Mickey. I can't get over it.' She laughed, unhappily. '*Get over it*. What a funny phrase that is! As if one's grief is a fallen house, and one has to pick one's way over the rubble to the ground on the other side . . . I've got lost in my rubble, Mickey. I can't seem to find my way across it. I don't think I *want* to cross it, that's the thing. The rubble has all my life in it still—'

For a second she couldn't go on. She looked

around the cabin of the boat; then spoke more quietly.

'Do you remember that night, when we all sat here? That night just before—? Sometimes I think about times like that. I bloody torture myself with thinking about times like that! *Do* you remember it?'

Mickey nodded. 'I remember it.'

'I'd been to that place in Bethnal Green. You made gin slings.'

'Gin gimlets.'

Kay looked up. 'Gin gimlets? Are you sure?'

Mickey nodded.

'Weren't there lemons?'

'Lemons? Where the hell would we have got lemons? We had lime juice, remember, in a bottle of Binkie's?'

Kay did remember it, now. The fact that she'd misremembered before – misremembered to the extent that she'd been able to picture Mickey actually cutting up the lemons, squeezing out the juice – made her uneasy.

'Lime juice,' she said, frowning, 'in a bottle. Why should I have forgotten that?'

'Don't think about it, Kay.'

'I don't want to think about it! But I don't want to forget it, either. Sometimes I can think of nothing else but things like that. My mind has hooks in it. Little hooks.'

But now she sounded almost crazy. She turned her head again, and looked out of the window. The sunlight made patterns on the water. A slick of oil had colours in, silver and blue . . . She turned back into the cabin, and found Mickey checking her watch.

'Kay,' said Mickey. 'I'm sorry, mate. I've got to get back to Sandy's.'

'Of course you have.'

'Why don't you stay here till I get home?'

'Don't be silly. I'm all right, really. It's a bore, that's all.'

She finished her tea. Her hand was quite steady now. She brushed crumbs from her lap, got to her feet, and helped clear away the plates.

'What'll you do now?' Mickey asked her, as they made their way down the Harrow Road.

Kay became a debutante again. She made a flighty gesture. 'Oh, I've heaps of things.'

'Have you, really?'

'Yes, of course.'

'I don't believe you. Have a think about what I said – about coming to live with me. Will you? Or come out, some time! We could go for a drink. We could go to Chelsea. There's no one there these days, the crowd's all changed.'

'All right,' said Kay.

She got out her cigarettes again, took one for herself, gave one to Mickey; and tucked another behind one of Mickey's boyish little ears. Mickey caught hold of her hand when she had done it, and gave it a squeeze; they stood for a second, smiling into each other's eyes.

They had kissed once, Kay remembered – years ago, and without success. They'd both been drunk. They'd ended up laughing. That's what happened, of course, when you were both, as it were, on the same side.

Mickey moved away. 'Ta-ta, Kay,' she said. Kay watched her running back to the garage. She saw her turn, once, to wave. Kay raised her hand, then started to walk, back in the direction of Bayswater.

She walked briskly, for as long as she thought that Mickey might be watching; but as soon as she'd turned a corner, she slowed her step. And when she got to Westbourne Grove and the street grew busy, she found a doorstep in the shadow of a broken wall, and sat down. She thought of what she'd said to Mickey, about standing in a crowd, stretching out her hand. And she studied the faces of the people as they passed, thinking, *What did you lose? How about you? How do you bear it? What do you do?*

'I knew that girl from Enfield was trouble the second she walked in,' Viv was saying, as she sprinkled Vim on the cloth. 'They always are, that brassy type.'

She and Helen had just been about to take their lunches out to the fire-escape when they'd spotted pencil-marks on the lavatory wall.

A long and thin goes right in
But a short and thick does the trick!

142

somebody had written, on the paint above the roller-towel. Helen had not, for a second, known where to look. Viv seemed hardly less embarrassed. 'This is what comes,' she said now, rubbing madly, 'of advertising in those local magazines.'

She stepped back, flushed and blinking. The wall was pale where she had cleaned it, but the words *thick* and *does the trick!* still showed, scored faintly into the paint. She rubbed again, then she and Helen moved about, narrowing their eyes, holding their heads at different angles to the light.

They became aware, all at once, of what they were doing. They looked at each other and started to laugh.

'Dear me,' said Helen, biting her lip.

Viv rinsed out the cloth and put away the Vim, her shoulders shaking. She dried her hands, then lifted her knuckles to her eyes, afraid for her mascara. 'Don't!' she said.

Still laughing, they opened the window and clambered out. They sat and unwrapped their sandwiches, sipped their tea and grew calmer at last; then caught one another's gaze and started laughing all over again.

Viv set down her spilling cup. 'Oh, what would the clients think?'

Her mascara had run after all. She got out a handkerchief, made a twist of it, put the twist to the tip of her tongue, then held up a mirror and widened her eyes, rubbing beneath them almost as savagely, Helen thought, as she'd rubbed at the marks on the lavatory wall. The blood, in rushing into her face, had made her seem youthful. Her hair was disarranged by laughter; she looked tousled, full of life.

She tucked the handkerchief into her sleeve and picked up her sandwich; and her laughter faded into sighs. She put back a corner of the bread, and the sight of the vivid meat inside it – and the taste of it, when she'd bitten – seemed for some reason to subdue her. Her face lost its flush. Her eyes dried. She chewed very slowly, and finally put the sandwich down. She was wearing a cardigan over her dress, and began fastening up its buttons.

It was almost two weeks since that warm Saturday, when Helen had lain with Julia in Regent's Park. That had been the last warm day of the summer, though they hadn't known it then. The season had turned. The sun was moving in and out of clouds. Viv put back her head to look at the sky.

'Not quite so warm today,' she said.

'No, not quite,' said Helen.

'I suppose we'll all be complaining, soon, about the cold.'

Helen saw winter, drawing nearer, like a long dark tunnel on a railway line. She said, 'It won't be so cold as last year, will it?'

'I hope not.'

'It won't be, surely!'

Viv rubbed her arms. 'A man in the *Evening Standard* said our winters will go on getting colder and colder, and longer and longer; that in another ten years we'll all be living like Eskimos.'

'Eskimos!' said Helen, picturing fur hats and wide, friendly faces; quite fancying the idea.

'That's what he said. He said it was something to do with the angle of the earth – that we'd knocked it off-balance with all those bombs. It makes sense, if you think about it. He said it served us all right.'

'Oh,' said Helen, 'people in newspapers are always writing things like that. Do you remember someone, at the start of the war, saying the whole thing was a punishment on us for letting our king abdicate?'

'Yes!' said Viv. 'I always thought that was a bit hard on everyone in France and Norway and places like that. I mean, it wasn't their king, after all.'

She turned her head. The door to the wig-maker's downstairs had opened, and a man had come out into the yard with a wastepaper basket under his arm. The basket was filled to overflowing with dark fibres – a mixture, probably, of netting and hair. Viv and Helen watched him cross to a dustbin, lift its lid, and empty the mess of fibres into it. Then he wiped his hands, and went back in. He didn't look up. When the door was closed, Viv made a face.

But Helen was still thinking about the war. She took another little bite of her sandwich, then said, 'Isn't it odd, how everyone talks about the war as if it were a thing – oh, from years ago. It feels almost quaint. It's as though we all got together in private and said to each other, "Now don't, for God's sake, let's mention *that*!" When did that happen?'

Viv shrugged. 'We all got tired of it, I suppose. We wanted to forget it.'

'Yes, I suppose so. I never would have thought we'd all forget it, though, so quickly. When it was on— Well, it was the only thing, wasn't it? The only thing you talked about. The only thing that mattered. You tried to make other things matter, but it was always that, you always came back to that.'

'Imagine if it started again,' said Viv.

'Christ!' said Helen. 'What an awful thought! It'd be an end to this place, anyway. Would you go back to your old job?'

Viv considered it. She had worked at the Ministry of Food, just around the corner in Portman Square. 'I don't know,' she said. 'Maybe. It felt – important. I liked that. Even though all I was doing was typing, really . . . I had a good friend there, a girl called Betty; she was loads of fun. But she married a boy from Australia at the end of the war, and he took her back home. I envy her, now. If it really started again I might go into one of the services. I'd like to travel, get away.' She looked wistful. Then, 'How about you?' she asked Helen. 'Would you go back to your old job?'

'I suppose so, though I was glad enough to leave it. It was funny work – a bit like this, in a way: unhappy people all expecting impossible things. You tried to do your best for them, but you got tired; or you had things of your own to think about. I don't think I'd want to stay in London, though. London will get flattened, won't it, when the next war comes? But then, everywhere will get flattened. It won't be like last time. Even when things were so awful, right in the middle of the blitz, I wanted to stay – didn't you? I hadn't been here very long, yet I felt a sort of – a sort of loyalty to the city, I suppose. I didn't want to let it down. It seems crazy, now! A loyalty to bricks and mortar! And then, of course, there were people I knew. I felt a loyalty to them, too. They were in London; and I wanted to be near them.'

'People like Julia?' asked Viv. 'Were you friends with her, then? Was she in London, too?'

'She was in London,' said Helen, nodding; 'but I only knew her at the end of the war. We shared a flat together, even then – a tiny little flat, in Mecklenburgh Square. I remember that flat so vividly! All the mismatched bits of furniture.' She closed her eyes, recalling surfaces and scents. 'It had boards across its window. It was falling down, really. There was a man upstairs, who used to pace and make the floor creak.' She shook her head, opening her eyes. 'I remember it clearer than anywhere else I ever lived; I don't know why. We were only there for a year or so. For most of the war I was—' She looked away again; picked up her sandwich. 'Well, for most of it I was somewhere else.'

Viv waited. When Helen didn't go on she said, 'I lived in a boarding-house for Ministry girls. Down by the Strand.'

Helen looked up. 'Did you? I didn't know that. I thought you lived at home, with your father.'

'I did at weekends. But during the week they liked to have us there, so we could get to work if the railways were hit. It was an awful place. So many girls! Everyone running up and down the stairs. Everyone pinching your lipstick and your stockings. Or someone would borrow your blouse or something, and when you got it back it was a different colour or a different shape, they'd dyed it or taken the sleeves off!'

She laughed. She moved her feet to a higher step on the metal ladder – drew up her knees, tucked in her skirt, rested her chin upon her fists. Then her laughter, as it had before, faded. Her gaze grew distant, serious. *Here comes that curtain*, Helen thought . . . But instead Viv said, 'It's funny, thinking back. It's only a couple of years but, you're right, it seems ages away. Some things were easier, then. There was a way of doing things, wasn't there? Someone else had decided it for you, said that was the best way to do it; and that's what you did. It got me down, at the time. I used to look forward to peace, to all the things I'd be able to do then. I don't know what I thought those things would be. I don't know what I thought would be different. You expect things to change, or people to change; but it's silly, isn't it? Because people and things don't change. Not really. You just have to get used to them.'

Her expression, now, was so stripped, so solemn, Helen reached and touched her arm. 'Viv,' she said. 'You look so awfully sad.'

Viv grew self-conscious again. She coloured, and laughed. 'Oh, don't mind me. I've been feeling a bit sorry for myself lately, that's all.'

'What's the matter? Aren't you happy?'

'Happy?' Viv blinked. 'I don't know. Is anybody happy? Really happy, I mean? People pretend they are.'

'I don't know either,' said Helen, after a moment. 'Happiness is such a fragile sort of thing these days. It's as though there's only so much to go round.'

'As if it's on the ration.'

Helen smiled. 'Yes, exactly! And so you know, when you've got some, that it's going to run out soon; and that keeps you from enjoying it, you're too busy wondering how you're going to feel when it's all gone. Or you start thinking about the person who's had to go without so that you can have your portion.'

Her own mood sank, as she thought this. She began picking at blisters of paint on the metal platform, exposing fibres of rust beneath. She went on quietly, 'Maybe it's right, after all, what the newspaper prophets say: that one gets paid back in the way one deserves. Maybe we've all forfeited our right to happiness, by doing bad things, or by letting bad things happen.'

She looked at Viv. They'd never spoken to each other quite so freely before, and she realised, as if for the first time, just how fond she was of Viv, and how much she liked doing this – just this – sitting out here, talking, on this rusting metal platform. And she thought of something else. *Were you friends with Julia then?* Viv had asked lightly, before – as if it were the most natural thing in the world that Helen should have been; as if it were perfectly normal that Helen should have stayed in London, in a war, for a woman's sake . . .

Her heart began to beat faster. She wanted, suddenly, to be able to confide in Viv. She wanted to, desperately! She wanted to say, *Listen to me, Viv. I'm in love with Julia! It's a marvellous thing, but terrible, too. Sometimes it makes a sort of child of me. Sometimes it feels like it's almost killing me! It leaves me helpless. It makes me afraid! I can't control it! Can that be right? Is it like this with other people? Has it ever been like this, with you?*

She felt her breath rising, until it seemed trapped in her chest. Her heart was beating wildly now, in her cheeks and fingertips. 'Viv—' she started.

But Viv had turned away. She'd put her hands to the pockets of her cardigan and, 'Oh, heck,' she said. 'I've left my cigs inside. I'll never get through the afternoon without one.' She started to rise, seizing hold of the rail of the platform and making the whole thing rock. She said, 'Will you give me a push-up?'

Helen got to her feet more quickly. 'I'm closer,' she said. 'I'll get them.'

'Are you sure?'

'Yes, of course. It'll only take a moment.'

Her breath still seemed to be crushed in her chest. She clambered awkwardly over the sill and landed with a thud beside the lavatory. There was still time, she thought, to say something. She wanted to more than ever now. And a cigarette would steady her nerves. She straightened her skirt. Viv called through the window: 'They're in my handbag!'

Helen nodded. She went quickly across the landing and up the short flight of stairs into the waiting-room. She kept her head down as she went, only glancing up at the last minute.

She found a man standing at Viv's desk, looking idly over the papers.

She started so violently at the sight of him, she almost screamed. Startled himself, the man stepped back. Then he began to laugh. 'Good Lord! Am I so terrifying as that?'

'I'm sorry,' said Helen, her hand at her breast. 'I had no idea— But the office is closed.'

'Is it? The door downstairs was open.'

'Well, it really oughtn't to have been.'

'I just walked in and up the stairs. I did wonder where everyone was. I'm sorry to have frightened you, Miss—?'

He looked frankly into her face as he said this. He was young and well-spoken, handsome, fair-haired, quite at his ease – so unlike their usual run of client that she felt at a disadvantage with him. She was aware of herself, breathless and flushed, her hair uncombed. She pictured Viv, too, waiting out on the fire-escape . . . *Balls*, she thought. But there was still time.

She calmed herself down, and turned to the diary on Viv's desk. 'Well,' she said. 'You don't have an appointment, I suppose?' She ran her finger down the page. 'You're not Mr Tiplady?'

'Mr Tiplady!' He smiled. 'No, I'm rather glad to say I'm not.'

'The fact is, we don't see anyone without an appointment.'

'So I see.' He had turned when she had, and was looking at the page over her shoulder. 'You're certainly doing a roaring trade. That's thanks to the war, I suppose.' He folded his arms and stood more easily. 'Just out of interest, how much do you charge?'

Helen glanced at the clock. *Go away. Go away!* But she was too polite to let the thought show. 'We charge in the first instance,' she said, 'a guinea—'

'As much as that?' He looked surprised. 'And, what will my guinea get me? I suppose you show me an album of girls, do you? Or, you don't actually bring the girls in?'

His manner had changed. He seemed really interested, yet was smiling, too, as if at some joke of his own. Helen grew cautious. It was just possible, she thought, that he was some kind of charming lunatic: one of those men – like Heath – driven insane by the mood of the times. She didn't know whether or not to believe him about the door. Suppose he had forced it? She'd often thought how vulnerable she and Viv were, so close to Oxford Street and yet cut off, up here, from the bustle of the pavement.

'I'm afraid I really can't discuss it with you now,' she said, her anxiety and impatience making her prim. 'If you'd care to come back in ordinary hours, I'm sure my colleague' – she glanced involuntarily towards the stairs, the lavatory – 'will be happy to explain the whole procedure to you.'

But that seemed to pique his interest even more. 'Your colleague,' he said, as if seizing on the word, and following her gaze with his own; even lifting and weaving his head, and clicking his tongue against his lower lip, thoughtfully, as he did it. 'I suppose your colleague's not available right now, by any chance?'

'I'm afraid we're closed for lunch just now,' said Helen firmly.

'Yes, of course. You said that. What a pity.' He said it vaguely. He was still gazing over at the stairs.

She turned a page in the diary. 'If you could come back tomorrow at, say, four—'

But now he'd looked round, and realised what she was doing. His manner changed again. He almost laughed. 'Look here, I'm sorry. I think I've given you the wrong impression.'

At that moment, Viv came up the stairs and into the office. She must have heard his voice after all, and wondered what was going on. She looked at him as if in amazement; and then, unaccountably, she blushed. Helen caught her eye, and made what she hoped was a little gesture of warning and alarm. She said, 'I was just finding this gentleman an appointment. Apparently the door downstairs was open—'

The man, however, had stepped forward and begun to laugh. 'Hello,' he said, giving Viv a nod. Then he turned back to Helen. 'I'm afraid,' he said to her, in real apology, 'I really did give you the wrong idea. It isn't a wife I'm after, you see. Just Miss Pearce.'

Viv's colour had deepened. She glanced at Helen as if nervous. She said, 'This is Mr Robert Fraser, Helen, a friend of my brother's. Mr Fraser, this is Miss Giniver . . . Is Duncan all right?'

'Oh, it's nothing like that,' said the man easily. 'Nothing at all. I was just passing, and thought I'd look in.'

'Duncan asked you to come?'

'I was just hoping you'd be free, to tell you the truth. It was just— Well, it was just a whim.'

He laughed again. There was a moment's awkward silence. Helen thought of the little warning gesture she'd made to Viv a minute ago; and felt a fool. For everything had changed, suddenly. It was just as though someone had taken a piece of chalk and, swiftly but firmly, bent to the floor and drawn a line: a line that had Viv and this man, Robert Fraser, on one side, and herself on the other. She made a vague kind of movement. 'Well,' she said, 'I ought to get on.'

'No, it's all right,' said Viv quickly. Her eyelids fluttered. 'I'll – I'll take Mr Fraser outside. Mr Fraser—?'

'Of course,' he said, moving with her towards the stairs. He nodded pleasantly to Helen as he went by. 'Goodbye! I'm sorry to have disturbed you. If I ever change my mind about that wife, I'll be sure to let you know!'

He went quickly down the staircase with a boyish irregular tread. When the door at the bottom was opened she heard him say to Viv, in a lower but carrying tone: 'I'm afraid I've rather landed you in it—'

There was a thump, as the door was closed.

Helen kept still for a moment, then stepped into her office and got out her cigarettes; but threw the packet down, unopened. She felt more of a fool than ever, now. She recalled the way that, on first coming up the stairs from the lavatory, she'd almost screamed – like some comedy spinster in a play!

Just as she thought this she heard laughter, down in the street. She went to the window and looked out.

The window had had cheesecloth varnished to it at some point in the war; a few scraps of net and some scrapings of varnish remained stuck to the glass, distorting the view. But she could see clearly enough the top of Fraser's head and his wide shoulders, lifting and tilting as he gestured and shrugged. And she could see, too, the curve of Viv's pink cheek and the tip of her ear, the spread of her fingers on the sleeve of her folded arm.

She let her head sink, until her brow met the varnished glass. How easy it was, she thought unhappily as she did it, for men and women. They could stand in a street and argue, flirt – they could kiss, make love, do anything at all – and the world indulged them. Whereas she and Julia—

She thought of what she'd been meaning to do,

out on the fire-escape. *I'm in love with Julia*, she'd been going to say. *And my love is almost killing me!*

She couldn't imagine saying it now. It seemed an absurd thing to say, now! She stood at the window, looking down, until she saw Fraser step forward to shake Viv's hand, as if in farewell; then she moved quickly back to her desk and took up a folder of papers.

She heard the click of the latch being fastened on the street-door, and the sound of footsteps. Viv came slowly up the stairs and through the waiting-room. She stood in the doorway of Helen's office. Helen didn't raise her head. Viv was silent for a moment, then said awkwardly, 'I'm sorry about that.'

'You've nothing to be sorry for,' said Helen, looking up at last and making herself smile. 'He frightened the life out of me, though! Was the door really unlocked?'

'Yes, it was.'

'Well, then I suppose we can't blame him for coming up.'

'He just thought it would be all right to call in,' said Viv. 'I don't know him at all, really. He turned up at my brother's when I was there last week. We only talked for a little while. He knew my brother, ages ago. I don't know why he should have come here.'

She'd started biting at one of her fingers, at the skin beside a nail. Her head was bowed, and her thick dark hair had slightly fallen across her face.

Helen watched her for a second, then went back to picking through the papers in the folder.

At last Viv said, rather thinly, 'Do you want to come back out, Helen?'

Helen looked up again. 'Back outside? Do we have time?' She looked at the clock. 'Only ten minutes . . . I don't know. Shall we?'

'Well,' said Viv, 'not if you don't want to.'

They gazed at each other, as if meaning to speak; but the moment for confidences had passed. Helen shuffled the papers. 'I ought to look these over, I suppose,' she said.

And, 'Yes,' said Viv, at once. 'Yes, all right.'

She stood in Helen's doorway a little longer, as if she might say more; then she went out to the waiting-room. Soon there came the sound of her straightening up the magazines on the table, shaking out the sofa cushions.

Everyone has their secrets, after all, Helen thought. The thought depressed her, horribly. It made her think of Julia. She put the papers down and sat at her desk, with her head in her hands, her eyes closed. If only Julia were here, right now! She began to long for the sound of Julia's voice, for the comforting touch of her hand. What would she be doing, at this sort of hour? Helen tried to visualise her. She pressed her hands into the sockets of her eyes and sent her thoughts across the streets of Marylebone until she had a sense of Julia's presence, fantastically vivid and real. She saw her sitting in her study at home: silent, solitary, perhaps bored or restless, perhaps thinking of Helen herself. She began to miss Julia so badly, the missing felt like an ache or a sickness. She opened her eyes, and saw the telephone. But she oughtn't to call, in a mood like this. She wouldn't do it, anyway, with Viv so close, able to overhear every word; and she couldn't bring herself to go tiptoeing across the floor and silently close her office door.

If Viv goes down to the lavatory, she thought, *I'll do it. Only then.*

She sat tensely, listening as Viv brushed dust from the carpet and rearranged chairs. Then she heard heels on the staircase, fading. Viv must have taken the teapot down to the basin to rinse out the leaves.

At once, she picked up the telephone and dialled.

There was a tinny electric burr. She imagined the telephone on Julia's desk, beginning to ring; imagined Julia giving a start, putting down her pen, lifting her hand – holding it, perhaps, for a moment or two, above the receiver, because of course everyone preferred to let a telephone ring a little than answer it at once. But the ringing went on. Perhaps Julia was downstairs in the kitchen; or down on the floor below that, in the lavatory. Now Helen saw her running up the narrow stairs to her study, in her flapping espadrille slippers; she saw her tucking back a lock of hair that had come bouncing out from behind her ear, reaching breathlessly for the phone . . .

Still the ringing went on. Maybe Julia, after all,

had decided not to answer. Helen had known her do that, when she was in the middle of writing a scene. But if she guessed it was Helen calling, then surely she'd pick the receiver up? If Helen would only let the thing ring for long enough, Julia would realise, Julia would answer.

Burr, burr. Burr, burr. The hateful noise went on and on. At last, after almost a minute, Helen put the receiver down, unable to bear the image of the telephone shrieking, forlorn and abandoned, in her own empty house.

'I haven't got long,' said Viv, looking up and down Oxford Street.

'It's very kind of you,' answered Fraser, 'to spare me any time at all.'

It was just after six. She had told him, at lunchtime, to come back; and had met him here, in front of the wrecked John Lewis building. She was anxious that Helen might still be about, and might see them; but when he saw her glancing nervously around, he misunderstood. The pavement was filled with people going briskly home from work or queuing for buses, and he thought she was bothered by the crowd. He said, 'No, we can't talk here, can we? Let me take you to a café, somewhere quiet.' He touched her arm.

But she said she didn't have time for that; that she was meeting someone in forty-five minutes, in another part of town. So they walked, instead, around the corner to one of the benches in

Cavendish Square. The bench was covered with fallen leaves, golden and glossy as scraps of yellow mackintosh. He swept them away so that she could sit.

She sat rather rigidly, with her hands in her pockets and her coat buttoned up. When he offered her a cigarette she shook her head. He put the cigarettes away and took out a pipe.

She watched him thumbing in the tobacco. He was like a kid, she thought, mucking about. She said, without smiling, 'I wish you hadn't come to my office today, Mr Fraser. I don't know what Miss Giniver thought.'

'She looked as though she thought I was going to fling her to the floor and ravish her, to tell you the truth!' he said. And then, when Viv wouldn't smile: 'I'm sorry. It just seemed the most straightforward way to see you.'

'I still don't know why you felt you needed to see me at all. Has my brother done something to you?'

'It's nothing like that.'

'He didn't ask you to come?'

'It's just as I told you earlier on. Your brother had nothing to do with it. He doesn't even know I'm here. He only mentioned to me, in passing, where you work. But he speaks so warmly of you. It's clear' – he held a flame to the pipe, sucking on the stem of it – 'it's clear you mean a great deal to him. It was the just the same, I remember, when we were in prison.'

160

He made no attempt to muffle the word, and Viv flinched. He saw, and lowered his voice. 'It was the same, I should have said, when I first knew him. He used to look forward to your visits more than to anything else in the world.'

She looked away. At the words 'your visits' she'd had a very clear and unpleasant memory of herself, her father and Duncan at one of the tables in the visiting-room at Wormwood Scrubs. She remembered the press of other visitors, the look of the men, the awful babble, the sour, airless feel of the room. She remembered Fraser himself from those days, too – for she'd seen him, more than once. She recalled his brash public-schoolboy's laugh; she remembered one of the other visitors saying, 'Isn't it a shame?' and a man actually calling out to him: '*Can't you take it, conchy?*' She'd felt rather sorry for him, then. She'd thought him brave, but brave in a pointless kind of way. He hadn't changed anything, after all. She'd felt more sympathy for his parents. She could still picture his mother, at the scratched prison table: a smart, kind, softly spoken woman, dreadfully wounded-looking and pale.

Duncan, of course, even then, had thought Fraser marvellous. He thought anyone marvellous who could talk cleverly, in a well-bred voice. Viv had arrived at Mr Mundy's on Tuesday night, and he had come to let her in, his dark eyes flashing with excitement. 'Guess who I met! You never will! He's coming round here, later on.' He'd sat listening out for Fraser, all evening; and when, a little later, Fraser had actually turned up, he'd leapt to his feet and gone rushing to the door . . .

It had all filled Viv with dismay. She and Mr Mundy had sat, uncomfortable, self-conscious, hardly knowing where to look.

Now she watched Fraser fiddling about with the pipe, and said, 'I still don't know what it is you want me to do.'

He laughed. 'To be perfectly honest with you, neither do I.'

'You said you're writing for a newspaper or something like that. You're not going to write about Duncan, are you?'

He looked as if the idea hadn't occurred to him. 'No,' he said. 'Of course not.'

'Because if that's what all this is about—'

'It's not "about" anything at all. How suspicious you are!' He began to laugh again. But when she still looked grave, he put back his hair, and changed his tone.

'Look,' he said. 'I know it's queer, my coming along out of the blue like this. I suppose it seems odd to you, my taking an interest in your brother after so long. I don't quite know myself why I should feel so strongly about it. It was just, coming across him so suddenly at the candle-works that time; thinking of somebody like him having to work in a place like that! And then – my God! Seeing him with Mr Mundy! I couldn't believe it. He'd told me where he was living and I thought he was joking! I can't tell you the start it gave me, the first time he took me to the house. I've been back there since, two or three times, and it still unnerves me. Has your brother really been there ever since his release? Right from the day he got out? It seems incredible.'

'It's what he wanted,' said Viv. She added: 'Mr Mundy's been very kind.'

It sounded feeble, even to her. Fraser raised his eyebrows. 'He's certainly got things nice and cosy. I'm just thinking back, to when we were inside. He was plain Mr Mundy then, of course. There was none of this "Uncle Horace" business. I thought I was hearing things, the first time I heard that!'

'It doesn't matter, does it?'

'Don't your family mind?'

'Why should they?'

'I don't know. It seems an odd sort of life, that's all, for a boy like Duncan. He's not even a boy any more, is he? And yet it's impossible to think of him as anything else. He might have got stuck. I think he has got stuck. I think he's made himself be stuck, as a way of – of punishing himself, for all that happened, years ago, all that he did and didn't do . . . I think Mr Mundy is taking very good care to keep him stuck; and – if you don't mind my saying so – after seeing the way you were with him on Tuesday night, I don't think anyone else is doing anything to, as it were, unstick him. All that fascination of his with things from the past, for instance.'

'That's just a hobby,' said Viv.

'It's a pretty morbid one, don't you think? For a boy like him?'

She lost her patience suddenly. '"A boy like him,"' she said. '"A boy like him." People have always said that about Duncan, ever since he was little. "A boy like him shouldn't be at a school like this, he's too sensitive for it." "A boy like him should go to college."'

Fraser frowned at her. 'Did it occur to you that those people might have been saying it, because it was true?'

'Of course it was true! But what was the point of it? And look where it got him! We had to deal with all that, Mr Fraser – my family and I, not you. Four years, going back and forth to that awful place. Four years, and more, fretting about it. It nearly killed my father! Perhaps if Duncan had been like you when he was young – had the things you had, I mean, the same sort of people around him, the same sort of start – perhaps things would have been different. He went to Mr Mundy's when he came out because he felt he'd nowhere else. Where were you, then? If you're so big a friend of his, where were you?'

Fraser looked away, lowered the pipe, turned it in his fingers; and didn't answer. She went on more quietly, 'Anyway, it doesn't matter now. But I can't help thinking your coming along like this— Well, what's it going to do? When Duncan told me he'd met you, I'll be quite honest with you, I wished he hadn't. What's the good of it? It's not going to get him anywhere. It's just going to give him ideas again; it's just going to stir things up and upset him.'

He was fishing for matches, and spoke stiffly. 'You could let him decide that for himself, of course.'

'But you know what he's like. You said, just now. He's got a sort of – a sort of wisdom about some things; but in so many ways he's still more or less a boy. He can be pushed into things, like a boy can. He can be—'

She stopped. Fraser had the box of matches in his hand but had turned, and was looking at her. 'What do you think,' he asked her slowly, 'I'm going to push him into?'

She swallowed, and dropped her gaze. 'I don't know.'

He went on, 'You're thinking of that boy, aren't you? The boy who died? Alec?' And then, when she looked up, he nodded. 'Yes. You see, I know all about him . . . You don't think I'm like him, though, surely?' She didn't answer. He coloured, as if angry. 'Is that what you think? Because if you do—Well, I could give you a list of girls, you know, who could put you straight on that!'

He said it seriously, but then must have caught the earnestness in his own voice. He blushed harder, put his hand again to his hair, and ducked his head. The gesture, unstudied and a little gauche, was the most appealing thing he'd done. She let herself see, for the first time, how nice-looking he

165

was, how smooth and unmarked. He was young, after all: younger than her.

He still had the pipe and the matches in his hand, but was sitting still, with his hands slackly in his lap. He said, 'I'm sorry. I only wanted to see you as a way of helping your brother.'

'Well, I think you might help him best just by leaving him alone.'

'But, is that really what you'd like? To just leave him there, living with Mr Mundy in that peculiar way?'

'There's nothing peculiar about it!'

'Are you quite sure?' He held her gaze; and when she looked away he said slowly, 'No, you're not, are you? I saw it in your face, last week. And what about that job, that factory? You want to see him working at it for the rest of his life? Making night lights, for nurseries?'

'People work in factories; it doesn't matter what they make. My father's worked in a factory for thirty years!'

'Is that any reason your brother should?'

'So long as he's happy,' she said. 'That's what you don't seem to understand. I just want Duncan to be happy. We all do.'

Her words, as before, sounded weak. And she knew, in her heart, that he was right. She knew that part of the reason she'd been so dismayed to see him arrive at Mr Mundy's last week was that she'd looked at the house with him in it, and seen it all as if through his eyes . . . But, she was tired.

She said to herself, as she always ended up saying to herself, about Duncan – *It's not my fault. I did my best. I've got my own problems to think about.*

And even as these words glided familiarly into her mind, she heard the quarter hour struck out on a nearby clock; and remembered the time.

'Mr Fraser—'

'Oh, call me Robert, will you?' he said, beginning to smile again. 'I'm sure your brother would want you to. I certainly do.'

So she said, 'Robert—'

'And may I call you Vivien? Or – what Duncan calls you – Viv?'

'If you like,' she said, feeling herself blush. 'I really don't care. It's kind of you to try and help Duncan like this. But the fact is, I can't talk about it now. I haven't got time.'

'No time for your brother?'

'I've got time for my brother; but not for this.'

He narrowed his eyes. 'You don't think much of my motives, do you?'

She said, 'I still don't know what your motives are.' And she added: 'I'm not sure you do.'

That made him colour slightly again. For a moment they sat in silence, both of them blushing. Then she changed her pose, getting ready to go, putting her hands into the pockets of her coat. The pockets had old bus tickets in them, stray coins and paper wrappers – but then her fingers found something else: that little parcel of cloth, with the heavy gold ring inside it.

Her heart gave a jolt. She stood up, abruptly. 'I've got to go,' she said. 'I'm sorry, Mr Fraser.'

'Robert,' he corrected, getting to his feet.

'I'm sorry, Robert.'

'That's all right. I ought to go, too. But, look here. I don't like you misunderstanding me. Let me walk with you and we can talk as we go.'

'I'd really rather—'

'Which way are you going?'

She didn't want to tell him. He saw her hesitate, and chose to take it, she supposed, as an invitation. When she started to walk he walked alongside her; once his arm brushed hers, and he made a show of apologising and moving further away. But an odd thing had happened between them. Somehow, in letting him go with her, she'd managed to put their relationship on a subtly different footing. As they headed back to Oxford Street they had to pause at a kerb alongside a window; she saw the two of them reflected in it, and met his gaze through the glass. He started to smile, seeing what she did: that they looked like a couple – a simple, nice-looking, young courting couple.

His manner changed. As they wove through the traffic at Oxford Circus he struggled to keep up with her and said, in a different tone from any he'd used with her yet, 'You know where you're going, anyway. I like that in a woman. Are you meeting a girlfriend?'

She shook her head.

'A boyfriend, then?'

'It's nobody,' she said, to shut him up.

'You're meeting nobody? Well, that shouldn't take long, in a town like this . . . Look, you've got me all wrong, you know. What do you say to us starting again – this time, with a drink?'

They had drawn near a pub on the edge of Soho. She shook her head and kept going. 'I can't.'

He touched her arm. 'Not just for twenty minutes?'

She felt the pressure of his fingers, and slowed, and met his gaze. He looked young and earnest again. She said, 'I can't. I'm sorry. There's something I've got to do.'

'Couldn't I do it with you?'

'I'd rather you didn't.'

'Well, I could wait.'

The awkwardness must have shown on her face. He looked around, at a loss. He said, 'Where the hell are you making for, anyway? Your evening job in a leg-show? You don't need to be bashful, if that's what it is. You'll find me a broadminded sort of bloke. I could sit in the audience and keep off the rowdies.' He pushed back his long hair, and smiled. 'Let me go a bit further with you, at least. I couldn't think of myself as a gentleman, and leave you on your own in streets like these.'

She hesitated, and then, 'All right,' she said. 'I'm going to the Strand. You can come with me, if you really want to, as far as Trafalgar Square.'

He bowed. 'Trafalgar Square it is.'

He offered her his arm. She didn't want to take

it, then thought of the minutes ticking by. She put her hand, lightly, in the crook of his elbow, and they moved off together. His arm was amazingly firm to the touch, the muscles shifting, beneath her fingers, with the rhythm of his walk.

As he'd hinted, the streets they were entering now were rather sleazy ones: a mixture of boarded-up houses and fenced-off ground, depressed-looking nightclubs, pubs and Italian cafés. The smell was of rotting vegetables, brick-dust, garlic, parmesan cheese; here and there an open doorway or window let out the blare of music. Yesterday she'd come this way on her own and a man had plucked at her arm and said in a phoney New York accent, 'Hey, Bombshell, how much for a grind?' He'd meant it as a sort of compliment, too. But tonight men looked but called nothing, because they assumed she was Fraser's girl. It was half amusing, half annoying. She noticed it more, perhaps, because she was unused to it. She never came anywhere like this with Reggie. They never went to nightclubs or restaurants. They only ever went from one lonely place to another; or they sat in his car with the radio on. She thought of bumping into somebody she knew, and grew nervous. Then she realised she had nothing to be nervous of.

While they walked, Fraser spoke about Duncan. He spoke as if he and she were agreed on the whole issue; as if all they had to do was put their heads together, spend a little time on it, and they'd be able to sort Duncan out. They had to do something, for a start, he said, about his job at that factory. He had a friend who worked in a printing-shop in Shoreditch; he thought this friend might be able to find Duncan a place, learning the trade. Or he knew another man who ran a bookshop. The pay would be negligible, but maybe that sort of work would appeal to Duncan more. Did she think it would?

She frowned, not really listening; still aware of the ring in its parcel in her pocket; conscious of the time. 'Why don't you ask Duncan,' she said at last, 'instead of me?'

'I wanted your opinion on it, that's all. I thought we might— Well, I hoped we'd be friends. If nothing else, we'll be bound to run into each other again at Mr Mundy's, and—'

They had reached the northwest corner of Trafalgar Square, and begun to slacken their pace. Viv turned her head, searching for a clock. When she looked back into Fraser's face she found him gazing at her with an odd expression.

'What?' she said.

He smiled. 'You look so like your brother some-times. You looked like him just then. You really are remarkably like him, aren't you?'

'You said that at Mr Mundy's.'

'You don't think so?'

'It's one of those things, I suppose, that you can't really see for yourself.' She caught sight of the clock on St Martin's church: twenty to seven. 'Now, I really must go.'

'All right. But, just a minute.'

He fished about in his jacket pocket and got out a piece of paper and a pencil. He quickly wrote something down: the telephone number of the house he was living in. 'You'll give me a call,' he said, as he handed it over, 'if you ever want to talk to me, in private? Not just about your brother, I mean.' He smiled. 'About other things, too.'

'Yes,' she said, stuffing the paper in her pocket. 'Yes, all right. I—' She gave him her hand. 'I'm sorry, Mr Fraser. I've got to go, now. Goodbye!'

And she turned and left him, went hurriedly across the rest of the square without looking back. Probably he stood and watched her running, wondering who on earth she was meeting, and why; she didn't care. She ran on, through a break in the traffic, and headed into the Strand.

The evenings were drawing in at last. The street was darker than it had been when she'd driven through it that time with Reggie: the thickness of the twilight gave everyone flat, featureless faces and she found herself peering at people, as she hurried, with a mixture of frustration, excitement, dread. It wasn't true, what she'd told Fraser. She didn't have an appointment to keep. She was looking for Kay, that was all. This was the fifth or sixth time she'd come here in the past two weeks. She was hoping to see her; just hoping to pick her out of the crowd . . .

She drew close to the Tivoli cinema, keeping to the north side of the street, where the view was widest. She slowed her step, then moved into a doorway, out of the way.

She must have looked crazy to anyone watching, gazing so keenly from face to face. She kept seeing figures she thought were Kay's; she kept moving forward, her heart thudding. But each time, as they drew nearer, the figures turned out to be not Kay at all, turned out to be wildly unlikely people, teenage boys or middle-aged men.

The cinema queue dwindled. The programme, she guessed, must have already begun. But there'd be the news-films first, and then, say, Mickey Mouse. Maybe it was silly, standing here. She might have missed Kay already. All that mucking about with Fraser! She tapped her foot. Perhaps she should cross over, buy a ticket, go inside; go up and down the aisles; or find a spot where she could watch the latecomers, more closely, as they came in.

But then, she thought suddenly, what was the point? Was it really likely that Kay would come back here? She might have come just that one time, for that one film. She could be anywhere in London! What were Viv's chances of seeing her, really?

The queue had shrunk to nothing now. A group of boys and girls came hurrying up to the doors, and that was it. Viv put her hand again to her pocket, feeling the ring in its bit of cloth, turning it over and over with her fingers, knowing it was stupid to keep waiting, but not wanting to leave, unable just to give it up, go home—

Then a man's voice sounded, close beside her.

'Still looking for nobody, I suppose?'

She jumped. It was Fraser.

'God!' she said. 'What do you want, now?'

He put up his hands. 'I don't want anything! I've been sitting where you left me – in Trafalgar Square, watching the pigeons. Awfully soothing on a bloke's nerves, those pigeons. I found myself quite losing track of time. Then I thought I'd be like Burlington Bertie, and walk down the Strand. I didn't expect to find you still here, honestly. And I can see by your face just how welcome I am. Don't worry, you'll find I'm quite the gentleman in matters like this. I won't hang about, and spoil your chances with the other bloke.'

She was looking over his shoulder, still scanning the faces of passers-by. Then she took in what he'd said – and the contrast between what he was thinking and the real reason she was here seemed, all at once, to defeat her. She lowered her head and said, 'It doesn't matter, anyway. The person's not coming.'

'Not coming? How do you know?'

'I just do,' she said bitterly. 'It was stupid, my waiting here at all.'

She turned away. He put out his hand, just touched her arm. 'Look here,' he said quietly, seriously. 'I'm sorry.'

She drew in her breath. 'I'm all right.'

'You don't look all right. Let me take you in somewhere, get you a drink—'

'You mustn't trouble.'

174

'It's no trouble.'

'You must have somewhere to be, don't you?'

He looked rueful. 'Well, as it happens, I said I'd look in on your brother, at Mr Mundy's. He won't mind waiting an extra hour though, I'm sure. Come on.'

He drew at her arm. She'd gone back to looking up and down the street; she couldn't help it. But she let him lead her along the pavement. He said, 'There's a pub just up there.'

She shook her head. 'Not a pub.'

'Not a pub, all right. A café? Here's one, look, with a window on the street. We'll go in here. And then, if your friend turns up after all . . .'

They went into the café and found a table near the door. He ordered coffees, a plate of cakes. And when, after a few minutes, another table became free, right next to the window, he moved her to that.

The café was busy. The door kept opening and closing as people passed in and out. From behind the counter there came the regular clatter of crockery, the hiss of steam. Viv kept her head turned to the street. Fraser sometimes looked with her; more often, though, he kept his gaze on her face. He said once, to try and make her laugh, 'I've changed my mind about you. I don't think you work in a legshow at all. I think you're a private detective. Am I close to the mark?'

She let her coffee sit in front of her and grow cool. The cakes arrived, nasty-looking things, the colour of luminous paint in daylight, each with a swirl of artificial cream on top, already turning back to water. She wasn't hungry. She still kept seeing, from the corner of her eye, people she thought might be Kay. She almost forgot about Fraser; she was vaguely aware that he'd fallen silent, that was all . . . But after another few minutes he spoke again; and his voice, this time, was quite flat.

He said, 'You know, I hope he's worth it.'

Viv looked at him, not understanding. 'Who?'

'This guy you're waiting for. From where I'm sitting, to tell you the truth, it rather looks as though he isn't. Since he's put you to all this trouble—'

'You think it's a he, of course,' she said, turning back to the window. 'It's like a man, to think that.'

'Well, isn't it a he?'

'No. If you must know, it's a woman.'

He didn't believe her at first. But she could see him, thinking it over. And then he leant back, nodding, and his expression changed. 'Ah,' he said. 'I see. The wife.'

He said it in such a cynical, knowing sort of way; and his comment was so far from the truth – yet in another way, so near it – that Viv felt stung. She wondered what Duncan might have told him, about her and Reggie. Her face grew warm. She said, 'It's not – it's not what you're thinking.'

He spread his hands. 'I told you before, I'm a broadminded bloke.'

'But, it's nothing like that. It's just—'

His eyes were on her. They were blue, still rather knowing but, apart from that, quite guileless; and as she gazed into them it struck her that he was the first person, in what must have been years and years, to whom she'd spoken for more than about a minute without telling some sort of lie. When the café door opened and a couple of boys came in and started joking with the man behind the counter, she said quietly, under cover of their laughter, 'I saw someone here. I saw someone here, the week before last; and I've been hoping to see her again. That's all it is.'

He could tell she was serious. He moved closer to the table again and said, 'A friend?'

She looked down. 'Just a woman. A woman I knew once, when the war was on.'

'And you made an arrangement with her, for tonight?'

'No. I just saw her there, outside the cinema. I've been back, and waited, on different nights. I thought, if I did that—' She grew self-conscious. 'It sounds barmy, doesn't it? I know it does. It *is* barmy. But, you see, when I saw her here, before, I sort of – ran away. Then I wished I hadn't. She was kind to me once. She was terribly kind. She did something for me.'

'You lost touch with her?' Fraser asked, in the little silence which followed. 'That happened all the time in wartime.'

'It wasn't that. I could have found out where she was if I'd wanted to; it would have been easy. But what she'd done for me, you see, made me think of something else, that I didn't want to remember.'

She shook her head. 'It's stupid really, because of course I remembered it anyway.'

He didn't press her to tell him more. They sat with the silly-looking cakes between them; he stirred the remains of his cooling coffee as if thinking over her words. Then he said, still rather musingly, 'Wartime is a time of kindness. We all tend to forget. I've worked with people in the past few months, people who've come here from Germany and Poland. Their stories— God! They told me terrible things, atrocious things; things I couldn't believe an ordinary man, in ordinary clothes, in the world I knew, could be telling me . . . But they told me marvellous things, too. The courage of people, the impossible goodness. I think it was having heard stories like that that made me, when I saw your brother again – I don't know. He was kind to me, in prison; I can tell you that. Just as it sounds like your friend, this woman, was kind to you.'

Viv said, 'She wasn't even a friend, really. We were strangers.'

'Well, sometimes it's easier to be kinder to strangers than to the people we're closest to. She might have forgotten you, though – have you thought of that? Or she might not want to be reminded. Are you even sure it's her?'

'It's her,' said Viv. 'I know it is. I just know. And yes, perhaps she has forgotten me, and perhaps I oughtn't to bother her. It's just – I can't explain it. It just seems the right thing to do.' She looked at him, suddenly afraid she'd said too much. She

178

wanted to say: 'You won't tell Duncan?' But what would that do, but make yet another secret? – a secret between him and her? You had to trust someone, after all; and perhaps he was right, and it was easiest to trust strangers . . . So she said nothing. She reached for one of the cakes and began to crumble it up. Then she turned her head, and gazed out into the street. She gazed idly, now; not looking for Kay; still sure, in her heart, that she'd had that single chance and lost it.

And even before her gaze had settled a figure came sauntering along the pavement from the direction of Waterloo Bridge: a slim, tall, quite striking figure, not at all like a boy or a middle-aged man, with its hands in its trouser pockets and a cigarette dangling nonchalantly from its lip . . . Viv moved closer to the window. Fraser saw, and leant to look too.

'What is it?' he said. 'You haven't seen her? Which one are you looking at? Not the tailored type, with the swagger?'

'Don't!' said Viv, moving back, reaching across the table to pull him back with her. 'She'll see.'

'I thought that was the point! What's the matter with you? Aren't you going to go over?'

She'd lost her nerve. 'I don't know. Shall I?'

'After you've put me through all this?'

'It's so long ago. She'll think I'm crackers.'

'But you want to, don't you?'

'Yes.'

'Go on, then! What are you waiting for?'

Again, it was the youth and the excitement in his blue eyes that made her do it. She got to her feet, and went out of the café; she ran across the street and reached Kay's side just as Kay herself had reached the cinema's swing doors. She took out the ring, in its cloth, from her pocket; and just touched Kay's arm . . .

It only took a minute or two. It was the easiest thing she'd ever done. But she came back to the café feeling elated. She sat, and smiled and smiled. Fraser watched her, smiling too.

'Did she remember you?'

Viv nodded.

'Was she pleased to see you?'

'I'm not sure. She seemed – different. I suppose everyone's different from how they were in those days.'

'Will you see her again? Are you glad you did it?'

'Yes,' said Viv. Then she said it again. 'Yes, I'm glad I did it.'

She looked back over at the cinema. There was no sign of Kay now. But her feeling of elation persisted. She felt capable of anything! She finished her coffee, her mind racing. She was thinking of all the things she could do. She could give up her job! She could leave Streatham, take a little flat all to herself! She could call up Reggie! Her heart jumped. She could find a telephone box, right now. She could call him up and tell him – what? That she was through with him, for ever! That she forgave him; but that forgiving wasn't enough . . . The possibilities made her giddy. Maybe she'd never do any of these things. But oh, how marvellous it was, just to know that she could!

She put down her cup and started to laugh. Fraser laughed, too. His smile had a frown mixed up in it; and as he looked her over, he shook his head.

'How extraordinarily like your brother you are!' he said.

The house, when Helen got home that night, was empty. She stood in the hall, calling Julia's name; but became aware, even as she was calling, of a sort of deadness to the place. The lights were off; the stove and kettle, up in the kitchen, were quite cold. Her first, wild, idiotic thought was, *Julia's gone*; and she went with a feeling of dread into their bedroom and slowly drew back the wardrobe door, certain that Julia's clothes would have all been cleared away . . . She did this before she'd taken her own coat off, and when she saw that Julia's clothes were still there; that none of her suitcases was missing; that her hairbrush and jewellery and cosmetics were all still scattered on top of the dressing-table, she sat awkwardly down on the bed and shook with relief.

You bloody idiot, she said to herself, almost laughing.

But then, where *was* Julia? Helen went back to the wardrobe. After a little calculation she worked out that Julia had gone out in one of her smartish dresses and one of her nicer coats. She'd taken her decent-looking bag, as opposed to her scuffed one. She might have gone to visit her parents, Helen thought. She might be out with her literary agent or her publisher. *She might be with Ursula Waring*, said a gnomish voice, from a dark, grubby corner of Helen's mind; but Helen wouldn't listen to that. Julia would be out with her editor or agent; probably her agent had rung up at the last minute, as he often did, and asked her to run into the office and sign some paper – something like that.

If that were the case, of course, Julia would have left a note. Helen got up and took her coat off – quite calm, now – and began to look around the house. She went back to the kitchen. Beside the pantry, hanging up from a nail, they kept a hinged brass hand with scraps of paper clasped in it, for writing lists and messages on; but all the messages gripped in it now were old ones. She searched the floor, in case a scrap of paper had fallen out. She looked on the kitchen counters and shelves and, finding nothing, began to look in all sorts of other, improbable places: in the bathroom, under the cushions on the sofa, in the pockets of one of Julia's cardigans. At last she could feel her searching taking on an edge of panic or compulsion. Again that grubby voice rose inside her, just pointed out to her that here she was, picking her way through bits of dust like an imbecile, when all the time Julia was out with Ursula Waring or some other woman, laughing at the very thought of her—

She had to thrust this voice back down. It was

like pressing down the spring of a grinning jack-in-the-box. But she wouldn't give in to thoughts like that. It was seven o'clock, an ordinary evening, and she was hungry. Everything was perfectly all right. Julia had gone out without expecting to be so late. Julia had been delayed, that was all. People got delayed, for God's sake, all the time! She decided to start cooking their dinner. She gathered together the ingredients for a shepherd's pie. She said to herself that by the time the pie had gone into the oven, Julia would be home.

She put the wireless on as she cooked, but kept the volume very low; and all the time that she boiled water, fried the mince, mashed the potato, she stood quite tensely, listening out for the sound of Julia's key being put into the lock of the door downstairs.

When the dish was ready, she didn't know whether to keep on waiting for Julia or not. She served it up on two plates; she put the plates to keep warm in the oven, and slowly did all the washing-up and the drying. Surely by the time she'd finished that, Julia would be back, and they could sit down and eat together? By now she was starving. When the washing-up was done she got her plate back out, put it to rest on top of the stove, and began to pick at the potato with a fork. She only meant to eat a morsel or two, just to blunt her hunger; she ended up eating the whole thing – eating it like that, standing up, with her pinnie on, with the steam running down the kitchen window, and the man and the woman, out in the yard, starting up a fresh argument, or a new version of an old one.

'*Work it up your arse!*'

She'd been so long in the bright kitchen, when she went out into the rest of the house she found it gloomy. She moved swiftly from room to room, turning on lights. She went down to the sitting-room and poured herself a glass of gin and water. She sat on the sofa and got out her knitting; she knitted for five or ten minutes. But the wool seemed to catch at her dry fingers. The gin was souring her mood, making her clumsy, unsettling her. She threw the knitting down and got to her feet. She wandered back up to the kitchen, still looking, vaguely, for some sort of note. She reached the bottom of the narrow staircase leading up to Julia's study. The urge came over her to go up there.

There was no reason, she thought, as she climbed the stairs, for feeling self-conscious about it. Julia had never said, for example, that she would prefer it if Helen left her study alone. The subject had never arisen between them; on the contrary, there were times when Julia had gone out to some meeting or other and had telephoned to say, 'I'm sorry Helen, I've been an idiot and left a paper behind. Would you mind running up to my room and fishing it out?' That showed she didn't mind the thought even of Helen going through the drawers of her desk; and certainly, though the drawers had keys to them, the keys were never turned.

Still, there was something furtive, something

troubling, about visiting Julia's study when Julia wasn't there. It was like going alone to your parents' bedroom when you were a child: you suspected that things went on there – precise, unguessable things, that were both about you and yet excluded you utterly . . . So Helen felt, anyway. She'd feel this even while, as now, she was simply standing in the room – not lifting up papers or peering gingerly into unsealed envelopes, just standing still in the middle of the room and looking around.

The room took up almost all of the attic floor. It was dim, quiet, with sloping ceilings – a real writer's garret, she and Julia liked to joke. The walls were a pale shade of olive; the carpet was a genuine Turkey rug, only slightly worn. A desk like a bank-manager's, and a swivel chair, were in front of one of the windows; an aged leather sofa was in front of the other – for Julia wrote in bursts, and in between liked to doze or read. A table at the sofa's end held dirty cups and glasses, a saucer of biscuit crumbs, an ashtray, ash. The cups and stubs of cigarettes had Julia's lipstick on them. A tumbler had a smudge left by her thumb. Everywhere, in fact, there were bits of Julia – Julia's dark hairs on the sofa cushions and the floor; her kicked-off espadrilles beneath the desk; a clipping of nail beside the waste-paper basket, an eye-lash, powder from her cheek.

If I were to hear, Helen said to herself, *that Julia had died today, I'd come in here, in exactly this way, and all this rubbish would be the stuff of tragedy.* As it was, she gazed from thing to thing and felt the chafing within her of a familiar but uneasy mix of emotions: fondness, annoyance, and fear. She thought of the haphazard way in which Julia had used to write, in that studio flat in Mecklenburgh Square she'd been describing to Viv, today, on the fire-escape. She remembered lying on a divan bed while Julia worked at a rickety table by the light of a single candle – her hand, as it rested on the page, seeming to cradle the flame, her palm a mirror, her handsome face lit up . . . She would come to bed at last, after writing for hours like that, and lie tired-out but sleepless, distracted and remote; Helen would sometimes softly lay a hand on her forehead and seem to be able to feel the words jostling and buzzing about behind it like so many bees. She didn't mind. She almost liked it. Because the novel after all was *only* a novel; the people in it weren't real; it was she, Helen, who was real, she who was able to lie at Julia's side like that and touch her brow . . .

She moved closer to Julia's desk. It was, like everything of Julia's, untidy, the blotting-paper over-inked, a pot of treasury-tags upturned, a heap of papers mixed with dirty handkerchiefs and enve-lopes, dried apple peel and tape. In the middle of it all was one of Julia's cheap blue Century note-books. *Sicken 2*, she had put on its cover: it held her plans for the novel she was working on now, a novel set in a nursing-home and called *Sicken and So Die*. Helen had come up with that title. She knew all the ins and outs of the complicated plot.

She opened the book and looked inside it, and the apparently cryptic jottings – *Inspector B to Maidstone – check RT*, and *Nurse Pringle – syrup, not needle!!* – made perfect sense to her. There was nothing here that she didn't understand. It was all as ordinary and as familiar to her as her own lopsided face.

Why, then, did Julia seem to recede from her, the closer she drew to objects like this? And where the hell was Julia now? She opened the notebook again and began to look more desperately through its pages, as if searching for clues. She picked up an inky handkerchief and shook it out. She looked beneath the blotting-pad. She opened drawers. She lifted a paper, an envelope, a book—

Underneath the book was the *Radio Times* from a fortnight before, folded open at the article about Julia.

URSULA WARING introduces Julia Standing's thrilling new novel—

And there, of course, was the little photograph. Julia had gone to a Mayfair man to have it done, and Helen had gone with her, 'for the fun of it'. The afternoon had been no fun at all. Helen had felt like a dowdy schoolgirl accompanying a good-looking friend to the hairdresser's – holding Julia's bag while the man made her pose and move about; having to watch while he smartened her hair, tilted her jaw, took her hands in his, the better to place

187

them. The finished pictures were flattering, though Julia pretended not to like them; they made her look glamorous – but not glamorous, Helen thought, in the way she really, effortlessly was – as she lounged about the flat, say, in her unironed trousers and patched shirts. They made her look *marriageable*; Helen didn't know if there was any better term. And she had thought, in great dismay, of all the ordinary people who must have picked up the *Radio Times* and opened it at Julia's face and said to themselves, idly and admiringly, 'What a handsome woman!' She'd pictured them as so many grubby fingers, rubbing down the image on a coin; or as quarrelling birds, pecking at Julia, taking her away, crumb by crumb . . .

She had been secretly glad when that issue had gone out of date and been replaced by another. Now, however, she looked at the magazine – at Julia's picture, at Ursula Waring's name – and all the old anxiety rose up in her as if fresh. She got into a squat, and closed her eyes, and bowed her head until her brow met the edge of Julia's desk; she moved her face so that the edge ground into her and hurt her. *I'd suffer more pain than this*, she thought as she did it, *to be sure of Julia!* She thought of the things she'd readily give up – the tip of a finger, a toe, a day from the end of her life. She thought there ought to be a system – a sort of medieval system – whereby people could earn the things they passionately wanted by being flogged or branded or cut. She almost wished that Julia had failed. She thought the words: *I wish she'd failed!* What a little shit she must be! How the hell had she got to this place? This place where she wished things like that on Julia? *But it's only,* she said wretchedly to herself, *because I love her—*

As she said the words, she heard the rattling of Julia's key in the lock of their front door. She scrambled to her feet, switched off the light and dashed downstairs; she went into the kitchen and pretended to be doing something at the sink, turning on the tap, filling a glass with water and emptying it out again. She didn't look round. She was thinking, *Don't make a fuss. Everything's all right. Be perfectly natural. Be quite calm.*

Then Julia came to her, and kissed her; and she smelt wine and cigarette smoke on Julia's mouth, and saw the bright, flushed, pleased expression on her face. And then her heart – for all that she was trying so desperately to hold back its jaws – her heart shut tight inside her, like a trap.

Julia said, 'Darling! I'm so sorry.'

Helen spoke coldly. 'What are you sorry for?'

'It's so late! I meant to be back hours ago. I had no idea.'

'Where have you been?'

Julia turned away. She said lightly, 'I've been with Ursula, that's all. She invited me over for afternoon tea. Somehow, you know how it is, the tea turned into supper—'

'Afternoon tea?'

189

'Yes,' said Julia. She was heading back into the hall, taking off her coat and hat.

'That's not like you, to cut into your working day like that.'

'Well, I'd got heaps done earlier on. I worked like a demon, from nine until four! When Ursula rang, I thought—'

'I called you at ten to two. Were you working then?'

Julia didn't answer for a moment. She said at last, from out in the hall, 'Ten to two? How very precise. I suppose I must have been.'

'You don't remember the phone ringing?'

'Probably I was downstairs.'

Helen went out to her. 'You heard Ursula Waring's ring, though.'

Julia was tidying her hair at the hall mirror. She said, as if patiently, 'Helen, don't do this.' She turned and looked, frowning, into Helen's face. 'What's the matter with your forehead? It's all red. Look, here.'

She came to Helen, her hand outstretched. Helen hit the hand away. 'I had no idea where the hell you were! Couldn't you have left me a note, even?'

'I didn't think to leave a note. One doesn't suppose, when one goes out to lunch—'

Helen pounced. 'To lunch? Not afternoon tea, then, after all?'

Julia's flushed cheeks grew pinker. She put down her head and moved past Helen into the bedroom. 'I just said *lunch* as an example. For God's sake!'

'I don't believe you,' said Helen, following her in. 'I think you've been out with Ursula Waring all day.' No reply. 'Well, have you?'

Julia had gone to the dressing-table and was getting herself a cigarette. Catching Helen's bullying tone, she paused with the cigarette at her lips, and narrowed her eyes, and shook her head, as if in distaste and disbelief. She said, 'Did this sort of thing seem flattering, once? Did it, ever?' She turned, struck a match and coolly lit the cigarette. When she turned back, her face had changed, become set, as if carved from coloured marble or a length of blemishless wood. She took the cigarette from her mouth and said, in a level, warning tone: *'Don't*, Helen.'

'Don't what?' asked Helen, as if amazed. But a part of her, too, was cringing from the words, utterly shamed by the monster she was making of herself. 'Don't what, Julia?'

'Don't start on all this— Christ! I'm not hanging around in here to listen to this.' She pushed her way past Helen and went back into the kitchen.

Helen went after her. 'You're not hanging around, you mean, to let me catch you out in a lie. There's a supper for you, but I don't suppose you'll need it. I suppose Ursula Waring took you to some chic restaurant. Full of BBC types, I expect. How jolly for you. I had to have dinner all on my own. I stood right here, at the bloody oven, and ate it with my apron on.'

The look of distaste reappeared on Julia's face;

191

but she laughed, too. She said, 'Well, why for God's sake did you do that?'

Helen didn't know. It seemed absurd to her, now. If only she could laugh along with Julia. If only she could say, *Oh Julia, what a fool I'm being!* She felt like a person fallen overboard from a ship. She looked at Julia smoking her cigarette, putting the kettle on to boil: it was like seeing people doing ordinary things, strolling, sipping drinks, on the ship's deck. There was still time, she thought, to put up her hand, to call out, *Help!* There was still time, and the ship would turn for her and she would be saved . . .

But she didn't call, and in another moment there was no time at all; the ship had accelerated away and she was alone and helpless in a flat grey disc of sea. She started to thrash. She started to bluster. She spoke in a mad sort of hiss. It was all right for Julia, she said. Julia did just as she pleased. If Julia supposed Helen didn't know what she got up to, behind Helen's back, while Helen was at work— If Julia thought she could make a fool of her— Helen had known, from the moment she'd got home, that Julia was out with Ursula Waring! Did Julia imagine—? And so on. She'd pushed away that grubby, grinning jack-in-the-box, earlier on. Now it had sprung up again and its voice had become her own.

Julia, meanwhile, moved stonily around the kitchen, making tea. 'No, Helen,' she said, wearily, from time to time, 'that's not how it was,' and, 'Don't be ridiculous, Helen.'

'When was it arranged, anyway?' Helen asked now.

'God! What?'

'This *tryst* of yours, with Ursula Waring.'

'*Tryst!* She called me up, some time this morning. Does it matter?'

'Apparently it does matter, if you have to go creeping and sneaking about. If you have to *lie* to me—'

'Well, what do you expect?' cried Julia, losing her temper at last, putting down her cup so that the tea spilled. 'It's because I know you'll behave like this! You twist everything so. You expect me to be guilty. It makes me appear to be guilty, even— Christ! Even to myself!' She lowered her voice, mindful, even in her anger, of the couple downstairs. She went on, 'If every time I meet some woman, make a friend— God! I got a call, the other day, from Daphne Rees. She asked me to have lunch with her – just an ordinary lunch! – and I said no, I was too busy; because I knew what *you*'d imagine. Phyllis Langdale wrote to me a month ago. No, you didn't know that, did you? She said how nice it had been to meet us both, at Caroline's supper-party. I thought of writing back and telling her what hell you'd given me over it in the taxi home! What a letter *that* would have made! "Dear Phyllis, I'd love to have drinks with you some time, but you see the thing is my girlfriend's what they call a jealous type. If you were married, or extremely ugly, or some sort of cripple, I dare say things would be different. But a single, even vaguely attractive woman – my dear, I couldn't risk it! Never mind if the girl's not queer; apparently I'm so irresistible that if she's not a raving Lesbian when she sits down with me for a gin and French, she will be when she stands up again!"'

'Shut up,' said Helen. 'You're making me out to be a fool! I'm not a fool. I know what you're like, how you are. I've seen you, with women—'

'You think I'm interested in other women?' Julia laughed. 'Christ, if only!'

Helen looked at her. 'What does that mean?'

Julia turned her head. 'Nothing. Nothing, Helen. It always amazes me, that's all, that it should be you who has this fucking – this fucking fixation. Is there something about affairs? Is it like – I don't know – Catholicism? One only spots the other Romans when one's practised it oneself?'

She met Helen's gaze, and looked away again. They stood in silence for a moment. Then, 'Work it up your arse,' said Helen. She turned, and went back downstairs to the sitting-room.

She spoke quietly, and walked calmly; but the violence of her feelings appalled her. She couldn't sit, she couldn't be still. She drank the rest of her gin and water, and poured herself another glassful. She lit herself a cigarette – but put it out almost at once. She stood at the mantelpiece, trembling; she was afraid that, at any second, she might go shrieking and whirling about the house, pulling books from their shelves, ripping up cushions. She thought she could easily take hold of the hair on her own head and start tearing it out. If someone had handed her a knife, she would have jabbed it into herself.

After a minute she heard Julia going up to her study and closing its door. Then there was silence. What was she doing? What could she be doing, that she needed to close the door on it like that? She might be using the telephone . . . The more Helen thought about it, the more certain she began to feel that that was what Julia was doing. She was calling up Ursula Waring – calling her up to complain, to laugh, to make some fresh arrangement to meet . . . It was terrible, thought Helen, not to know! She couldn't bear it. She went with diabolical stealth to the bottom of the stairs, and held her breath, trying to hear.

Then she caught sight of herself in the hall mirror: saw her flushed, contorted face; and felt filled with disgust. The disgust was worse than anything. She put up a hand to cover her eyes, and went back into the sitting-room. She didn't think of going up to Julia. It seemed natural to her, now, that Julia should loathe her, should want to turn away from her; she loathed herself, she wished she could turn away from her own skin. She felt utterly trapped, suffocated. She stood for a moment not knowing what to do with herself, then went to the window and put back the curtain. She looked at the the street, the garden, the houses with their peeling stucco façades. She saw a world of devious things out to trick and mock her. A man and a woman walked by, hand in hand, smiling: it seemed to her that they must have a secret, to safety and ease and trust, that she had lost.

She sat, and switched off the lamp. Down in the basement the man, the woman and their daughter called out, from room to room; the girl started playing a recorder, going over and over the same halting nursery tune. There was no sound from the rooms upstairs until, at ten o'clock or so, Julia's door was opened and she went quietly down to the kitchen. Helen followed her movements with horrible distinctness: heard her pass back and forth from the kitchen to the bedroom; saw her come down to use the lavatory, go to the bathroom, wash her face; saw her go up again to the bedroom, switching off the lights behind her as she went; heard her moving across the creaking bedroom floor as she took off her clothes and got into bed. She didn't attempt to speak to Helen, or come to the sitting-room at all, and Helen didn't call out. The bedroom door was pushed to, but not closed: the light from the reading-lamp showed in the stairwell for a quarter of an hour, and then was extinguished.

The house was perfectly dark after that, and the darkness, and the silence, made Helen feel worse than ever. She only had to reach for the switch of the lamp, the dial of the wireless, to change the mood of the place, but she couldn't do it; she was quite cut off from ordinary habits and things. She sat a little longer, then got up and began to pace.

The pacing was like something an actress might do in a play, to communicate a state of despair or dementedness, and didn't feel real. She got down on the floor, drew up her legs, put her arms before her face: this pose didn't feel real, either, but she held it, for almost twenty minutes. *Perhaps Julia will come down and see me lying on the floor*, she thought, as she lay there; she thought that if Julia did that, then she would at least realise the extremity of the feeling by which she, Helen, was gripped.

Then she saw at last that she would only look absurd. She got up. She was chilled, and cramped. She went to the mirror. It was unnerving, gazing at your face in a mirror in a darkened room; there was a little light from a street-lamp, however, and she could see by this that her cheek and bare arm were marked red and white, as if in little weals, from where she'd lain upon the carpet. The marks were satisfying, at least. She had often longed, in fact, for her jealousy to take some physical form; she'd sometimes thought, in moments like this, *I'll burn myself*, or *I'll cut myself*. For a burn or a cut might be shown, might be nursed, might scar or heal, would be a miserable kind of emblem; would anyway be *there*, on the surface of her body, rather than corroding it from within. Now the thought came to her again, that she might scar herself in some way. It came, like the solution to a problem. *I won't be doing it*, she said to herself, *like some hysterical girl. I won't be doing it for Julia, hoping she'll come and catch me at it. It won't be like lying on the sitting-room floor. I'll be doing it for myself, as a secret.*

She didn't allow herself to think what a very poor secret such a thing would be. She went quietly up to the kitchen and got her sponge-bag from the cupboard; came back down to the bathroom, softly closed and locked the door, and turned on the light; and at once felt better. The light was bright, like the lights you saw in hospital operating-rooms in films; the bare white surfaces of the bath and basin contributed, too, a certain clinical feeling, a sense of efficiency, even of duty. She was not in the least like some hysterical girl. She saw her face in the mirror again and the scarlet had faded from her cheek; she looked perfectly reasonable and calm.

She proceeded, now, as if she'd planned the entire operation in advance. She opened the neck of the sponge-bag and drew out the slim chromium case which held the safety razor she and Julia used for shaving their legs. She took the razor out, unwound its screw, lifted off the little hub of metal, and eased out the blade. How thin it was, how flexible! It was like holding nothing – a wafer, a counter in a game, a postage stamp. Her only concern was, where she might cut. She looked at her arms; she thought perhaps the inside of the arm, where the flesh was softer and might be supposed to yield more easily. She considered her stomach, for a similar reason. She didn't think of her wrists, ankles or shins, or any hard part like that. Finally she settled on her inner thigh. She put up a foot to the cold rounded lip of the bath; found the pose too cramped; lengthened her stride and braced her foot against the farther wall. She drew back her skirt, wondered about tucking it into her knickers, thought of taking it off entirely. For, suppose she should bleed on it? She had no idea how much blood to expect.

Her thigh was pale, creamy-pale against the white of the bath-tub, and seemed huge beneath her hands. She'd never contemplated it in just this way before, and she was struck now by how perfectly featureless it was. If she were to see it in isolation, she'd hardly know it as a functioning piece of limb. She didn't think she would even recognise it as hers.

She put a hand upon the leg, to stretch the flesh tight between her fingers and her thumb; she listened once, to be sure that there was no one out in the hall able to hear her; then she brought the edge of the blade to the skin and made a cut. The cut was shallow, but impossibly painful: she felt it, like stepping in icy water, as a hideous shock to the heart. She recoiled for a moment, then tried a second time. The sensation was the same. She literally gasped. *Do it again, more swiftly!* she said to herself; but the thinness and flexibility of the metal, which had seemed almost attractive before, now struck her, in relation to the springing fatness of her thigh, as repulsive. The slicing was too precise. The cuts she'd made were filling with blood; the blood rose slowly, however – as if grudgingly – and seemed to darken and congeal at once. The edges of flesh were already closing: she put the razor blade down and pulled them apart. That made the blood come a little faster. At last it spilled from the skin and grew smeary. She watched, for a minute; two or three times more worked the flesh around the cuts, to make the blood flow again; then she rubbed the leg clean, as best she could, with a dampened handkerchief.

She was left with two short crimson lines, such as might have been made by a hard but playful swipe from the paw of a cat.

She sat down on the edge of the bath. The shock of cutting, she thought, had produced some change in her, some almost chemical change: she felt quite unnaturally clear-headed, alive, and chastened. She'd lost the certainty that the cutting of her leg was a sane and reasonable thing to do; she would have hated, for example, for Julia, or any of their friends, to have come upon her as she was doing it. She would have died of embarrassment! And yet— She kept looking at the crimson lines, in a half-perplexed, half-admiring way. *You perfect fool*, she thought; but she thought it almost jauntily. At last she took up the blade again, washed it, screwed it back beneath its metal hub, and put the razor back in its case. She switched off the light, allowed her eyes to grow used to the darkness, then let herself into the hall and went up to the bedroom.

Julia lay on her side, turned away from the door, her face in darkness, her hair very black against her pillow. It was impossible to say whether she was sleeping or awake.

'Julia,' said Helen, quietly.

'What?' asked Julia after a moment.

'I'm sorry. I'm sorry. Do you hate me?'

'Yes.'

'You don't hate me as much as I hate myself.'

Julia rolled on to her back. 'Do you say that as some sort of consolation?'

'I don't know,' said Helen. She went closer, put her fingers to Julia's hair.

Julia flinched. 'Your hand's freezing. Don't touch me!' She took Helen's hand. 'For God's sake, why are you so cold? Where have you been?'

'In the bathroom. Nowhere.'

'Get into bed, can't you?'

Helen moved away to take off her clothes, unpin her hair, draw on her nightdress. She did it all in a creeping, craven sort of way. Julia said again, when she'd got into the bed beside her, 'You're so cold!'

'I'm sorry,' said Helen. She hadn't noticed the chill, before; but now, feeling the warmth of Julia's body, she began to shake. 'I'm sorry,' she said again. Her teeth chattered in her head. She tried to make herself rigid; the trembling grew worse.

'God!' said Julia; but she put her arm around Helen and drew her close. She was wearing a boy's striped nightshirt: it smelt of sleep, of unmade beds, of unwashed hair – but pleasantly, deliciously. Helen lay against her and shut her eyes. She felt exhausted, emptied out. She thought of the evening that had passed, and it was astonishing to her that a single set of hours could contain so many separate states of violent feeling.

Perhaps Julia thought the same. She lifted a hand and rubbed her face. 'What a ridiculous night!' she said.

'Do you really hate me, Julia?'

'Yes. No, I don't suppose so.'

'I can't help myself,' said Helen. 'I don't know myself, when I'm like that. It's like—'

But she couldn't explain it; she never could. It sounded childish, every time. She could never convey to Julia how utterly dreadful it was to have that seething, wizened little gnome-like thing spring up and consume you; how exhausting, to have to tuck it back into your breast when it was done; how frightening, to feel it there, living inside you, waiting its chance to spring again . . .

She said only, 'I love you, Julia.'

And Julia answered: 'Idiot. Go to sleep.'

They were silent after that. Julia lay tensely for a time, but soon her limbs began to slacken and her breaths to deepen and slow. Once, as if startled by a dream, she jumped, and that made Helen jump, too; but then she settled back into slumber. Out in the street, there were voices. Someone ran laughing along the pavement. In the house next door a plug was drawn from an electric socket, a window went squealing against its frame and was closed with a bang.

Julia stirred in her sleep, made uneasy by dreams

again. Who, wondered Helen, was she dreaming of? Not Ursula Waring, after all. *But not of me, either,* Helen thought. For, wakeful, chastened, she saw it all very plainly now: Julia's staying out so late, when she might so easily have left a note; when she might so easily have done it differently, done it in secret, not done it at all . . . *Don't, Helen,* Julia said, in exasperation, every time. But if she didn't want bluster and fuss, why did she make it so easy for Helen to create them? With some part of herself, Helen thought, she must long for them. She must long for them because she knew that, beyond them, there was nothing: deadness, blankness, the arid surface of her own parched heart.

When did Julia stop loving me? Helen wondered now. It was too frightful a thought to pursue, however; and she was too exhausted. She lay open-eyed, still pressed close to Julia, still feeling the heat of her limbs, the rising and falling of her breaths. But in time she changed her pose, and moved away.

And as her hand slid across the cotton of Julia's nightshirt, she thought of something else – a silly thing – she thought of a pair of pyjamas she'd once owned, when the war was on, and then had lost. They were satin pyjamas, the colour of pearls: the most beautiful pyjamas, it seemed to her now, as she lay alone and untouched in the darkness at Julia's side; the most beautiful pyjamas she'd ever seen.

Duncan had come home from work that night and heated a kettle full of water; he'd taken the kettle up to his room, stripped down to his vest, and washed his hands, his face and his hair – trying to get the feel of the factory out of them, wanting to look his best for his evening with Fraser.

Still in his vest and trousers he'd gone downstairs, to polish his shoes, to put a towel on the kitchen counter and iron a shirt. The shirt had a soft collar to it, like the shirts that Fraser wore; and when Duncan put it on, still hot from the iron, he left it unbuttoned at the throat – just as Fraser wore his. He thought, too, of leaving the Brylcreem off his hair. He went back up to his bedroom and stood at his mirror, combing the hair this way and that, trying out different partings, different ways of letting it tumble over his brow . . . But the hair, as it dried, began to grow downy; he began to remind himself of the little boy in the 'Bubbles' advert for Pears soap. So he put the Brylcreem on after all, worrying that he'd left it too late, spending five or ten more minutes with the comb, trying to get the waves to sit right.

When he'd finished he went downstairs again and Mr Mundy said, with a dreadful forced sort of brightness, 'My word! The girls are in for a treat tonight, all right! What time's he coming for you, son?'

'Half-past seven,' said Duncan shyly, 'the same as last time. But we're going to a different pub, on a different bit of the river. They sell a better sort of beer, Fraser says.'

Mr Mundy nodded, his face still stretched in a

ghastly smile. 'Yes,' he said, 'the girls won't know what's hit them tonight!'

He had not been able to believe it when Duncan had brought Fraser home, that other time, two weeks before. Fraser had not been able to believe it, either. The three of them had sat in the parlour together, at a loss for things to say; in the end the little cat had come trotting innocently in, and that had saved them. They'd spent twenty minutes making her chase after bits of string. Duncan had even got down on the floor and shown Fraser his trick of letting her walk up his body. Mr Mundy had gone around since then like a wounded man. His limp had worsened; he'd begun to stoop. Mr Leonard, in his crooked house in the street off Lavender Hill, had been very dismayed at the change in him. He spoke more passionately to him than ever about the necessity of resisting the lure of Error and False Belief.

Tonight, once Fraser arrived, Duncan planned to get out as quickly as he could. He and Mr Mundy ate their tea, then stood together washing up the dishes; and as soon as the dishes were stacked away, he put on his jacket. He sat in the parlour, at the very front of his chair, ready to spring up the moment he heard Fraser's knock. But he picked up a book, too, to pass the time, and to make himself look careless. The book was a library book on antique silver, with a table of hallmarks: he worked his finger down the page, trying to memorise the significance of anchors, crowns, lions, thistles – all the time, of course, listening out for that tap at the door . . . Half-past seven came and went. He began to grow tense. He started to imagine all the ordinary things that might be keeping Fraser away. He pictured Fraser coming breathlessly to the door, just as he had come breathlessly up to the factory gate, that other time. His face would be pink, his hair would be bouncing over his brow, and he'd say, 'Pearce! Had you given up on me? I'm so sorry! I've been—' The excuses grew wilder as the minutes ticked by. He'd been stuck in an Underground train, going out of his mind with frustration. He'd seen a person get hit by a car, and had to send for an ambulance!

By quarter-past eight Duncan had begun to worry that Fraser might have come, have knocked, and gone away unheard. Mr Mundy had switched the wireless on, and the programme was rather noisy. So, on the pretext of getting himself a glass of water, he went out into the hall and stood quite still, cocking his head, listening for footsteps; he even, very softly, opened the front door and looked up and down the street. But there was no sign of Fraser. He went back into the parlour, leaving the door propped open. The radio programme changed, then changed again a half-hour later. The grandfather clock kept sending out its heavy, hollow chimes.

It took him until half-past nine to understand that Fraser wasn't going to come. The disappointment was dreadful – but then, he was used to disappointment; the first sting of it faded, turned instead into a settled blankness of heart. He put down his book, the table of hallmarks unlearnt. He was aware of Mr Mundy's gaze, but couldn't bring himself to meet it. And when Mr Mundy got up, came awkwardly to him, and lightly patted his shoulder and said, 'There. He's a busy chap, I expect. He'll have run into a couple of pals. That's what's happened, you mark my words!' —when Mr Mundy said that, he couldn't answer. He found he almost hated the feel of Mr Mundy's hand. Mr Mundy waited, then moved off. He went out to the kitchen. He let the parlour door close behind him, and Duncan suddenly felt the closeness and the airless-ness of the dim, small, crowded room. He had a horrible sense of himself falling, falling, as if down the narrow shaft of a well.

But the panic, like the disappointment, flared in him and died. Mr Mundy returned in time with a cup of cocoa: Duncan took it from his hands and meekly drank it. He carried the cup out to the kitchen and washed it himself, turning it over and over in the stream of cold water. The milk that was left in the pan he put down in a saucer on the floor, for the cat. He went out to the lavatory and, for a little while, just stood there in the yard, looking up at the sky.

When he went back into the parlour Mr Mundy was already going about shaking cushions, getting ready for bed. As Duncan watched, he started turning off the lamps. He moved from one lamp to the next. The parlour grew dark, the faces in the

pictures on the walls, the ornaments on the mantelpiece, drawing back into shadow. It was just ten
o'clock.

They went upstairs together, slowly, taking one
step at a time. Mr Mundy kept his hand in the
crook of Duncan's elbow; and at the top he had to
pause, still with his hand on Duncan's arm, to get
his breath back.

When he spoke, his voice was husky. He said,
without looking at Duncan, 'You'll come in, son,
in a minute, to say goodnight?'

Duncan didn't answer straight away. They stood
in silence, and he felt Mr Mundy stiffen as if
afraid . . . Then, 'Yes,' he said, very quietly. 'All
right.'

Mr Mundy nodded, his shoulders drooping with
relief. 'Thank you, son,' he said. He drew off his
hand and made his slow, shuffling way along the
landing to his bedroom. Duncan went into his own
room and started to undress.

This room was small: a boy's room – the very
room, in fact, in which Mr Mundy himself had used
to sleep, when he was young and lived in this house
with his parents and sister. The bed was a high
Victorian one, with polished brass balls at each of
its corners; Duncan had once unscrewed one of
these and found a slip of paper inside it, marked in
a smudged childish hand: *Mabel Alice Mundy twenty
dredful curses on you if you read this!* The books in
the book-case were boys' adventure stories with
broad, colourful spines. On the mantelpiece, set out

as if to fight, were some badly painted old lead soldiers. But Mr Mundy had put up shelves, too, for Duncan to display his own things, the things he'd bought in markets and antique shops. Duncan usually spent a moment, before he went to bed, looking over the pots and jars and ornaments, the teaspoons and tear-bottles, picking them up and delighting in them all over again; thinking about where they'd come from and who'd owned them before.

But he looked at it all, tonight, without much interest. He briefly picked up the bit of clay pipe he'd found on the beach by the riverside pub, that was all. He put his pyjamas on slowly, buttoning the jacket, then tucking it tidily into the trousers. He cleaned his teeth, and combed his hair again – combed it differently this time, making it neat, putting a parting in it like a child's. He was very aware, as he did all this, of Mr Mundy waiting patiently in the room next door; he pictured him lying very still and straight, his head propped up on feather pillows, the blankets drawn up to his armpits, his hands neatly folded, but ready to pat the side of the bed, invitingly, when Duncan went in . . . It wasn't much. It was almost nothing. Duncan thought of other things. There was a picture, hanging over Mr Mundy's bed: a scene of an angel, safely leading children over a narrow, precipitous bridge. He'd look at that until it was over. He'd look at the complicated folds in the angel's gown; at the children's large, innocent-spiteful Victorian faces.

He put down his comb and picked up the bit of clay pipe again; and this time touched it to his mouth. It was chill and very smooth. He closed his eyes and moved it lightly across his lips, backwards and forwards – liking the feel of it, but made miserable by it too; aware of the uneasy stir of sensations it was calling up inside him. If only Fraser, he thought, had come! Perhaps, after all, he'd simply forgotten. It might be something as ordinary as that. *If you were another sort of boy*, he said bitterly to himself, *you wouldn't have sat around here just waiting for him to turn up, you'd have gone out to find him. If you were a proper sort of boy you'd go out to his house right now—*

He opened his eyes – and at once met his own gaze in the mirror. His hair was combed in its neat white parting, his pyjama jacket buttoned up to the chin; but he wasn't a boy. He wasn't ten years old. He wasn't even seventeen. He was twenty-four, and could do what he liked. He was twenty-four, and Mr Mundy—

Mr Mundy, he thought suddenly, could go to hell. Why shouldn't Duncan go out and get Fraser, if that's what he wanted? He knew the way to Fraser's street. He knew the very house Fraser lived in, because Fraser had taken him past the end of his road, once, and pointed it out to him!

He moved about very quickly now. He messed up the parting in his hair. He put on his trousers and his jacket, pulling them on right over his pyjamas, not wanting to waste even a minute by taking the pyjamas off. He put on his socks and his polished shoes, and as he stooped to tie his laces he realised that his hands were shaking; but he wasn't afraid. He felt almost giddy.

His shoes must have sounded loudly against the floor as he walked about. He heard the uneasy creaking of Mr Mundy's bed, and that made him move faster. He stepped out of his room and glanced just once across the landing to Mr Mundy's door; then he went quickly down the stairs.

The house was dark, but he knew his way through it as a blind man would, putting out his hand and finding doorknobs, anticipating steps and slippery rugs. He didn't go to the front door, because he knew that Mr Mundy's bedroom overlooked the street, and he wanted to go more secretly. For even in the midst of his excitement – even after having said to himself that Mr Mundy, for all he cared, could go to hell! – even after that, he thought it would be horrible to look back and see Mr Mundy at the window, watching him go.

So he went the back way, through to the kitchen and out, past the lavatory, to the end of the yard; and only when he got to the yard door did he remember that it was kept shut with a padlock. He knew where the key was, and might have run back for it; but he couldn't bear to go back now, not even as far as the scullery drawer. He dragged over a couple of crates and clambered up them, like a thief, to the top of the wall; he dropped to the other side, landing heavily, hurting his foot, hopping about.

But the feeling, suddenly, of having a locked door behind him, was wonderful. He said to himself, in Alec's voice: *There's no going back now, D.P.!*

He made his way along the alley at the back of Mr Mundy's house, and emerged in a residential street. The street was one he walked down often, but it seemed transformed to him now, in the darkness. He moved more slowly, taken with the strange aspect of it all: very aware of the people in the houses that he passed; seeing lights put out in downstairs rooms and springing on in bedrooms and on landings, as the people went to bed. He saw a woman lift a white net curtain to reach for a window latch: the curtain draped her as a veil would a bride. In a modern house, a frosted bathroom window was lit up and showed, very clearly, a man in a vest: he sipped from a glass, put back his head to gargle; then jerked forward to spit the gargle out. Duncan caught the ring of the glass as it was set down on the basin, and when the man turned on a tap, he heard the water rushing through a waste-pipe, spluttering as it struck the drain below. The world seemed full, to him, of extraordinary new things. Nobody challenged him. Nobody seemed even to look at him. He moved through the streets as a ghost might.

He walked, in this unreal, fascinated way, through Shepherd's Bush and Hammersmith, for almost an hour; then slowed his step and grew more wary, finding the end of Fraser's street. The houses here were rather grander than the ones that he was used to; they were that kind of red-brick Edwardian villa you saw turned into doctors' surgeries, or homes for the blind, or – as in this street – boarding-houses. Each had its own name, set above its door in leaded letters. Fraser's house, Duncan saw as he drew close to it, was called *St Day's*. A sign said, *No Vacancies*.

Duncan stood, hesitating, at the gate to the shallow front garden. He knew that Fraser's room was the one on the ground floor, on the left-hand side. He remembered that, because Fraser had made a joke of the fact that his landlady called this room *front bottom*; he said it was like something one's nurse would say. The curtains at the window were drawn together. They were old black-out curtains, and perfectly dark. But there was a slim, brilliant blade of colour where Fraser hadn't pulled them quite shut. Duncan thought he could hear a voice, too, talking monotonously, in the room beyond.

The sound of the voice made him suddenly uncertain. Suppose Mr Mundy was right, and Fraser had spent the evening with his friends? What would he think of Duncan turning up in the middle of it all? What sort of people would the friends be? Duncan imagined university types, clever young men with pipes and spectacles and knitted ties. Then he had an even worse thought. He thought that Fraser might be in there with a girl. He saw the girl very clearly: stout, blowsy, with a tittering laugh; with wet red lips and cherry-brandy breath.

Until he'd had this dreadful vision he'd been going to walk to the front door, like a proper visitor, and ring the bell. Now, as he grew nervous, the temptation to tiptoe over to the window and just quickly peer inside was too much for him. So he unlatched the gate and pushed it open; it swung noiselessly on its hinge. He went up the path, then made his way between rustling bushes to the window. With his heart thudding, he put his face to the glass.

He saw Fraser at once. He was sitting in an armchair at the back of the room, beyond the bed. He was dressed in his shirt-sleeves, and had his head put back; beside his chair was a table with a mess of papers on it, and his pipe in an ashtray, and a glass, and a bottle of what looked like whisky. He was sitting quite still, as if dozing, though the voice that Duncan had heard before was still going monotonously on . . . But now the voice gave way to a low burst of music, and Duncan realised that it was coming from a radio, that was all. The music, in fact, seemed to wake Fraser up. He got to his feet and rubbed his face. He went across the room, moved just out of Duncan's vision, and the sound was abruptly cut off. As he walked, Duncan saw that he'd taken his shoes off. His socks had holes in them: great big holes, showing his toes and uncut toe-nails.

The sight of the holes and the toenails gave Duncan courage. When Fraser moved back towards his chair as if meaning to sink down in it again, he tapped on the glass.

At once, Fraser stopped and turned his head, frowning, searching for the source of the sound.

He looked at the gap in the curtains – looked right, as it seemed to Duncan, into Duncan's eyes; but couldn't see him. The sensation was unnerving. Again Duncan felt, but less pleasantly this time, like a ghost. He lifted his hand and tapped harder – and that made Fraser cross the room and take hold of the curtain and pull it back.

When he caught sight of Duncan, he looked amazed. 'Pearce!' he said. But then he winced, and glanced quickly at the bedroom door. He thumbed back the catch of the window and quietly raised the sash, putting a finger to his lips.

'Not too loudly. I think the landlady's in the hall. What the hell are you doing here? Are you all right?'

'Yes,' said Duncan quietly. 'I just came looking for you. I've been waiting at Mr Mundy's. Why didn't you come? I waited for you all night.'

Fraser looked guilty. 'I'm sorry. The time ran away with me. Then it was late, and—' He made a hopeless gesture. 'I don't know.'

'I was waiting for you,' Duncan said again. 'I thought something must have happened to you.'

'I'm sorry. Truly I am. I didn't suppose you'd come and find me! How did you get here?'

'I just walked.'

'Mr Mundy let you?'

Duncan snorted. 'Mr Mundy couldn't stop me! I've been walking in the streets.'

Fraser looked him over, peering at his jacket, frowning again but beginning to smile. He said, 'You've got – you've got your pyjamas on!'

'So?' said Duncan, touching his collar self-consciously. 'What's wrong with that? It'll save me time.'

'What?'

'It'll save me time, later, when I go to bed.'

'You're crazy, Pearce!'

'You're the crazy one. You smell of drink. You smell awful! What have you been doing?'

But bafflingly, Fraser had started to laugh. 'I've been out with a girl,' he said.

'I knew you had! What girl? What's so funny?'

'Nothing,' said Fraser. But he was still laughing. 'It's just – this girl.'

'Well, what about her?'

'Oh, Pearce.' Fraser wiped his lips and tried to speak more soberly. 'It was your sister,' he said.

Duncan stared at him, growing cold. 'My sister! What are you talking about? You can't mean Viv?'

'Yes, I mean Viv. We went to a pub. She was awfully nice – laughed at all of my jokes; even let me kiss her, in the end. Had the grace to blush, too, when I opened my eyes and found her sneaking a glance at her wrist-watch . . . I put her on the bus and sent her home.'

'But, how?' asked Duncan.

'We just walked to a bus-stop—'

'You know what I mean! How did you meet her? Why did you do it? Take her out, I mean, and—?'

Fraser was laughing again. But his laughter had changed. It was rueful now, almost embarrassed. He lifted a hand, to cover his mouth.

And, after a moment, Duncan began to laugh too. He couldn't help it. He didn't know what he was laughing at, even – whether it was Fraser, or himself, or Viv, or Mr Mundy, or all of them. But for almost a minute he and Fraser stood there, on either side of the window-sill, their hands across their mouths, their eyes filling with tears, their faces flushing, as they tried, hopelessly, to stifle their laughter and snorts.

Then Fraser grew a little calmer. He glanced over his shoulder again and whispered, 'All right. I think she's gone up now. Come in though, for God's sake! Before a policeman or somebody spots us.'

And then he moved back, and put aside the black-out curtain, so that Duncan could climb in.

'Ah, Miss Langrish,' said Mr Leonard, drawing open his door.

Kay gave a jump. She had been going softly up the darkened staircase, but a creaking board must have given her away. Mr Leonard, she guessed, had been sitting up alone in his treatment-room, making his night watch, sending out prayers. He was dressed in his shirt-sleeves, the cuffs rolled back. He had put on the indigo-coloured lamp he used when healing at night, and the blue of it lit the landing strangely.

He stood in his doorway, his face in shadow. He said quietly, 'I've been thinking of you tonight, Miss Langrish. How are you?'

She told him she was well. He said, 'You've been

out, I imagine, enjoying the evening?' He tilted his head and added, 'You've seen old friends?'

'I've been to a cinema,' she answered quickly.

He nodded, as if sagely. 'A cinema, yes. Such curious places, I always think. Such instructive places . . . Next time you go to a cinema, Miss Langrish, you ought to just try something. Just turn your head and look over your shoulder. What will you find? So many faces, all lit by the restless, flickering light of impermanent things. Eyes fixed, and wide, with awe, with terror or with lust. Just so, you see, is the unevolved spirit held in thrall by material sense; by fictions and by dreams . . .'

His voice was low, level, compelling. When she said nothing, he came closer to her and gently caught hold of her hand. He said, 'I think you are one of those spirits, Miss Langrish. I think you are searching, but held in thrall. That is because you are searching with your eyes cast down, seeing nothing but dust. You must lift up your gaze, my dear. You must learn to look away from perishable things.'

His palm and fingertips were soft, and his grip seemed gentle; even so, she had to make a little effort in order to draw her hand away. She said, 'I will. I— Thank you, Mr Leonard', sounding ridiculous to herself, her voice thick, uncertain, not at all like her own. She moved from him: went gracelessly up the staircase to her room; fumbled with the lock of it before she got the door open and went inside.

She waited for the click of Mr Leonard's door

downstairs and then, without putting on the light, crossed to her armchair and sat down. Her foot struck something as she went, and sent it rustling over the rucked-up rug: she'd left a newspaper, open, on the floor. On the arm of her chair was a dirty plate and an old tin pie-dish, overflowing with ash and cigarette stubs. A shirt and some collars that she had recently washed were hanging from a string in the fireplace, pale and flimsy-looking in the gloom.

She kept still for a moment, then put her hand to her pocket and brought out that ring. It felt bulky to her touch, and the finger on which she'd used to wear it was too slim, now, to keep it in place. When she had taken it, in the street, it had still been warm from Viv's hand. She had sat in the cinema, staring unseeingly at the roaring, twitching pantomime being played out on the screen, turning the gold band over and over, running her finger-tips across all its little scratches and dents . . . At last, unable to bear it, she'd clumsily put the ring away and got to her feet; had stumbled along the cinema row, gone quickly through the foyer, and out into the street.

Since then she had been walking. She'd walked to Oxford Street, to Rathbone Place, to Bloomsbury – restless and searching, just as Mr Leonard had guessed. She'd thought of going back to Mickey's boat, had got as far as Paddington, even, before she'd given the idea up. For, what was the point? She'd gone into a pub instead, and had a couple of whiskys. She'd bought a drink for a blond-haired girl; that had made her feel better.

After that she'd come wearily home to Lavender Hill. Now she felt exhausted. She turned the ring in her fingers as she'd turned it in the cinema, but even the slight weight of it seemed too heavy for her hand. She gazed about, listlessly, for somewhere to put it, and finally dropped it into the pie-dish, amongst the cigarette stubs.

But it lay there gleaming, undimmed by ash; it kept drawing her eye, and after a minute she fished it out again and rubbed it clean. She put it back on her slender finger; and closed her fist, to keep it from slipping.

The house was still. All London seemed still. Only, presently, did there rise, from the room below, the muffled throb of Mr Leonard's murmur, which told her he was hard at work again; and she pictured him, bathed in indigo electric light, hunched and watchful, sending out his fierce benediction into the fragility of the night.

1944

CHAPTER 1

Every time Viv and her father came out of the prison they had to stop for a minute or two so that Mr Pearce could rest, could get out his handkerchief and wipe his face. It was as though the visits knocked the breath from him. He'd gaze back at the quaint, grey, medieval-looking gate like a man who'd just been punched. 'If I'd ever thought,' he'd say, or, 'If someone had told me.'

'Thank God your mother's not here, Vivien, to have to see this,' he said today.

Viv took his arm. 'At least it's not for much longer.' She spoke clearly, so that he would hear. 'Remember what we said, at the start? We said, "It's not for ever."'

He blew his nose. 'That's right. That's true.'

They started to walk. He insisted on carrying her satchel for her, but she might as well have been holding it herself: he seemed to lean against her with all his weight, and every so often he let out his breath in a little puff. He could have been her grandfather, she thought. All this business with Duncan had made an old man of him.

The February day had been cold, but bright. Now

it was quarter to five and the sun was setting: there were a couple of barrage balloons up and they were the only things that still caught the light, drifting pinkly, vividly, in the darkening sky. Viv and her father walked along towards Wood Lane. There was a café, close to the station, where they usually stopped. When they reached it today, however, they found women there whose faces they recognised: the girl-friends and wives of men in other parts of the prison. They were freshening up their make-up, peering into compacts; laughing their heads off. Viv and her father walked on to another place. They went in, and bought cups of tea.

This café was not so nice as the other. There was one spoon, to be used by all, tied to the counter by a piece of string. The tables were covered with greasy oilcloths, and the steamed-up window had patches and smears where men must have leant their heads against it as they lolled in their chairs. But her father, Viv thought, saw none of this. He still moved as though winded or bewildered. He sat, and lifted his cup to his mouth, and his hand was shaking: he had to dip his head and quickly sip at the tea before it should spill. And when he rolled himself a cigarette the tobacco fell from the paper. She put down her own cup and helped him pick up the strands from the table – using her long nails, making a joke of it.

He was a little calmer after his smoke. He finished his tea, and they walked together to the Under-ground, going quickly now, feeling the cold. He had a long journey home to Streatham, but she was going, she said, back to work at Portman Square – working extra hours to make up for the ones she'd taken off in order to visit Duncan. They sat side by side in the train, unable to talk because of the roar and rattle of it. When she got out at Marble Arch he got out with her, to say goodbye on the platform.

The platform was one that was used as a shelter in the night. There were bunks, buckets, a litter of papers, a sour uriney smell. People were already coming in, kids and old ladies, settling down.

'There we are,' said Viv's father, as they waited. He was trying to make the best of things. 'It's another month done, I suppose.'

'Yes, that's right.'

'And how did you think he was looking? Did you think he was looking all right?'

She nodded. 'Yes, he looked all right.'

'Yes . . . And what I always think to myself, Vivien, is this: at least we know where he is. We know he's being looked after. There's plenty fathers can't say that of their sons in wartime, can they?'

'No.'

'There's plenty fathers would envy me.'

He took out his handkerchief again and wiped his eyes. But his look grew bitter rather than sad. And after a moment he said, in a different voice, 'God help me, though, for talking ill of the dead; but it ought to be that other boy in there, not Duncan!'

She pressed his arm, saying nothing. She saw the anger in him, tightening, then draining away. He let out his breath, patted her hand.

'Good girl. You're a good girl, Vivien.'

They stood without speaking until another train roared in. Then, 'Here you are,' she said. 'Go on, now. I'll be all right.'

'You don't want me to walk you up to Portman Square?'

'Don't be daft! Go on, look. And give my love to Pamela!'

He didn't hear her. She watched him board but, the windows being all blacked out, when he moved further in to find a seat she lost sight of him. But she didn't want him to glimpse her rushing away: she waited for the doors to close and the train to start up, before moving off herself.

Then, however, it was as though she became a different girl. The slightly exaggerated manner she had to adopt when speaking to her father – the mouthing, the gestures – fell away. She was suddenly neat, smart, guarded: she looked at her watch and went quickly, her heels clicking on the concrete floor. Anyone watching her, after hearing the conversation she'd just had, would have been baffled: for she didn't head for the steps that would have taken her up to the street; she didn't even glance that way. Instead she went purposefully across to the westbound platform and waited there for a train; and when the train drew in, she got on it and travelled back in the direction she'd just come from. And at Notting Hill Gate she changed to the Circle Line, and rode to Euston Square.

She didn't have to go back to work, after all. She

was going to a hotel in Camden Town. She was meeting Reggie. He'd sent her the address of a place and a rough sort of map, and she'd memorised it, so that now, when she left the train, she could go quickly and not hang about. She was dressed in her sober office clothes and a navy mackintosh and scarf, and the day had darkened properly. She moved like a shadow through the blacked-out streets around Euston, heading north.

These streets were full of small hotels. Some were nicer than others. Some were not nice at all: they looked like places that tarts would use; or they had refugee people in them, families from Malta, Poland, Viv wasn't sure where else. The one she wanted was in a street off Mornington Crescent. It smelt of gravy dinners and dusty carpets. But the woman at the desk was all right. 'Miss Pearce,' she said, smiling, looking at Viv's identification card, then going through her book for the reservation. 'Just passing through? That's right.'

For there were a thousand reasons, these days, why a girl should spend a night on her own in a London hotel.

She gave Viv a key with a wooden tag on it. The room was a cheap one, up three flights of creaking stairs. There was a single bed, an ancient-looking wardrobe, a chair with cigarette burns, and a little wash-basin in the corner that was coming away from the wall. A radiator, painted over and over with different kinds of paint, gave off a tepid heat. On the bedside table was an alarm clock, fastened down with a length of wire. The clock said ten past six. She thought she had thirty or forty minutes.

She took off her coat, and opened her satchel. Inside were two bulky buff Ministry of Food envelopes, marked *Confidential*. One held a pair of evening shoes. In the other was a dress, and real silk stockings. She had been worried about the dress all day, because it was crêpe and easily creased: she took it carefully from the envelope and let it hang from her hands, then spent a few minutes tugging at it, trying to flatten out the folds. The stockings she had worn and washed many times; there were patches of darning, the stitches tiny and neat, like fairy-work. She ran them over her fingers, liking the feel of them, looking for faults.

She wished she could bathe. She thought she could feel the sour prison smells still clinging to her. But there wasn't time for it. She went down the hall and used the lavatory, then came back to her room and stripped to her brassière and knickers, to wash herself at the little basin.

There was no hot water, she discovered: the tap went round and round in her hand. She ran the cold, and splashed her face, then lifted her arms and leant to the wall and rinsed her armpits – the water running down to her waist, making her shiver, wetting the carpet. The towel was yellowy-white and thin, like a baby's napkin. The soap had fine grey seams in it. But she'd brought talcum powder with her; and she dabbed scent, from a little bottle, on her wrists and throat and collarbones, and between her breasts. When she put on the flimsy crêpe dress, and replaced her lisle winter stockings with the flesh-coloured silk ones, she felt as though she was in her nightie, light and exposed.

So she went a little self-consciously down to the bar, and got herself a drink – a gin and ginger – to settle her nerves.

'It's only one each miss, I'm afraid,' the barman said; but he made the measure, it seemed to her, a large one. She sat at a table, keeping her head down. It was nearly dinner-time, and people were just beginning to come in. If some man were to catch her eye, drift over, insist on joining her, it would spoil everything. She'd brought a pen and a piece of paper with her, and now spread the paper out. She actually started to write a letter to a girl she knew, in Swansea.

> *Dear Margery –*
> *Hello there, how are you getting along? This is just a word to let you know that I am still alive, despite Hitler doing his best, ha ha. Hope things are a bit quieter where you are—*

He arrived at just after seven. She'd been glancing slyly over at every man who had appeared, but had heard a step and, for some reason not thinking it was his, looked up unguardedly: she met his gaze as he crossed the doorway, and blushed like crazy. A moment later she heard him talking with the woman at the desk – telling her that he was meeting someone, a man. Would they mind if he waited? The woman said they wouldn't mind it one little bit.

He came into the bar, had a joke with the barman – 'Just pour me a drop of that stuff there, will you?' – nodding to one of the fancy bottles that were kept, for show, on the shelves behind the counter. In the end he got gin, like everyone else. He brought it to the table next to hers and set it down on a beer-mat. He was dressed in his uniform, wearing it badly, as he always did, the jacket looking as though it was meant for someone half a size bigger. He plucked at his trousers, and sat; then got out a packet of service cigarettes and caught her eye.

'How do you do?' he said.

She changed her pose, drew in her skirt. 'How do you do?'

He offered the cigarettes. 'Care to smoke?

'No, thank you.'

'You won't mind if I do?'

She shook her head, and went back to her letter, though with the nearness of him, the excitement of it all, she'd lost the sense of what she'd been writing . . . After a second she saw him tilt his head: he was trying to read the words over her shoulder. When she turned to him, he straightened up as if caught out.

'Must be the hell of a fellow,' he said, nodding to the page, 'to get all that.'

'It's a lady-friend, actually.' She sounded prim.

'Well, my mistake. – Oh, now don't be like that!'

For she'd folded the paper, begun to screw to-gether the pen. 'Don't leave on my account, will you?'

She said, 'It's nothing to do with you. I've got an appointment.'

He rolled his eyes, then winked at the barman. 'Why do girls always say something like that when I appear?'

He loved all this. He could spin it out for hours. It only put her on edge: she thought they must be like a pair of painful amateur actors. She was always afraid she'd start laughing. Once, in ano-ther hotel, she *had* started laughing; and that had made him laugh; they'd sat there, giggling like kids . . . She finished her drink. This was the worst part. She picked up her paper, her pen, her bag, and—

'Don't forget this, miss,' he said, touching her arm and taking up her key. He held it out to her by its flat wooden tag.

She blushed again. 'Thank you.'

'Don't mention it.' He straightened his tie. 'That's my lucky number, as it happens.'

Perhaps he winked at the barman again, she didn't know. She went out of the bar and up to her room – so excited now, she was practically breathless. She put on the lamp. She looked in the mirror and recombed her hair. She began to shiver. She'd got chilled from sitting in the bar in her dress: she put her coat over her shoulders and stood at the tepid radiator, hoping to warm up, feeling the

231

goose-pimples rising on her bare arms and trying to rub them away. She watched the tethered alarm clock, and waited.

After fifteen minutes there was a gentle tapping at the door. She ran to open it, throwing off the coat as she went; and Reggie darted inside.

'Jesus!' he whispered. 'This place is crawling! I had to stand about for ages on the stairs, pretending to tie my shoelaces. A chamber-maid passed me, twice, and gave me the hell of a funny look. I think she thought I was peeping through keyholes.' He put his arms around her and kissed her. 'God! You glorious girl, you.'

It was so wonderful to stand in his arms, she felt suddenly almost light-headed. She even thought, for an awful moment, that she might cry. She kept her cheek against his collar, so that he shouldn't see her face; and when she could speak again what she said was: 'You need a shave.'

'I know,' he answered, rubbing his chin against her forehead. 'Does it hurt?'

'Yes.'

'Do you mind?'

'No.'

'Good girl. To have to start messing about with razors, now, would just about kill me. God! I had a bloody awful time of it getting down here.'

'Are you sorry you came?'

He kissed her again. 'Sorry? I've been thinking of this all day.'

'Only all day?'

'All week. All month. For ever. Oh, Viv.' He kissed her harder. 'I've missed you like hell.'

'Wait,' she whispered, pulling away.

'I can't. I can't! All right. Let me look at you. You look beautiful, you fabulous girl. I saw you downstairs and, I swear to God, it was all I could do to keep my hands off you; it was like torture.'

They moved further into the room, hand in hand. He stood rubbing his eyes, looking about. The bulb in the lamp was dim; even so, he saw enough, and made a face.

'This joint is a bit of a hole, isn't it? Morrison said it was OK. I think it's worse than the Paddington one.'

'It's all right,' she said.

'It's not all right. It breaks my heart. You wait till after the war, when I'm back on a proper man's pay. It'll be the Ritz and the Savoy then, every time.'

'I won't care where it is,' she said.

'You wait, though.'

'I won't care where it is, so long as you're there.'

She said it almost shyly. They looked at each other – just looked at each other, getting used to the sight of one another's faces. She hadn't seen him for a month. He was stationed near Worcester, and got to London every four or five weeks. That was nothing, she knew, in wartime. She knew girls with boyfriends in North Africa and Burma, on ships in the Atlantic, in POW camps. But she must be selfish, because she hated time, for keeping him from her even for a month. She hated it for making them

233

strangers to each other, when they ought to be closest. She hated it for taking him away from her again, when she'd just got used to him.

Perhaps he saw all this in her face. He pulled her to him, to kiss her again. But when he felt the press of her against him he moved back, remembering something.

'Hang on,' he said, unbuttoning the flap of his jacket pocket. 'I've got a present for you. Here.'

It was a paper case of hair-grips. She'd been complaining, when she saw him last, about how she had run out. He said, 'One of the boys at the base was selling them. It's not much, but—'

'They're just the thing,' she said shyly. She was touched by his having remembered.

'Are they? I thought they would be. And look, don't laugh.' He'd coloured slightly. 'I brought you these, too.'

She thought he was going to give her cigarettes. He'd produced a bashed-up packet. But he opened it very carefully, then took hold of her hand and gently tipped the contents out into her palm.

They turned out to be three wilting snowdrops. They fell in a tangle of fine green stems.

He said, 'They're not broken, are they?'

'They're beautiful!' said Viv, touching the tight bud-like white flowers, the little ballerina skirts. 'Where did you get them?'

'The train stopped for forty-five minutes, and half of us blokes got out for a smoke. I looked down and there they were. I thought— Well, they made me think of you.'

She could see he was embarrassed. She pictured him stooping to pick the flowers, then putting them into that cigarette packet – doing it quickly, so that his friends wouldn't see. Her heart seemed too big, suddenly, for her breast. Again she was afraid that she might cry. But she mustn't do that. Crying was stupid, was pointless! Such a dreadful waste of time. She lifted a snowdrop and gently shook it, then looked at the basin.

'I should put them in water.'

'They're too far gone. Pin them to your dress.'

'I haven't got a pin.'

He took up the hair-grips. 'Use one of these. Or— Here, I've a better idea.'

He fixed the flowers to her hair. He did it rather fumblingly; she felt the point of the grip cut slightly into her scalp. But then he held her face in his swarthy hands, and looked her over.

'There,' he said. 'I swear to God, you get more beautiful every time I see you.'

She went to the mirror. She didn't look beautiful at all. Her face was flushed, her lipstick smeared by his kisses. The stems of the flowers had got crushed by the grip and hung rather limply. But the white of them was vivid, lovely, against the black-brown of her hair.

She turned back to the room. She oughtn't to have moved away from his arms. They seemed to feel the distance, suddenly; and grew shy with each other again. He went to the armchair and sat down, unfastening the top two buttons of his jacket and loosening the collar and tie beneath. After a little silence he cleared his throat and said, 'So. What do you want to do tonight, glamour girl?'

She lifted a shoulder. 'I don't know. I don't mind. Whatever you like.' She just wanted to stay here with him.

'Are you hungry?'

'Not really.'

'We could go out.'

'If you want to.'

'I wish we had some drink.'

'You've just had one!'

'Some whisky, I mean.'

Another silence. She felt herself getting chilly again. She moved to the radiator, and rubbed her arms, as she had before.

He didn't notice. He'd gone back to looking around the room. He asked, as if politely, 'You didn't have any trouble finding this place?'

'No,' she said. 'No, it was easy.'

'Were you working today, or what?'

She hesitated. 'I went to see Duncan,' she said, looking away, 'with Dad.'

He knew about Duncan – at least, he knew where Duncan was. He thought he was in for stealing money. His manner changed. He looked at her properly again.

'Poor baby! I thought you seemed a bit blue. How was it?'

'It was all right.'

'It's stinking, you having to go to a place like that!'

'He doesn't have anyone else, except Dad.'

'It's lousy, that's all. If it was me, and my sister—'

He stopped. There had come the bang of a closing door, amazingly close; and now voices started up, on the other side of the wall. A man's and a woman's, slightly raised, perhaps in argument: the man's sounding most clearly, but both of them muffled, fitful, like the squeals made by a cloth as it polished a table.

'Hell!' whispered Reggie. 'That's all we need.'

'Do you think they can hear us?'

'Not if we're quiet; and not if they carry on like that. Let's hope they do! The fun'll start if they decide to kiss and make up.' He smirked. 'It'll be like a race.'

'I know who'd win,' she said, at once.

He pretended to be hurt. 'Give a fellow a chance!'

He looked her over, in a new sort of way; then held out his hand and said, in a coaxing voice, 'Come here, glamour girl.'

She shook her head, smiling, and wouldn't go to him.

'Come here,' he said again; but she still wouldn't go. So he rose, and reached for her fingers, and drew her to him – pulling at her arm as a sailor pulls on a rope, hand over hand. 'Look at me,' he murmured as he did it. 'I'm a drowning man. I'm a goner. I'm desperate, Viv.'

He kissed her again, lightly enough, at first; but then, as the kiss went on, they both grew serious, almost grim. The stir of feelings which, a moment before, had been gathered about her heart, expanded further. It was as if he were drawing all the life of her to the surface of her flesh. He began to move his hands over her, cupping and working her hips and buttocks, pressing her to him so that she could feel, through her flimsy dress, the points and bulges of his uniform jacket, the buttons and the folds. He began to grow hard: she felt the movement of it, inside his trousers, against her belly. An amazing thing, she thought it, even now; she'd never got used to it. Sometimes he'd move her hand to it. 'That's thanks to you,' he might say, jokily. 'That's all yours. That's got your name on it.' But today he said nothing. They were both too serious. They pulled and pressed at one another as if ravenous for each other's touch.

She was aware of the voices, still sounding fitfully in the neighbouring room. She heard someone walk, whistling a dance-tune, past the door. Down in the stairwell a gong was rung, calling guests to dinner. She and Reggie kissed on, at the centre of it all, silent and more or less still, but, as it seemed to her, enveloped by a storm of motion and noise: the rushing of breath, of blood, of moisture, the straining of fabric and of skin.

She began to move her hips against his. He let her do it for a moment, then pulled away.

238

'Jesus!' he whispered, wiping his mouth. 'You're killing me!'

She drew him back. 'Don't stop.'

'I'm not going to stop. I just don't want to finish before I've started. Hang on.'

He took off his jacket and threw it down, then shrugged off his braces. He put his arms around her again and walked her to the bed, meaning to lie her down on it. As soon as they sank upon it, however, it creaked. It creaked, whichever spot they tried. So he spread his jacket out on the floor and they lay down together on that.

He pulled up her skirt and ran his hand over the bare part of her leg, beneath her buttock. She thought of the crêpe dress getting creased, her precious fairy-worked stockings snagging, but let the thought go. She turned her head, and the snow-drops tumbled from her hair and were squashed, and she didn't care. She caught the dusty, nasty smell of the hotel carpet; she pictured all the men and women who might have embraced on it before, or who might be lying like this, now, in other rooms, in other houses – strangers to her, just as she and Reggie were strangers to them . . . The idea was lovely to her, suddenly. Reggie lowered himself properly upon her and she let her limbs grow loose, giving herself up to the weight of him; but still moving her hips. She forgot her father, her brother, the war; she felt pressed out of herself, released.

★   ★   ★

239

The waiting about, Kay thought, was the hardest part; she had never got used to it. When the Warning went, at just after ten, she actually felt better. She stretched in her chair and yawned, luxuriously.

'I'd like a couple of simple fractures tonight,' she told Mickey. 'Nothing too bloody; I've had enough blood and guts for a while. And no one too heavy. I nearly broke my back last week, on that policeman in Ecclestone Square! No, a couple of slim little girls with broken ankles would just about do it.'

'I'd like a nice old lady,' said Mickey, yawning too. She was lying on the floor, on a camping-mattress, reading a cowboy book. 'A nice old lady with a bag of sweets.'

She had just put the book aside and closed her eyes when Binkie, the station leader, came into the common-room clapping her hands. 'Wake up, Carmichael!' she told Mickey. 'No snoozing on the job. That was the Yellow, didn't you hear? I should say we've an hour or two before the fun starts, but you never know. How about making a tour of the fuel stores? Howard and Cole, you can go too. And put the water on, on your way, for the bottles in the vans. All right?'

There were various curses and groans. Mickey climbed slowly to her feet, rubbing her eyes, nodding to the others. They got their coats, and went out to the garage.

Kay stretched again. She looked at the clock, then glanced around for something to do: wanting to keep herself alert, and take her mind off the waiting. She found a deck of greasy playing cards, picked them up and gave them a shuffle. The cards were meant for servicemen, and had pictures of glamour girls on them. Over the years, ambulance people had given the girls beards and moustaches, spectacles and missing teeth.

She called to Hughes, another driver. 'Fancy a game?'

He was darning a sock, and looked up, squinting. 'What's your stake?'

'Penny a pop?'

'All right.'

She shuffled her chair over to his. He was sitting right beside the oil-stove, and could never be persuaded away from it, for the room – which was part of the complex of garages under Dolphin Square, close to the Thames – had a concrete floor and walls of whitewashed brick, and was always chilly. Hughes wore a black astrakhan coat over his uniform and had turned up the collar. His hands and wrists, where they projected from his long, voluminous sleeves, looked pale and waxy. His face was slender as a ghost's, his teeth very stained from cigarettes. He wore glasses with dark tortoiseshell frames.

Kay dealt him a hand, and watched him sorting delicately through his cards. She shook her head. 'It's like gaming with Death,' she said.

He held her gaze, and extended a hand – pointed a finger, then turned and crooked it. '*Tonight*,' he whispered in horror-film tones.

She threw a penny at him. 'Stop it.' The coin bounced to the floor.

'Hey, what's the idea?' said someone – a woman called Partridge. She was kneeling on the concrete, cutting out a dress from paper patterns.

Kay said, 'Hughes was giving me the creeps.'

'Hughes gives everyone the creeps.'

'This time he was actually meaning to.'

Hughes did his Death-act, then, for Partridge. 'That's not funny, Hughes,' she said. When two more drivers passed through the room, he did it for them. One of them shrieked. Hughes got up and went to the mirror and did it for himself. He came back looking quite unnerved.

'I've had a whiff of my own grave,' he said, picking up his cards.

Presently Mickey came back in.

'Any sense of what it's like out there?' they asked her.

She was rubbing her cold hands. 'A few wallops over Marylebone way, according to R and D. Station 39 are out already.'

Kay caught her eye. She said quietly, 'Rathbone Place all right, d'you think?'

Mickey took off her coat. 'I think so.' She blew on her fingers. 'What's the game?'

For a time there was relative silence. A new girl, O'Neil, got out a First Aid manual and started testing herself on procedure. Drivers and attendants drifted in and out. A woman who by day was tutor in a dancing-school changed into a pair of woollen knickerbockers and started exercising: bending, stretching, lifting her legs.

At quarter to eleven they heard the first close explosion. Shortly after that, the ack-ack started up in Hyde Park. Their station was a couple of miles away from the guns: even so, the booms seemed to rise up from the concrete into their shoes, and the crockery and cutlery, out in the kitchen, began to rattle.

But only O'Neil, the new girl, exclaimed at the sound. Everyone else simply got on with what they were doing without looking up – Partridge pinning her paper patterns a little more swiftly, perhaps; the dancing-tutor, after a moment, going off to change back into her trousers. Mickey had taken off her boots; now, lazily, she pulled them on again and began to lace them. Kay lit a cigarette, from the stub of an old one. It was worth smoking more cigarettes than you really wanted, she felt, at this stage, to make up for the frantic time to come, when you might have to go without for hours at a stretch.

There was the rumble of another explosion. It seemed closer than the last. A teaspoon which had been travelling eerily across a table, as if pushed by spirits, now flew right off.

Somebody laughed. Somebody else said, 'We're in for it tonight, kids!'

'Could be nuisance raiders,' said Kay.

Hughes snorted. 'Could be my Aunt Fanny. They dropped photograph flares last night, I swear it.

They'll be back for the railway lines, if nothing else—'

He turned his head. The telephone, in Binkie's office, had started to ring. Everyone grew still. Kay felt a quick, sharp stab of anxiety, deep in her breast. The phone was silenced, as Binkie picked it up. They heard her voice, very clearly: 'Yes, I see. Yes, at once.'

'Here we go,' said Hughes, getting up, taking off his astrakhan coat.

Binkie came briskly into the common-room, pushing back her white hair.

'Two incidents so far,' she said, 'and they're expecting plenty more. Bessborough Place, and Hugh Street. Two ambulances and a car to the first; an ambulance and car to the second. Let's make it' – she pointed from person to person, thinking it over as she spoke – 'Langrish and Carmichael, Cole and O'Neil, Hughes and Edwards, Partridge, Howard . . . All right, off you go!'

Kay and the other drivers at once went out into the garage, putting on their tin hats as they ran. The grey vans and cars stood parked and ready; Kay climbed into the cabin of hers and started its engine, pressing and easing off the accelerator pedal, warming it up. After a moment, Mickey joined her. She'd been to Binkie, to pick up the chit that would tell them more precisely what was needed and where they must go. She came quickly, hopping on to the running-board and climbing into the cabin as Kay moved off.

'Which one did we get?'

'Hugh Street.'

Kay nodded, swinging the van out of the garage and up the slope to the street, going slowly at first, so that Partridge, in the car behind, could catch up and follow, then putting her foot down. The van was an old commercial one that had been converted at the start of the war; she had to double-declutch with every gear change – a rather tiresome business. But she knew the vehicle and all its quirks, and went smoothly, confidently. Ten minutes before, playing cards with Hughes, she'd been almost dozy. At the ring of the telephone there had come that stab of anxiety around her heart. Now she felt – not unafraid, because only a fool would be unafraid in a job like this; but awake, alert, alive in all her limbs.

They had to go north-west to get to Hugh Street, and the route was a grim one, the shabby houses at the heart of Pimlico giving way, with dismal regularity, to patches of devastated land, to mounds of rubble, or hollowed-out terraces. The ack-ack guns still pounded on; between bursts of fire Kay could make out, too, the dreary throb of aircraft, the occasional whistle and whizz of bombs and rockets. The sounds were very like those of an ordinary Guy Fawkes night, from before the war; the smells, however, were different: not the simple-minded smell – as Kay thought of it now – of ordinary gunpowder, but the faint stink of burning rubber from the guns, and the putrid scent of exploded shells.

The streets were deserted, and lightly fogged. In raids, like this, Pimlico had an odd sort of haunted feel – the feel of having until recently swarmed with lives, which had all been violently extinguished or chased off. And when the guns stopped, the atmosphere could be even weirder. Kay and Mickey had once or twice walked along the edge of the river after their shift was finished. The place was uncanny: quieter, in its way, than the countryside would have been; and the view down the Thames, to Westminster, was all of humped, irregular masses – as if the war had stripped London back, made a series of villages of it, each of them defending itself against unknown forces, darkly and alone.

They arrived at the top of St George's Drive and found a man – a Police Reserve – looking out for them, waiting to direct them to the site. Kay raised her hand to him, and wound down her window; he ran over to the van – ran lumpishly, because of the weight of his uniform, his hat, the canvas bag that was strapped to his chest and swung as he moved. 'Around to the left,' he said. 'You'll see it all right. Keep well out, though, because of glass.'

He ran off, then, to flag down Partridge and say the same thing to her.

Kay went on more cautiously. As soon as she turned into Hugh Street there began to come, as she knew there would, specks and smuts upon the windscreen of the van: dust, from pulverised brick and stone, plaster and wood. The light from her head-lamps – which was poor enough, because

246

the lamps were dimmed – seemed to thicken, to cloud and swirl, like stout settling down in a glass. She leant forward, trying to see, driving more and more slowly, hearing the crunch and snap of things beneath her wheels; afraid for the tyres. Then she made out another faint light, fifty yards ahead: the beam from the torch of an ARP man. He slightly raised it, hearing her come. She parked the van, and Partridge drew up behind her.

The warden came over, taking off his hat, wiping beneath it with a handkerchief, then blowing his nose. Behind him was a line of houses, dark against the almost-dark of the sky. Peering through the swirling dust, Kay could see now that one of the houses had been almost demolished – its front compressed, reduced to rubble and beams, as if under the carelessly placed boot of a roving giant.

'What was it?' she asked the warden as she and Mickey got out. 'HE?'

He was putting his hat back on, and nodded. 'Hundred pounder at least.' He helped them get blankets, bandages, and a stretcher from the back of the van, then began to lead them over the rubble, shining his torch about as he went.

'This place caught all of it,' he said. 'Three flats. The top and the middle we think were empty. But the people from the other were all at home – had been in their shelter and were just coming out again, if you can believe it. Thank God they never made it to the house! The man's pretty cut about with glass from one of the windows. The others were all more or less knocked flying, you'll be able to tell how badly. One old lady's got the worst of it: she's the one I think you'll need the stretcher for. I told them all to keep in the garden till you arrived. They ought to have a doctor look at them, really; but Control say the doctor's car's been caught in a blast—'

He lost his footing, then righted himself and went on without speaking. Partridge was coughing because of the dust. Mickey was rubbing grit from her eyes. The chaos was extraordinary. Every time Kay put down her feet, things cracked beneath them, or wrapped themselves around her ankles: broken window-glass mixed up with broken mirrors, crockery, chairs and tables, curtains, carpets, feathers from a cushion or a bed, great splinters of wood. The wood surprised Kay, even now: in the days before the war she'd imagined that houses were made more or less solidly, of stone – like the last Little Pig's, in the fairy tale. What amazed her, too, was the smallness of the piles of dirt and rubble to which even large buildings could be reduced. This house had had three intact floors to it, an hour before; the heap of debris its front had become was no more than six or seven feet high. She supposed that houses, after all – like the lives that were lived in them – were mostly made of space. It was the spaces, in fact, which counted, rather than the bricks.

The rear of the house, however, was more or less intact. They went through a creaking passageway and emerged, bizarrely, into a kitchen, still with cups and plates on its shelves and pictures on its walls, its electric light burning and its black-out curtain up. But part of the ceiling had come down, and streams of dust were tumbling from cracks in the plaster behind; beams were still falling, the warden said, and the place was expected to collapse.

He took them out to the little garden, then went back through the house to the street, to check on the neighbours. Kay put up the brim of her hat. It was hard to see, through the darkness, but she made out the figure of a man, sitting on a step with his hands at his head; and a woman, lying flat and very still on a blanket or rug, with another woman beside her, perhaps chafing her hands. A girl behind them was going dazedly about. A second girl was sitting in the open doorway of a shelter. She had a whimpering, yelping thing in her arms – Kay took it at first to be an injured baby. Then it wriggled and gave a high-pitched bark, and she saw that it was a dog.

The dust was still swirling, making everyone cough. There was that queer, disorientating atmosphere that Kay had always noticed at sites like this. The air felt charged, as if with a rapidly beating pulse – as if still ringing, physically vibrating – as if the atoms that made up the house, the garden, the people themselves, had been jolted out of their moorings and were still in the process of settling back. Kay was aware, too, of the building behind her, threatening its collapse. She went very quickly from person to person, tucking blankets over their shoulders, and shining her torch, looking into their faces.

Then, 'Right,' she said, straightening up. One of the girls, she thought, might have a broken leg or ankle; she sent Partridge to look at her. Mickey went to the man on the step. Kay herself went back to the woman who was lying on the rug. She was very elderly, and had taken some sort of blow to the chest. When Kay knelt beside her and felt for her heart, she let out a moan.

'She's all right, isn't she?' asked the other woman, loudly. She was shivering, and her long greyish hair was wild about her shoulders; probably she'd had it in a plait or a bun and the blast had ripped it free. 'She hasn't said a word since she lay down. She's seventy-six. It's all on account of her we were out here at all. We'd been sitting in there' – she gestured to the shelter – 'as good as gold, just playing cards and listening to the wireless. Then she said she wanted the lavatory. I brought her out, and the dog came tearing out behind us. Then the girls started crying, and then *he* comes out' – she meant her husband – 'with no more sense than to start running round the garden, in the black-out, like a fool. And then – Honest to God, miss, it was like the end of the world had come.' She clutched the blanket, still shivering. Now that she'd started talking, she couldn't stop. 'Here's his mother,' she went on, in the same loud, chattering, complaining way, 'and here's me, and the girls, with God knows how many broken bones between us. And what about the house? I think the roof's come off, hasn't it? The warden won't say a word, wouldn't let us back into the kitchen, even. I'm afraid to go and look.' She put a jumping hand on Kay's arm. 'Can you tell me, miss? Are the ceilings down?'

None of them had seen the front of the house yet; from the back, and in the darkness, it looked almost untouched. Kay had been moving her hands quickly over the elderly lady, checking her arms and legs. She said now, without looking up, 'I'm afraid there's rather a lot of damage—'

'What?' said the woman. She was deaf, from the blast.

'I'm afraid it's hard to say, in the dark,' said Kay, more clearly. She was concentrating on what she was doing. She thought she'd been able to feel the jut of broken ribs. She reached for her bag and brought out bandages, and began, as swiftly as she could, to bind the lady up.

'It's all on account of her, you know—' the woman started again.

'Help me with this, if you can!' Kay shouted, to distract her.

Mickey, meanwhile, had been examining the man. His face had seemed black to Kay, at first; she'd imagined it covered with earth or soot. Once she'd shone her torch on it, however, the black had become brilliant red. His arms and chest were the same, and when she'd moved the light over him it had sent back dainty little glints. He had shards of glass sticking out of him. Mickey was trying to get out the worst before bandaging him up. He was wincing as she did it, and moving his head as if blind. His eyes were half-closed, stuck together with thickening blood.

He must have felt Mickey hesitating. 'Is it bad?' Kay heard him ask.

'It's not so bad,' answered Mickey. 'It's made a bit of a hedgehog of you, that's all. Now, don't try and speak. We've got to stop up those holes. You'll never be able to drink a pint again, otherwise; it'll all come sprinkling out.'

He wasn't listening, or couldn't hear. 'How's Mother?' he said, over the end of her words. He called hoarsely to Kay. 'That's my mother.'

'Do try and not speak,' said Mickey again. 'Your mother's all right.'

'How are the girls?'

'The girls, as well.'

Then the dust caught in his throat. Mickey held his head so that he could cough. Kay imagined his cuts reopening as he shuddered and jerked, or the glass that was still in him moving in deeper . . . She was aware, too, of the buzz of planes, still sounding monotonously overhead. And once there came the slithering, splintering sound of a falling roof, from a street nearby. She worked more quickly. 'OK, Partridge?' she called, as she tied off the bandage. 'How much longer?'

'Nearly there.'

'And you, Mickey?'

'We'll be ready when you are.'

'Right.' Kay unfolded the stretcher she'd brought from the van. The warden reappeared as she was doing it; he helped her lift the lady on and tuck the blanket around her.

'Which way can we take her?' Kay asked him, when she was in place. 'Is there a way to the street through the garden?'

The warden shook his head. 'Not this garden. We'll have to go back through the house.'

'Through the house? Hell. We'd better go right now. Ready to lift? OK. One, two—'

As she felt herself rise, the old lady opened her eyes at last and looked about her in amazement. She said in a whisper, 'What you doing?'

Kay felt for a firmer grip on the arms of the stretcher. 'We're taking you to hospital. You've hurt your ribs. But you'll be all right.'

'To hospital?'

'Can you lie still for us? It won't take long, I promise. We must just get you out to the ambulance.' Kay spoke as she might to a friend – to Mickey, say. She had heard policemen and nurses address injured people as though they were idiots: 'All right, dearie.' 'Now then, Ma.' 'Don't you worry about that.'

'Here's your son coming, too,' she said, when she saw Mickey helping up the bleeding man. 'Partridge, are you ready with the girls? OK, everybody. Come now. Quickly, but softly.'

They trooped raggedly into the kitchen. The

253

light made them wince and cover their eyes. And then the girls, of course, saw how filthy and cut about they were – and how dreadful their father looked, with the blood and the bandages on his face. They began to cry.

'Never mind,' their mother said, shaken. She was still shivering. 'Never mind. We're all right, aren't we? Phyllis, turn the key in the door. Bring the tea, Eileen. And cover up that tin of corned beef! Just to be on the safe— Oh, my Lord!' She had reached the door that led from the kitchen and seen the chaos that lay beyond. She couldn't believe it. She stood with her hand at her heart. 'Oh, my good Lord!'

The girls, behind her, let out screams.

Kay's feet slid about again, as she and the warden tried to manoeuvre the elderly lady over the rubble. Every step they took sent up a new cloud of dust, feathers, soot. But finally they got her to the edge of what was once the front garden. They found a couple of schoolboys swinging from the handles of the ambulance doors.

'Need any help, mister?' the boys said, to the warden or, perhaps, to Kay.

The warden answered them. 'No, we don't. You clear off back to your shelter, before you get your bloody heads blown off. Where are your mothers? What do you think those planes are, bumble-bees?'

'Is that old Mrs Parry? Is she dead?'

'Get out of it!'

'Oh, my Lord!' the woman was still saying, as

she made her way through the wreckage of her flat.

The ambulance had four metal bunks, of the kind used in shelters. There was a dim light, but no form of heating, so Kay tucked another blanket around the elderly lady and fastened her into the bunk with a canvas belt, then put one of the hot-water bottles under her knees, and another next to her feet. Mickey brought the man. His eyes were gummed shut completely now, with blood and dust; she had to guide his arms and his legs as if he'd forgotten how to use them. His wife came after. She had started picking little things up: a single tartan slipper, a plant in a pot. 'How can I leave all this?' she said, when the warden tried to get her into Partridge's car so that she could be driven to the First Aid Post. She'd started crying. 'Won't you run and get Mr Grant, from out of his house across the road? He'll watch our things. Will you, Mr Andrews?'

'We can't let you bring it,' Partridge was saying, meanwhile, to the girl with the dog.

'I don't want to go, then!' cried the girl. She gripped the dog harder, making it squeal. Then she looked down at her feet. 'Oh, Mum, here's that picture you had from Uncle Patrick, all smashed to bits!'

'Let her take the dog, Partridge,' said Kay. 'What harm can it do?'

But it was Partridge's decision, not hers; and there wasn't time, anyway, to stay and debate it. She left them all arguing, just nodding to Mickey in the back of the van, closing the doors, then running round to the front and wiping off the windscreen: for in the twenty minutes or so that the vehicle had been sitting idle in the street it had got thickly coated with dust. She got in the cabin and started the engine.

'Andrews,' she called to the warden, as she began to turn, 'watch my tyres for me, will you?' A puncture now would be disastrous. He moved away from the woman and the girls and shone his torch about her wheels, then raised his hand to her.

She went cautiously at first, speeding up when the road grew clearer. They were supposed to keep to a steady sixteen miles per hour when carrying casualties – but she thought of the elderly lady with her broken ribs, and the bleeding man, and drove faster. Now and then, too, she'd lean closer to the windscreen to peer up into the sky. The drone of aeroplanes was still heavy, the thumping of the guns still loud, but the sound of the engine was loud, too, and she couldn't tell if she was driving into the worst of the action or leaving it behind.

In the wall of the cabin behind her head was a sliding glass panel: she was aware of Mickey, moving about in the back of the van. Keeping her eyes on the road ahead she turned slightly and called, 'All right?'

'Just about,' answered Mickey. 'The old lady's feeling the bumps, though.'

'I'll do what I can,' said Kay.

She peered at the surface of the road, trying

desperately to avoid the breaks and potholes, until her eyes began to smart.

When she pulled up at the stretcher entrance of the hospital on the Horseferry Road, the reception nurse came running out to greet her, ducking her head as if it were raining. The ward sister, however, followed at an almost leisurely pace, apparently quite unperturbed by the flashes and the bangs.

'Can't keep away from us, Langrish?' she said, over a new burst of gunfire. 'Well, and what do you have for us this time?'

She was large-bosomed and fair, and the wings of her cap curled into points: they always struck Kay as being like the Viking horns worn by certain opera singers. She sent for a trolley and a wheeled chair, chivvying the porters as though they were geese. And when the man who'd been cut about by glass came dazedly out of the van, she chivvied him, too: 'Quickly, please!'

Kay and Mickey lifted out the elderly lady and set her gently on the trolley. Mickey had pinned a label to her, saying where and when she'd been hurt. She was putting out her hand as if frightened, and Kay took hold of her fingers. 'Don't worry, now. You'll be all right.'

Then they helped the man into the wheeled chair. He reached to pat Mickey's arm, saying, 'Thank you, son.' He'd caught a glimpse of her at the start and had thought her a boy, all this time.

'Poor bloke,' she said, when she and Kay had got back in the van. She was trying to wipe the worst of his blood from her hands. 'He'll be scarred like anything, won't he?'

Kay nodded. But the fact was, having handed the man and his mother over safely, she was already beginning to forget them. She was fixing her mind, instead, on her route back to Dolphin Square; and she was conscious, too, of the continuing row of aeroplanes and guns. She leant forward again, to peer at the sky. Mickey peered too, and, after a minute, wound down her window and stuck out her head.

'How's it look?' asked Kay.

'Not very clever. Just a couple of planes, but they're right overhead. They look like they're going round in a circle.'

'A circle with us in it?'

' 'Fraid so.'

Kay speeded up. Mickey's tin helmet bounced against the frame of the window; she raised her hand to steady it. 'The searchlight's got him, now,' she said. 'Now they've lost him. Now— Whoops.' She drew in her head, very quickly. 'Here's the guns again.'

Kay turned a corner, and looked up. She could make out now the beam of a searchlight and, in it, the shining body of a plane. As she watched, a line of shells rose towards the aircraft, apparently in silence – for though she could hear and feel the pounding of the guns, it was hard, somehow, to attach that clamour to the string of darting lights, or to the little puffs of smoke produced when the lights were extinguished. Soon, anyway, she was distracted by falling shrapnel. It struck the roof and the bonnet of the van with a series of clatters – as if the bombers had brought their cutlery drawers with them, and were emptying them out.

But then there was a more substantial thud, and then another; and the road ahead, suddenly, was lit by a fierce white light. The plane was dropping incendiaries, and one had burst.

'Great,' said Mickey. 'What'll we do?'

Automatically Kay had slowed, and her foot was hovering over the brake. They were meant to keep going, whatever they passed. If you got involved in some new incident, it could prove fatal. But she found it hard, every time, simply to drive away from danger.

She made a decision, and stopped the van, as close as she dared get to the spluttering cylinder. 'I'm not going to leave this street to catch fire,' she said, opening her door and jumping out. 'I don't care what Binkie'll have to say about it.'

She looked around, saw a heap of sandbags before the window of a house, and, shielding her face and hands from the incendiary's mad magnesium frothing, she dragged one over and let it sink. The white light disappeared. But then another bomb, further down the street, started up. She took a second sandbag to that. The incendiaries that were only smouldering she kicked; they went out in a shower of viscous sparks. Mickey came and helped her, and after a minute a man and a girl emerged from a house and joined in, too: they all went capering up and down the street like crazy foot-ballers . . . But some of the incendiaries had fallen on to roofs and into gardens, where they couldn't get at them; one had lodged in a wooden *To Let* sign, which was already beginning to burn.

'Where the hell's your warden?' Kay asked the man.

'You tell me,' he said, panting. 'This street's on the border of two posts. They sit there arguing about who's supposed to patrol it. Do you think we need firemen?'

'A couple of stirrup-pumps would do it, if we only had ladders or ropes.'

'Shall I run to a telephone?'

Kay looked around in frustration. 'Yes,' she said. 'Yes, I think you ought to.'

He went off. Kay turned to the girl. 'You should get back under cover.'

The girl was dressed in a man's teddy-bear coat, and a pixiehood. She shook her head, grinning. 'I like it out here. It's more lively.'

'Well, it may be too bloody lively in a minute. There, what did I tell you?'

There had come a bang, a sort of *whump*, from one of the houses farther down the street, followed by the tinkling of falling glass. Kay and Mickey ran towards it, and the girl ran after them. They found a ground-floor window with its shutters blown open and its curtains sagging on a broken rod; the curtains were black with soot or smoke, and a black cloud, with scraps of plaster in it, was billowing out, but with no sign of flame.

'Watch out,' said Kay, as she and Mickey got onto the window-sill and looked in. 'It might be a timed one.'

'I dunno,' answered Mickey. She shone in her torch. The room was a kitchen: quite wrecked, with chairs and crockery flung about and the wallpaper scorched, and the kitchen table thrown against the wall and upended. Just beyond the table they could see the figure of a man sprawled in the chaos. He was wearing pyjamas and a dressing-gown, and was clutching his thigh. 'Oh! Oh!' they heard him say. 'Oh, to fuck!'

Mickey gripped Kay's arm. She was peering through the dust. 'Kay,' she said huskily. 'I think his leg's gone. I think it's blown clean off! We'll need a strap, for the bleeding.'

'What's that?' called the man, beginning to cough. 'Who's there? Help!'

Kay turned and ran to the ambulance. 'Don't look,' she said to the girl, who was hovering about outside. The drone of aeroplanes had faded, but the little fires that had been started up and down the street were taking proper hold now, the flames of them yellow, orange, red, rather than white. They would bring more planes, with real explosives, but she could do nothing at all about them. She got out a box of dressings and hurried back to the house. She found Mickey in the room with the wounded man. She had pushed back some of the mess and was ripping open the man's pyjamas.

'Help me up,' he was saying.

'Don't try and talk.'

'It's just, my leg—'

'I know. It's all right. We need to put a tourniquet on you.'

'A what?'

'To keep you from bleeding.'

'Bleeding? Am I bleeding?'

'You must be, mate,' said Mickey grimly.

She gave a final tug on the seam of the pyjamas and swung the beam of her torch on to the man's bare thigh. The flesh ended a little way above the knee. The stump, however, was pink, smooth, almost shiny . . . 'Hang on,' said Kay, putting her hand on Mickey's shoulder. The man let out his breath. He began to laugh, and then to cough again.

'Fuck me,' he said. 'If you find a leg on the end of that you'll be a fucking magician. I lost that in the last war.'

The leg he was missing was a cork one. On top of that, the blast that had knocked him down had come not from a bomb, but only from a faulty gas-cooker. He'd been bending down to put a match to the ring beneath a kettle, and the whole thing had gone up. His artificial leg had been ripped from him and sent flying with everything else: they looked around and found it, hanging by one of its buckles from the picture-rail.

Mickey handed it to him in disgust. 'As if there

262

aren't enough bangs going off just now, without you having to make more.'

'I was only after a cup of tea,' he said, still coughing. 'A man's entitled to his cup of tea, isn't he?'

When they got him upright, they saw how badly shaken he was. He had burns on his face and on his hands, and part of his hair, and his brows and lashes, had been singed away. They thought they might as well take him to hospital as leave him here; they carried him out into the street and put him into the ambulance.

All around the square, fires were still burning, but the girl who'd helped extinguish the incendiaries had started banging on the doors of houses; one or two people appeared with pails of water, and pumps, and buckets of sand. The man with the artificial leg called to someone he knew, to ask him to board up the window of his flat.

'Looks like we're well out of here,' he said to Kay and Mickey, watching the figures running about. 'I hope they don't turn their pumps on my house, though. I'd rather a fire than a flood, any day. – What's this?' he went on, as Kay pushed the door closed. 'You're not going to lock me up in this van with her, are you?' He meant Mickey.

'I think you'll be all right,' said Kay.

'That's what you say. You didn't see the way she went for my pyjamas . . .'

'Proper caution he was,' Mickey said, when they'd dropped the man at the hospital.

'Laugh?' said Kay.

'Honestly, though, a cork leg! If the others should find out—'

Kay tittered. ' "Kay! Kay!" ' she said throatily. ' "I think it's blown clean off!" '

Mickey lit them cigarettes. 'Get lost.'

'Don't mind it, dear. Anyone would have thought the same.'

'Maybe. Still, didn't that girl have lovely brown eyes?'

'Did she?'

'You never notice the dark ones.'

The guns, for the moment, had fallen silent. The plane that had dropped the incendiaries had been chased off. It was like the lifting of a weight. Kay and Mickey chatted and laughed, all the way back to Dolphin Square. But they were met in the garage by Partridge, who gave them a warning look. 'You're in trouble, girls.'

Binkie appeared. She had a sheaf of chits in her hand.

'Langrish and Carmichael, where the hell have you been? You were seen heading back almost an hour ago. I was just about to call Control and report you missing.'

Kay explained about the incendiaries and the wounded man.

'That's too bad,' said Binkie. 'You're to come straight back between jobs. You've been in this business too long not to know that, Langrish.'

'You'd like me to leave a street to burn and bring more bombs? We'd have lots of jobs, then.'

'You know the procedure. I'm warning you. You'll do this sort of thing once too often.'

She was called back to her office by the ring of the telephone, and returned, in another moment, to send Kay and Mickey out again. The bombers had moved away from Pimlico, but there was trouble in Camberwell and Walworth. A couple of the section's ambulances had been struck and put out of service: Kay and Mickey, and four other drivers from Dolphin Square, went over the river to take their place. The jobs were rather grisly ones. In Camberwell a house had fallen and its occupants been struck by beams: Kay had to help a doctor fix splints to a child's crushed legs, and the child screamed and screamed whenever they touched her. In another street, a little later, two men were hit by flying shrapnel: they were so cut about, they looked as though some sort of maniac had gone at them with knives.

By quarter-past two – almost the end of their shift at the station – Kay and Mickey had been out five times. They drew into Dolphin Square, more or less exhausted. Kay switched off the engine as she turned in from the street, and let the vehicle coast down the slope into the garage under its own speed. When she tugged on the brake, she and Mickey put back their heads and closed their eyes.

'What can you see?' she asked.

'Bandages,' answered Mickey. 'You?'

'The road, still moving.'

Their van was now filthier than ever: they spent

another quarter of an hour filling bucket after bucket with freezing water, rinsing it out and washing it down. Then they had to clean themselves off. There was an unheated room, its door marked DECONTA- MINATION: FEMALE, where they were expected to do that. The room had a sort of trough in it, and more cold water. The combination of dust and blood was terribly hard to remove from clothes and skin. Mickey's fingers, at least, were bare. Kay wore a ring of plain gold on her smallest finger, which she never liked to take off; she had to ease it up to her knuckle to get the dirt from underneath.

When they'd done the best they could with their hands, they took off their hats. Where the straps had gripped, across their brows and under their chins, there was clean pink flesh, but the skin between was reddish-black from brick-dust and smoke, only showing lighter where they'd wiped sweat away, or in channels where water had run from their eyes. Their lashes had grit in them: they paid attention to that, because sometimes the grit contained little pieces of glass. They took it in turns to examine each other in the light: 'Look up . . . Look down . . . Lovely!'

Kay went through to the common-room. Most of the drivers were already home. Hughes was having his hand bandaged by O'Neil, the new girl.

'Not so tight, ducks.'

'Sorry, Hughes.'

'What's up?' asked Kay, sitting down beside them.

'This?' said Hughes. 'Oh, nothing. O'Neil's just practising.'

Kay yawned. It was always a mistake to sit before the All Clear had sounded: she felt suddenly tired to death. 'What kind of a shift have you two had?' she asked, in an effort to stay awake.

Hughes shrugged, his gaze on the winding bandage. 'Not too bad. Ruptured stomach, and a lost eye.'

'And you, O'Neil?'

'Four broken bones in Warwick Square.'

Kay frowned. 'That's a music-hall song, surely?'

'Howard and Larkin,' O'Neil went on, 'got a man who fell down a flight of steps, on Bloomfield Terrace. It wasn't even blast; he was whizzed, that's all.'

'Whizzed!' said Kay, liking the word, beginning to laugh. The laugh became another yawn. 'Well, good luck to him. Anyone who can put their hands, these days, on enough booze to get whizzed by, deserves a medal.'

Out in the kitchen, Mickey was making tea. Kay listened to the clink of china for a moment, then hauled herself up and went to help. They added fresh leaves to the filthy-looking black mixture that was kept, almost permanently, in the bottom of the pot; but then had to wait for the water to boil on a shrunken flame, because the gas pressure was low. The All Clear sounded just as they were pouring out, and the last of the drivers appeared. Binkie went from room to room, counting heads.

The mood of the place began to grow jolly. It was a sort of exhilaration, at having survived, got through, taken on another raid and beaten it. Everyone was streaked with blood and dust, impossibly weary from wading through rubble, from stooping and lifting, from driving through the dark; but they turned the ghastly things they'd seen and done into jokes. Kay took in the mugs, and was greeted with cheers. Partridge picked up a teaspoon and used it to fire paper pellets around the room. O'Neil had finished bandaging Hughes's hand and started on his head. She put his spectacles back on him, on top of the crêpe.

When the telephone rang, no one grew quiet and tried to listen: they supposed it was Control, calling with confirmation of the All Clear. But then Binkie came in again. She raised her hands, and had to shout to make herself heard.

'There's a single ambulance needed,' she said, 'up at the north end of Sutherland Street. Who's been back longest?'

'Drat,' said O'Neil, taking a safety-pin from her mouth. 'That's Cole and me. Cole?'

Cole yawned and got to her feet. There were more cheers.

'Good for you, girls,' said Kay, settling back.

'Yes, cheerio girls!' said Hughes, pushing up the bandage from one of his eyes. 'Splint one for me!'

'Just a minute,' said Binkie. 'O'Neil, Cole' – she lowered her voice – 'I'm afraid it's a mortuary run. No survivors at all. One body for certain, and they think two more. A mother and children. The parts are to be carried to storage. Think you can take it?'

The room fell silent. 'Christ,' said Hughes, letting the bandage fall back down, and drawing up his collar.

O'Neil looked sick. She was only seventeen. 'Well—' she said.

There was a moment's stillness. Then, 'I'll do it,' said Kay. She got to her feet. 'I'll partner Cole instead. Cole, you won't mind?'

'I won't mind at all.'

'Look here,' said O'Neil. She had grown white before, but was now blushing. 'It's all right. I don't want you nannying me, Langrish.'

'No one's doing that,' said Kay. 'But you'll see enough awful things in this job, that's all, without being made to see them when you don't have to. Mickey, you'll be OK with O'Neil, if another call comes through?'

'Sure,' said Mickey. She nodded to O'Neil. 'Kay's right, O'Neil. Forget it.'

'Yes, think yourself lucky,' said Hughes. 'Do the same when it's my turn, Langrish!'

O'Neil was still blushing. 'Well,' she said, 'thanks, Langrish.'

Kay followed Cole out to the garage. Cole started up her van, and moved off slowly. 'No point in rushing, I suppose . . . Do you want a smoke? There are some in there.'

She gestured to a pocket in the dashboard. Kay fished about inside it and brought out a flat

269

gun-metal case marked, in nailvarnish, *E.M. Cole, Hands Off!* She lit two cigarettes and handed one over.

'Thanks,' said Cole, taking a puff. 'God, that's better. That was nice, by the way, what you did for O'Neil.'

Kay rubbed her eyes. 'O'Neil's just a kid.'

'Still. – Hell, this engine pinks like crazy! I think the ignition's buggered.'

They rode the rest of the way in silence, concentrating on the route. The site they wanted was back up towards Hugh Street. 'Is this really the place?' asked Kay, as Cole put the brake on; for the house looked fine. The damage, they found when they got out, was all in the back garden – a direct hit on a shelter. People who must recently have emerged from shelters of their own were gathered at the garden wall, trying to see. Policemen had set up a tarpaulin. A man led Kay and Cole around it, to show them what had been recovered: a woman's body, clothed and slippered but minus its head; and the naked, sexless torso of an oldish child, still tied round with its dressing-gown cord. These lay under a blanket. Wrapped in an oilcloth sheet beside them were various body-parts: little arms, little legs; a jaw; and a chubby jointed limb that might have been a knee or an elbow.

'We thought at first: a woman, a daughter and a son,' said the policeman quietly. 'But there are, frankly—' He wiped his mouth. 'Well, there are more limbs than we can account for. We think now that there must have been three children, perhaps four. We're talking to the neighbours . . . Do you think you can manage?'

Kay nodded. She turned, and went back to the van. It was better to be moving, doing something, after sights like that. She and Cole got stretchers: they lifted on the woman's body and the torso and fixed labels to them with string. The limbs they wanted to keep in their oilcloth sheet, but the policeman said he couldn't spare it. So they brought a crate, and lined it with newspaper, and put the arms and legs in that. The worst thing to handle was the jaw, with its little milk-teeth. Cole picked it up, then almost threw it into the box – overcome, in the end, not with sadness, but simply with the horror of the thing.

'All right?' asked Kay, touching her shoulder.

'Yes. I'm all right.'

'Walk about over there. I'll see to this.'

'I said I'm all right, didn't I?'

They took the crate to the ambulance, labelled it up and put it on board. Kay made sure to tie a strap around it. Once she'd carried a load like this from a mortuary to Billingsgate, where unidentified body parts were stored. She hadn't fastened down the crate, and when she'd opened the ambulance doors at the market a man's head had rolled out and landed at her feet.

'What a pissing awful job,' said Cole, as they climbed into the van.

They got back to the station at quarter-past four.

271

The shift had changed by then: Mickey, Binkie, Hughes – everyone had gone. The new people, not knowing where they'd been, laughed at them. 'What's this, Langrish? Your own shift not enough for you that you have to do ours too?' 'Yes, want to stay and take my place, Langrish? Cole, how about you?'

'We'd make a better bloody show of it than you lot,' said Kay, 'that's for certain!'

She joined Cole in the wash-room. They stood side by side in silence, cleaning their hands, not catching each other's eye. When they'd put on their coats and started to walk together towards Westminster, Cole looked up at the sky.

'Wasn't it lucky that the rain held off?' she said.

They went different ways at St James's Park, and after that Kay walked more swiftly. Her flat was north of Oxford Street, in a sort of mews or yard off Rathbone Place. She had a route to it through the little streets of Soho – a fine, quick route, if you didn't mind, as she didn't, the loneliness of it at this time of night, and the eeriness of so many knocked-about houses and silent restaurants and shops. Tonight she saw nobody much at all except, close to home, her warden, Henry Varney.

'All right, Henry?' she called quietly.

He lifted his hand. 'All right, Miss Langrish! I saw Jerry buzzing about over Pimlico, and thought of you. Keep you on your toes, did he?'

'Just a bit. Anything doing round here?'

'Very quiet.'

'That's what we want, isn't it? Good night.'

272

'Good night, Miss Langrish. Put your ear-plugs in just in case, though!'

'I will!'

She went on, still quickly, to Rathbone Place; only at the mouth of the mews did she begin to step more lightly – for she had a secret, persistent dread of coming back and finding that the place had been hit, was in flames or ruins. But all was quiet. Her flat was at the blank far end of the yard, above a garage, beside a warehouse; she had to go up a flight of wooden steps to get to its door. At the top she paused, to take off her jacket and her boots; she let herself in with her latchkey and passed inside very softly. She made her way into the sitting-room and switched on a table-lamp, then tiptoed to the bedroom door and gently pushed it open. With the light of the lamp she could just make out the bed, and the sleeping figure in it – the flung-out arms, the tangled hair, the sole of a foot, thrust out from underneath the bedclothes.

She pushed the door further, went to the bed and squatted beside it. Helen stirred, opening her eyes: not quite awake, but awake enough to put up her arms, be kissed.

'Hello,' she said, in a blurred kind of way.

'Hello,' murmured Kay.

'What time is it?'

'Horribly late – or horribly early, I don't know which. Have you been here all this time? You didn't go over to the shelter?' Helen shook her head. 'I wish you would.'

'I don't like it, Kay.' She touched Kay's face, checking for cuts. 'Are you all right?'

'Yes,' said Kay, 'I'm fine. Go back to sleep now.'

She smoothed Helen's hair away from her brow, watching for the stilling of her eyelids: feeling the rising of emotion in her own breast; and made almost afraid, for a moment, by the fierceness of it. For she thought of the little bits of bodies she and Cole had had to collect, tonight, from the garden on Sutherland Street, and felt the ghastliness of them, suddenly, as she had not felt it then – the awful softness of human flesh, the vulnerability of bone, the appalling slightness of necks and wrists and finger-joints . . . It seemed a sort of miracle to her that she should come back, from so much mayhem, to so much that was quick and warm and beautiful and unmarked.

She kept watch for another minute, until she was sure that Helen had sunk back into sleep; then she rose and tucked the bedclothes around her shoulders and lightly kissed her again. She shut the bedroom door as softly as she had opened it, and went back into the sitting-room. She pulled at her tie, undid her collarstud. When she rubbed at her neck with her fingers, she felt grit.

Against one of the walls of the sitting-room was a little bookcase. Behind one of the books was a bottle of whisky. She got herself a tumbler and fished the bottle out. She lit a cigarette, and sat down.

She was fine, for a moment or two. But then the whisky began to shiver in the glass as she raised it to her mouth, and the cigarette to shed ash over her knuckles. She'd started to shake. Sometimes it happened. Soon she was shaking so hard she could barely keep the cigarette in her mouth or sip from her drink. It was like the passing through her of a ghost express-train; there was nothing to be done, she knew, but let the train rattle on, through all its boxes and cars . . . The whisky helped. At last she grew calm enough to finish her cigarette and sit more comfortably. When she was perfectly steady, and sure the express train wouldn't come back again, she'd go to bed. She mightn't sleep, for an hour or more. Instead, she'd lie and listen to Helen's steady breathing in the darkness. She might put her fingers to Helen's wrist, and feel for the miraculous tick-tick-ticking of her pulse.

It was extraordinary how still the prison could get at this time of night; fantastic, to think of the number of men who lay in it – three hundred, in Duncan's hall alone – so quietly and without fuss. And yet it was always at about this hour that Duncan woke: as if a certain point of stillness, when reached in the atmosphere of the place, acted on him like a sound or a vibration.

He was awake, now. He was lying on his bunk, on his back, with his hands behind his head; he was gazing into the blackness made by Fraser's bunk, a yard above his face. He felt clear-headed and quite calm: relieved of an awful burden, now that visiting-day had come and gone – now that he'd managed to get through his father's visit without arguing or sulking, without breaking down or making a fool of himself in some way. There was a whole month, now, until visiting-day came round again. And a month in prison was an age. A month in prison was like a street with a fog in it: you could see the things that were near to you clearly enough, but the rest was grey, blank, depthless.

He said to himself, *How changed you are!* For he'd used to brood over all the little details of his father's visits, for days at a time; he'd lie tormented, seeing his father's face, hearing his father's voice and his own – like a mad projectionist with a picture, making it play over and over. Or else he'd compose wild letters, telling his father not to come again. One time he had thrown off the bed-clothes, sprung from his bunk, sat down at his table and actually, in the near-pitch darkness, started to write a letter to Viv. He had written feverishly, with a stub of pencil, on a sheet of paper torn from the back of a library book; and when he looked next morning at what he'd done it was like the work of a lunatic, the lines all running across each other, the same ideas and phrases coming up again and again: *The filth of this place – I can't describe it – I'm afraid, Viv – the filth – I'm afraid—* He'd been put on report, then, for damaging the book.

He turned on to his side, not wanting to remember it.

The moon had set, but there must be starlight: he and Fraser had drawn back the black-out, and the window – a series of ugly little panes – cast an interesting shadow on the floor. You could see it move, Duncan had found, if you watched hard enough; or you could lie looking up, with your head at a tiring angle, and see the stars themselves, see the moon, the odd sparkle of gunfire. The lights made you shiver. The cell was cold. Low in the wall beneath the window was an opening in the bricks with a piece of Victorian fretwork across it: it was meant to circulate heat, but the air that rose from it was always freezing. Duncan was wearing his prison pyjamas, his vest and his socks; the rest of his clothes – his shirt, his jacket and trousers and cape – he'd spread on top of the blankets which covered him, for extra warmth. In the bunk above, Fraser had done the same.

But Fraser had moved in his sleep, and his cape or his shirt was hanging slightly to one side. He'd flung out his arm, too, and the fingers of his hand showed: shapely, dark, like the legs of some impossibly large and well-muscled spider. As Duncan watched, the fingers gave a twitch – as if feeling for a purchase, trying for a spring . . . *Don't look at it*, Duncan said to himself, because he sometimes found that small, idiotic things like that could get a grip on his thoughts at night, and really unnerve him. He turned the other way, and that was better. If he stretched out his own hand now and touched the wall, he could feel where the plaster had been scratched away by men who'd lain here years before: *J.B. December 1922, L.C.V. nine months ten days*

1934 . . . The dates were not old enough to be really quaint, but he liked to think of the men who had made them, and the little instruments they must have used, the stolen needles and nails, the broken bits of china. *R.I.P. George K, a fine screwsman*: that made him wonder if a prisoner had died in this cell, been killed, or killed himself. One man had scored a calendar, but he had given every month thirty days, so the calendar was next to useless. Another had written verses: *Five lonely years I must walk my cell, I wish my wife was here as well* – and underneath this someone else had put, *She don't you cunt, shes getting stuffed by your best pal ha ha.*

Duncan closed his eyes. Who else, he wondered, was awake, in the whole of the building? Perhaps only the officers. You could hear them pass: back and forth they went, once every hour, like figures on an old-fashioned clock. Their shoes were soft, but made the metal landings ring: a chilly, shivering sound with a steady beat to it, like the pulsing of icy blood. You rarely heard it during the day, probably the place was too noisy then; to Duncan it seemed part of the special feel of the night, as if produced by the stillness and the dark. He would wait, to catch it. It meant another sixty minutes of prison time done, after all. And if he were the only man awake and knowing, then those sixty minutes, he felt, belonged exclusively to him: they went into his account, with a slither and a chink, like coins in the back of a china pig. Hard luck on the men who slept! They got nothing . . . But if someone stirred – if someone coughed, or banged on his door for an officer to come; if a man started weeping or calling out – then Duncan would share the minutes with him, fifty-fifty, thirty minutes each. That was only fair.

It was stupid, really, because of course, your time passed quickest of all when you were asleep; and lying awake, as Duncan was now, only made things worse. But you had to have little schemes, little tricks like this; you had to be able to turn your waiting into something more palpable – a piece of work or a puzzle. It was all you had to do. It was all that prison was: not a china pig after all, but a great, slow machine, for the grinding up of time. Your life went into it, and was crushed to a powder.

He lifted his head, then changed his pose again, rolled back on to his other side. The shivering sound had started up on the landing, and this time the beat was so slight, so subtle, he knew that it must be Mr Mundy who walked there; because Mr Mundy had been at the prison longer than any other officer and knew how to walk in a careful way, so as not to disturb the men. The beat came closer, but began to slow; like a fading heartbeat it came, until at last it stopped completely. Duncan held his breath. Beneath the door to his cell was a bar of sickly blue light, and in the vertical centre of the door, five feet from the floor, was a covered spy-hole. Now, as he watched, the bar of light was broken and the spy-hole, for a second, grew bright, then dimmed. Mr Mundy was standing, looking in. For,

279

just as he knew how to walk so gently, so he also knew, he said, when any of his men were troubled and couldn't sleep . . .

He stood there, quite still, for almost a minute. Then, 'All right?' he called, very softly.

Duncan didn't answer at first. He was afraid that Fraser would wake. But finally, 'All right!' he whispered. And then, when Fraser didn't stir, he added: 'Good night!'

'Good night!' Mr Mundy answered.

Duncan closed his eyes. In time he heard the shivering beat start up again and grow faint. When he looked again, the bar of light beneath his door was unbroken, and the pale little circle of the spy-hole had been snuffed out. He rolled on to his other side, and put his hands beneath his cheek – like a boy in a picture-book, waiting patiently for sleep.

CHAPTER 2

'Helen!' Helen heard somebody call, above the snarl of traffic on the Marylebone Road. 'Helen! Over here!'

She turned her head, and saw a woman in a blue jeans jacket and dungarees, rather filthy at the knee, with her hair done up in a dusty turban. The woman was smiling, and had lifted her hand. 'Helen!' she called again, beginning to laugh.

'Julia!' said Helen, at last. She crossed the road. 'I didn't recognise you!'

'I'm not surprised. I must look like a chimney-sweep, do I?'

'Well, a little.'

Julia got up. She'd been sitting in the sun, on a stump of wall. She had a Gladys Mitchell novel in one hand and a cigarette in the other: now she took a hasty final draw on the cigarette and threw it away. She rubbed her hand across the bib of her dungarees, so that she could offer it to Helen. But when she glanced at her palm, she looked doubtful.

'I think the dirt's there permanently. Do you mind?'

'Of course not.'

They shook hands. Julia said, 'Where are you going?'

'I'm going back to work,' answered Helen, a little self-consciously; for something about Julia – Julia's manner, Julia's clear, upper-class voice – always made her shy. 'I've just had lunch. I work just over there, in the Town Hall.'

'The Town Hall?' Julia peered along the street. 'We've probably passed one another before, then, and not noticed. My father and I've been working our way through all the streets around here. We've set up a sort of headquarters, in a house on Bryanston Square. We've been there for a week. He's just gone off to see a warden, and I'm making it an excuse for a little sit down.'

Julia's father, Helen knew, was an architect. He was making a survey of bomb-damaged buildings, and Julia was helping. But Helen had always imagined them working miles away, in the East End or somewhere like that. She said, 'Bryanston Square? How funny! I walk through there all the time.'

'Do you?' asked Julia.

They looked at each other, for a second, frowning and smiling. Then Julia went on, more briskly, 'How are you, anyway?'

Helen shrugged, rather shy again. 'I'm all right. A bit tired, of course; like everyone. How are you? Are you writing?'

'Yes, a little.'

'You manage to do it, in between bangs?'

'Yes, in between bangs. It keeps my mind off them,

I think. I'm just reading this' – she showed the book – 'as a way of checking out the competition. But tell me, how's Kay?'

She asked it, perfectly easily; but Helen felt herself blush. She nodded. 'Kay's all right.'

'Still at the Station? At Dolphin Square?'

'Yes. Still there.'

'With Mickey? And Binkie? They're quite a pair, aren't they?'

Helen laughed, agreeing that they were . . . The sun grew brighter, and Julia lifted the book to her brow, to make a shade. But she kept her gaze on Helen's face as she did it, as if turning something over in her mind.

Then, 'Look,' she said. She tugged at her wrist-watch, which had worked its way around her arm. 'My father will be ten minutes yet. I was just about to go and get myself a cup of tea. There's a canteen thing up by the station. Care to join me? Or do you have to get back to work?'

'Well,' said Helen, surprised. 'I ought to be back at my desk, as it happens.'

'Ought you? But, look at it this way. The tea will make you work harder.'

'Well, perhaps,' said Helen.

She was still aware of having blushed; and she didn't want Julia to suppose that she couldn't stand in a street and talk about Kay, as if the whole thing weren't perfectly natural, perfectly fine . . . And Kay herself would be pleased to hear they'd met up; she thought of it like that. So she glanced at her own watch, then smiled and said, 'All right, so long as we're quick. I'll brave the wrath of Miss Chisholm, just this once.'

'Miss Chisholm?'

'A colleague of mine, and frightfully proper. Her pursed lips are something awful. She scares the life out of me, to be honest.'

Julia laughed. They started to walk. They went very quickly up the street and joined a short line of people waiting to be served at the window of a mobile canteen.

The day, though sunny and almost breezeless, was cold. The winter so far had been a very bitter one. But that made the blueness of today's sky, Helen thought, more lovely. Everyone looked cheerful, as if reminded of happier times. A soldier in khaki had leant his kitbag and rifle against the canteen van and was lazily rolling a cigarette. The girl in front of Helen and Julia was wearing sunglasses. The elderly man in front of her had on a cream Panama hat. But he and the girl had gas-mask boxes hung over their shoulders, too: people had dug them out, Helen had noticed, and started carrying them again. And fifty yards further along the Marylebone Road an office building had been freshly bombed: an emergency water tank had been set up; there were scraps of wet, charred paper clinging to the pavements, a coating of ash on walls and trees, and muddy tracks leading in and out of the wreckage where hoses had been dragged across the street.

The queue moved forward. Julia asked for teas

from the girl behind the counter. Helen took out her purse, and there was the usual women's quarrel over who should pay. In the end, Julia did; she said it was her idea in the first place. The tea looked ghastly, anyway: greyish, probably made from chlorinated water, and the milk was powdered and formed lumps. Julia picked up the cups and led Helen a little way off, to a heap of sandbags underneath a boarded window. The bags had had the sun on them; they smelt, not unpleasantly, of drying jute. Some had split, and showed pale earth, the limp remains of flowers and grass.

Julia pulled on a broken stalk. '"Nature triumphant over war",' she said, in a wireless voice; for it was the sort of thing that people were always writing about to the radio – the new variety of wildflower they had spotted on the bomb-sites, the new species of bird, all of that – it had got terribly boring. She sipped her tea, then made a face: 'God, this is awful.' She got out a packet of cigarettes and a lighter. 'You won't mind my smoking in the street?'

'Of course not.'

'Want one?'

'I've got my own here somewhere—'

'Don't be silly. Here.'

'Well, thanks.'

They shared the flame, their heads coming rather close together, the smoke rising up and into their eyes. Without thinking, Helen touched her fingers, very lightly, to Julia's hand.

'Your knuckles are grazed,' she said.

Julia looked. 'So they are. That must be from broken glass.' She lifted the knuckles to her mouth and sucked them. 'I had to lower myself through the fanlight of a house this morning.'

'Goodness!' said Helen. 'Like Oliver Twist!'

'Yes, just like that.'

'Isn't that illegal?'

'So you might think. But we have a sort of special dispensation, my father and I. If a house is empty and we can't get hold of the keys, we're allowed to get in however we can. It's a filthy business, not at all as exciting as it sounds: the rooms all smashed, the carpets wrecked, the mirrors in splinters. The water-pipes might have had it: the water runs and turns the soot to sludge. I went into places last month and found things frozen: sofas and table-cloths and things like that. Or, things get burned. An incendiary will land on a roof: it might burn right through, quite neatly, from one floor to the next; you can stand in the basement and look at the sky . . . I find damage like that more miserable, somehow, than if a house has been blasted to bits: it's like a life with a cancer in it.'

'Is it frightening?' asked Helen, very taken with Julia's description. 'I think it would frighten me.'

'It spooks me a bit. Then there's always the chance, of course, of discovering someone – a looter, who's got in the same way you did. Boys who've gone in for a lark. You see rotten drawings on the walls, sometimes; you pity the family that must come back. Then again, sometimes the house hasn't been abandoned at all. My father got into one, a few months ago: he went into every room to look at the damage, and in the last room of all was a very old woman, in a yellow nightdress and with silver hair, asleep in a four-poster bed with tattered curtains.'

Helen saw the scene, quite clearly. She said, fascinated, 'What did your father do?'

'He left her to it – went silently back downstairs; then told the local warden. The warden said the old woman had a girl who came and cooked her dinners for her, and lit her fires; that she was ninety-three, and could never be got to come out when a raid was on. That she remembered seeing Prince Albert with Queen Victoria once in a carriage in Hyde Park.'

The sun, all the time that Julia was speaking, was moving in and out of cloud. When it grew bright she put her hand to her eyes or, as she had before, lifted her book; now, its growing brighter than ever, she stopped talking, shut her eyes completely for a moment and put back her head.

How lovely she is! thought Helen suddenly, jolted out of the story about the old woman; for the sun lit Julia as a spotlight might, and the blue of the dungarees and the jacket set off the tan of her face, the dark of her lashes and neat, straight brows; and because her hair was swept up by the turban you saw more clearly the graceful lines of her jaw and her throat. She had parted her lips. Her mouth was full, slightly crowded, the teeth not quite even. But even that was lovely, somehow: one of those flaws of feature that mysteriously render a handsome face more handsome than genuine flawlessness could.

No wonder, Helen thought, with an unsettling mix of feelings – envy, and admiration, and a slight sinking of heart – *No wonder Kay was in love with you.*

For that was all the connection she and Julia had. They could not be said, even, to be friends. Julia was Kay's friend, as Mickey was – or rather, not at all as Mickey was, for she did not, as Mickey did, spend time with Kay and Helen, at their flat, in pubs, at parties. She wasn't open and easy and kind. She had a sort of mystery to her – a sort of glamour, Helen thought it.

The mystery and glamour had been there, right from the start. 'You must meet Julia,' Kay had used to say, after Helen had moved into her flat. 'I do so want you two to meet up.' But there had always been something in the way of it: Julia was busy, Julia was writing; Julia kept odd hours and could never be pinned down. They'd met, at last, about a year before, by accident: bumped into each other at the theatre, after a performance of – of all things – *Blithe Spirit*. Julia had been handsome, charming, frightening, remote: Helen had taken one look at her, noted the awkward, slightly flustered manner with which Kay introduced her; and guessed everything.

Later that night she'd asked Kay: 'What was there, between you and Julia?' – and Kay had instantly grown awkward again.

'Nothing,' she'd said.

'Nothing?'

'A sort of – misaffection, that was all. Ages ago.'

'You were in love with her,' Helen had said, bluntly.

And Kay had laughed – 'Look here, let's talk of something else!' – but also, what was rare for her, had blushed.

That blush was all the link there was, between Helen and Julia – a funny sort of link, when you thought about it.

Julia smiled and tilted her head. They were only fifty yards or so from the entrance to Marylebone Station, and through a lull in the traffic there had come a sudden burst of noise from one of the platforms: a blown whistle, followed by the letting out of steam. She opened her eyes. 'I like that sound.'

'So do I,' said Helen. 'It's a holiday sound, isn't it? A buckets-and-spades sort of sound. It makes me long to get away, get out of London, just for a bit.' She swilled the tea in the bottom of her cup. 'No chance of that, I suppose.'

'No?' said Julia, looking at her. 'Can't you fix something up?'

'Where's there to go to? And then, the trains . . . And, anyway, I'd never persuade Kay. She's working extra shifts, now, at Dolphin Square. She'd never take time off, while things are so bad.'

Julia drew on her cigarette, then threw it down and covered it over with her shoe. 'Kay's such a heroine, though, isn't she?' she said, blowing out smoke. 'Kay's such a brick.'

She meant it jokingly, Helen supposed; but her tone was not quite light, and she looked at Helen, as she said it, from the corner of her eye, almost slyly – as if testing her, weighing up her response.

Helen remembered, then, something she'd once heard Mickey say about Julia: that she longed to be admired; that she couldn't bear to have anyone liked over herself; and that she was hard. And she thought, with a flicker of dislike, *It's true, you are hard.* She felt suddenly, in that one moment, exposed, unsafe.

But the queer thing was, the sensation of unsafeness, even of dislike, was almost exciting. She glanced again at Julia's smooth, handsome, upper-class face and thought of jewels, of pearls. Wasn't hardness a condition of glamour, after all?

And then Julia changed her pose, and the moment passed. She caught hold of her wrist-watch again; Helen saw how late it was and said, 'Damn.' She quickly finished her cigarette, dropped the stub into her almost empty cup, and heard it hiss. 'I must get back to work.'

Julia nodded, drinking off her tea. She said, 'I'll go with you.'

They went quickly back to the canteen, to leave their cups on the counter, then walked the couple of hundred yards to Helen's office.

'Will your Miss Prism give you hell, for staying out so long?' asked Julia, as they went.

'Miss Chisholm,' said Helen, smiling. 'She might.'

'You'd better put the blame on me, then. Say I'm an emergency case. That I've – what? Lost my house, and everything in it?'

'Everything?' Helen thought it over. 'That's about six separate departments, I'm afraid. I could only help you with a grant for light repairs. You'd have to see someone over at the War Damage Commission about rebuilding work; they're just as likely, however, to send you back to us. Miss Links, on the third floor, might be able to give you some assistance with the cleaning of any salvageable items – curtains, carpets, things like that. But be sure to bring your cleaners' bills with you; and the chit we gave you, when you first filed your report of the incident. – What's that? You've lost the chit? Oh, dear. You must get another, and start all over again . . . It's like snakes and ladders, you see. And this is always assuming, of course, that we've found time to see you in the first place.'

Julia grimaced. 'You enjoy your job.'

'It's frustrating, that's all. You hope to make some sort of difference. But now the people we rehoused three years ago are coming back; they've been bombed out all over again. We've less money than ever. And still the war is costing us – how much do they say? Eleven million a day?'

'Don't ask me,' said Julia. 'I've given up reading the papers. Since the world's so obviously bent on killing itself, I decided months ago to sit back and let it.'

'I wish I could,' said Helen. 'But I find I feel even worse, not knowing, than I do when I know it all.'

But now they had reached the Town Hall; and paused, at the bottom of the steps, to say goodbye.

The steps were flanked by two anxious-looking stone lions, furred grey with a coating of ash. Julia reached to pat one, and laughed.

'I'm awfully tempted to hop up on the back of it. What do you think Miss Chisholm would say about that?'

'I think you'd give her a heart attack,' said Helen. 'Goodbye, Julia.' She held out her hand. 'Don't climb through any more fanlights, will you?'

'I'll do my best. Goodbye, Helen. It's been nice. That's an awful word, isn't it?'

'It's a grand word. It's been nice to see you, too.'

'Has it? I hope I'll bump into you again, then. Or, you must have Kay bring you over, some time, to Mecklenburgh Square. We could have dinner.'

'Yes,' said Helen. For after all, why shouldn't they? It seemed easy now. 'Yes, I will.' They moved apart. 'And, thanks for the tea!'

'We've rather a lot of people waiting, Miss Giniver,' said Miss Chisholm, when she went in.

'Have we?' asked Helen. She went through the office, and down the staff corridor to the lavatory, to take off her coat and hat, to stand at the mirror and repowder her face. She saw again, as she did it, Julia's smooth, striking features: the slender throat, dark eyes, neat brows; the full, irregular, distracting mouth.

The door opened, and Miss Links came in.

'Oh, Miss Giniver, I'm glad I caught you. Rather sad news, I'm afraid. Mr Piper, at the Mayor's Fund: his wife's been killed.'

'Oh, no,' said Helen, lowering her hand.

'Yes, a timed one. Got her early this morning. Awfully bad luck. We're sending a card. We won't ask everyone to sign it – gets rather monotonous after a while – but I thought you'd like to know.'

'Yes, thanks.'

Helen closed her compact and put it away, and went sadly back to her desk – and hardly thought of Julia again, after that; hardly thought of her at all.

'Well,' said the prisoner in front of Duncan in the dinner-queue, an awful old pansy called Auntie Vi, 'and what have we today? Lobster Thermidor, perhaps? Pâté? Veal?'

'It's mutton, Auntie,' said the boy dishing up the food.

Auntie Vi tutted. 'Doesn't even have the imagination to dress itself as lamb, I suppose. Heigh ho. Give me a plateful, darling. I hear the lunches at Brooks are hardly much better these days.'

She said this last to Duncan, rolling her eyes and touching her hair. Her hair was blonded at the front with a bit of peroxide, and beautifully waved – for she slept every night with strings around her head, to put the kinks in. Her cheeks were rouged, and her lips as red as a girl's: you couldn't pick up a scarlet-bound book in the library without finding pale little patches on it, where men like her had sucked at the boards for lipstick.

Duncan couldn't stand her. He got his food, saying nothing, and after a moment she moved on. But,

'My,' she murmured as she went, 'aren't *we* proud today?' And when he glanced her way again he saw her setting down her dinner on her table and touching her hand to her breast. 'My dears!' he heard her cry to her cronies. 'I've just been cut! Cut to the quick! Who? Why, Little Miss Tragedy Pearce over there . . .'

He put down his head, and took his plate across the hall in the other direction. He shared a table, near the gates, with Fraser and eight other men. Fraser was there already. He was talking animatedly to the man who had the seat across from him, a man called Watling, another Objector. Watling was sitting with folded arms, and Fraser was leaning forwards and tapping at the oilcloth cover on the table to make his point. He didn't notice Duncan come and draw out a chair, a few places away. The other men, however, looked up and nodded, pleasantly enough: 'Hello, Pearce.' 'All right, son?'

They were mostly older men. Duncan and Fraser were two of the youngest prisoners there. Duncan, in particular, was liked, and often looked out for. 'How are you?' the elderly man beside him asked him now. 'Had a visit lately, from your nice sister?'

'She came on Saturday,' said Duncan, as he sat.

'She's good to you. Nice-looking, too.' The man winked. 'And that never hurts, does it?'

Duncan smiled, but then started sniffing, screwing up his face. 'What's that awful smell?'

'What do you think?' said the man on his other side. 'That blasted recess has blocked again.'

294

A few yards away from their table was the sink where the men from the ground-floor cells on this side had to empty their chamber-pots. The sink was always getting blocked; Duncan glanced over at it now, incautiously, and saw it brimming over with a nauseating stew of urine and rigid brown turds.

'God!' he said, turning his chair. He started picking at his dinner. But that made him feel sick, too. The mutton was fatty, the potatoes grey; the unwashed, overboiled cabbage still had soil clinging to it.

The man sitting opposite saw him struggling, and smiled. 'Appetising, isn't it? Do you know, I found mouse-droppings in my cocoa last night.'

'Evans, from the Threes,' said someone else, 'says he once found toe-nails in his bread! Those buggers in C Hall do it on purpose. The worst thing was, Evans said, he was so bloody hungry he had to keep eating! He just picked the toe-nails out as he went along!'

The men made faces. Duncan's elderly neighbour said, 'Well, it's like my old dad used to say: "Hungry dogs will eat dirty puddings." I tell you, I never knew the truth of that until they put me in here.'

They chatted on. Duncan scraped more dirt from his cabbage and loaded up his fork. As he ate, he caught snatches of Fraser's conversation with Watling, carrying over the other men's talk: 'But you don't mean to tell me, that with so many COs here and at Maidstone—?' The rest was lost. The table they were sitting at was one of fifteen, laid out on the concrete floor of their hall. Each table held ten or twelve men, so that the noise of conversation and laughter, the scrape of chairs, the shouts of the officers, was almost unbearable – and it was made much worse, of course, by the queer acoustics of the place, which turned any sort of cry into that of a platform announcer at King's Cross.

Now, for example, a sudden commotion made everyone flinch. Mr Garnish, the PO, had gone galloping down the hall and started screaming and swearing into some man's face – *'You little git!'* – and all because the man had dropped a potato, or spilt his gravy, or something like that. The curses were like the dreadful bayings of a furious beast; but men turned to look, and at once turned back, as if bored. Fraser, Duncan noticed, didn't turn at all. He was still arguing with Watling. He gripped his cropped hair and said, laughing, 'We shall never agree!'

His voice carried clearly now; the hall had quietened down a little after Mr Garnish's outburst. The man on Watling's right – a man named Hammond; a deserter, in for robbery – looked at Fraser very sourly. 'Why don't you fucking well stop arguing, then,' he said, 'and give the rest of us a break? Gas, gas, gas, it's all you do. It's all right for you to talk, anyhow. It's your sort who'll do all right out of this war – just as you've done all right out of peace.'

'You're right,' answered Fraser, 'we will. Because *my* sort – as you call them – can rely on *your* sort thinking exactly that. While working men can see

296

no good in peace-time, they'll have no reason *not* to go to war. Give them decent jobs and houses, give their children decent schools, and they'll soon get the point of pacifism.'

'For fuck's sake!' said Hammond in disgust; but despite himself, he was drawn into arguing. The man on the other side of him was drawn in, too. Someone else said Fraser seemed to think that the ordinary working man could do no wrong. 'You ought to try managing a factory load of them,' he said. He was in for embezzlement. 'That will soon change your politics, believe me.' Then Hammond said, 'And what about the Nazis? They're ordinary working men too, aren't they?'

'Indeed they are,' said Fraser.

'And what about the Japs?'

'Now, the Japs,' said the man next to Fraser – another deserter, called Giggs – 'ain't human. Everybody knows that.'

The conversation ran on for several minutes. Duncan ate his filthy dinner, listening but saying nothing. From time to time he glanced at Fraser, who, having started the whole thing off, having stirred the table up, was leaning back in his chair with his hands behind his head, looking delighted. His uniform, Duncan thought, fitted him about as badly as everyone else's fitted them; the grey of the jacket, with its grubby red star, sucked the colour from his face; the collar of his shirt was black with dirt; and yet he managed, somehow, to look hand-some – to look merely slender, say, where everyone else looked pinched and underfed. He'd been at Wormwood Scrubs three months, and only had another nine to do; but he'd already done a year at Brixton Prison, and Brixton was known to be harder than here. He'd once told Duncan, too, that even Brixton wasn't so much worse than his old public school. But only his hands had really suffered, from life in the Scrubs – for he was in the Basket Shop, and he hadn't yet got the knack of handling the tools. His fingers had blisters on them the size of shillings.

Now, turning his head, he caught Duncan watching him; and smiled. 'You don't join in our discussion, Pearce?' he called down the table. 'What's your opinion on all this?'

'Pearce hasn't got an opinion on anything,' said Hammond, before Duncan could answer. 'He just keeps his head down – don't you, cock?'

Duncan moved, self-conscious. 'I don't see the point of going on about things all the time, if that's what you mean. We can't change anything. Why should we try? It's someone else's war, not ours.'

Hammond nodded. 'It's someone else's fucking war, all right!'

'Is it?' Fraser asked Duncan.

'It is,' said Duncan, when you're in here. Just like everything else is someone else's, too. Everything that counts, I mean: nice things, as well as bad—'

'Bloody hell,' said Giggs, yawning. 'You sound like a right old lag, son. You sound like a fucking lifer!'

'In other words,' said Fraser, 'you're doing just what they want you to do. Garnish, and Daniels, I mean, and Churchill, and all the rest of them. You're giving up your right to think! I don't blame you, Pearce. It's hard, in here, when there's no encouragement to do anything else. When they don't let you listen, even, to the news! As for this—' He reached down the table. There was a newspaper lying there, the *Daily Express*. But when he opened it up, it was like one of those Christmas snowflakes made by children at school: pieces of news had been clipped out of it, and virtually all that was left were the family pages, the sporting pages, and cartoons. Fraser threw it down again. 'That's what they'll do to your mind,' he said, 'if you let them. Don't let them, Pearce!'

He spoke very passionately, holding Duncan's gaze with his clear blue eyes; and Duncan felt himself colour. 'It's easy for you,' he started to say.

But Fraser's gaze had moved to a point behind Duncan's shoulder, and his look had changed. He'd seen Mr Mundy, making his way between the tables. He lifted his hand.

'Why, Mr Mundy, sir!' he called, in a stagey kind of way. 'You're just the man!'

Mr Mundy ambled over. He saw Duncan and gave him a nod. But he looked more warily at Fraser and said in his soft, pleasant voice, 'Now, what's the matter?'

'Nothing's the matter,' Fraser answered. 'I just thought you might be able to explain to us why the prison system seems so keen on turning its inmates into morons, when it might – oh, I don't know – educate them?'

Mr Mundy smiled tolerantly, but would not be drawn. 'There you are,' he said, starting to move on. 'You grumble all you like. Prison lets a man do that, anyway.'

'But it won't let him think, sir!' pursued Fraser. 'It won't let him read the papers, or listen to the wireless. What's the point of that?'

'You know what the point is, son. It does you men no good to hear about things from the world outside that you've got no part in. It stirs you up.'

'It gives us minds and opinions of our own, in other words; and makes us harder for you to manage.'

Mr Mundy shook his head. 'You got a grievance, son, you take it up with Mr Garnish. But if you'd been in the service as long as I have—'

'How long *have* you been in the service, Mr Mundy?' broke in Hammond. He and Giggs had been listening. The other men at the table were listening, too. Mr Mundy hesitated. Hammond went on, 'Mr Daniels told us, sir, that you'd been here for forty years, something like that.'

'Well,' said Mr Mundy, slowing his step, 'I've been here twenty-seven years; and before that, I was at Parkhurst for ten.'

Hammond whistled. Giggs said, 'Christ! That's more than murderers get, ain't it? What was it like here in the old days, though? What were the men like, Mr Mundy?'

300

They sounded like boys in a classroom, Duncan thought, trying to distract the master into talking about his time at Ypres; and Mr Mundy was too kind to walk away. Probably, too, he would rather talk to Hammond than to Fraser. He shifted his pose, to stand more comfortably. He folded his arms and thought it over.

'The men, I should say,' he said at last, 'were about the same.'

'About the same?' said Hammond. 'What, you mean there've been blokes like Wainwright, going on about the grub – and Watling and Fraser, boring everyone's arse off about politics – for thirty-seven years? Blimey! I wonder you haven't gone right off your chump, Mr Mundy. I wonder you haven't gone clean round the twist!'

'What about the twirls, sir?' asked Giggs excitedly. 'I bet they was cruel men, wasn't they?'

'Well,' said Mr Mundy fairly, 'there's good officers and bad, kind and hard, everywhere you go. But prison habits—' He wrinkled his nose. 'Prison habits were awfully hard in those days; yes, awfully hard. You fellows think you have it rough; but your days are like lambswool, compared to those. I've known officers would whip a man as soon as look at him. I've seen lads flogged – lads of eleven, twelve, thirteen, it'd break your heart. Yes, they were awfully brutal days . . . But, there it is. What I always say is, in prison you see men at their worst, and at their best. I've known plenty of gentlemen, in my time here. I've known fellows come in as villains and leave as saints and the other way around. I've walked with men to the gallows, and been proud to shake their hands.'

'That must have cheered them up no end, sir!' called Fraser.

Duncan looked at Mr Mundy and saw him flush, as if caught out. Hammond said quickly, 'Who was the hardest man you ever had in here, sir? Who was the biggest villain?' But Mr Mundy would not be drawn again. He unfolded his arms, straightened up.

'All right,' he said, as he moved off. 'You men ought to get on and finish your dinners, now. Come on.'

He started his circuit of the hall again, going slowly, and limping slightly, because of his hip.

Giggs and Hammond snorted with laughter.

'He's a soft fucking git!' said Hammond, when Mr Mundy was out of earshot. 'He's a fucking peach, isn't he? I tell you what though, he must be out of his fucking mind to have stood it in prison for – how long did he say? Thirty-seven years? Thirty-seven days was enough for me of this fucking place. Thirty-seven minutes. Thirty-seven seconds—'

'Look!' said Giggs. 'Look at him go! What's he walk like that for? He walks like a fucking old duck. Imagine if some bloke was to have it away over the wall while Mr Mundy was with him! Imagine Mr Mundy starting off after him!'

'Leave him alone,' said Duncan suddenly, 'can't you?'

Hammond looked at him, amazed. 'What's it matter to you? We're only having a bit of a laugh. Christ, if you can't have a laugh in this place—'

'Just leave him alone.'

Giggs made a face. 'Well, pardon us. We forgot you and him were so fucking thick.'

'We're not anything,' said Duncan. 'Just—'

'Yes, give it a rest, can't you?' said another man, the embezzler. He'd been trying to read the cut-up *Daily Express*. He gave it a shake, and a bit of it fell out. 'It's like feeding time in the blasted zoo.'

Giggs pushed back his chair and got up. 'Come on, mate,' he said to Hammond. 'This table fucking stinks, anyhow.'

They picked their plates up and moved off. After a moment the embezzler and another man went, too. The men left at Duncan's end of the table shifted closer together. One of them had a little set of dominoes made from cast-off pieces of wood, and they began setting out the pieces for a game.

Fraser stretched in his chair again. 'Just another dinner-hour,' he said, 'at Wormwood Scrubs, D Hall.' He looked at Duncan. 'I never thought I'd see you take on Hammond and Giggs, Pearce. And all on Mr Mundy's behalf! He'd be quite touched.'

Duncan was trembling a little, as it happened. He hated arguments, confrontations; he always had. He said, 'Hammond and Giggs get on my nerves. Mr Mundy's all right. He's better than Mr Garnish and the others, anybody will tell you that.'

But Fraser curled his lip. 'Give me Garnish over

Mundy, any day. Give me an honest sadist, I mean, rather than a hypocrite. All that bloody nonsense about shaking hands with the condemned man.'

'He's only doing a job, like everyone else.'

'Like state-paid bullies and murderers everywhere!'

'Mr Mundy's not like that,' said Duncan stubbornly.

'He certainly,' said Watling, glancing at Duncan but addressing Fraser, 'has some very queer ideas about Christianity. Have you ever heard him talk on the subject?'

'I think I have,' said Fraser. 'He's one of the Mary Baker Eddy crowd, isn't he?'

'He said something to me once, when I was over at the infirmary with some very painful boils. He said the boils were simply *manifesting* – these were the very words he used, mind – they were *manifesting my belief in pain*. He said, "You believe in God, don't you? Well then, God is perfect and He made a perfect world. So how can you have boils?" He said, "*What the doctors call your boils is really only your false belief! Make your belief a true one, and your boils will disappear!*"'

Fraser gave a shout of laughter. 'What poetry!' he cried. 'And what a comfort, to a man who's just had his leg blown off, or his stomach bayoneted!'

Duncan frowned. 'You're as bad as Hammond. Just because you don't agree with it.'

'What's there to agree with?' Fraser said. 'You can't agree, or disagree, with gibberish. And gibberish it

304

is, most certainly. One of those things dreamed up to pacify sex-starved old women.' He sniggered. 'Like the WVS.'

Watling looked prim. 'Well, I don't know about that.'

'He's not so different, anyway, from you,' said Duncan.

Fraser was still smiling. 'What do you mean?'

'It's like Watling said. You both think the world can be perfect, don't you? But at least he's doing something to *make* it perfect, by willing bad things away. Instead of just – well, instead of just sitting in here, I mean.'

Fraser's smile faded. He looked at Duncan, then looked away. There was an awkward little silence. Then Watling moved forward again. 'Let me ask you this, Fraser,' he said, with an air of continuing a conversation in which Duncan had no part. 'If at your tribunal they had told you . . .'

Fraser folded his arms and listened, and gradually started smiling again – his good humour, apparently, quite restored.

Duncan waited, then turned away. The men on the other side of him had just finished a game. Two of them were lightly clapping. 'Well played,' said one, politely. He and his neighbour passed over the tiny twists of tobacco they were using as wagers; then the three of them began to flip the dominoes over and mix them up, to start again. 'Care to join us?' they asked, seeing Duncan sitting more or less alone; but Duncan shook his head. He had the impression that he'd hurt Fraser's feelings, and was sorry. He was going to wait another minute, to see if Fraser might give up the argument with Watling and turn back to him . . .

But Fraser didn't turn; and soon the stink of the blocked recess grew too much to bear. Duncan put his knife and fork together and, 'See you later,' he said to the domino players.

'Yes, see you later Pearce. Don't—'

Their words were interrupted by a cry: '*Yoo hoo! Miss Tragedy! Yoo hoo!*'

It was Auntie Vi, and a couple of her friends – two boys a few years older than Duncan, called Monica and Stella. They were mincing down the hall between the tables, smoking, and waving their hands. They must have noticed Duncan getting to his feet. Now they called again: 'Yoo hoo! What's the matter, Miss Tragedy? Don't you like us?'

Duncan pushed in his chair. Fraser, he saw, had looked up as if irritated. Watling was making another prim, repressive sort of face. Auntie Vi, and Monica and Stella, minced closer. Duncan took up his plate and moved off with it just as they drew level with his table.

'Off she trips, look!' he heard Monica say, behind his back. 'Where's she going in such a hurry? Do you think she has a husband, up in that flowery of hers?'

'Not her, my dears,' said Auntie Vi, puffing on her roll-up. 'Not while she's still in black for the last one. Why, she's sitting like Patience on a Monument, positively *grinning* at Grief! You know her story, don't you? Haven't you ever seen her in Mailbags One? Stitch, stitch, stitch she goes, with her little white hand; and at night, my dears I swear she creeps back over there and pulls all the stitches out.'

Their voices faded as they moved on. But Duncan felt himself blushing at their words, blushing horribly, guiltily, from his throat to his scalp. And, what was worse, he glanced back to his table and saw Fraser's face; and Fraser's expression was such an unpleasant one – such a mixture of awkwardness and anger and distaste – he grew almost sick.

He scraped the uneaten food from his plate, then swilled the plate and his knife and fork in the tub of soapless cold water that was provided for them to wash their dinner-things in. He went across the hall to the staircase and began to climb it, as quickly as he could.

He grew breathless almost at once. Any sort of exercise left them all winded. At the Threes he had to pause to catch his breath. At his own landing he leant on the rail outside his cell, waiting for his heart to slow. He folded his arms and rested on his elbows and looked back down into the hall.

The din of quarrelling voices, of laughter and shouts, was milder up here. The view was horribly impressive. For the hall was as long as a small city street, with a roof of blacked-out glass. Strung right across it, at the level of the first landing, was a net: Duncan saw the men through a haze of wire and cigarette smoke and sickly, artificial light; it was like gazing at creatures in a cage or under water; they were like strange, pallid things that never saw daylight. And what you noticed most, he thought, from this height, was the drabness of it all: the concrete floor, the lustreless paint upon the walls, the shapeless grey uniforms with their single spots of red, the spew-coloured oilcloths on the tables . . . Only Fraser, it still seemed to him, stood out as a single point of brightness: for his cropped hair was fair, where most of the other men's was dark or dull brown; and he moved animatedly, where others slouched; and when he laughed – as he did again now – he laughed with a shout that carried even to here.

He was talking to Watling, still; he was listening hard to something Watling was saying, and occasionally nodding his head. He didn't like Watling much, Duncan knew; but the fact was he'd talk to anyone, for hours at a time, just for the sake of it: it didn't mean anything when he looked at you, spoke passionately to you; he was passionate about everything.

'That boy Fraser oughtn't to be here,' Mr Mundy had said to Duncan, privately. 'Coming from a family like that, with all the advantages he's had!' He took Fraser's being here as a sort of insult to the other men. He said he was playing at being in prison. He didn't like the fact that Duncan had to share a cell with him; he said that he'd end up giving Duncan queer ideas. If he could have found a way to do it, he would have got Duncan a cell all to himself.

Perhaps Mr Mundy was right, Duncan thought, looking again at Fraser's smooth fair head. Perhaps Fraser was only playing at being in prison – like a prince, dressing up as a pauper. But then, what was the difference, in a place like this, between playing at something and doing it for real? It was like playing at being tortured, or being killed! It was like going into the army and saying you were only doing it for fun: the soldiers shooting at you from the other side wouldn't know you were only pretending.

Fraser stretched right back in his chair again, raising his arms, putting out his long legs. But he kept his back to Duncan; and Duncan suddenly found himself wishing that he would turn and look up. He stared at the back of Fraser's head and tried to will him to turn around. He concentrated all his mind on it, sent out the words as a sort of ray. *Look, Fraser!* he thought. *Look, Robert Fraser!* He even used Fraser's prison number. *Look, 1755 Fraser! 1755 Robert Fraser, look at me!*

But Fraser didn't look. He kept on talking with Watling, and laughing; and at last Duncan gave it up. He blinked, and rubbed his eyes. And when he looked again, it was Mr Mundy's gaze he met: for Mr Mundy must have spotted him leaning there, and been watching him. He gave Duncan a nod, and then moved on slowly between the tables. Duncan turned and went into his cell and lay down, exhausted.

★   ★   ★

'You're late,' said Viv's friend Betty, as Viv ran down the stairs to the cloakroom at Portman Court.

'I know,' said Viv breathlessly. 'Has Gibson noticed?'

'She's in with Mr Archer. They sent me all the way to the basement, for these.' Betty held up files. 'If you hurry you'll be OK. Where've you been, anyway?'

Viv shook her head, smiling. 'Nowhere.'

She ran on, pulling off her gloves and her hat as she went; throwing back the locker door when she got to it and bundling her coat inside. Miss Gibson let them keep their handbags at their desks, so she held on to that; but before she closed the locker door she quickly opened the handbag up and looked inside it, to be sure she had what she thought she might need – because her period was due, and her breasts and stomach were sore – a sanitary towel and a box of aspirin. She'd have liked to go to the lavatory and put the towel in place right now, but there wasn't the time. She took an aspirin, anyway, as she started back up the stairs, chewing it up without any water and swallowing it down, making a face against the bitter chalky taste of it.

She had been all the way back to John Allen House, in her lunch-hour; she'd gone back there to check the post. For she knew there'd be a card for her, from Reggie: he always sent her a note after one of their Saturdays; it was the only way he had of telling her he was all right. The card, this time, was a picture postcard with a daft illustration on it, a soldier and a pretty girl in the blackout, the soldier winking and the caption underneath saying, *Keeping it dark*. Next to this Reggie had written, *Lucky ****ers!!!* And on the back he'd put: *G.G.* – that meant Glamour Girl. *Looked for brunette, but could only find blondes. Wish I was him & she was you! xxx.* She had the card in her bag now, beside the box of aspirin.

It was quarter-past two, and her room was up on the seventh floor. She might have taken the lift, but the lifts were slow, and she'd got stuck waiting about for them before; she kept to the stairs. She went quickly, steadily, like a distance runner: folding her arms beneath her breasts; keeping her heels up, because the stairs were hard, of marble, and heels made a row. When she passed a man, he laughed. 'I say! What's the rush? Do you know something the rest of us don't?' That made her slacken her pace slightly, until he'd moved on; then she speeded up again. Only at the turn of the seventh floor did she slow right down, to catch her breath, to blot her face with her handkerchief and smooth her hair.

A mad sort of noise began to reach her now, a *crackety-crack-crack-crack!* – it was like the bursting of midget shells. She went quickly down a corridor and opened a door, and the noise grew almost deafening: the room beyond was crowded with desks, each with a girl at it, furiously typing. Some wore earphones; most were typing from shorthand notes. They were plunging away so vigorously

311

because their machines held not just one sheet of paper, but two or three and sometimes four, with carbons in between. The room was large, but stuffy. The windows had been gas-proofed years before. The panes had strips of brown paper gummed to them in case of blast.

The smell was a rather overpowering one: a mixture of talcum powder, permanent waves, typewriter ink, cigarette smoke, BO. On the walls were posters from various Ministry campaigns: pictures of Potato Pete and other cheery root vegetables, imploring you to boil them up and eat them; slogans, like old religious samplers.

PLANT NOW!
SPRING and SUMMER will come as usual – EVEN in WARTIME.

At the head of the room was a table, separated from the others; its chair was empty. But a minute after Viv had sat down, taken off her typewriter cover and started work, the door to Mr Archer's office opened and Miss Gibson looked in. She glanced once around the room and, seeing the girls all typing away, disappeared again.

The moment the door was closed, Viv felt something small and light strike her on the shoulder and bounce to the floor. Betty had thrown a paperclip at her from her desk ten feet away.

'You lead a charmed life, Pearce,' she mouthed, when Viv looked over.

Viv stuck out her tongue, and went back to her work.

She was typing up a table, a list of foodstuffs and their calorific values – a fiddly job, since you had to type the vertical columns first, with the right sort of space between them, and then you had to take the papers out and put them back in horizontally and type the lines. And you had to do it all, of course, without letting the papers slide about against each other, otherwise the top sheet would look all right, but the copies underneath would turn out crazy.

What with the effort of getting it right, and the noisiness and stuffiness of the room, you might as well, Viv thought, be working in a factory, making precision parts for planes. You'd probably earn more in a factory. And yet people thought it glamorous, when you told them you were a typist at a Ministry; and lots of the girls were upper-class – they had names like Nancy, Minty, Felicity, Daphne, Faye. Viv had nothing much in common with any of them. Even Betty – who chewed gum, and liked to talk like a wise-cracking New York waitress in a film – even Betty had been to a finishing school, and had money coming out of her ears.

Viv, by contrast, had come to the job after completing a secretarial course at a college in Balham; she'd had a nice instructor there, who'd encouraged her to apply. 'There's really no reason, these days,' the instructor had said, 'why a girl with a background like yours shouldn't do just as well for

herself as a girl from a better sort of family.' She'd
advised Viv to take elocution lessons, that was all;
and so, for half an hour each week for three months,
Viv had stood blushing in front of an elderly actress
in a basement room in Kennington, reciting poetry.
She could still remember whole chunks of Walter
de la Mare.

'Is there anybody there?' said the Traveller,
Knocking on the moonlit door;
And his horse in the silence champed the grasses
Of the forest's ferny floor.

On the day of her interview, the sight and sound
of the wellbred young women in the Ministry
waiting-room had absolutely appalled her. One had
said carelessly, 'Oh, it'll be a cinch, girls! They'll
just want to see that our hair's not dyed, and that
we don't use words like *dad* and *toilet* and horrors
like that.'

The interview had passed off all right, as it
happened. But Viv could never hear the word 'toilet',
even now, after so long, without remembering that
moment, and that girl.

When all the trouble with Duncan had started
up, she had kept it to herself. No one, not even
Betty, knew she had a brother at all. Early on in
the war girls at John Allen House had now and
then asked her, in the blunt, casual way that people
asked you things like that: 'Don't you have a
brother, Viv? Lucky you! Brothers are awful, I can't

bear mine.' These days, however, no one asked after brothers, boyfriends, husbands – just in case.

She finished the table she'd been typing, and started on another. The girl at the desk in front of her – a girl named Millicent – leant back in her chair and shook her head. A hair came flying on to the paper in Viv's machine: it was long, and brown, quite dry through having been over-waved, but it had a blob of grease on it like a pinhead, where it had been fixed to Millicent's scalp. Viv blew it to the floor. She'd discovered that if you looked closely at the floor at this time of day, you could see that it was full of hairs like that. She thought, sometimes, of the amazing amount of tangled hair that must end up in the char-ladies' brooms, when they'd gone through the building and finished sweeping. The thought, just now, on top of the smells and general stuffiness of the room, depressed her rather. For how fed-up she was, she realised, of living with women! How absolutely sick to death she was, of the closeness of so many girls! Of powder! Of scent! Of lipstick marks on the rims of cups and the ends of pencils! Of razored armpits and razored legs! Of bottles of veramon and boxes of aspirin!

That made her think of the aspirin in her bag; and her mind moved from that to Reggie's card. She pictured Reggie writing it, posting it. She saw his face, heard his voice, felt the touch of him – and began to miss him, dreadfully. She started to count up all the different dingy hotel rooms they'd made love in. She thought of all the times he'd had to leave her, to go to his mother-in-law's, to his wife. 'I wish it was you I was going home to,' he always said. She knew he meant it. God knows what his wife thought about it. Viv wouldn't let herself wonder. She'd never been the sort to ask things about his family, to pry and make digs. She'd seen a picture of his wife and little boy, but that was years ago. Since then, she might have passed them on the street! She might meet them in a bus, on a train, get talking. *'What nice, handsome children.' – 'Do you think so? They're the image of their dad. Let me show you a snapshot—'*

Milk, eggs, cheese, bugger, she had typed. She quickly looked up; and had to pull the papers out and start again. What was Reggie doing, she wondered, as she turned the reel, right now? Was he thinking of her? She tried to reach out to him with her mind. *My darling*, she called him, in her thoughts. She'd never call him that to his face. *My darling, my darling . . .* She flicked closed the paper guard and started typing again; but she typed fluently, and one of the advantages – or disadvantages – of being able to type so well was that, while your fingers flew over the keys, your thoughts could start racing. If you had something on your mind, it could seem to pick up the typewriter's rhythm and run like a train . . . Now her mind ran with the idea of Reggie. She remembered the feel of him in her arms. She remembered the working of his hands over her thighs. She felt the memory in her own fingers, in her breasts, her mouth, and in between her legs . . .

Awful to be thinking things like that, so vividly, with all these upper-class girls about, and in the arid *crack-crack-cracking* of so many typewriters. But— She glanced around the room. Weren't any of these girls in love? Really in love, like she was with Reggie? Even Miss Gibson must once have been kissed. A man must have wanted her; a man might have lain with her on a bedroom floor, taken off her knickers, put himself inside her, pushed and pushed—

Abruptly, the door to Mr Archer's office opened again and Miss Gibson herself reappeared. Viv blushed, and put her head down. *Pork, bacon, beef, lamb, poultry,* she typed. *Herring, sardine, salmon, shrimp—*

But Miss Gibson, having caught her eye, called her over.

'Miss Pearce,' she said. She had a roneo stencil in her hand. 'You seem for some reason to have time to spare. Take this down to the ink room, will you, and have them run off two hundred copies? Quickly as you can, please.'

'Yes, Miss Gibson,' said Viv. She took the stencil and went out.

The ink room was two floors down, at the end of another marble corridor. Viv spoke to the girl in charge of it, a plain-faced girl in spectacles, whom no one much liked. She was turning the handle of one of the machines; she looked at Miss Gibson's stencil and said, with great contempt, 'Two hundred? I'm making a batch of a thousand here, for Mr Brightman. The trouble with all you people is, you

317

seem to think that copies can be whistled up by magic. You'll have to turn them out yourself, I'm afraid. Ever worked one of these machines? The last girl I had in here made such a muck of things, the drum was unusable for days.'

Viv had been shown how to fit a stencil, but months before. She fumbled about with the cradle now, the girl, still turning her own machine, looking over and calling, witheringly: 'Not *that* way!' and, 'There, look! *There!*'

At last the stencil and the paper and the ink were all in place; and all Viv had to do then was stand and turn the handle, two hundred times . . . The motion hurt her tender breasts. She felt herself begin to grow sweaty. And to make things worse, a man from another department came in, and stood, smiling, and watched her.

'I always like to see you girls doing that,' he said, when she'd finished. 'You look just like milkmaids, churning butter.'

He only had a few copies of his own to make. By the time she'd counted out her sheets and let them dry he had finished, and he held the door for her when she went out. He did it rather awkwardly, because he walked with a cane: he'd been an airman, she knew, at the start of the war, and had been lamed in some sort of smash. He was young, quite fair: the kind of man of whom girls said, 'He's got nice eyes,' or, 'He's got nice hair' – not because his eyes or his hair were especially handsome, but because the rest of his face wasn't handsome at all, and yet you wanted to find something pleasant to say about him. They set off together down the corridor and she felt obliged to walk at his pace.

He said, 'You're one of Miss Gibson's girls, aren't you? Up on the top floor? I thought so. I've noticed you about the place before.'

They got to the staircase. Her arm was aching, from turning the handle of the machine. She had an uncomfortable, moistish feeling between her legs. It was probably sweat, but might, she thought, be something worse. If the man hadn't been with her, she would have run downstairs; but she didn't want him to see her dashing off to the lavatory. He took the staircase one step at a time, steadying himself by gripping the banister; perhaps he was laying it on a bit thick, too, to give himself a few extra minutes with her . . .

'That must be your room along there,' he said, when they got to the top. 'I can tell by the clatter.' He moved his cane from his right hand to his left, so that he could shake hands with her. 'Well, goodbye, Miss—?'

'Miss Pearce,' said Viv.

'Goodbye, Miss Pearce. Perhaps I'll see you churning milk again, some time? Or else— Well, if you'd care to make it a stiffer drink—?'

She told him she'd think about it; because she didn't want him to suppose she wouldn't, because of his leg. She might even let him take her on a date. She might let him kiss her. Where was the harm? It wouldn't mean anything. It was just what you did. It wouldn't be what she had with Reggie.

She gave the papers to Miss Gibson; but on the way back to her seat she hesitated, still thinking of the lavatory. She remembered a girl who, a few weeks before, had been seen all over the building with blood on her skirt. She picked up her handbag, went back to Miss Gibson, and asked if she could be excused.

Miss Gibson looked at the clock, and frowned. 'Oh, very well. But this is why you girls have lunch-hours, don't forget.'

This time, to keep herself from being jolted about by the stairs, Viv took the lift. But then she almost ran into the cloakroom: she went into one of the lavatory stalls, pulled up her skirt, lowered her knickers; she pulled a couple of sheets of paper from the box and pressed them between her legs.

When she drew the paper away, however, it was quite unmarked. She thought maybe peeing would bring the blood down. But she peed, and it made no difference.

'Hell,' she said, aloud. For periods were annoying enough when they came; but waiting around for them was almost worse. She got the sanitary towel out and pinned it in place, just to be on the safe side; she looked in her bag, and saw Reggie's card, and was almost tempted to take it out and read it again . . .

But beside the card there was her little pocket diary: a slim blue Ministry diary, with a pencil in its spine. And when she saw that, she checked herself. She thought of dates. How long had it been since her last period, anyway? It seemed like ages, suddenly.

She got the diary out and opened it up. The pages looked cryptic, like a spy's, for there were all sorts of codes on them: a symbol for the days she'd visited Duncan, another for her Saturdays with Reggie; and a discreet little asterisk, every twenty-eight or twenty-nine days. She began now to count up the dates from the last asterisk: she got to twenty-nine, and counted on – to thirty, thirty-one, thirty-two, thirty-three.

She couldn't believe it. She went back and counted again. She'd never been so late before. She'd never really been late at all; she always joked to other girls that she was like a clock, like a calendar. She said to herself: *It's because of the raids.* That must be what it was. The raids mucked everybody up. It stood to reason. She was tired. She was probably run-down.

She pulled more paper from the box and pressed it between her legs again; and when, again, the paper came away unmarked, she even got to her feet and did a couple of little jumps, trying to jolt the blood out. But jumping made her breasts hurt: they hurt so much they were almost stinging, and when she put her hands to them she felt how swollen they were, how stretched and full.

She picked up the diary again, and went through it a third time. Maybe she'd made some mistake with the last date.

There was no mistake, she knew it. She thought, *I can't be. I can't!* But if she were . . . Her mind was racing. For if she were, then it must have happened not this last time with Reggie, but the time before; and that was already a month ago—

No, she thought. She wouldn't believe it. She said to herself, *You'll be all right.* She straightened her clothes. Her hands were shaking. *Every girl gets scares; but not you. Reggie's too careful. You're OK. You're all right. You can't be!*

'Here she is at last,' said Binkie, as Kay stepped on to Mickey's boat and opened up the cabin doors. 'Kay! We thought you weren't coming.'

The boat rocked about.

'Hello, Bink. Hello, Mickey. Sorry I'm late.'

'Never mind. You're just in time for a drink. We're making gimlets.'

'Gimlets!' said Kay, putting down her bag. She looked at her watch. It was only quarter-past five.

Binkie saw her expression. 'Oh, balls to that! I can't speak for your liver, but mine's still on peace-time hours.'

Kay took off her cap. She was dressed, as Mickey and Binkie were, in uniform, ready for work. But the cabin had a stove in it, and a hissing lamp, and was very warm: she sat down across from Binkie, undid her jacket, and loosened her tie.

Mickey was busy bringing out tumblers, spoons, a siphon of soda water. She put them on an upturned beer crate between Binkie and Kay, then got the gin and opened the lime. The gin was some nameless, cheap variety, and instead of cordial she had real lime juice: it was in a brown medicine bottle with a white screw cap; Binkie had bought it from a chemist's, she said, as a food supplement.

Mickey stirred the ingredients together and handed the glasses over, keeping one for herself. They raised them up, then tasted and winced.

'It's like battery acid!' said Kay.

'Never mind that, dear girl,' said Binkie. 'Think of the Vitamin C.'

She offered round cigarettes. She favoured a rough Turkish brand, difficult to get hold of. She had them in a fancy gold case, but had cut each one in half to make a packet last longer; she smoked with a tarnished ivory holder. Mickey and Kay each took a stub – pinching them, as they had to, between their forefingers and thumbs; leaning very close to the lighter.

'I feel like my father,' said Mickey, puffing, moving back. Her father was a bookmaker.

'You look like a gangster,' said Kay. 'Talking of which—' Her heart gave a little flutter of excitement. 'Doesn't either of you want to know what it was that made me late?'

Mickey put the cigarette down. 'God, I forgot all about it. You've been to see those spiv friends of Cole's! You didn't go and get yourself arrested, did you?'

'Not those beastly black-market boys?' said Binkie,

taking the ivory holder from her mouth. 'Oh Kay, how could you?'

'I know,' said Kay, raising her hands. 'I know. I *know*. It's perfectly lousy. But I've been getting whisky from them for months.'

'Whisky doesn't count. Whisky's practically medicinal in a job like ours. Anything else—'

'But Bink, it's for Helen. It's her birthday at the end of the month. Have you looked in the shops lately? They're worse than ever. I wanted to get her – I don't know, something handsome. A bit of glamour. This filthy war's knocked all the glamour out of life for women like her. It's all right for us, we can just kick about in the muck and pretty well like it—'

'But stolen goods, Kay! Stolen goods!'

'Cole says the insurers take care of all that. Anyway, most of it's stuff from before the war – left over, lying useless. Not actually looted. Good God, I'd never touch looted stuff.'

'I'm glad to hear it! But you can hardly expect me to approve. And if Headquarters should find out—'

'I don't approve, either,' said Kay. 'You know I don't. It's just—' She grew self-conscious. 'Well, I'm sick of gazing into Helen's face and seeing it look more and more tired and worn. If I were her husband I'd be off fighting; there wouldn't be a thing I could do about it. But the fact is, I'm here—'

Binkie put up a hand. 'Save the hearts and flowers,' she said, 'for your tribunal. God knows it'll be my tribunal, too, if it gets out that I've been a party to something like this.'

'You haven't been a party to anything, yet!' said Mickey impatiently. 'What did you get, Kay? What was it like?'

Kay described the place she had been to, a room in the basement of a ruined shop in Bethnal Green.

'They were perfectly polite,' she said, 'once they knew I was a friend of Cole's and not a lady detective. And oh! if you could see the things they have there! Crates and crates of cigarettes! Soaps! Razor blades! *Coffee!*'

'Coffee!'

'And stockings. I was tempted by the stockings, I must admit. But you see, I had in mind a nightdress. Helen's nightdress is absolutely falling to bits; it breaks my heart. They picked through all the things they had – cotton bedjackets, flannel pyjamas . . . And then, I saw this.'

She had picked up her bag, and opened it now to bring out a flat rectangular box. The box was pink, with a silk bow across it. 'Look at it,' she said, as Binkie and Mickey leant in to see. 'It looks like the kind of thing – doesn't it? – that a fellow in an American picture would be carrying under his arm, when he calls on a chorus-girl, backstage.'

She set the box flat upon her lap – paused a moment, for effect – then carefully lifted off the lid. Inside were layers of silver paper. She put them back, and revealed a satin pyjama-suit, the colour of pearls.

'Wow,' said Mickey.

'Wow, and how,' said Kay. She lifted up the jacket and shook it out. It was as heavy, in her hands, as a girl's full head of hair; and though it was cold, from having been carried about in its box, she felt it warming even as she held it. Something about it – the smoothness of it, the lustre of it – had made her think of Helen. She thought of Helen again, now, as she shook it again to watch it ripple.

'Look at its shine!' she said. 'Look at the buttons!' For the buttons were bone, fine as wafers, and amazingly pleasing to the finger and the eye.

Binkie moved her cigarette-holder from one hand to the other, so that she could lift up the jacket's cuff and run her thumb over the satin. She said, 'It's damn fine stuff, I'll give you that.'

'D'you see the label? It's French, look.'

'French?' said Mickey. 'There you are, then. Helen'll be doing her bit for the Resistance, just by wearing it.'

'Dear girl,' said Binkie. 'She won't be putting up any resistance once she's in this.'

They laughed. Kay turned the jacket about, to marvel at it a little longer; she even stood, and held it and the trousers against herself: 'They look absurd on me, of course, but you get the idea.'

'They're lovely,' said Mickey, sitting back. 'I bet they cost a fortune, though, didn't they? Come on, tell us the truth: how much did you give for them?'

Kay had started to fold the suit up; and felt herself

colour. 'Oh,' she said, without lifting her head. 'You know.'

'No,' said Mickey watching her. 'Not really.'

'One doesn't expect a quality thing like this to come cheaply. Not in wartime—'

'How much? Kay, you're blushing!'

'It's warm, that's all. It's that damn stove!'

'Five pounds? Six?'

'Well, I've got to squander the Langrish family fortune on something! And what the hell else is there, these days, to spend one's money on? There's no liquor in the pubs, no tobacco in the tobacconists'.'

'Seven pounds? Eight?' Mickey stared at her. 'Kay, not more?'

Kay said quickly, but rather vaguely, 'No. About eight.'

In fact she'd paid ten for the pyjamas, and another five pounds for a bag of coffee beans and a couple of bottles of whisky; but didn't want to admit it.

'Eight pounds!' Mickey cried. 'Are you barmy?'

'But think how happy it'll make Helen!'

'Not half as happy as you made those spivs.'

'Oh, so what!' said Kay, feeling the effect of the gin suddenly, and growing belligerent. 'All's fair in love and war, isn't it? Especially this war; and more especially' – she lowered her voice – 'more especially, our sort of love. Christ! I've done my bit, haven't I? It's not even as if Helen would get any kind of pension if I were killed—'

'The trouble with you, Langrish,' said Binkie, 'is you have a gallantry complex.'

'So? Why shouldn't I? We have to be gallant, people like us. No one else is bloody well going to be gallant on our behalf.'

'Well, but don't take it too far. There's more to love than grand gestures.'

'Oh, spare me,' said Kay.

She had folded the pyjamas away, and now checked her watch again, suddenly afraid that Helen, who was due to join the three of them here for a drink, after work, might turn up early and spoil the surprise. She held the box out to Mickey. 'Look after this for me, will you? Just until the beginning of next month? If I keep it at home, Helen might find it.'

Mickey carried it down to the other end of the cabin, and stowed it away under her bed.

When she came back, she mixed more drinks. Binkie took a fresh glassful but sat swirling the gin, gazing down into it, looking suddenly gloomy. After a minute or so she said, 'All this stuff about gallantry, girls, has rather depressed me.'

'Oh, Bink!' said Mickey. 'Don't say that.'

'But I'm afraid it has. It's all very well, Kay, for you to set yourself up as some kind of champion – the Queers' Best Friend – you, with your dear little Helen, your silk pyjamas, all of that. But your sort of story is awfully rare. Most of us— Well, take Mickey and me. What do we have?'

'Speak for yourself!' said Mickey, coughing.

'The gin's made you maudlin,' said Kay. 'I knew cocktails before six was a bad idea.'

'It's not the gin. I'm quite serious. Tell me truly: doesn't the life we lead ever get you down? It's all right when one is young. It's positively thrilling, when one is twenty! The secrecy, the intensity – being keyed up, like a harp. Girls were fabulous things to me, once – all that flying into rages over bits of nonsense; threatening to slash their wrists in the lavatories at parties, that sort of thing. Men were like shadows, like paper puppets, like little boys! compared with that. But one gets to an age where one sees the truth of it. One gets to an age where one is simply exhausted. And one realises one has finished with the whole damn game . . . Men begin to seem almost attractive after that. Sometimes I think quite seriously of finding some nice little chap to settle down with – some quiet little Liberal MP, someone like that. It would be so restful.'

Kay had once felt something similar, as it happened. But that was before the war, and before she'd met Helen. Now she said drily, 'The deep, deep peace of the marital bed, after the hurly-burly of the Sapphic chaise longue.'

'Precisely.'

'What rubbish.'

'I mean it!' said Binkie. 'You wait till you're my age' – she was forty-six – 'and wake every morning to gaze on the vast tract of uncreased linen that is the other side of the divan. Try being gallant to

329

that . . . We shan't even have children, don't forget, to look after us in our old age.'

'God!' said Mickey. 'Why don't we just cut our throats right now and get it over with?'

'If I had the spunk,' said Binkie, 'I might do just that. It's only the station I keep going for. Thank God for the war, is what I say! The thought of peace starting up again, I don't mind telling you, fills me with horror.'

'Well,' said Kay, 'you'd better get used to the idea. Now we're only seventeen miles from Rome – or whatever it is – it's surely only a matter of time.'

They discussed the state of things in Italy for the next ten minutes or so; then got on – as people did get on, these days – to the subject of Hitler's secret weapons.

'You know there are absolutely gigantic guns,' said Binkie, 'being put in place in France? The government's trying to keep it hush-hush, but Collins, at Berkeley Square, knows a chap in one of the Ministries. He says the shells from those guns will make it as far as north London. They'll take out entire streets, apparently.'

'I heard the Germans,' said Mickey, 'are putting together a kind of ray—'

The boat tilted, as someone stepped on to it from the tow-path. Kay, who'd been listening out for footsteps, leant forward to put down her glass. She said in a whisper, 'That'll be Helen. Remember, now: not a word about pyjamas, birthdays, or anything like that.'

There was a knock, the doors were opened, and Helen appeared. Kay rose to take her hand and help her down the couple of steps into the cabin, and to kiss her cheek.

'Hello, darling.'

'Hello, Kay,' said Helen, smiling. Her cheek was cold, curved, soft and smooth as a child's. Her lips were dry beneath their lipstick, slightly roughened by the wind. She looked around, at the clouds of smoke. 'Goodness! It's like a Turkish harem in here. Not that I've ever been in a Turkish harem.'

'Dear girl, I have,' said Binkie. 'I can tell you, they're awfully overrated.'

Helen laughed. 'Hello, Binkie. Hello, Mickey. How are you both?'

'All right.'

'Fighting fit, dear girl. And you?'

Helen nodded to the glasses that were sitting about. 'I shall be fine, with something like that inside me.'

'We're drinking gimlets – sound all right?'

'Right now I'd drink powdered glass if it had a splash of alcohol in it.'

She took off her coat and hat, and glanced about for a mirror. 'Do I look awful?' she said, not finding one, and trying to tidy her hair.

'You look wonderful,' said Kay. 'Come and sit down.'

She slipped an arm around Helen's waist, and they sat. Binkie and Mickey leant forward to make a fresh round of cocktails. They were still debating secret weapons. 'I don't believe it for a second,' Binkie was saying. 'Invisible rays—?'

'All right, darling?' murmured Kay, touching her lips to Helen's cheek again. 'Did you have a lousy day?'

'Not really,' said Helen. 'How was yours? What have you been doing?'

'Nothing at all. Thinking of you.'

Helen smiled. 'You always say that.'

'That's because I'm always doing it. I'm doing it now.'

'Are you? What are you thinking?'

'Ah,' said Kay.

She was thinking, of course, of the satin pyjamas. She was imagining buttoning up the pyjama jacket over Helen's bare breasts. She was thinking of the look and the feel of Helen's bottom and thighs, in the pearl-coloured silk. She moved her hand to Helen's hip, and began to stroke it – enchanted, suddenly, by the lovely swell and spring of it; remembering what Binkie had said, and feeling the force of her own good fortune; marvelling that Helen was here, right here, in this funny little clog-shaped boat, warm and pink and rounded and alive, in the curve of her arm.

Helen turned her head, and met her look. She said, 'You're tight.'

'I believe I am. Here's a thought. Get tight too.'

'Get tight, for forty-five minutes with you? Then have to sleep it off all by myself?'

'Come over to the station with us when we go,'

said Kay. She raised and lowered her eyebrows. 'I'll show you the back of my ambulance.'

'You nit,' said Helen, laughing. 'What on earth's the matter with you?'

'I'm in love, that's all.'

'I say, you two,' said Binkie loudly, handing Helen a glass. 'If I'd known this was going to turn into a petting-session, I might not have come. Stop making wallflowers of Mickey and me, will you?'

'We were just being friendly,' said Kay. 'I might get my head blown off later on. I've got to make the most of my lips while I still have them.'

'I've got to make the most of mine, then,' said Binkie, raising her glass. 'Here's how.'

At six o'clock they heard the wireless starting up on the barge next door: they opened the doors, to listen to the news. Then a programme of dance-music came on; it was too cold to keep the doors open, but Mickey slid back a window so that they could still hear the music a little, mixed up with the buzz and splutter of passing engines, the bumping of the boats. The song was a slow one. Kay kept her arm around Helen's waist, still lightly stroking and smoothing it, while Mickey and Binkie chatted on. The heat from the stove, and the gin in her cocktail, had made her dozy.

Then Helen moved forward, to reach for her drink again; and when she sat back, she turned and caught Kay's eye, a little awkwardly.

'Who do you think I saw today?' she said.

'I don't know. Who?'

'A friend of yours. Julia.'

Kay stared at her. 'Julia?' she said. 'Julia Standing?'

'Yes.'

'You mean, you saw her in the street?'

'No,' said Helen. 'That is, yes. But then we had a cup of tea together, from a van near my office. She'd been to a house nearby – you know, that job she has, with her father?'

'Yes, of course,' said Kay slowly.

She was trying to push away the mix of feelings that the sound of Julia's name always conjured up in her. She said to herself, as she always did, *Don't be silly. It was nothing. It was too long ago.* But it wasn't nothing, she knew that. She tried to picture Helen and Julia together: she saw Helen, with her round child's face, her untidy hair and chapped lips; and Julia, smooth and self-possessed as a cool dark gem . . . She said, 'Was it all right?'

Helen laughed, self-conscious. 'Yes. Why shouldn't it have been?'

'I don't know.'

But Binkie had heard. She knew Julia too, but only very slightly. 'Is that Julia Standing you're talking about?'

'Yes,' said Kay, reluctantly. 'Helen saw her today.'

'Did you, Helen? How is she? Still looking as though she's spent the entire war eating steak tartare and drinking glasses and glasses of milk?'

Helen blinked. 'Well,' she said, 'I suppose so.'

'She's so frightfully handsome, isn't she? But— I don't know. I've always found looks like hers rather chilling, somehow. What do you think, Mickey?'

'She's all right,' said Mickey shortly, glancing at Kay; knowing more than Binkie.

But Binkie went on. 'Is she still doing that thing of hers, Helen, going over bombed houses?'

'Yes,' said Helen.

Mickey picked up her drink and narrowed her eyes. 'She ought,' she murmured, 'to try pulling somebody out from underneath one, some time.'

Kay laughed. Helen lifted her own drink again, as if not trusting herself to answer. Binkie said to Mickey, 'Dear girl, talking of pulling out bodies – did you hear what happened to the crew over at Station 89? Jerry struck a cemetery and hit the graves. Half of the coffins were blown wide open.'

Kay drew Helen close again. 'I don't know, I'm sure,' she said very quietly, 'why one's chums should like each other, just because they *are* one's chums; and yet one expects them to, somehow.'

Helen said, without looking up, 'Julia's the vivid kind of person people either like or don't like, I suppose. And Mickey's loyal to you, of course.'

'Yes, perhaps that's it.'

'It was only a cup of tea. Julia was perfectly nice about it.'

'Well, good,' said Kay, smiling.

'I don't expect we'll do it again.'

Kay kissed her cheek. She said, 'I hope you do.'

Helen looked at her. 'Do you?'

'Of course,' said Kay – thinking, actually, that

she rather hoped they wouldn't, since the whole idiotic situation clearly made Helen so uneasy.

But Helen laughed, and kissed her back – not uneasy, suddenly, at all.

'You darling,' she said.

CHAPTER 3

'Miss Giniver,' said Miss Chisholm, putting her head around Helen's door, 'there's a lady to see you.'

It was a week or so later. Helen was fastening papers together with a clip, and didn't look up. 'Does she have an appointment?'

'She asked in particular for you.'

'Did she? Blast.' This was what came of giving out your name too freely. 'Where is she?'

'She said she wouldn't come in, as she's rather shabby.'

'Well, she can hardly be too shabby to come in here. Tell her we're not fussy. She must make an appointment, though.'

Miss Chisholm came further into the room and held out a folded piece of paper. 'She wanted me to give you this,' she said, with a hint of disapproval. 'I told her we weren't in the habit of accepting personal post.'

Helen took the note. It was addressed to *Miss Helen Giniver*, in a hand she didn't recognise, and there was a dirty thumb-print on it. She opened it up. It said:

Are you free for lunch? I have tea, and rabbit-meat sandwiches! What do you say? Don't worry, if not. But I'll be outside for the next ten minutes.

And it was signed *Julia*.

Helen saw the signature first, and her heart gave an astonishing sort of fillip in her breast, like a leaping fish. She was horribly aware of Miss Chisholm, watching. She closed the paper smartly back up.

'Thank you, Miss Chisholm,' she said, as she ran her thumbnail along the fold. 'It's just a friend of mine. I'll— I'll go out to her, when I've finished here.'

She slipped the note under a pile of other papers and picked up a pen, as if meaning to write. But as soon as she heard Miss Chisholm going back to her desk in the outer office, she put the pen down. She unlocked a drawer in her own desk and took out her handbag, to tidy her hair, put on powder and lipstick.

Then she squinted at herself in the mirror of her compact. A woman could always tell, she thought, when a girl had just done her face; she didn't want Miss Chisholm to notice – worse, she didn't want Julia to think she had put on make-up especially for her. So she got out her handkerchief and tried to wipe some of the powder away. She drew in her lips and bit repeatedly at the cloth, to blot off the lipstick. She slightly disarranged her hair. *Now*, she thought, *I look like I've been in some sort of tussle—*

For God's sake! What did it matter? It was only Julia. She put the make-up away, got her coat and hat and scarf; went lightly past Miss Chisholm's desk and out along the Town Hall corridors to the lobby and the street.

Julia was standing in front of one of the grey stone lions. She had on her dungarees and her denim jacket again, but this time, instead of a turban, her hair was tied up in a scarf. She had her hands looped around the strap of a leather satchel, slung over her shoulder, and she was gazing at nothing, rocking slightly from foot to foot. But when she heard the swinging back of the bomb-proofed doors she looked round and smiled. And at the sight of her smile, Helen's heart gave another absurd lurch – a twitch, or wriggle, that was almost painful.

But she spoke calmly. 'Hello, Julia. What a nice surprise.'

'Is it?' asked Julia. 'I thought that, since I know where you work now . . .' She looked up at the sky, which was clouded and grey. 'I was hoping for a sunny day, like last time. It's pretty chilly, isn't it? I thought— But tell me, if this sounds like a lousy idea. I've been working so long among ruins, on my own, I've forgotten all the social niceties. But I thought you might like to come and look at the house I've pitched up in, in Bryanston Square – see what I've been up to. The place has been empty for months, I'm sure no one would mind.'

'I'd love to,' said Helen.

'Really?'

'Yes!'

'All right,' said Julia, smiling again. 'I won't take your arm, as I'm so filthy; but this way is nicest.'

She led Helen along the Marylebone Road, and soon made a turn into quieter streets. 'Was that the famous Miss Chisholm,' she said as they went, 'who took my note? I see what you mean about those pursed lips. She looked at me as though she thought I had designs on the office safe!'

'She looks at me like that,' said Helen.

Julia laughed. 'She ought to have seen this.' She opened her satchel and brought out an enormous bunch of keys, each with a tattered label attached. She held it up and shook it like a gaoler. 'What do you think? I got these from the local warden. I've been in and out of half the houses around here. Marylebone has no more secrets from me. You'd think people would have got used to the sight of me ferreting around – but, no. A couple of days ago someone saw me having trouble with a lock, and called the police. She said an "obviously foreign-looking" woman was trying to force her way into a house. I don't know if she took me for a Nazi, or a vagrant refugee. The police were pretty decent about it. Do you think I look foreign?'

She had been sorting through the keys, but raised her head as she asked this. Helen looked into her face, then looked away.

'It's your dark colouring, I suppose.'

'Yes, I suppose so. I should be all right, anyway, now you're with me. You've those English flower looks, haven't you? No one could mistake you for anything but an Ally. – Here we are. The place we want is just over there.'

She took Helen to the door of a grim, tall, dilapidated house, and put one of her keys into its lock. A stream of dust fell from the lintel as she pushed the door open, and Helen went gingerly inside. She was met at once by a bitter, damp smell, like that of old wash-cloths.

'That's just from rain,' said Julia, as she closed the door and fiddled with the latch. 'The roof's been hit, and most of the windows blasted out. Sorry it's so dark. The electricity's off, of course. Go through that doorway over there, it's a little lighter.'

Helen moved across the hall and found herself at the entrance to a sitting-room, cast in a sort of flat twilight by a partly shuttered window. For a moment, until her eyes had grown used to the gloom, the room looked almost all right; then she began to see more clearly, and stepped forward, saying, 'Oh! What an awful shame! This lovely furniture!' For there was a carpet on the floor, and a handsome sofa and chairs, and a footstool, a table – all of it dusty, and heavily marked by flying glass and fallen plaster, or else damp, the wood with a bloom on it and beginning to swell. 'And the chandelier!' she cried softly, looking up.

'Yes, watch your step,' said Julia, coming to her and touching her arm. 'Half the lustres have fallen and smashed.'

'I thought, from what you'd said, that the place

would be quite empty. Why on earth don't the people who own it come back, and fix it up, or take these things away?'

'They think there's no point, I suppose,' said Julia, 'since it's half-way wrecked already. The woman's probably holed up with relatives in the country. The husband might be fighting; he might even be dead.'

'But these lovely things!' said Helen again. She thought of the men and women who came into her office. 'Somebody else could live here, surely? I see so many people with absolutely nothing.'

Julia tapped with her knuckles against the wall. 'The place isn't sound. Another close hit, and it may collapse. It probably will. That's why my father and I are in here. We're recording ghosts, you see, really.'

Helen moved slowly across the room, looking in dismay from one spoiled handsome thing to another. She went to a set of high double doors and carefully pulled them ajar. The room beyond was just as wretched as this one – its window smashed, its velvet curtains marked with rain, spots on the floor where birds had dirtied, soot and cinders blasted from the hearth. She took a step, and something crunched beneath her shoe – a piece of burnt-out coke. It left a smudge of black on the carpet. She looked back at Julia and said, 'I'm afraid to kccp going. It doesn't seem right.'

'You get used to that; don't worry. I've been tramping up and down the stairs for weeks and not given it a thought.'

'You're absolutely sure there's no one here? No one like the old lady you told me about last week? And no one's likely to come back?'

'No one,' said Julia. 'My father may put his head in later, that's all. I've left the door unlocked for him.' She held out her hand, in a beckoning gesture. 'Come downstairs, and you can see what he and I have been doing.'

She went back into the hall, and Helen followed her down a set of unlit stairs to a basement room, where she had laid out, on a trestle table in the light of a barred but broken window, various plans and elevations of the houses of the square. She showed Helen how she was marking the damage – the symbols she was using, the system of measurement, things like that.

'It looks very technical,' said Helen, impressed.

But Julia answered, 'It's probably no more technical than the kind of thing you're used to doing at that office of yours – balancing books, filling in forms and whatnot. I'm utterly useless at things like that. I should hate, too, to have to deal with people coming in and out, wanting things; I don't know how you bear it. This suits me because it's so solitary, so silent.'

'You don't find it lonely?'

'Sometimes. I'm used to it, though. The author's temperament, and all that . . .' She stretched. 'Shall we eat? Let's go through to the next room. It's cold, but not so damp as upstairs.'

She picked up her satchel and led the way along

a passage into the kitchen. There was an old deal table in the middle of the room, thick with fallen flakes of plaster; she began to clear the plaster off.

'I really do have rabbit-meat sandwiches, by the way,' she said, as the plaster tumbled. 'One of my neighbours has a gardener, who traps them. Apparently they're all over London now. He said he caught this one in Leicester Square! I'm not sure I believe him.'

Helen said, 'A friend of mine who firewatches says she saw a rabbit, one night, on the platform at Victoria Station; so perhaps he did.'

'A rabbit at Victoria! Was it waiting for a train?'

'Yes. Apparently it was looking at its pocket-watch, and seemed awfully het-up about something.'

Julia laughed. The laughter was different from the sort of laughter Helen had heard from her before. It was real, unforced – like water welling briefly from a spring, and to have called it up made Helen feel pleased as a child. She said to herself, *For goodness' sake! You're like a second-former swooning over a prefect!* She had to move about to hide her feelings, looking across the dusty jars and pudding moulds on the kitchen shelves while Julia set her bag on the table and rummaged inside it.

The kitchen was an old Victorian one, with long wooden counters and a chipped stone sink. The window had bars before it, like the other, and in between the bars curled ivy. The light was green and very soft. Helen said, as she walked about,

'You can see the cook and the scullery maids in here.'

'Yes, can't you?'

'And the local policeman, slipping in in the middle of his beat, for his cup of tea.'

'"No Followers",' said Julia, smiling. 'Come and sit down, Helen.'

She had got out a wax-paper packet of sandwiches, and a nightwatchman's bottle of tea. She'd drawn up chairs, but looked dubiously from the dusty seats to Helen's smartish coat. She said, 'I could put paper down, if you like.'

'It's all right,' said Helen. 'Really.'

'Sure? I'll take you at your word, you know. I won't be like Kay about it.'

'Like Kay?'

'Laying down my cloak, all of that, like Walter Raleigh.'

It was the first time they had mentioned Kay, and Helen sat without answering. For Kay *would* have made a fuss about the dust, she thought; and she knew instinctively how tiresome that sort of thing would seem to Julia. It made her aware, more than ever, of the curious situation she was in: that she had accepted a love, a sets of attentions, that Julia herself had had the chance to accept first, and had rejected . . .

Julia unwrapped the sandwiches, drew out the cork from the steaming tea; she'd had the bottle wrapped in a pullover, she said, to keep it hot. She poured a little of the tea into two dainty porcelain cups from one of the cupboards; then swilled it around, to warm the china, threw that away and poured out more.

The tea was sugary, and very creamy. It must have had all Julia's ration in it. Helen sipped it, closing her eyes, feeling guilty. When Julia offered her a sandwich she said, 'I ought to give you money or something for this, Julia.'

Julia said, 'Really.'

'I could give you a coupon—'

'For God's sake! Is that what this war has done to us? You can buy me a drink some time, if you feel as badly about it as all that.'

They began to eat. The bread was coarse, but the meat sweet and very tender; the flavour was a heavy, distinctive one. Helen realised, after a moment, that it must be garlic. She had tasted garlic in restaurants, but had never cooked with it herself; Julia had bought it, she said as they ate, from a shop on Frith Street, Soho. She'd managed, too, to get macaroni, olive oil, dried parmesan cheese. And she had a relative in America who sent her parcels of food. 'You can get more Italian food in Chicago,' she said, swallowing, 'than you can in Italy. Joyce sends me olives, and black salad vinegar.'

'How lucky you are!' said Helen.

'I suppose I am. You don't have any people abroad who could do something like that for you?'

'Oh, no. My family are all still in Worthing, where I grew up.'

Julia looked surprised. 'You grew up in Worthing?

I didn't know that. Though I suppose, now I think about it, you had to grow up somewhere . . . My family has a house near Arundel; we used to swim at Worthing sometimes. Once I ate too many whelks or cockles – or toffee apples, or something – and was vilely sick, all over the pier. What was it like there, growing up?'

'It was all right,' said Helen. 'My family— Well, they're very ordinary. Did you know that? They're not— They're not like Kay's.' *They're not like yours*, was what she really meant. 'My father's an optician. My brother makes lenses for the RAF. My parents' house—' She looked around. 'It isn't like this house, it isn't anything like this.'

Perhaps Julia saw that she was embarrassed. She said quietly, 'Well, but nothing like that matters any more, does it? Not these days. Not now we all dress like scarecrows, and talk like Americans – or else, like chars. "Here's your grub, ducks," a girl in a café said to me the other day; I swear she'd been to Roedean, too.'

Helen smiled. 'It makes people feel better, I suppose. It's another kind of uniform.'

Julia made a face. 'I hate this passion for uniforms, too. Uniforms, armbands, badges. I thought the military impulse, as it's grown up in Germany, was what we were against!' She sipped her tea, then almost yawned. 'But perhaps I take the whole thing too seriously.' She looked at Helen over the rim of her cup. 'I ought to be like you. Well adjusted, and so on.'

Helen stared, amazed to think that Julia had formed any sort of opinion of her, much less one like that. She said, 'Is that how I seem? It isn't how I feel. *Well adjusted*. I'm not even sure I know what it means.'

'Well,' said Julia, 'you always give the impression of being pretty thoughtful, pretty measured. That's what I mean. You don't say much; but what you do say seems to be worth listening to. That's quite rare, isn't it?'

'It must be a trick,' said Helen lightly. 'When you're quiet, people imagine you're awfully deep. In fact all you're doing is thinking – I don't know – how tight your bra is; or wondering whether or not you need the lavatory.'

'But that,' said Julia, 'sounds exactly like good adjustment, to me! Thinking about yourself, rather than the effect you might be having on other people. And the whole—' She hesitated. 'Well, the whole grisly "L" business. You know what I mean . . . You seem to handle *that* awfully coolly.'

Helen looked down into her cup, and didn't answer. Julia said, more quietly, 'How impertinent of me. I'm sorry, Helen.'

'No, it's all right,' said Helen quickly, looking up again. 'I'm not very used to talking about it, that's all. And I'm not sure, you know, that I've ever really thought of it as being much of a *business*. It was just how things turned out. I didn't think about it at all, to tell you the truth, when I was younger. Or if I did, I suppose I thought the usual sort of thing: spinster teachers, earnest girls . . .'

'There was no one, in Worthing?'

'Well, there were men.' Helen laughed. 'That makes me sound like a call-girl, doesn't it? There was only one boy, really. I moved to London to be near him; but it didn't work out. And then I met Kay.'

'Ah, yes,' said Julia, sipping her tea again. 'And then you met Kay. And in such terribly romantic circumstances.'

Helen looked at her, trying to gauge her tone and expression. She said shyly, 'It did seem romantic. Kay's rather glamorous, isn't she? At least, she seemed glamorous to me. I'd never met anyone like her before. I'd been in London less than six months then. She made such a – such a fuss of me. And she seemed so certain of what she wanted. That was terribly exciting somehow. It was hard to resist, anyway. It never felt strange, as perhaps it ought to have done . . . But then, so many impossible things were becoming ordinary, just then.' She thought back, with a slight shudder, to the night that she and Kay had met. 'And as impossible things go, being with Kay was, I suppose, quite a mild one.'

She was speaking, she realised, in almost a tone of apology; for she was conscious, still, of what she thought of as a gaucheness in herself, conscious that all the things she was describing to Julia as attractive in Kay were things that Julia herself must have found it easy to resist. Part of her wanted to defend

Kay; but part of her, too, wanted to confide in Julia, almost as one wife to another. She'd never spoken like this to anyone. She'd left her own friends behind, when she moved in with Kay; or she kept Kay a secret from them. And Kay's friends were all like Mickey – all like Kay, in other words. Now she wanted to ask how it had been for Julia, with Kay. She wanted to know if Julia had felt what she herself sometimes, guiltily, felt: that Kay's constant fussing, which had once been so appealing, so exciting, could also be rather like a burden; that Kay made an absurd kind of heroine of you; that Kay's passion was so great there was something unreal about it, it could never be matched . . .

But she didn't ask any of these things. She looked down into her cup again, and was silent. Julia said, 'And when the war's over? And everything goes back to normal?' And she took refuge, then, in briskness. She shook her head.

'It's pointless thinking about that, isn't it?' It was what everybody said, to all sorts of questions. 'We might get blown to bits tomorrow. Until then – well, I'd never want to advertise it. I'd never dream, for example, of telling my mother! But, why should I? It's a thing between Kay and me. And we're two grown women. Who does it harm?'

Julia watched her for a moment, then poured more tea from the bottle. She said, as if with a touch of sarcasm, 'You *are* well adjusted.'

So then Helen grew embarrassed again. She thought, *I've said too much, and bored her. She preferred me before, when I was quiet and she thought I was deep . . .*

They sat without speaking, until Julia shivered and rubbed her arms. 'God!' she said. 'This isn't much fun for you, is it? Me, giving you the third degree, in the basement of a ruined house! It's like lunch with the Gestapo!'

Helen laughed, her embarrassment fading. 'No. It's nice.'

'Are you sure? I could— Well, I could show you over the whole place, if you like.'

'Yes, I'd like that.'

They finished their sandwiches and their tea, and Julia tidied away the bottle and the paper and rinsed out the cups. They went back upstairs, going past the doors to the sitting-room and the room behind it, and up the dimly lit staircase to the floors above.

They went softly, sometimes murmuring together over some particular detail or piece of damage, but more often moving about in silence. The rooms on these higher floors were bleaker, even, than the ones downstairs. The bedrooms still had their beds and wardrobes in them, and the wardrobes were damp, because of the broken windows, the ancient clothes inside them eaten through by moths or growing mouldy. Sections of the ceilings had come down. Books and ornaments lay about, ruined. And in the bathroom, a mirror hung on the wall with a weird, blank face: its glass had shattered and fallen, and filled the basin beneath it in a hundred silvery shards.

351

As they climbed up to the attic floor there was a scuttling, fluttering sound. Julia turned. 'Pigeons, or mice,' she said softly. 'You won't mind?'

'Not rats?' asked Helen apprehensively.

'Oh, no. At least, I don't think so.'

She went on, and opened a door. The scuttling changed, became the sound of clapping hands. Peering over Julia's shoulder, Helen saw a bird fly up and then, as if by magic, disappear. The sloping ceiling had a hole in it, where an incendiary had burned through. The bomb had landed on a feather mattress underneath and made a crater: it looked like an ulcerated leg. You could still smell the bitter scent of burnt, damp feathers.

The room was a housekeeper's or maid's. There was a photograph in a frame, on the bedside table, of a little girl. And on the floor was a single slim leather glove, much nibbled by mice.

Helen picked the glove up and did her best to smooth it out. She put it neatly down beside the photograph. She stood for a second looking up through the hole in the ceiling at the close, gun-coloured sky. Then she went with Julia to the window, and gazed out at the yard at the back of the house.

The yard was ruined, like everything else: its paving-stones broken, its plants run wild, the column of a sundial blown from its base and lying in pieces.

'Isn't it sad?' said Julia quietly. 'Look at the fig tree.'

'Yes. All that fruit!' For the tree was lolling with broken branches, and the ground beneath it was thick with rotting figs that must have fallen from it and gone uncollected the summer before.

Helen got out cigarettes, and Julia moved closer to her, to take one. They smoked together, their shoulders just touching, the sleeve of Julia's jacket just catching at Helen's coat as she raised and lowered her cigarette. Her knuckles were still marked, Helen noticed, from where she'd grazed them the week before; and Helen thought of how, that time, she'd lightly touched them with her fingertips. She and Julia had only been standing together – just standing together, like this. Nothing had happened to make a change. But she couldn't imagine, now, touching any part of Julia so carelessly as that.

The thought was thrilling, but also frightening. They chatted a little, about the houses which backed on to Bryanston Square; Julia pointed out the ones she had visited, and described the things she'd seen in them. But her sleeve still caught against Helen's, and it was that brushing and clinging of fabric, rather than Julia's words, which held Helen's attention; at last she began to feel the flesh of her arm rising up – as if Julia, or the nearness of Julia, was somehow tugging, drawing at it . . .

She shivered and moved away. She'd almost finished her cigarette, and made that the excuse. She looked around for somewhere to stub it.

Julia saw. 'Just drop it, and stamp on it,' she said.

'I don't like to,' said Helen.

'It'll hardly make things worse.'

'I know, but—'

She took the cigarette to the fireplace, to crush it out there; and she did the same with Julia's, when Julia had finished. But then she didn't want to leave the two stubs behind in the empty grate: she waved them about to cool them down, and put them back, with the fresh ones, in her packet.

'Suppose the people come back?' she said, when Julia stared at her in disbelief. 'They won't like to think that strangers have been in here, looking at their things.'

'You don't think they'd be a shade more troubled by the rainwater, the broken windows, the bomb in the bed?'

'Rain and bombs and windows are just things,' said Helen. 'They're impersonal, not like people . . . You think I'm silly.'

Julia was gazing at her, shaking her head. 'On the contrary,' she said quietly. She was smiling, but sounded almost sad. 'I was thinking – well, how awfully nice you are.'

They looked at each other for a moment, until Helen lowered her gaze. She put away the packet of cigarettes, then went back across the room to the charred mattress. The room seemed small to her, suddenly: she was very aware of herself and Julia in it, at the top of this chill, silent house – the warmth and the life and the solidness of them, in comparison with so much damage. She could feel the rising, again, of goose-pimples, on her arms. She could feel the beating of her own heart, in her throat, her breast, her fingertips . . .

'I ought,' she said, without turning round, 'to get back to work.'

And Julia laughed. 'Now you're nicer than ever,' she said. But she still sounded sad, somehow. 'Come on. Let's go down.'

They went out to the landing and down one flight of stairs. They moved so quietly, still, that when a door was closed, somewhere at the bottom of the house, they heard it, and stopped. Helen's heart, instead of rushing, seemed to falter. 'What's that?' she whispered, nervously gripping the banister rail.

Julia was frowning. 'I don't know.'

But then a man called lightly up the stairs. 'Julia? Are you there?' – and her expression cleared.

'It's my father,' she said. She leant, and yelled cheerfully into the stairwell: 'I'm up here, Daddy! Right at the top! – Come and meet him,' she said, turning back, taking hold of Helen's hand and squeezing her fingers.

She went quickly down the stairs. Helen followed more slowly. By the time she got down to the hall, Julia was brushing dust from her father's shoulders and hair, and laughing. 'Darling, you're filthy!'

'Am I?'

'Yes! Look, Helen, what a state my father's in. He's been burrowing through coal cellars . . . Daddy, this is my friend Miss Helen Giniver. Don't shake her hand! She thinks we're a family of mudlarks as it is.'

Mr Standing smiled. He was wearing a dirty blue boiler suit with grubby medal ribbons on the breast. He'd taken off a crumpled-looking cap, and now smoothed down his hair where Julia had disarranged it. He said, 'How do you do, Miss Giniver? I'm afraid Julia's right about my hand. Been taking a look around, have you?'

'Yes.'

'Rum sort of job, isn't it? All dust. Not like the other war: that was all mud. Makes one wonder what the next one will be. Ashes, I expect . . . What I should really like to be doing, of course, is putting up new places, rather than grubbing around in these old ones. Still, it keeps me busy. Keeps Julia out of trouble, too.' He winked. His eyes were dark, as Julia's were, the lids rather heavy. His hair was grey, but darkened by dirt; his brow and temples were dirty, too – or else freckled, it was hard to see. As he spoke he ran his gaze, in a practised, casual way, over Helen's figure. 'Glad to see you taking an interest, anyway. Care to stay, and help?'

Julia said, 'Don't be silly, Daddy. Helen has a terribly important job already. She works for the Assistance Board.'

'The Assistance Board? Really?' He looked at Helen properly. 'With Lord Stanley?'

Helen said, 'Only in the local office, I'm afraid.'

'Ah. Pity. Stanley and I are old friends.'

He stood chatting with them for another few

moments; then, 'Jolly good,' he said. 'I'm off down to the basement, to take a quick look at those plans. If you'll excuse me, Miss—?'

He stepped around them and headed downstairs. As he moved out of the thickest of the shadows Helen saw that what she'd taken to be dirt, or freckles, on his face, were really the scars of old blisters, from fire or gas.

'Isn't he a darling?' said Julia, when he'd gone. 'Really, he's the most awful rogue.' She opened the door, and she and Helen stood together on the step. She shivered again. 'It looks like rain. You'll have to be quick! You know your way back all right? I'd come with you, only— Oh, hang on.'

She'd put her hand, suddenly, on Helen's shoulder, to keep her from moving on to the pavement, and Helen turned back to her, alarmed – thinking, almost, that Julia meant to kiss her, embrace her, something like that. But all she was doing was brushing dust from Helen's arm.

'There,' she said, smiling. 'Now, turn around and let me see the back of you. Yes, here's another bit. Now, the other way. How biddable you are! But we mustn't give Miss Chisholm any grounds for complaint.' She raised an eyebrow. 'Nor Kay, for that matter . . . There. That's splendid.'

They said goodbye. 'Come and find me some other lunch-time!' Julia called, as Helen moved off. 'I'll be here for two more weeks. We could go to a pub. You can buy me that drink!'

Helen said she would.

She began to walk. Once the door was closed she looked at her wrist-watch, and started to run. She got back to her office at a minute past two. 'Your first appointment's waiting, Miss Giniver,' Miss Chisholm told her, with a glance at the clock; so she didn't have time, even, to visit the lavatory or comb her hair.

She worked very steadily, for an hour and a half. The job was tiring in times like these. The sort of people she'd been interviewing in the past few weeks were like the people she'd got used to seeing during the big blitz, three years before. Some of them came fresh from the wreckage of their homes, with dirty hands, cut about and bandaged. One woman had been bombed out, she said, three times; she sat on the other side of Helen's desk and wept.

'It's not the house having gone,' she said. 'It's the moving about. I feel like a bit of tinder, miss. I haven't slept since all this happened. My little boy's got delicate health. My husband's in Burma; I'm all on my own.'

'It's awfully hard,' said Helen. She gave the woman a form, and patiently showed her how to complete it. The woman looked at it, not understanding.

'All this?'

'I'm afraid so.'

'But, if I could just have a pound or two —'

'I can't give you money, I'm afraid. You see, it's a rather lengthy process. We must send a valuer to assess the damage before we can make an advance.

We must have someone from our own department see your old home and make a report. I'll try to get them to the site as quickly as I can, but with all the new raids . . .'

The woman was gazing, still, at the pieces of paper in her hand. 'I feel like tinder,' she said again, passing her hand across her eyes. 'Just like tinder.'

Helen watched her for a second; then took the form back. She filled in the woman's details herself, backdating it all to the month before; and in the space requesting the date and serial number of the valuer's report, she wrote some likely but vaguely illegible inky figures. She put the form in a tray marked *Approved*, ready to be sent up to Miss Steadman on the first floor; and she clipped on a note, to say it was urgent.

But she didn't do anything like that for the next person, or for the people after him. She'd been struck by the woman's describing herself as being like tinder, that was all. In the first blitz, she'd tried to help everyone; she'd given money to people, sometimes, from her own purse. But the war made you careless. You started off, she thought sadly, imagining you'd be a kind of heroine. You ended up thinking only of yourself.

For at the back of her mind, all afternoon, was the idea of Julia. She was thinking of Julia even as she was comforting the crying woman, even as she was saying, 'It's awfully hard.' She was remembering the feel of Julia's arm as it brushed against hers; the closeness of Julia, in that small attic room.

Then, at a quarter to four, her telephone rang.

'Miss Giniver?' said the girl on reception. 'An outside call. A Miss Hepburn. Shall I put her through?'

Miss Hepburn? thought Helen, distractedly. Then she understood, and her stomach fluttered with anxiety and guilt. 'Just a second,' she said. 'Ask the caller to hold, will you?' She put the receiver down, and went to her door and called out: 'Miss Chisholm? No more applicants, please, just for a minute! I've got the Camden Town office on the line.' She sat back at her desk, and willed herself steady. 'Hello, Miss Hepburn,' she said quietly, when the call had been put through.

'Hello, you.' It was Kay. They had a sort of game, with names, like that. 'This is just a nuisance call, I'm afraid.' Her voice sounded deep, and rather lazy. She was smoking a cigarette: she moved the receiver, to blow out smoke . . . 'How's life in Assistance?'

'Pretty hectic, actually,' said Helen, glancing at the door. 'I can't talk long.'

'Can't you? I oughtn't to have rung, ought I?'

'Not really.'

'I've been kicking my heels at home. I— Just a minute.'

There was a little puff of air, and then a sense of deadness: Kay had put her palm over the receiver and started to cough. The cough went on. Helen pictured her as she'd often seen her – doubled over, her eyes watering, her face scarlet, her lungs filled up with smoke and brick-dust. She said, 'Kay? Are you all right?'

'Still here,' said Kay, coming back. 'It's not so bad.'

'You oughtn't to be smoking.'

'The smoking helps. Hearing your voice helps.'

Helen didn't answer. She was thinking of the switchboard girl. A friend of Mickey's had lost her job, when a girl had listened in on a private call between her and her lover.

'I wish you were here, at home,' Kay went on. 'Can't they get along without you?'

'You know they can't.'

'You have to go, don't you?'

'I do, really.'

Kay was smiling: Helen could hear it in her voice. 'All right. Nothing else to report, though? No one tried to storm the office? Mr Holmes still giving you the eye?'

'No,' said Helen, smiling too. Then her stomach fluttered again, and she drew in her breath. 'Actually—'

'Hang on,' said Kay. She moved the receiver, and began to cough again. Helen heard her wiping her mouth. 'I must let you go,' she said, when she came back.

'Yes,' said Helen leadenly.

'I'll see you later. You're coming straight home? Come quickly, won't you?'

'Yes, of course.'

'Good girl . . . Goodbye, Miss Giniver.'

'Goodbye, Kay.'

Helen put the receiver down and sat very still. She had a clear image of Kay, getting up, finishing her cigarette, wandering restlessly around the flat, perhaps coughing again. She might stand at the window with her hands in her pockets. She might whistle or hum, old songs from the music hall, 'Daisy, Daisy,' songs like that. She might put down paper on the sitting-room table, to polish her shoes. She might get out a funny little sailor's sewing-kit she had, and darn her socks. She didn't know that Helen, a few hours before, had been standing at a window, feeling the flesh on her arm rise up like the petals of a flower to the sun, because Julia was beside her. She didn't know that Helen, in a little attic room, had had to turn away from Julia's gaze, because the quickening of her own blood had made her afraid . . .

Helen snatched up the telephone again and gave the girl a number. The phone rang twice, and then, 'Hello,' said Kay, surprised by Helen's voice. 'What did you forget?'

'Nothing,' said Helen. 'I— I wanted to hear you again, that's all. What were you doing?'

'I was in the bathroom,' said Kay. 'I'd just started to cut my hair. I've dropped hair everywhere, now. You'll hate it.'

'No I won't. Kay, I just wanted to tell you—You know, that thing.'

She meant, *I love you*. Kay was silent for a second, and then said, '*That* thing.' Her voice had thickened. 'I wanted to tell you that, too . . .'

362

What an absolute idiot I've been! thought Helen, when she'd put the phone down again. Her heart felt, now, as though it was swollen inside her, was rising up, like dough, into her throat. She was almost trembling. She got out her handbag and looked for her cigarettes. She found the packet and opened it up.

Inside the packet were those two stubs. She'd put them in there and forgotten. There was lipstick on them, from her own mouth, and from Julia's.

She put them in the ashtray on her desk. Then she found that the ashtray kept drawing her eye. In the end she took it from the room, and tipped it out into one of the wire bins in Miss Chisholm's office.

At half-past six, Viv was in the cloakroom at Portman Court. She was standing in a lavatory cubicle, being sick into the bowl. She was sick three times, then straightened up and closed her eyes and, for a minute, felt wonderfully tranquil and well. But when she opened her eyes and saw the lumpy brown mess she'd brought up – a mixture of tea and half-digested garibaldi biscuits – she retched again. The cloakroom door was opened just as she was coming out to rinse her mouth. It was one of the girls from her own department, a girl called Caroline Graham.

'I say,' said the girl, 'are you all right? Gibson sent me to find you. What's up? You look rotten.'

Viv wiped her face, gingerly, on an edge of roller-towel. 'I'm OK.'

'You don't look it, honestly. Do you want me to go with you to the nurse?'

'It's nothing,' said Viv. 'Just— Just a hangover.'

Caroline heard that, and her manner changed. She leant her hip comfortably against one of the basins, and got out a stick of chewing-gum. 'Oh,' she said, folding the stick into her mouth, 'I know all about *those*. And crikey, it must have been bad if you're still throwing up at this hour! I hope the chap was worth it. It's not so rotten, I always think, if you've had a really good time. The worst is, when the boy's a dud, and you sort of drink just in the hope that it'll start to make him look better. You want to eat a raw egg or something.'

Viv felt her stomach quiver again. She moved away from the sight of the tumbling grey gum in Caroline's mouth. 'I don't think I could.' She glanced into the mirror. 'God, look at the state of me! Have you got any powder on you?'

'Here,' said Caroline. She got out a compact and handed it over; and when Viv had used it she took it back and used it herself. Then she stood at the mirror, recurling her hair, the chewing-gum still for a moment; the tip of her tongue showing pinkly between her painted lips, her face smooth and plump with health and youth and the absence of worry: so that Viv looked at her and thought miserably, *How bloody mean and unfair life is! I wish I was you.*

Caroline caught her gaze. 'You do look rotten,' she said, beginning to chew again. 'Why don't you stay longer? It's no skin off my nose. We've only got another half-hour, anyway. I could tell Gibson I looked and couldn't find you. You could say you were collared by Mr Brightman, something like that. He's always sending girls out for soda-mints.'

'Thanks,' said Viv, 'but I'll be OK.'

'Are you sure?'

'Yes.'

But she'd lowered her head to straighten the waistband of her skirt; and now, in looking up too quickly, she grew queasy again. She put her hand out to one of the basins and closed her eyes – swallowing, swallowing, feeling the gathering of sickness in her stomach and fighting to keep it from rushing up . . . All at once, it surged. She darted back into the lavatory cubicle and retched drily into the bowl. In that narrow space, the sounds she made seemed dreadful. She tugged on the chain to try and disguise them. When she went back out to the basins, Caroline looked anxious.

'I think you ought to let me take you to the nurse, Viv.'

'I can't go to the nurse with a hangover.'

'You ought to do something. You look terrible.'

'I'll be all right,' said Viv, 'in a minute.'

Then she thought of the little journey she'd have to make back up to the typing room: the hard flights of stairs, the corridors. She imagined being sick on one of the polished marble floors. She pictured the typing room itself: the chairs and tables all crowded together, the black-outs up, making everything stuffy, the smells of ink and hair and make-up worse than ever.

'I wish I could just go home,' she said miserably.

'Well, why don't you? There's only twenty minutes now.'

'Shall I? What about Gibson?'

'I'll tell her you're poorly. It's the truth, isn't it? Look here, though, what about getting home? Suppose you faint on the way or something?'

'I don't think I'll faint,' said Viv. But didn't women faint, when they were—? *God!* She turned away. She was suddenly afraid that Caroline, in looking at her, would see what the real matter was. She looked at her watch and said, with an effort at calmness, at brightness, 'Will you do me a favour? I think I'll wait for Betty Lawrence and walk home with her. Will you tell her, after you've told Gibson? Will you say I'll meet her here?'

'Of course,' said Caroline, straightening up, getting ready to go. 'And don't forget, about that raw egg. I know it sounds like an awful waste of the ration, but I had a colossal hangover once, on some filthy cocktails a boy mixed up for me at a party; the egg did the trick like you wouldn't believe. I think Minty Brewster's got her hands on a couple of eggs; ask her.'

'I will,' said Viv, trying to smile. 'Thanks, Caroline. Oh, and if Gibson asks what the matter is, don't tell her I've been sick, will you? She's bound to guess – about the hangover, I mean.'

Caroline laughed. She blew out a little grey

chewing-gum bubble, and burst it with a pop. 'Don't worry. I'll be frightfully female and mysterious, and she'll think it's the curse. Will that do?'

Viv nodded, laughing too.

The moment Caroline went out, her laughter died. She felt the flesh on her face sink, grow heavy. The cloakroom had hot pipes running through it, and the air was dry; it felt under pressure, like a room in a submarine. Viv wanted more than anything to be able to open the window and put her face in a breeze. But the lights were on, and the curtain was already drawn: all she could do was go to the side of it and pull the dusty, scratchy cloth around her head like a sort of hood, and get what she could of the chill evening air that was seeping in through gaps in the window-frame.

The window opened on to a courtyard. She could hear typing, the ring of telephones, from rooms on the floors above. If she listened carefully, too, she could just make out, beyond those sounds, the ordinary sounds of Wigmore Street and Portman Square: cars and taxis, and men and women going shopping, going out, going home from work. They were the sort of sounds, Viv thought, that you heard a thousand, thousand times, and never noticed – just as, when you were well, you never thought about being well, you could only really feel what it was like to be healthy for about a minute, when you stopped being sick. But when you were sick, it made you into a stranger, a foreigner in your own land. Everything that was simple and ordinary to everyone else became like an enemy to you. Your own body became like an enemy to you, plotting and scheming against you and setting traps . . .

She stood at the window, thinking all this, until, at just before seven, the sound of typing faded and was replaced, across the building, by the scrape of wooden chairs on bare floors. A minute after that, the first of the women appeared: they came bowling into the cloakroom to visit the lavatory and get their coats. Viv went out to her locker and, very slowly, put on her own coat, her hat and gloves. She moved between the women like some sort of phantom, gazing at the dullest of them, the plainest of them, the plump and bespectacled, with a mad sort of ravening envy; feeling herself impossibly separated from them and alone. She listened to their clear, confident voices and thought, *This is what happens to people like me. I'm just like Duncan, after all. We try to make something of ourselves and life won't let us, we get tripped up—*

Betty appeared. She came in frowning, turning her head. When she saw Viv, she came straight over.

She said, 'What's up? Caroline Graham said you couldn't make it back upstairs. She laid it on as thick as anything for Gibson – said you'd been taken by surprise by something. Now word's gone round you've got the squits.' She looked Viv over. 'Hey, you do look bad.'

Viv tried to move away from her gaze as, earlier, she'd tried to move from Caroline's. She said, 'I just felt a bit sick.'

'Poor kid. You need bucking up. I've got just the thing for that, too. Jean, from Shipping, has been spreading the word about an MOI party. One of their boys got his divorce papers through today, and they say they need girls. They've been hoarding for weeks by the sound of it, so it should be a pretty good blow. We've just got time to change; come on.'

Viv looked at her, appalled. 'You're joking,' she said. 'I can't manage that. I look like a wreck!'

'Oh, throw on a bit of Max Factor,' said Betty as she shrugged on her coat, 'and the Ministry boys won't notice.'

She took Viv's arm and led her out of the room, and they began the journey up to the lobby. Climbing the stairs, Viv found, was awful, like being at sea; but there was a comfort to be had from the feel of Betty's arm in hers, from being helped and guided. They got to the desk and signed themselves out. The street was not quite dark enough for them to have to switch on their torches. But the evening was cold. Betty stopped for a moment to get out a pair of gloves.

She caught sight of another girl, and lifted one of the gloves and waved it.

'Jean! Jean, come over here! Tell Viv about this do tonight, will you? She needs persuading.'

The girl called Jean started to walk with them. 'It should be terrific, Viv,' she said. 'They told me to bring as many pals as I could get hold of.'

Viv shook her head. 'I'm sorry, Jean. I can't, tonight.'

'Oh, but Viv!'

'Don't listen to her, Jean,' said Betty. 'She's not herself.'

'I'll say she's not herself! Viv, they've been hoarding for absolute weeks—'

'I told her that.'

'I can't,' said Viv again. 'Honestly, I don't feel up to it.'

'What's there to be up to? All those boys are after is a few swell-looking girls in tight sweaters.'

'No, really.'

'It isn't every day a chap gets his divorce through, after all.'

'No, honestly,' said Viv, her voice beginning to break, 'I can't. I can't! I—'

She stopped walking, put her hand across her eyes; and there, in the middle of Wigmore Street, she began to cry.

There was a moment's silence. Then Betty said, 'Uh-oh. Sorry, Jean. Looks like the party'll have to do without us after all.'

'Well, it's hard luck on those fellows. They'll be awfully disappointed.'

'Look at it this way: there'll be more for you.'

Jean said, 'That's a thought, I suppose.' She touched Viv's arm. 'Cheer up, Viv. He must be a rotter, you know, if he makes you feel like this. I'm going to fly back to Johnnie Allen House, girls! If you change your minds, you know where to find me!' She went off, almost running.

Viv took out her handkerchief and blew her nose.

She raised her head, and saw people watching her, mildly curious, as they passed by.

'I feel such a fool.'

'Don't be daft,' said Betty gently. 'We all cry, sometimes. Come on, kid.' She drew Viv's arm through hers again, and squeezed her hand. 'Let's get you home. What you need's a nice hot-water bottle, and a gin with a couple of aspirin in it. Come to think of it, that's what I need, too.'

They began to walk again, more slowly. Viv's limbs seemed to tingle, almost to buzz, with tiredness. The thought of going back to John Allen House at this time of night, when the place would be in chaos, with chairs being dragged across the dining-room floor, the lights blazing, the wireless blasting out dance-music, girls running up and down the stairs in their underwear, ripping curlers from their hair, calling to each other at the top of their voices – the thought exhausted her.

She pulled at Betty's arm. 'I can't face going back just yet. Let's go somewhere else, somewhere quiet. Can we?'

'Well,' said Betty, doubtfully, 'we could go to a café, something like that.'

'I can't face a café, either,' said Viv. 'Can we just sit down somewhere? Just for five minutes?' Her voice was rising, threatening to break again.

'All right,' said Betty, leading her off.

They found themselves, after a short walk, in one of the area's residential squares, and went into the garden. It was the sort of place that would have been locked to them in the years before the war; now, of course, the railings had gone and they went straight in. They found a bench away from the thickest bushes, on the quietest side of the square. It was not quite dark, but getting darker all the time, and Betty, looking around, said, 'Well, we'll either get raped, or someone'll think we're a couple of good-time girls and offer us money. I don't know about you, but if the price was right I might be tempted to take it.' She still had hold of Viv's arm. 'All right, kid,' she said, as they sat and drew close their coats. 'Tell me what's wrong. And remember: I've given up the chance of getting groped by an MOI divorcé for this, so it had better be good.'

Viv smiled. But the smile grew almost painful, almost at once. She felt the rising of tears in her throat just as, before, she'd felt the rushing up of sickness. She said, 'Oh, Betty—' and her voice dissolved. She put a hand across her mouth, and shook her head. After a second she said in a whisper, 'I'll cry, if I say it.'

'Well,' said Betty, 'I'll cry if you don't!' Then, more kindly: 'All right, I'm not stupid. I've a pretty good idea what this is about. Or who, I should say . . . What's he done now? Come on, there's a limit to the kind of thing a man can do to a girl to make her cry. They just don't have the imagination. He either stands her up, or chucks her over, or knocks her down.' She snorted. 'Or knocks her up.'

She said it jokingly, beginning to laugh. Then she met Viv's gaze through the gathering darkness, and her laughter faded.

'Oh, Viv,' she said quietly.

'I know,' said Viv.

'Oh, Viv! When did you find out?'

'A couple of weeks ago.'

'A couple of weeks? That's not so much. Are you sure it's not just – you know, just a bit late? With all these raids—'

'No,' said Viv. She wiped her face. 'I thought that, at first. But it's not just that. I know it's happened. I just know. Look at the state of me . . . I've been sick.'

'You've been sick?' said Betty, impressed. 'In the mornings?'

'Not in the mornings. In the afternoons and at night. My sister was like that. All her friends were sick first thing, but she was sick nearly every night, for three months.'

'Three months!' said Betty.

Viv glanced around. 'Shush, will you?'

'Sorry. But crikey, kid. What are you going to do?'

'I don't know.'

'Have you told Reggie?'

Viv looked away. 'No, I haven't.'

'Why not? It's his fault, isn't it?'

'It's not his fault,' said Viv, looking back. 'I mean, it's my fault as much as his.'

'Your fault?' said Betty. 'How's that? For giving him' – she lowered her voice even further –

'permission to come aboard? That's all very well, but he should, you know, have worn his rain-coat.'

Viv shook her head. 'It's been all right, until now. We never use those. He can't stand them.'

They sat in silence for a second. Then, 'I think you should tell him,' said Betty.

'No,' said Viv firmly. 'I'm not telling anyone except you. Don't you tell anyone, either! God!' The idea was awful. 'Suppose Gibson finds out? Remember Felicity Withers?'

Felicity Withers was a Ministry of Works girl who'd got herself pregnant by a Free French airman the year before. She'd thrown herself down the stairs at John Allen House; there'd been the most awful row about it. She'd been dismissed from the Ministry, sent home, back to her parents – a vicar and his wife – in Birmingham.

'We all said what a nit she was,' said Viv. 'God, I wish she was here now! She got—' She looked around, and spoke in a murmur. 'She got some pills, didn't she? From a chemist's?'

'I don't know,' said Betty.

'She did,' said Viv. 'I'm sure she did.'

'You could take Epsom salts.'

'I've done that. It didn't work.'

'You could try a red-hot bath, and gin.'

Viv almost laughed. 'At John Allen House? I'd never get the water hot enough. And then, imagine if someone saw, or smelt the gin. I couldn't do it at my father's, either.' She shuddered, just thinking about it. 'Isn't there anything else? There must be other things.'

Betty thought it over. 'You could squirt yourself with soapy water. That's supposed to work. You have to hit the right spot, though. Or you could use – you know – a knitting needle—'

'God!' said Viv, growing sick again. 'I don't think I could bear to. Could you, if you were me?'

'I don't know. I might, if I was worried enough. Can't you just – lift weights?'

'What weights?' said Viv.

'Sandbags, things like that? Can't you jump up and down on the spot?'

Viv thought of the various uncomfortable ordinary journeys she'd had to make in the past two weeks: the bumping about on trains and buses, the flights of stairs she'd climbed at work. 'That kind of thing won't do it,' she said. 'It doesn't want to come out like that, I know it doesn't.'

'You could soak pennies in drinking-water.'

'That's just an old wives' tale, isn't it?'

'Well, don't old wives know a thing or two? That's why they're old wives, after all, and not—'

'And not old you-know-whats, like me?'

'That's not what I meant.'

Viv looked away. It was quite dark now. From the pavements beyond the garden there was the occasional blur of shaded torch-light, the shrinking and spreading and darting about of beams. But the tall, flat houses that edged the square were perfectly still. She felt Betty shiver, and shivered herself. But they didn't get up. Betty drew in her collar and folded her arms. She said, again, 'You could talk to Reggie.'

'No,' said Viv. 'I'm not going to tell him.'

'Why not? It's his, isn't it?'

'Of course it is!'

'Well, I'm only asking.'

'What a thing to say!'

'You ought to tell him, though. I'm not being funny, Viv, but the fact is, well, him being a married man . . . He ought to have an idea of what you could do.'

'He won't have a clue,' said Viv. 'His wife – she's kid-crazy. It's all she wants him for. What he gets from me, it's different.'

'I'll bet it is.'

'It is!'

'Well, not in nine months' time it won't be. Eight months' time, I mean.'

'That's why I've got to fix it by myself,' said Viv. 'Don't you see? If it turns out that, after all, I'm just like her—'

'And you really want to fix it? You couldn't— Well, you couldn't have it, and keep it, or—?'

'Are you kidding?' said Viv. 'My father— It would kill my father!'

It would kill him, she meant, *after everything with Duncan*. She couldn't say that, however, to Betty; and suddenly the burden of so many secrets, so much caution and darkness and care, seemed unbearable. 'Oh!' she said. 'It's so bloody unfair!

Why does it have to be like this, Betty? As if things weren't hard enough already! Then this comes along, to make things harder. It's such a little thing—'

'I hate to break this to you, kid,' said Betty, 'but it won't be little for long.'

Viv looked at her, through the darkness. She folded her arms across her stomach. 'That's what I can't bear,' she said quietly, 'the thought of it inside me, getting bigger and bigger.' She seemed, all at once, to be able to feel it, sucking at her like a leech. She said, 'What's it like? It's like a fat little worm, isn't it?'

'A fat little worm,' answered Betty, 'with Reggie's face.'

'Don't say things like that! If I start thinking about it like that, it'll make it worse. I've got to try the pills that Felicity Withers tried.'

'But they didn't work for her. That's why she chucked herself down the stairs! And didn't they make her sick?'

'Well, I feel sick anyway! What's the difference?'

She didn't exactly feel sick now, however. She felt agitated, almost feverish. It seemed to her, suddenly, that she'd been living in a kind of trance. She couldn't believe it. She thought of the days and days that had slipped by, while she'd done nothing. She sat up straighter and looked around.

'I need a chemist's shop,' she said. 'Where can I find that kind of chemist's? Betty, come on.'

'Hang on,' said Betty. She'd opened her bag. 'Hell,

you can't just drop this sort of thing on a girl, and then expect her to— Let me just have a cigarette.'

'A cigarette?' repeated Viv. 'How can you be thinking about a cigarette?'

'Calm down,' said Betty.

Viv pushed her. 'I can't calm down! Do you think you'd be able to calm down, if you were me?'

But all at once she felt exhausted. She slumped back again, and closed her eyes. When she looked up, she found Betty watching her. Her expression, in the darkness, was hard to read. There might have been pity in it, or fascination; even a touch of scorn.

'What are you thinking?' Viv asked quietly. 'You're thinking I'm soft, aren't you? Like we said Felicity Withers was.'

Betty shrugged. 'Any girl can get caught out.'

'You never have.'

'God!' Betty took off her glove and tapped like mad at the bench. 'Touch wood, can't you? That's all it is, after all: just luck, good luck and bad . . .' She fished about in her bag again, looking for her lighter. 'I still say, anyway, that you should tell Reggie. What's the point of going with a married man, if you can't tell him things like this?'

'No,' said Viv, almost soundlessly. They'd gone back to speaking in murmurs. 'I'll try the pills first; and if they don't work, I'll tell him then. And then, if they do, he'll be none the wiser.'

'Unlike you, hopefully.'

'You *do* think I'm soft.'

'All I'm saying is, if he had worn his raincoat—'

'He doesn't like it!'

'That's too bad. You can't muck about, Viv, when you're a chap in Reggie's shoes. If he was a single boy it would be different, you could take chances; the worst thing would be, you'd end up married sooner than you meant.'

'You're making it sound,' said Viv miserably, 'like it's something you think about, something you plan – like buying a bedroom suite! You know how we feel about each other. It's like you said just now, about touching wood. He's only married to another girl through rotten luck, through bad timing. Some things just can't be helped, that's all; it's just how they are.'

'And it'll go on being just how things are, for years and years,' said Betty. 'And he'll be grand, thank you very much; and how will you be?'

'You can't think like that,' said Viv. 'Nobody thinks like that! We might all be dead tomorrow. You have to take what you want, don't you? What you really want? You don't know what it's like. There isn't anything else for me, except Reggie. If I didn't have him—' Her voice thickened. She took out her handkerchief and blew her nose. 'He makes me happy,' she said, after a minute. 'You know he does. He makes me laugh.'

Betty finally found her lighter. 'Well,' she said, as she struck it, 'you're not laughing now.'

Viv watched the spurting up of the flame; she blinked against the plunge back into darkness, and didn't answer. She and Betty sat almost without speaking until it grew too cold to sit any longer; then they linked arms, wearily, and stood.

They had just moved off across the garden when they heard the sirens go. Betty said, 'There you are. That'd put an end to all your problems – a nice fat bomb.'

Viv looked up. 'God, it would. And no one would know, except for you.'

She'd never thought of that before, about all the secrets that the war must have swallowed up, left buried in dust and darkness and silence. She had only ever thought of the raids as tearing things open, making things hard. She kept glancing up at the sky as she and Betty walked to John Allen House, telling herself that she wanted to see the searchlights go up; that she wanted the planes to come, the guns to start, all hell to break loose . . .

But when the first of the guns began to pound, up in north London somewhere, she grew tense, and made Betty walk faster – afraid of the bombing, even in her wretchedness; afraid of getting hurt; not wanting to die, after all.

'Hey, Jerry!' Giggs was calling out of his window, two hours later. *'Hey, Fritz! This way! This fucking way!'*

'Shut up, Giggs, you gobshite!' called someone else. *'This way, Jerry! Over here!'*

Giggs had heard of a prison being bombed, and all the men with less than six months left to serve in it being released; he only had four and a half still to do, and so, every time a raid started up, he'd drag his table across his cell, climb up on to it, and call to the German pilots out of his window. If the raid was a bad one, Duncan found, the shouts could really unsettle you: you began to picture Giggs as something like a great big magnet, sucking bullets and bombs and areoplanes out of the sky. Tonight, however, the raid seemed distant, and no one was much bothered by it. The thuds and flashes were occasional, and soft; the darkness thickened and thinned slightly, that was all, as searchlights swept over the sky. Other men had got up on to their tables and were calling to each other, about ordinary things, across Giggs's shouts.

'*Woolly! Woolly, you owe me half a dollar, you git!*'

'*Mick! Hey, Mick! What are you doing?*'

There wasn't an officer to make them be silent. The officers went straight down into their shelter as soon as a raid started up.

'*You owe me—!*'

'*Mick! Hey, Mick!*'

The men had to shout themselves almost hoarse, in order to be heard; someone might call from a window at one end of the hall, and be answered by a man fifty cells away. Lying in bed and hearing them yell was like going through the wireless, finding stations in the dark. Duncan almost liked it; he found, at least, that he could filter the voices out when they began to get on his nerves. Fraser, on the other hand, was driven mad by them, every time. Now, for example, he was moving restlessly about,

381

grumbling and cursing. He raised himself up, and punched out the lumps of horsehair in his mattress. He plucked at the bits of uniform he'd laid on his blanket for extra warmth. Duncan couldn't see him, because the cell was too dark; but he could feel the movement of him through the frame of the bunks. When he lay heavily back down, the bunks rocked from side to side, and creaked and squealed slightly, like bunks in a ship. *We might be sailors*, Duncan thought.

'*You owe me half a dollar, you cunt!*'

'God!' said Fraser, raising himself again and punching the mattress more violently. 'Why can't they be quiet? *Shut up!*' he shouted, slapping the wall.

'It's no good,' said Duncan, yawning. 'They won't be able to hear you. Now they're after Stella, listen.'

For someone had begun calling out: '*Ste-lla! Ste-lla!*' Duncan thought it was a boy named Pacey, down on the Twos. '*Ste-lla! I've got something to tell you . . . I saw your twat, in the bath-house! I saw your twat! It was black as my hat!*'

Another man whistled and laughed. '*You're a fucking poet, Pacey!*'

'*It looked like a fucking black rat with its throat cut! It looked like your old man's beard, with your old girl's fat fucking lips in the middle! Ste-lla! Why don't you answer?*'

'*She can't answer,*' came another voice. '*She's got her gob on Mr Chase!*'

'*She's got her gob round Chase,*' said someone else,

'*and Browning is slipping her a length from the back. She's got her fucking hands full, boys!*'

'*Shut up, you naughty things!*' cried a new voice. It was Monica, on the Threes.

Pacey started on her, then. '*Moni-ca! Moni-ca!*'

'*Shut up, you beasts! Can't a girl get her beauty sleep?*'

This was followed by the *crump!* of a distant explosion and, '*Jerry!*' Giggs called again. '*Fritz! Adolf! This way!*'

Fraser groaned and turned his pillow. Then, 'Hell!' he said. 'That's all we need!'

For on top of everything else, somebody had started singing.

'*Little girl in blue, I've been dreaming of you . . . Little girl in blue . . .*'

It was a man called Miller. He was in for running some sort of racket from a nightclub. He sang all the time, with horrible sincerity, as if crooning into a microphone at the front of a band. At the sound of his voice now, men up and down the hall began to complain.

'*Turn it off!*'

'*Miller, you bastard!*'

Duncan's neighbour, Quigley, began to beat with something – his salt-pot, probably – on the floor of his cell. '*Shut up*,' he roared as he did it, '*you fucking slags! Miller, you cunt!*'

'*I've been dreaming of you . . .*'

Miller sang on, through all the complaints, through all the distant roar of the raid; and the worst of it was, the song was tuneful. One by one, the men fell silent, as if they were listening. Even Quigley, after a while, threw down his salt-pot and stopped roaring.

> *I hear your voice, I reach to hold you,*
> *Your lips touch mine, my arms enfold you.*
> *But then you're gone: I wake and find*
> *That I've been drea-ming . . .*

Fraser, too, had grown still. He'd lifted his head, the better to hear. 'Hell, Pearce,' he said now. 'I think I danced to this tune once. I'm sure I did.' He lay back down. 'I probably laughed at the bloody thing, then. Now— Now it seems stinkingly apt, doesn't it? Christ! Trust Miller and a popular song to be so honest about longing.'

Duncan said nothing. The song went on.

> *Though we're apart, I can't forget you.*
> *I bless the hour that I first met you—*

Abruptly, another voice broke across it. This one was deep, tuneless, lusty.

> *Give me a girl with eyes of blue,*
> *Who likes it if you don't but prefers it if you do!*

Someone cheered. Fraser said, in a tone of disbelief, 'Who the hell is that, now?'

Duncan tilted his head, to listen. 'I don't know. Maybe Atkin?'

Atkin, like Giggs, was a deserter. The song sounded like something a serviceman would sing.

Give me a girl with eyes of black,
Who likes it on her belly but prefers it on her back!

'Cause I'll be seeing you again, when you—

Miller was still going. For almost a minute the two songs ran bizarrely together; then Miller gave in. His voice trailed away. '*You wanker!*' he yelled. There were more cheers. Atkin's voice – or whosever it was – grew louder, lustier. He must have been cupping his hands around his mouth and bellowing like a bull.

Give me a girl with hair of brown,
Who likes it going up but prefers it coming down!
Give me a girl with hair of red,
Who likes it in the hand but prefers it in the bed!
Give me a—

But then the 'Raiders Past' siren started up. Atkin turned his song into a whoop. Men on every landing joined in, drumming with their fists on their walls, their window-frames, their beds. Only Giggs was disappointed.

'*Come back, you gobshites!*' he called, hoarsely. '*Come back, you German cunts! You forgot D Hall! You forgot D Hall!*'

'*Get down out of those fucking windows!*' roared

385

someone out in the yard, and there was the rapid *crunch, crunch* of boots on cinders, as the officers emerged from their shelter and started heading towards the prison. From all along the hall, then, there came the thump and scrape of tables: the men were leaping down from their windows, hurling themselves back into their bunks. In another minute, the electric lights were switched on. Mr Browning and Mr Chase came pounding up the stairs and started racing down the landings, hammering on doors, flinging open spy-holes: *'Pacey! Wright! Malone, you little shit— If I catch any of you fuckers out of your beds, the whole lot of you'll be banged up from now till Christmas, do you hear?'*

Fraser turned his face into his pillow, groaning and cursing against the light. Duncan drew up his blanket over his eyes. Their door was thumped, but the racing footsteps went past. They faded for a moment; stopped; grew loud, then faded again. Duncan had a sense of Mr Browning and Mr Chase turning snarling about, thwarted and furious, like dogs on chains. *'You shit-cakes!'* one of them cried, for show. *'I'm warning you—!'*

They paced back and forth along the landings for another minute or two; eventually, however, they tramped down the stairs. In another moment, with a little *phut*, the lights in the cells were switched off again.

Duncan quickly put down his blanket and moved his head to the edge of his pillow. He liked the moment when the current was cut. He liked to see the bulb in the ceiling. For the light faded slowly, and for three or four seconds, if you watched for it, you could make out the filament inside the glass, a curl of wire that turned from white to furious amber, to burning red, to delicate pink; and then, when the cell was dark, you could still see the yellow blur of it inside your eye.

A man gave a whistle, quietly. Someone shouted to Atkin. He wanted Atkin to carry on singing. He wanted to know about the girl whose hair was yellow – what did she like? What about her? He called it twice, three times; but Atkin wouldn't answer. The matey, mischievous feeling that had gripped them all, ten minutes before, was losing its hold. The silence was deepening, growing daunting, and to try to break into it, now, was to make it seem worse. For after all, thought Duncan, you could sing or bellow as much as you liked; it was only a way of putting off this moment – this moment that always, finally, came – when the loneliness of the prison night rose up about you, like water in a sinking boat.

He could still hear the words of the songs, however – just as he'd still been able to see the glowing filament in the bulb against the darkness of his own eyelids. *Give me a girl*, he could hear in his head. *Give me a girl*, and *I'll be seeing you*, over and over.

Perhaps Fraser could hear it, too. He changed his pose, rolled on to his back, kept fidgeting. Now that the place was so quiet, when he passed his hand across the stubble on his chin – when he rubbed

his eye, even, with his knuckle – Duncan heard it . . .
He blew out his breath.

'Damn,' he said, very softly. 'I wish I had a girl,
Pearce, right now. Just an ordinary girl. Not the kind
of girls I used to meet – the brainy types.' He
laughed, and the frame of the bunks gave a shiver.
'God,' he said, 'isn't that a phrase to freeze a man's
blood? "A brainy girl".' He put on a voice. ' "You'd
like my friend, she's ever so brainy." As if that's what
one wants them for . . .' He laughed again – a sort
of snigger, this time, too low to make the bed-frame
jump. 'Yes,' he said, 'just an ordinary little girl is
what I'd like right now. She wouldn't have to be
pretty. Sometimes the pretty ones are no good – do
you know what I mean? They think too much of
themselves; they don't want to mess their hair up,
smudge their lips. I wish I had a plain, stout, stupid
girl. A plain, stout, stupid, grateful girl. Do you know
what I'd do with her, Pearce?'

He wasn't talking to Duncan, really; he was talking
to the darkness, to himself. He might have been
murmuring in his sleep. But the effect was more
intimate, somehow, than if he'd been whispering
into Duncan's ear. Duncan opened his eyes and
gazed into the perfect, velvety blackness of the cell.
There was a depthlessness to it that was so queer
and unnerving, he put up his hand. He wanted to
remind himself of the distance between his and
Fraser's bunk: he'd begun to feel as though Fraser
was nearer than he ought to have been; and he was
very aware of his own body as a sort of duplication

or echo of the one above . . . When his fingers found the criss-crossed wire underside of Fraser's bed, he kept them there. He said, 'Don't think about it. Go to sleep.'

'No, but seriously,' Fraser went on, 'do you know what I'd do? I'd have her, fully clothed. I wouldn't take off a stitch. I'd only loosen a button or two at the back of her dress – and I'd undo her brassière, while I was about it – and then I'd draw the dress and the brassière down to her elbows and get my fingers on to her chest. I'd give her a pinch. I might pull her about a bit – there wouldn't be a thing she could do if I did, for the dress – do you see? – the dress would be pinning her arms to her sides . . . And when I'd finished with her chest, I'd push up her skirt. I'd push it right up to her waist. I'd keep the knickers on her, but they'd be that silky, flimsy kind that you can work your way about, work your way up . . .' The words tailed away. When he spoke again, his voice had changed, was bare and not at all boastful. 'I had a girl like that, once. I've never forgotten it. She wasn't a beauty.'

He fell silent. Then, 'Damn,' he said softly again. 'Damn, damn.' And he moved about, so that the wires supporting his mattress flexed and tightened, and Duncan quickly drew back his fingers. He had rolled on to his side, Duncan thought; but though he lay still, there was a tension to him – something charged and furtive, as if he might be holding his breath, calculating. And when he moved again, to draw up the blanket, the movement seemed false,

389

seemed stagey: as if it was being made, elaborately, to conceal another, more secret . . .

He had put his hand, Duncan knew, to his cock; and after another moment he began, with a subtle, even motion, to stroke it.

It was a thing men did all the time, in prison. They made a joke of it, a sport of it, a boast of it; Duncan had once shared a cell with a boy who had done it, not even at night, with a blanket to cover him, but during the day, obscenely. He had learned to turn his head from it, just as he'd learned to turn his head from the sight and sound and smell of other men belching, farting, pissing, shitting into pots. Now, however, in the utter darkness of the cell, and in the queer, uneasy atmosphere raised by Miller's and Atkin's singing, he found himself horribly aware of the stealthy, helpless, purposeful, half-ashamed motion of Fraser's hand. For a moment or two he kept quite still, not wanting to betray the fact that he was awake. Then he found that his stillness only made his senses more acute: he could hear the slight thickening, now, of Fraser's breath; he could smell him as he sweated; he could even catch, he thought, the faint, wet, regular sound – like a ticking watch – of the tip of Fraser's cock being rhythmically uncovered . . . He couldn't help it. He felt his own cock give a twitch and begin to grow hard. He lay another minute, perfectly still save for that gathering and tightening of flesh between his legs; then he made the same sort of stealthy, stagey movements that Fraser had: pulled

390

up the blanket over himself, slid his hand into his pyjamas, and took the base of his cock in his fist.

But his other hand, he raised. He found the wires of Fraser's bed again and just touched them with his knuckles, lightly at first; then he caught the tension in them, the hectic little jolts and quivers they were giving in response to the regular jog-jog-jog of Fraser's fist. He worked one of his fingers about them – clinging to them, almost, with the tip of that one finger; bracing himself against them, as he tugged with his other hand at his cock.

He was aware, after a minute or so of this, of Fraser giving a shudder, and of the wires beneath his mattress growing still; but he couldn't have stopped his own hand, then, for anything, and a moment later his own spunk rushed: he felt the travelling and bursting of it as if it were hot and scalded him. He thought he made a sound, as it came; it might just have been the roaring of the blood through his ears . . . But when the roaring died, there was only the silence: the awful, aba-shing stillness of the prison night. It was like emerging from some sort of fit, a spell of madness; he thought of what he'd just done and imagined himself pounding, gasping, plucking at Fraser's bunk like some kind of beast.

Only after a minute did Fraser move. There was the rustle of bedclothes, and Duncan guessed he was wiping spunk from himself with his sheet. But the rustling went on, the movement became tense, almost savage; finally, Fraser struck his pillow.

'Damn this place,' he said, as he did it, 'for turning us all into schoolboys! Do you hear me, Pearce? I suppose you liked that. Did you, Pearce? Hey?'

'No,' said Duncan at last – but his mouth was dry, and his tongue caught against his palate. The word came out as a sort of whisper.

Then he flinched. The bed-frame had rocked, and something warm and light had struck him, in the face. He put up his hand, and felt a sticky kind of wetness on his cheek. Fraser must have leant over the edge of the bunk and flicked spunk at him.

'You liked it all right,' said Fraser bitterly. His voice was close, for a moment. Then he moved back beneath his blanket. 'You liked it all right, you blasted bugger.'

CHAPTER 4

'Goodness,' said Helen, opening her eyes. 'What's this?'

'Happy birthday, darling,' said Kay, putting down a tray at the side of the bed, and leaning to kiss her.

Helen's face was dry and warm and smooth, quite beautiful; her hair had frizzed up a little, like a sleepy child's. She lay for a moment, blinking, then pushed herself higher in the bed and drew up the pillow to the small of her back. She did it clumsily, still not quite awake; and when she yawned, she put her hands to her face and worked her fingers into the corners of her eyes, to remove the crumbs of sleep from them. Her eyes were slightly puffed.

'You don't mind that I've woken you?' asked Kay. It was a Saturday, still early, and she had worked the night before; but she'd been up for an hour and was already dressed, in a pair of tailored slacks and a jersey. 'I couldn't bear to wait any longer. Look, here.'

She brought the tray to Helen's lap. There was a spray of paper flowers in a vase, china pots and cups, an upturned bowl on a plate; and the pink box, with the silk bow, containing the satin pyjamas.

Helen went from item to item, politely, slightly self-conscious. 'What beautiful flowers. What a lovely box!' She looked as though she was struggling to wake up, be charmed and excited. *I should have let her sleep*, Kay thought.

But then she lifted the lids of the china pots. 'Jam,' she said, 'and *coffee*!' That was better. 'Oh, Kay!'

'It's real coffee,' said Kay. 'And, look here.'

She nudged the upturned bowl, and Helen picked it up. Underneath, on a paper doily, was an orange. Kay had worked on it for half an hour with the point of a vegetable knife, carving HAPPY BIRTHDAY into the peel.

Helen smiled properly, her dry lips parting over her small white teeth. 'It's wonderful.'

'The R's a bit ropey.'

'Not at all.' She took the orange up and held it to her nose. 'Where did you get it?'

'Oh,' said Kay vaguely. 'I coshed a small child for it, in the black-out.' She poured out coffee. 'Open your gift.'

'In a minute,' said Helen. 'I must pee first. Hold the tray, will you?'

She kicked off the blankets and ran to the bath-room. Kay drew the bed-covers back up so that the mattress should stay warm. Heat rose from the bed, even as she did it – rose palpably, against her face, like steam or smoke. She sat with the tray on her

lap, and rearranged the flowers, admired the orange
– fretting, slightly, over that crooked R.

'What a fright I looked!' said Helen, laughing,
coming back. 'Like Struwwelpeter.' She had washed
her face and brushed her teeth and tried to
calm her cloud of hair.

'Don't be silly,' said Kay. 'Come here.' She put
out her hand; Helen took it, and let herself be
drawn into a kiss. Her mouth was chill, from the
cold water.

She got back into bed, and Kay sat beside her.
They drank the coffee, ate toast and jam.

'Have your orange,' said Kay.

Helen turned it in her hands. 'Shall I? It seems
a shame. I ought to keep it.'

'What for? Go on.'

So Helen broke the skin, and peeled the orange,
and divided it into pigs. Kay took one, but said that
she must eat the rest herself. The fruit was slightly
sour, and dry – the segments tore too easily. But
the sensation of them yielding up their juice upon
the tongue was glorious.

'Now open your present,' said Kay impatiently,
when the orange was finished.

Helen bit her lip. 'I hardly dare. Such a beautiful
box!' She picked it up, self-conscious again. She
held it beside her ear, and playfully shook it. When
she began, very gingerly, to ease off the lid, Kay
laughed at her.

'Just pull it right off!'

'I don't want to spoil it.'

'It doesn't matter.'

'No,' said Helen. 'It's too pretty. – Oh!' She looked startled. She'd removed the lid at last and, the box being tilted against her knees, the folds of paper inside had parted and the pyjama-suit, like quick-silver, had come tumbling fluidly out. She gazed at it for a moment without moving; then, as if reluctantly, she caught hold of the jacket and lifted it up. 'Oh, Kay.'

'Do you like it?'

'It's beautiful. Too beautiful! It must have cost a fortune! Where ever did you get it?'

Kay smiled and wouldn't answer. She took a sleeve of the jacket and held it up. 'Do you see the buttons?'

'Yes.'

'They're bone. Here on the sleeve, too.'

Helen held the satin to her face, and closed her eyes.

'The colour suits you,' said Kay. And then, when Helen didn't answer: 'You do like it, really?'

'Darling, of course. But— I don't deserve it.'

'Don't deserve it? What are you talking about?'

Helen shook her head and laughed, opening her eyes. 'Nothing. I'm being silly, that's all.'

Kay took away the tray, the cups and plates and paper. 'Try it on,' she said.

'I oughtn't to. Not without bathing first.'

'Oh, rubbish. Put it on. I want to see you in it!'

So Helen got slowly out of bed, drew off her threadbare nightdress, stepped into the pyjama trousers and buttoned on the top. The trousers were fastened with a linen cord. The jacket tied at the waist: it was full like a blouse but, the satin being heavy, it showed very clearly the swell of her breasts, the tips of her nipples. The sleeves were long: she buttoned the cuffs and folded them back, but they slid out of the folds at once and fell almost to her fingertips. She stood, as if shyly, for Kay to look her over.

Kay whistled. 'How glamorous you look! Just like Greta Garbo in *Grand Hotel*.'

She didn't look glamorous really, however; she looked young, and small, and rather solemn. The room was cold, and the satin chill; she shivered and blew on her hands. She worked again at folding back the sleeves, almost fretfully – gazing once, as she did it, into the mirror, and then turning quickly away.

Kay watched her, with a sort of ache about her heart. She felt her love, at moments like this, as a thing of wonder – it was wonderful to her, that Helen, who was so lovely, so fair and unmarked, should be here at all, to be looked at and touched . . . Then again, it was impossible to imagine her in any other place, with any other lover. No other lover, Kay knew, would feel about her quite as Kay did. She might have been born, been a child, grown up – done all the particular, serious and inconsequential things she'd done – just so she could arrive at this point, now; just so she could stand, barefoot, in a satin pyjama-suit, and Kay could watch her.

But then she moved away from the mirror.

'Don't go,' said Kay.

'Just to start my bath off.'

'No,' said Kay. 'Not yet.'

She got off the bed and crossed the room and took Helen in her arms. She ran her fingers over her face, and kissed her lips. She slid her hands beneath the satin jacket to touch the smooth, warm flesh of her back and waist. Then she moved behind her and held her breasts, taking the weight of them against her palms. She felt the swell of Helen's buttocks, the sliding of the skin of her plump thighs inside the satin. She put her cheek against Helen's ear.

'You're beautiful.'

'No,' said Helen.

Kay turned her to face the mirror. 'Can't you see yourself? You're lovely. I knew you were, the first time I saw you. I held your face in my hand. You were smooth, like a pearl.'

Helen closed her eyes. 'I know,' she said.

They kissed again. The kiss went on. But then Helen drew away. 'I have to pee again,' she said. 'I'm sorry, Kay. And I really should bathe.'

The satin made her slippery: she moved from Kay's grasp, turning her head and laughing, playful but determined, like a nymph eluding a satyr. She went back to the bathroom and closed the door. There was the rush of the faucets, the whoosh of flame in the water-heater; and then, in a minute or so, the rub of her heels against the enamel of the tub.

Kay took the coffee-pot to the sitting-room fire and put it close to the grate. She went back to the bedroom, cleared away the tray, made up the bed, folded the torn tissue paper. The flowers she set, in their vase, on the sitting-room table, beside the cards that Helen had already received, by yesterday's post, from her family in Worthing. She moved a chair. Where the chair had stood she saw a sprinkling of crumbs. She got a brush and a pan from the kitchen, and swept them up.

Kay had lived in this flat for almost seven years. She'd got it from a woman she'd once been lovers with, a woman who'd worked here, more or less – though Kay had never told Helen this – as a prostitute. Kay's life had been rather chaotic in those days. She'd had too much money; she'd drunk too much; she'd careered from one unhappy love-affair to another . . . The woman had taken up with a businessman in the end, and moved to Mayfair; but she'd given Kay the flat as a parting gift.

Kay liked it here more than anywhere she'd ever lived. The flat's rooms were L-shaped; she liked those. She liked, too, the funny little mews or yard that the flat overlooked. The warehouse next door served some of the furniture stores on the Tottenham Court Road; before the war, Kay had been able to stand at her window and watch young men and women in the workshops painting swags and cupids on lovely old tables and chairs. Now the workshops had been closed down. The warehouse was used for holding utility furniture for the Board of Trade. The fact of there being so much wood there, and so much varnish and paint, made the mews a dreadfully unsafe place. But when Kay thought of moving, her heart sank. She felt about the flat rather as she felt about Helen: that it was secret, special, hers.

She checked the warmth of the coffee in its pot. On the mantelpiece was a box of cigarettes; that made her think of the case in her pocket. She took it out, and started to fill it. Presently she heard Helen come out of the bathroom and begin the business of getting dressed. She called to her, across the hall. 'What shall we do today, Helen? What would you like to do?'

'I don't know,' answered Helen.

'I might take you to a smart restaurant for lunch. How about that?'

'You've spent too much on me already!'

'Oh, balls to that! as Binkie might say. Wouldn't you like a fancy luncheon?'

There was no reply. Kay shut the cigarette case and put it back in her pocket. She poured more coffee into Helen's cup and took it through to the bedroom. Helen was dressed in her bra, her petticoat and stockings. She was combing her hair – combing it carefully, trying to turn the curls into waves. The pyjama-suit lay on the bed, very neatly folded.

Kay set the cup down on the dressing-table. 'Helen,' she said.

'Yes, darling?'

'You seem awfully distracted. Isn't there anywhere

you'd like to go? Not Windsor Castle, somewhere like that? The Zoo?'

'The Zoo?' said Helen, laughing, but also frowning. 'My goodness, I feel like a child being offered a day out by its aunt.'

'Well, that's how one's supposed to feel on one's birthday. And you did, you know, mention Windsor Castle – and the Zoo – when we talked about this last week.'

'I know I did,' said Helen. 'I'm sorry, Kay. But Windsor – oh, won't it take an age to get there? Won't the trains be awful?' She had gone to the wardrobe and was looking through her dresses. 'You'll have to be home for work at seven.'

'We have ages till seven,' said Kay. Then she saw the dress that Helen was taking from its hanger. 'That one?' she said.

'Don't you like it?'

'It's your birthday. Wear the Cedric Allen one. I like that one more.'

Helen looked doubtful. 'It's awfully smart.' But she put the first dress back and drew out another, a dark blue dress with cream lapels. It had cost two pounds, two years before; Kay had bought it, of course. Kay had bought most of Helen's things, especially in those days. A section of the hem was slightly puckered, where it had got worn and had to be darned; but apart from that, it looked almost new. Helen shook it open and stepped inside it.

Kay held out her hands. 'Come here,' she said, 'and I'll hook you up.'

So Helen came to her and turned her back, and lifted up her hair. Kay settled the dress more smoothly on her shoulders, drew close its panels and, starting at the bottom, began to fasten together its hooks. She did it slowly. She'd always liked the sight and the feel of a woman's back. She liked, for example, the look of an evening dress on naked shoulders – the tautness of it – the way, when the shoulder-blades were drawn together, it gaped, giving you a glimpse of the underclothes or the pink, pressed flesh behind . . . Helen's back was firm – not muscular, but plump, resilient. Her neck was handsome, with a down of fair hair. When Kay had closed the final hook and eye she bent her head and kissed it. Then she put her arms around Helen's waist, laid her hands upon her stomach and pulled her closer.

Helen moved her cheek against Kay's jaw. 'I thought you wanted to go out.'

'But you look so lovely in your dress.'

'Perhaps I ought to take it off, if you feel like that about it.'

'Perhaps I ought to take it off for you.'

Helen pulled away. 'Be sensible, Kay.'

Kay laughed and let her go. 'All right . . . Now, how about the Zoo?'

Helen had gone back to the dressing-table and was screwing on earrings. 'The Zoo,' she said, frowning again. 'Well, perhaps. But won't it look funny? Two women, our age?'

'Does that matter?'

'No,' said Helen, after a moment, 'I suppose not.'

She sat and drew on her shoes, bending her head, so that her hair fell before her face. 'You don't,' she added lightly, as Kay was turning from the room, 'want to ask other people?'

'Other people?' asked Kay, surprised, turning back. 'You mean, like Mickey?'

'Yes,' said Helen, after a second. Then, 'No, it was just a thought.'

'Would you like to call in on Mickey, on the way?'

'No. It's all right, really.' She straightened up, laughing at herself, her face quite pink from the effort of leaning forward and reaching to tie her laces.

They didn't go to the Zoo, in the end. Helen said she didn't, after all, like the idea of looking at so many poor little creatures in their cages and pens. They began to walk, and saw a bus marked up for Hampstead; and ran to catch that, instead. They got off at the High Street, and had a lunch of sardines and chips in a little café; they looked in a couple of second-hand bookshops, then made their way, through the handsome, higgledy-piggledy, red-brick streets, to the Heath. They walked arm in arm – Helen not minding the fact that they were two women, now, for one expected to see women, she said, on a Saturday afternoon on Hampstead Heath; it was a place for plain, brisk women, spinsters, and dogs.

Actually, there were many young couples about.

One or two of the girls wore trousers, like Kay; most were in service uniforms, or in the glamourless austere get-ups that passed, these days, for weekend best. The boys were in battledress: khaki and navy blue and every shade between – the uniforms of Poland, Norway, Canada, Australia, France.

The day was cold. The sky was so white it hurt the eye. Kay and Helen hadn't come to the Heath since the summer before last, when they'd gone bathing in the Ladies' pond; they remembered it as lush, green, lovely. But now the trees were utterly bare, revealing, here and there, the brutal, barbed-wired flanks of anti-aircraft batteries and military gear. The leaves that had fallen months before had turned to mulch, and the mulch had a rime of frost on it: it looked unhealthy, like rotting fruit. Much of the ground had been marked by shrapnel, or torn by the tyres of trucks; and in the west there were enormous canyons and pits where earth had been dug, at various points, for filling sandbags.

They tried to keep away from the worst of it, going more or less aimlessly, but following the more secluded routes. At the junction of two broad paths they turned north; the path led them up, then down through a wood, and they emerged, in another few minutes, at a lake. The water was frozen, right across. A dozen or so ducks were huddled together, like refugees, on an island of twigs.

'Poor things,' said Helen, squeezing Kay's arm. 'I wish we'd brought bread.'

They went closer to the water. The ice was thin,

but must have been strong, for it was littered with sticks and stones that people had thrown in an effort to break it. Kay bared her hands – for she was dressed against the cold, in gloves and a belted coat, a scarf and a beret – and picked up a stone of her own, and tossed it, just for the pleasure of seeing it skitter. Then she went right to the lake's edge and pressed at the ice with the toe of her shoe. A couple of children came to watch her: she showed them the silvery pockets of air that bulged beneath the ice's surface, then squatted and prised at the ice with her hands, bringing up great jagged sheets, which she broke into smaller pieces for the children to hold, and fling, or stamp on with their heels. When the ice was crushed, it became white powder – exactly the powder of broken glass at a bomb site.

Helen was standing where Kay had left her, watching. She'd kept her gloved hands in her pockets; the collar of her coat was turned up, and she was wearing a loose wool hat, like a tam-o'-shanter, pulled down low over her brow. Her expression was a queer one – a smile that was soft, but also troubled. Kay fished out a last piece of ice for the children and went back to her.

'What's up?' she asked.

Helen shook her head, and smiled properly. 'Nothing. I was enjoying looking at you. You looked like a boy.'

Kay was banging her hands together, to knock the chill and the dirt from them. She said, 'Ice turns everyone into boys, doesn't it? The lake at home, when I was a kid, used to freeze sometimes. It was much bigger than this. Or maybe it only seemed big to me, then. Tommy, Gerald and I used to go out on it. My poor mother! She used to hate it, she used to think we'd all be drowned. I didn't understand. All the boys she knew, of course, were getting killed, one after another . . . Are you cold?'

Helen had shivered. She nodded. 'A bit.'

Kay looked around. 'There's a milk-bar here somewhere. We could get a cup of tea. Would you like that?'

'Yes, perhaps.'

'You ought to have a cake or a bun, too, on your birthday. Don't you think?'

Helen wrinkled up her nose. 'I'm not sure I want one, really. It's sure to be awful, whatever we get.'

'Oh,' said Kay, 'but you must.'

She thought she knew where the milk-bar was. She put her arm through Helen's and drew her close and led her along a new path; they walked for another twenty minutes, however, without finding anything. So then they went back to the frozen lake, and tried another path. Then, 'There it is!' said Kay.

But when they drew close to the building they saw that it was half burnt-out, the window-frames glassless, the curtains in ribbons, the brickwork black. A notice on the door said, *Blitzed Last Saturday.* Underneath it someone had fixed a sad-looking paper Union Jack, the kind that had once, before the war, been stuck on sand-castles.

'Damn,' said Kay.

Helen said, 'It's all right. I didn't really want anything.'

'There's sure to be somewhere else.'

'If I have tea, it'll only make me need the lavatory.'

Kay laughed. 'Darling, you'll need the lavatory, whatever you do. And, it's your birthday. You ought to have a cake.'

'I'm too old for cakes!' said Helen, with a touch of impatience. She took out a handkerchief and blew her nose. 'God, it's cold! Let's keep walking.'

She was smiling again; but seemed distant to Kay, distracted. Perhaps it was only the weather. It was hard to be cheerful, of course, when it was as cold as this.

Kay lit them both cigarettes. They went back yet again to the lake, and up through the wood – going more quickly, to try and get warm.

The path, from this angle, began to look more familiar to Kay. She remembered, suddenly, an afternoon she'd spent here in the past . . . She said, without thinking, 'You know, I believe I came this way once, with Julia.'

'With Julia?' asked Helen. 'When was that?'

She spoke with a try at lightness; but self-consciously, too. Kay thought: *Bugger*. She said, 'Oh, years ago, I don't know. I remember a bridge, something like that.'

'What sort of bridge?'

'Just a bridge. A funny little bridge, quite rococo, overlooking a pond.'

'Where was it?'

'I thought it was this way, but now I'm not sure. It's the sort of thing, I expect, like Shangri-La, that you can only find by not really meaning to look for.'

She wished she'd said nothing. Helen, she thought, was pretending an interest in the bridge – overdoing it slightly, to make up for the awkwardness that had been conjured by the saying of Julia's name. They walked on. Kay tried one way, half-heartedly, and then another; she was about to give it up when the path they were walking on suddenly opened up and they found themselves in exactly the place she'd been looking for.

The bridge wasn't nearly as charming as she'd recalled; it was plainer, not rococo at all. But Helen went at once to the side of it and stood gazing down at the pond beneath, as if enchanted.

'I can see Julia here,' she said, smiling, when Kay joined her.

'Can you?' asked Kay.

She didn't want to think of Julia, especially. She stood for a second, looking down at the new pond; it was iced and littered like the other one, and had its own straggling band of refugee ducks. But then she turned to Helen and gazed at her profile, at her cheek and throat – which had pinked, at last, with what seemed real excitement and interest; and she caught a glimpse, beyond the turned-up collar of Helen's coat, of the cream lapel beneath it, and beneath that, the smooth, blemishless skin. She remembered standing in the bedroom, fastening up the handsome dress; she remembered the sliding of the silk pyjamas, the feel of the weight of Helen's hot, suspended breasts.

She grew warm with desire all over again. She took Helen's arm and drew her closer. Helen turned, saw her expression, and glanced about in alarm.

'Someone will come,' she said. 'Don't, Kay!'

'Don't what? All I'm doing is looking at you.'

'It's the way you're looking.'

Kay shrugged. 'I might be— Here.' She put her hands to one of Helen's earrings and began to unscrew it. She spoke more softly. 'I might be fixing your earring for you. Say your earring was caught? I'd have to unfasten it like this, wouldn't I? Anyone would do that. I'd have to put back your hair, that would only be natural. I might have to move closer . . .'

As she spoke, she was drawing the ornament from Helen's ear, and smoothing the chill, naked lobe with her fingers.

Helen flinched. 'Someone will come,' she said again.

'Not if we're quick.'

'Don't be silly, Kay.'

But Kay kissed her, anyway; then felt her break almost roughly away. For someone *had* come – a nice-looking woman, walking a dog. She'd appeared on the other side of the bridge, soundlessly, from nowhere.

Kay held up the earring and said, in an ordinary

voice, 'No, it's no good. I'm afraid you'll have to do it.' Helen turned her back to her and stood stiffly, as if absolutely riveted by some little detail in the scene below.

As the woman passed, Kay caught her eye and smiled. The woman smiled back – but smiled uncertainly, Kay thought. She must have glimpsed the end of their embrace, but was doubtful: puzzled and embarrassed. The dog came trotting over and sniffed at Helen's heels. He took ages to go.

'Smuts!' cried the woman, getting redder and redder in the face. 'Smuts! Bad dog!'

'God!' said Helen when they had gone. She tilted her head to put the earring back on, her hands at her jaw, her fingers working furiously at the little screw.

Kay was laughing. 'Oh, so what? It's not the nineteenth bloody century.'

But Helen wouldn't smile. Her mouth was set, almost grim, as she fumbled with the earring. And when Kay made to help her she moved sharply away. Kay gave it up. *What a lot of fuss*, she thought, *about nothing* ... She got out her cigarettes again, and offered the case. Helen shook her head. They went on with unlinked arms, in silence.

They rejoined the path they had come in on and, without debating it, crossed to another, heading south. This led, they saw after a moment, to the crest of Parliament Hill. The slope was gentle at first, but soon grew steep, and Kay glanced at Helen from the corner of her eye, and saw her moving brusquely, breathing hard; she looked as though she might be working herself into a temper, looking for a reason to start complaining, a way of somehow blaming Kay . . . But then they got to the top, and saw the view. Her expression changed, cleared, grew simple and pleased again.

For you could see right across the city from here, to all the landmarks of London; and because of the distance – and because of the smoke from so many chimneys, which hung in the chill, windless air like a net in water – even the patches of rubble and the hollowed-out, roofless buildings had a certain smudgy charm. Four or five barrage balloons were up, seeming to swell, and then to shrink, as they turned and drifted. They were like pigs in a barn-yard, Kay thought. They gave the city a jovial, cosy look.

A few people were taking photographs. 'There's St Paul's Cathedral,' a girl was saying to her American soldier boyfriend. 'There's the Houses of Parliament. There's—'

'Be quiet, will you?' a man said loudly to her. 'There might be spies about.'

The girl shut up.

Helen and Kay stood gazing at the view with everyone else, shading their eyes against the glare of the bleached-out sky. Then, a little way along the path, a bench became free, and Kay darted to claim it. Helen joined her, moving more slowly. She sat, leaning forward, frowning, still gazing hard across the city.

411

Kay said, 'Isn't it marvellous?'

Helen nodded. 'Isn't it. I wish it was clearer, though.'

'But then it wouldn't be so charming. It's romantic, like this.'

Helen still peered. She pointed. 'That's St Pancras Station, isn't it?' She spoke quietly, glancing about for the officious man.

Kay looked. 'Yes, it must be.'

'And there's the university building.'

'Yes. What are you looking for? Rathbone Place? I doubt we'd be able to see it from here.'

'There's the Foundling Estate,' said Helen, as if she hadn't heard.

'It's further west than the Coram's Fields, and further south.' Kay looked again, and pointed. 'There's Portland Place, I think. It's nearer to there.'

'Yes,' said Helen, vaguely.

'Can you see? You're not looking in the right direction.'

'Yes.'

Kay put her hand on Helen's wrist. 'Darling, you're not—'

'God!' said Helen, sharply moving her arm away. 'Must you call me that?'

She spoke almost in a hiss, glancing about as she had before. Her face was white, with cold and with annoyance. The lipstick was standing out on her lips.

Kay turned her head. She felt, suddenly, a rush not so much of anger as of disappointment: a

412

disappointment in the weather, in Helen, in the day – in the whole damn thing. 'For Christ's sake,' she said. She lit up yet another cigarette, without offering the case. The smoke was bitter in her mouth, like her own soured mood.

Helen said quietly, after a time, 'I'm sorry, Kay.' She'd clasped her hands together in her lap and was gazing down at them.

'What on earth's the matter with you?'

'I feel a bit blue, that's all.'

'Well, don't for God's sake start looking like that, or—' Kay threw away the cigarette, and lowered her voice – 'I shall have to put my arm around you; and think how much you'll hate it.'

Her mood had changed again. The bitterness had gone, had sunk as quickly as it had risen; the disappointment, after all, had been too huge a thing to bear. She felt filled, instead, with tenderness. She felt actually sore, about her heart. 'I'm sorry, too,' she said gently. 'I suppose that birthdays are never as much fun for the people having them, as they are for the people putting them together.'

Helen looked up and smiled, rather sadly. 'I must not like being twenty-nine. It's a funny age, isn't it? Much better to have got it over with and gone straight to thirty.'

'It's a perfect age,' said Kay, with some of her former gallantry, 'on you. Any age would be that—'

But Helen had flinched. 'Don't, Kay,' she said. 'Don't— Don't be so nice to me.'

'Don't be nice to you!'

'Don't—' Helen shook her head. 'I don't deserve it.'

'You said that this morning.'

'It's true, that's why. I—'

She looked out across London again, in the same direction she'd gazed in before; and wouldn't go on. Kay watched her, perplexed; then rubbed her arm, gently, with her knuckles.

'Hey,' she said quietly. 'It doesn't matter. I wanted to make the day a special one, that's all. But maybe you can't expect to have a special day in wartime. Next year – who knows? The war might have ended. We'll do it properly. I'll take you away! I'll take you to France! Would you like that?'

Helen didn't answer. She had turned to Kay and was holding her gaze, and her look had grown earnest. After a moment she said, in a murmur, 'You won't get tired of me, Kay, now that I'm a beastly bad-tempered old spinster?'

For a second, Kay couldn't reply. Then she said, in the same low tone, 'You're my girl, aren't you? I'll never grow tired of you, you know that.'

'You might.'

'I shan't ever. You're mine, for ever.'

'I wish I was,' said Helen. 'I wish— I wish the world was different. Why can't it be different? I hate having to sneak and—' She waited, while a woman and a man went silently by, arm in arm. She lowered her voice still further. 'I hate having to sneak and slink so grubbily about. If we could only be married, something like that.'

Kay blinked and looked away. It was one of the tragedies of her life, that she couldn't be like a man to Helen – make her a wife, give her children . . . They sat in silence for a moment, gazing out again at the view but not seeing any of it now. Kay said quietly, 'Let me take you home.'

Helen was pulling at a button on her coat. 'We'll only have an hour or two before you'll have to go out.'

Kay made herself smile. 'Well, I know a way to fill an hour or two.'

'You know what I mean,' said Helen. She looked up again, and Kay saw then that she was almost crying. 'Can't you stay home with me tonight, Kay?'

'Helen,' said Kay, appalled. 'What's the matter?'

'I just— I don't know. I wish you could stay with me, that's all.'

'I can't. I can't. I have to go in. You know I do.'

'You're always there.'

'I can't, Helen . . . God, don't look at me like that! If I have to think of you, at home, unhappy, I'll—'

They had drawn closer together. But now, as before, a man and a girl came strolling along the path, beside their bench, and Helen drew away. She took out a handkerchief and wiped her eyes. Kay watched the couple – who had paused to look at the view, like everyone else – and wanted to kill them. The urge to take Helen in her arms – and the consciousness that she must not do it – was making her twitch, making her ill.

When the couple moved on, she looked at Helen again and said, 'Tell me you won't be unhappy tonight.'

'I'll be ecstatic tonight,' said Helen unhappily.

'Tell me you won't be lonely. Tell me— Tell me you'll go to the pub and get canned, and pick up some boy, some soldier—'

'Would you like me to?'

'I'd love it,' said Kay . . . 'I'd hate it, you know I would. I'd jump in the river. You're the only thing that makes this bloody war bearable.'

'Kay—'

'Tell me you love me,' said Kay, in a whisper.

'I do love you,' said Helen. She closed her eyes, as if the better to feel it or show it; and her voice grew earnest again. 'I do love you, Kay.'

'Well, son,' said Duncan's father, as he and Viv sat down, 'how are you? Been treating you all right, have they?'

'Yes,' Duncan answered, 'I suppose so.'

'Eh?'

Duncan cleared his throat. 'I said, Yes, they have.'

His father nodded, grimacing awfully as he tried to follow the words. This was the worst sort of setting for him, Duncan knew. The room had six tables in it, and theirs was the last; but every table had two prisoners at one end, and the prisoners' visitors at the other; and everyone was shouting. Duncan's neighbour was a man named Leddy, a post-office clerk, in for forging money orders. Sitting next to

416

Viv was Leddy's wife. Duncan had seen her before. She gave Leddy hell, every time she came. 'If you think I'm happy,' she was saying now, 'about having a woman like that come into my home—' At the table next to her was a girl with a baby. She was jiggling the baby up and down, trying to get it to smile at its father. But the baby was crying: shrieking open-mouthed like a siren, then pulling in great shuddering breaths and shrieking again. The room was just an ordinary small prison room, with ordinary closed prison windows. It smelt of ordinary prison smells – unwashed feet, sour mops, bad food, bad breath. But above the regular smells were other ones, too, much more disturbing: perfume, make-up, permanent waves; the smells of children; the smells of traffic, dogs, pavements, open air.

Viv was taking off her coat. She was wearing a lavender-coloured blouse done up with little pearl buttons, and the buttons caught Duncan's eye. He'd forgotten about buttons like that. He'd forgotten what they felt like. He wished he could reach across the table, now, and take one, just for a second, between his finger and his thumb.

She saw him looking, and moved about as if self-conscious. She folded her coat across her lap. 'How are you, really?' she asked, when she'd done it. 'Are you all right?'

'Yes, I'm OK.'

'You look awfully pale.'

'Do I? You said that last time, though.'

'I always forget.'

'How've you liked this past month, son?' said his father loudly. 'Made you jump, has it? I said to Mrs Christie, Jerry's got us on the hop, he's caught us with our feet up. What a time of it we had, though, a night or two ago! Bangs so loud, they woke me up! That'll give you an idea how bad it was.'

'Yes,' said Duncan, trying to smile.

'Mr Wilson's place lost its roof.'

'Mr Wilson's place?'

'You know the one.'

'Where we used to go,' said Viv, seeing Duncan struggle, 'when we were little. That man and his sister, who used to give us sweets. Don't you remember? They had a little bird, in a cage. You used to ask to feed it.'

'—a great big lump of a girl,' Leddy's wife was saying now, 'with habits like that! It turned my stomach—'

'I don't remember,' said Duncan.

His father was shaking his head, a beat behind, because of his hearing. 'No,' he said, 'you hardly credit it when it all dies down. You'd think from the racket that the world had been smashed to nothing. It gives you a turn to see so many houses still standing up. Puts you right back in the blitz. —Well, they're calling it the Little Blitz, aren't they?' He said this last to Viv; then turned to Duncan again. 'You won't feel it so much, I suppose,' he said, 'in here?'

Duncan thought of the darkness, Giggs calling out, the officers going down to their shelter. He

418

moved in his chair. 'It depends what you mean,' he said, 'by "feel it".'

But he must have mumbled. His father tilted his head, grimaced again. 'What's that?'

'It depends what you— God! No, we don't feel it so much.'

'No,' answered his father mildly. 'No, I shouldn't have thought you would.'

Mr Daniels walked up and down behind the prisoners, scuffing his shoes. The baby still cried: Duncan's father started trying to catch its eye, making faces at it. A few tables on, Fraser was sitting; his mother and father had come to see him. Duncan could just make them out. His mother was dressed in black, with a hat with a veil, as if for a funeral. His father's face was brick-red. Duncan couldn't hear what they were saying. But he could see Fraser's hands where they rested on the table, the blistered fingers moving restlessly about.

Viv said, 'Dad's been moved to another shop at Warner's, Duncan.'

He looked back at her, blinking, and she touched their father's arm, spoke into his ear. 'I was just telling Duncan, Dad, that you've been moved to another shop.'

Duncan's father nodded. 'That's right.'

'Oh yes?' said Duncan. 'Is it all right?'

'It's not too bad. I'm working with Bernie Lawson now.'

'Bernie Lawson?'

'And Mrs Gifford's daughter, June.' Duncan's

father smiled. He started to tell Duncan some story . . . Duncan lost the thread of it almost at once. His father never realised. He spoke of all the little factory jokes and intrigues as if Duncan were still at home. 'Stanley Hibbert,' he was saying, and, 'Muriel and Phil. You should have seen their faces! I told Miss Ogilvy—' Duncan recognised some of the names, but the people were like ghosts to him. He watched the words being formed on his father's lips, and took his cue from his father's expressions and nodded and smiled, as if he were deaf himself.

'They said to give you their best, anyway,' his father finished. 'They always ask after you. And Pamela sends her love, of course. She said to tell you, she's sorry she can't get in to see you more.'

Duncan nodded again – forgetting, for a moment, who Pamela was. Then, with a little jolt, he remembered that she was his other sister . . . She'd come to see him about three times, in the three years he'd been in here. He didn't much mind; Viv and his father, however, always looked awkward about it.

Viv said, 'It's hard, when there are babies.'

'Oh yes,' said their father, seizing on this, 'that makes things hard. No, you don't want to be hauling kids about with you when you come here. Unless you're bringing them in to see their dads; that's a different thing, of course. Mind you' – he glanced at the girl with the crying baby, and tried, and failed, to lower his voice – 'I shouldn't have cared to have any of you kids see me in a place like this, if it'd been me. Well, it's not nice. It

420

doesn't give you nice things to think back on. I hardly liked to have you see your mother, up at the hospital that time.'

'It's nice for the fathers, though,' said Viv. 'It was nice for Mother, I expect.'

'Oh yes, there is that.'

Duncan glanced down the room again, to Fraser's parents. This time, too, he saw Fraser himself: Fraser was looking along the tables, as he was. He met Duncan's gaze, and slightly turned down the corners of his mouth. Then he looked at Duncan's father and at Viv, in an interested way . . . Duncan thought of his father's threadbare coat. He lowered his head and started picking bits of varnish from the table.

His hands were clean, because he'd taken care to wash them that morning, and to pare his nails. His trousers had a sharp crease down each leg, from where he'd slept with them beneath his mattress the night before. His hair was combed flat, and greased with a mixture of wax and margarine. He had a vision, every time, of how it would be when he was brought in here: he wanted his father and Viv to look at him and be somehow impressed by him; he wanted them to think, *He's a credit to us!* But always, at about this point in their visit, his mood began to plunge. He remembered that he and his father had never had anything to say to each other, even years before. And his disappointment – in his father, in himself, even in Viv – would start to rise up and almost choke him. He'd wish, perversely, that he'd come with dirty fingernails and uncombed hair. He'd realise that what he really wanted was for Viv and his father to see that he lived in filth: he wanted them to tell him that he was a sort of hero for doing it without complaining, without being turned by it into a beast. The fact that they talked to him, every time, about ordinary things – as if they'd come to visit him in a hospital or a boarding-school, rather than a prison – made his disappointment turn to rage. Sometimes it would be as much as he could do to look at his father's face without wanting to hurl himself across the room and hit it.

He felt himself begin to tremble. His hands were still before him, on the table, and he saw them jump. So he drew them back and folded them together in his lap. He glanced at the visiting-room clock. Eleven minutes still to go . . .

Duncan's father had been making faces at the baby again, and the baby had quietened. Now he and Viv were looking idly about the room. *They've got bored of me*, Duncan thought. He saw them as being like people in a restaurant who'd run out of things to say, who'd reached that point in a dull evening when it became all right to start studying the other diners, to pick out little quirks and flaws. He looked again at the clock. Ten minutes, now. But his hands still trembled. He felt himself, too, begin to sweat. The urge rose in him, suddenly, to muck things up, to do the worst he possibly could; to make Viv and his father hate him. His father turned back to him and said pleasantly, 'Who's that chap, son, right down at the end there?' and he answered with great scorn, as if the question were an utterly fatuous one: 'That's Patrick Grayson.'

'He's a nice-looking fellow, isn't he? Has he just come in?'

'No, he hasn't. You saw him last time. You said he was nice-looking, then. His time's almost up.'

'Is it? I bet he's pleased. I bet his wife is, too.'

Duncan curled his lip. 'Do you? He's going into the army as soon as he gets out. He might as well stay here. At least in here he gets to see her once a month; and there's no chance, of course, of him getting his head shot off.'

His father tried to follow the words. 'Well,' he said vaguely, 'he'll be glad to do his bit, I expect.' He turned his head again. 'Yes, he's a nice-looking chap all right.'

Duncan exploded. 'Why don't you go and sit with him, instead of me, if you like him so much?'

'What's that?' said his father, turning back.

'Duncan,' said Viv.

But Duncan went on. 'I expect you'd rather I was like him. I expect you'd rather I was going out, into the army, to get my head blown off. I suppose you'd rather the army was going to make a murderer of me—'

'Duncan,' said Viv again, looking startled but also tired. 'Don't be silly.'

His father, however, was losing his temper. 'Don't talk bloody nonsense,' he said. 'Going into the army to get your head blown off? What do you know about it? If you'd gone into the army when you were supposed to—'

'Dad,' said Viv.

He ignored her, or didn't hear her. 'A spell in the bloody army,' he said, moving about in his seat, 'is what he needs. Talking like that. Am I ashamed! Of course I'm bloody well ashamed!'

She touched his arm. 'Duncan didn't mean anything by it, Dad. Did you, Duncan?'

Duncan didn't answer. His father glared at him for a second, then said, 'You don't know what shame feels like, in here! You'll know it when you come out, though. You'll know it, the first time you have to pass that woman and her husband in the street—'

He meant Alec's parents. But he could never say Alec's name. He bit off the words now and, with an effort, swallowed them down. The colour had risen into his face. 'Am I ashamed!' he said again. He looked at Duncan. 'What do you want me to say to you, boy?'

Duncan shrugged. He felt ashamed himself, now; but curiously better, too, for having made this happen. He went back to picking at the table, saying lightly but clearly, 'Don't come, if you feel like that about it.'

That started his father off again. 'Don't come? What are you talking about, don't come? You're my own son, aren't you?'

'So?'

Mr Pearce looked away in disgust.

'Duncan,' said Viv.

'What? He doesn't have to come.'

'Duncan, for God's sake!'

But now he'd started to smile. The smile didn't come from a sense of pleasure. His feelings were plunging about like a madman's. They were like a kite, in a storm: it was all he could do keep his balance, hauling at the string . . . He put his hand across his mouth and said, 'I'm sorry.'

His father looked up, and his colour rose even higher. 'What's he smiling at?'

'He's not really smiling,' said Viv.

'If his mother was here—! No wonder you're poorly.'

'Just leave it, Dad.'

'Vivien's not well,' said Mr Pearce aggressively to Duncan. 'She had to stop, on the way here. The last thing she wants is some of your nonsense. You ought to be grateful she's come to see you at all! Plenty sisters wouldn't bother, I can tell you that.'

'They haven't a clue,' said Leddy's wife, chiming in. She'd heard it all, of course. 'They sit in here. They get their dinners brought to them. They don't give a thought to what it's like for us, out there.'

Viv made some gesture, but wouldn't answer. Her expression was grim. Duncan gazed into her face and noticed, what he hadn't seen before, that she was pale beneath her make-up, and her eyes were shadowed and red at the rims. He felt, suddenly, that his father was right. He felt sick with himself, for spoiling things. *She's the nicest, prettiest sister a fellow could have!* he thought, almost wildly, still looking at Viv. He wanted to draw the other men's attention to her. *Look here*, he wanted to be able to cry, *at my nice sister!*

It took all his strength and will just to sit there, wretchedly, in silence. He looked at Mr Daniels, longing for him to call out that visiting-time was up; and finally, with great relief, he saw him checking his watch against the face of the clock, then unlocking a cupboard and bringing out a handbell. He gave the bell a couple of half-hearted rings, and the muddle of voices at once grew louder. Chairs were pushed back. People got up quickly – as if, like Duncan, they were relieved. The baby gave a start in its mother's arms and started crying all over again.

Duncan's father rose, grimly, and put on his hat. Viv looked at Duncan in a way that said, *Well done*.

He said, 'I'm sorry.'

'You ought to be.' They were speaking too softly, now, for their father to hear. 'You're not the only one who's badly off, you know. You might just try thinking about that.'

'I do. It's just—' He couldn't explain it. He said instead, 'Are you really not well?'

She looked away. 'I'm all right. I'm just tired, that's all.'

'Because of the raids?'

'Yes, I expect so.'

He watched her stand and shrug on her coat.

Her lavender blouse, with its little pearl buttons, got covered over. Her hair fell forward as she dipped her head, and she tucked it back, behind her ear. He saw again how pale she was beneath her powder.

They weren't allowed to kiss or embrace, but before she moved off she reached her arm across the table and just touched her hand to his.

'Look after yourself, all right?' she said, without smiling, as she drew the hand back.

'I will. Look after yourself, too.'

'I'll try,' she said.

He nodded to his father, wanting to catch his eye, but afraid of it, too. He said, 'Goodbye, Dad. I'm sorry for the silly things I said.'

But perhaps he didn't say it clearly enough. His father turned away while he was still speaking, dipping his head, looking for Viv's arm so that he could link his own with it.

Ten minutes earlier Duncan had almost wanted to strike his face; now he stood with his thighs pressed hard against the table, watching Viv and his father find a place in the crowd of visitors; not wanting to leave the room until his father had left it, in case his father should look back.

But only Viv looked back – just once, very briefly. And a second later Mr Daniels came to Duncan and gave him a push.

'Into the line with you, Pearce. And you, Leddy. All right, you buggers, let's go.'

He took them out of the visiting-room, back to

427

the junction of passages that led to the workshops, and handed them over to Mr Chase. Mr Chase looked wearily at his watch. It was twenty to five. The men from the Basket Shop, he said, could make their way back to it by themselves; one of them was a Redband. As for the others – well, he was fucked if he was going to escort them all the way over to Mailbags One and Two, just for the sake of twenty minutes; he led them back to the hall instead. They walked without speaking: dejected, subdued; all of them, like Duncan, with neatly combed hair and pressed trousers and clean hands. The hall looked vast with no one in it. There were so few of them – eight men, only – that when they trudged up the staircases the landings made that chilly, shivering sound that Duncan listened for at night.

Each man went straight into his own cell, as if glad to get in there. Duncan sat on his bunk and put his head in his hands.

He stayed like that for three or four minutes. Then he heard firm, soft footsteps on the landing outside his door, and quickly tried to dry his eyes. But he couldn't do it quickly enough.

'Now, then,' said Mr Mundy gently. 'What's all this?'

That made Duncan cry properly. He covered his face and sobbed into his fingers, his shoulders shaking, making thc bcd-frame jump. Mr Mundy didn't try to stop him; he didn't come to him, put an arm on his shoulder, anything like that. He simply stood, and waited for the worst of the tears to be over; and then he said, 'There. Had a visit from your dad, haven't you? That's right, I saw the Order. Shook you up a bit, has it?'

Duncan nodded, wiping his face on his coarse prison handkerchief. 'A bit.'

'It always shakes a fellow up, seeing faces from home. Well, put it this way, it's hard to be natural. You go on and cry some more, if that's what you want. It won't trouble me. I've seen harder men than you cry, I can tell you.'

Duncan shook his head. His face felt hot, felt bruised and pulled about, from the contortions of his sobs. 'I'm all right, now,' he said unsteadily.

' 'Course you are.'

'I just— I make such a mess of things, Mr Mundy. I make such a mess of things, every time.'

His voice was rising. He bit his mouth, drew in his arms and clenched his fists, to keep himself from crying again. When the fit passed and he let himself relax, he felt exhausted. He groaned and rubbed his face.

Mr Mundy stood watching for another moment; then he caught hold of Duncan's chair and turned it and, slightly awkwardly, with a little sigh of discomfort, sat down. 'Tell you what,' he said, as he did it. 'Have a smoke. Look what I've got here.'

He brought out a packet of Player's cigarettes. He opened it up, and leant to offer it to Duncan. 'Go on,' he said, giving the cigarettes a shake.

Duncan drew a cigarette out. It seemed as fat as a small cigar compared to the usual prison roll-ups.

The tobacco was tight inside its smooth, cool sheath of paper – so nice in his hand, he turned it in his fingers and began to feel better.

'All right, isn't it?' said Mr Mundy, watching him.

'It's lovely,' said Duncan.

'Aren't you going to smoke it?'

'I don't know. I ought to keep it, to take the tobacco out. I could get four or five smokes from this.'

Mr Mundy smiled. He started to sing, in a tuneful old man's voice. '*Five little fags in a dainty little packet . . .*' He wrinkled up his nose. 'Smoke it now.'

'Shall I?'

'Go on. I'll keep you company. We can be two chaps, smoking together.'

Duncan laughed. But the laughter came too soon on top of his tears: it caught in his chest and made him tremble. Mr Mundy pretended not to notice. He got out a cigarette for himself, and a box of matches. He held the flame to Duncan first, then drew on it himself. They smoked, for half a minute, in silence. Then Duncan held the cigarette off and said, 'It's making my eyes sting. It's making me giddy! I'm going to faint!'

'Get away with you!' said Mr Mundy, chuckling.

'I am!' said Duncan. He sat back, pretending to swoon. He became like a boy, sometimes, with Mr Mundy . . . But then he grew serious again. 'God,' he said, 'what a state to be in! Knocked down by one little cigarette!'

He kept his feet on the floor but let himself fall right back, supporting himself on one of his elbows. He wondered where Viv and his father were, now. He tried to picture his father's journey back to Streatham; he couldn't do it. Then he tried to visualise the various rooms of his father's flat. He had, instead, a sudden, violent, vivid image of his father's kitchen on the day he'd last seen it, with the spreading mess of darkening scarlet on the walls and floor—

He sat up again, quickly. Ash fell from his cigarette. He brushed it away, then rubbed his still-aching face and, after a moment, without looking up, said quietly, 'Do you think I'll do all right, Mr Mundy, when I get out?'

Mr Mundy took another puff of his own cigarette. 'Of course you will,' he said comfortably. 'You'll just need time to – well, to find your feet.'

'To find my feet?' Duncan frowned. 'You mean, like a sailor?' He saw himself staggering about on a tilting pavement.

'Like a sailor!' Mr Mundy laughed, tickled by the idea.

'But what will I do, say, for work?'

'You'll be all right.'

'But why should I be?'

'There'll always be jobs for clever young fellows like you. You mark my words.'

It was the sort of thing that Duncan's father said, that made Duncan want to kill him. But now he bit at one of his fingernails and looked at Mr

431

Mundy across his knuckles and said, 'Do you think so?'

Mr Mundy nodded. 'I've seen all sorts of fellows come through here. They all felt like you, at one time or another. They did just fine.'

'But the sorts of fellows you've seen,' persisted Duncan, 'didn't they probably have wives and children, things like that, to go back home to? Were any of them – frightened, do you think?'

'Frightened?'

'Frightened of what was going to happen to them, how they were going to be—?'

'Now then,' said Mr Mundy again, but more sternly. 'What sort of talk is that? You know what sort it is, don't you?'

Duncan looked away. 'Yes,' he said, after a moment. 'It's letting Error in.'

'That's right. It's the worst thing a boy in your situation can do, to start thinking like that.'

'Yes, I know,' said Duncan. 'It's just— Well, you look so much at walls, in this place. I try to look into the future but that's like a wall, too; I can't see myself getting over it. I try to think of what I'll do, where I'll live. There's my dad's house' – he saw again that scarlet kitchen – 'but my dad's house is only two streets away from—' he lowered his voice, 'from Alec's. Alec, you know, the boy, my friend—? My father used to go down that street to go to work. Now he goes half a mile around it every time, my sister told me. How will it be, if I go back there? I keep thinking about it, Mr Mundy.

I keep thinking, if I was to see someone who knew Alec—'

'That boy Alec,' said Mr Mundy firmly, 'was a troubled boy, from everything you've told me. That boy lived in Error, if anybody ever did. He's free of all that now.'

Duncan moved, uncomfortable. 'You said that before. But it never feels like that. If you'd been there—'

'No one was there,' said Mr Mundy, 'but you. And that's what you might call your Burden. But I'd lay a pound against a penny Alec is looking at you right now, longing to pluck that Burden from you, saying, *Put it down, chum!* and wishing you could hear him. I'd bet you he is laughing, but also crying: laughing, to be where he is, in the sunshine; crying, because you are still in the dark.'

Duncan nodded, liking the comforting sound of Mr Mundy's voice; liking the quaintness of the words – *pluck, Burden, Error, chum*; but not, in his heart, believing any of it. He wanted to think that Alec was where Mr Mundy described: he tried to imagine him surrounded by sunlight and flowers, smiling . . . But Alec had never been like that, he'd said it was common to sit about in parks and gardens or go bathing; and he hardly ever really smiled, because his teeth were bad and he was ashamed of them.

Duncan looked up, into Mr Mundy's face. 'It's hard, Mr Mundy,' he said simply.

Mr Mundy didn't answer for a moment. Instead

he got slowly to his feet, then came to Duncan's bunk and sat beside him; and he put his hand – his left hand, with the cigarette in it – on Duncan's shoulder. He said, in a quiet, confidential tone, 'You think of me, when you get low; and I'll think of you. How's that? You and me are alike, after all: for I shall be out of here next year, just as you will. My date for retirement's coming up, you see; and the idea's as queer to me as it is to you – queerer, perhaps, for you know what they say, that if a prisoner does two years in gaol, then his guard does one . . . So you think of me, when you get low. And I'll think of you. I'll think of you – well, I won't say, as a father thinks of his son, for I know you've got your own dad to do that; but let's say, as a man might think of his nephew. How about that?'

He held Duncan's gaze, and patted his shoulder. When a little ash fell from the tip of his cigarette to Duncan's knee, he reached with his other hand and carefully brushed it away; then let the hand stay there.

'All right?' he asked.

Duncan lowered his gaze. 'Yes,' he answered quietly.

Mr Mundy patted him again. 'Good boy. For you're a special boy – you know that, don't you? You're a very special boy. And things have a way of turning out all right, for special boys like you. You see if they don't.'

He kept his hand on Duncan's knee for another

434

moment; then gave the knee a squeeze, and got up. The gates, at the end of the hall, had been thrown open: the men were being brought back from the workshops. There was the sound of many footsteps, the rattling of the stairs and iron landings. Mr Chase could be heard calling out: 'Keep moving. Keep moving! Every man to his own cell. Giggs and Hammond, stop pissing about!'

Mr Mundy pinched out his cigarette and put it back into its packet; then, as Duncan watched, he took out two fresh ones, lifted up the corner of Duncan's pillow and slipped them underneath. He gave Duncan a wink, and patted the pillow smooth, when he'd done it; he was just straightening up when the first of the men began to troop past Duncan's door. Crawley, Waterman, Giggs, Quigley . . . Then Fraser appeared. He had his hands in his pockets and was kicking his boots as he walked. He brightened up, however, when he saw Mr Mundy.

'Hello,' he said. 'This is an honour, sir, and no mistake! And do I smell real tobacco? Hello, Pearce. How was your visit? About as much fun as mine, from the look of it. That was a nice trick of Mr Chase's, too – sending us back to the Basket Shop, while you Mailbags got off early.'

Duncan didn't answer. Fraser wasn't listening, anyway. He was looking at Mr Mundy, who was moving past him to the door. 'You're not leaving us, sir?'

'I've got work to do,' said Mr Mundy stiffly. 'My day's not like you men's, that finishes at five.'

'Oh, but give us proper occupations,' said Fraser in his exaggerated way. 'Teach us trades. Pay us real men's wages, instead of the pittances we get now. I'm sure we'd work like billy-oh then! Heavens, you might even find you'd make decent men of us. Imagine a prison doing that!'

Mr Mundy nodded, rather sourly. 'You're clever, son,' he said, as he went out.

'So my father always tells me, Mr Mundy,' Fraser answered. 'So clever I'll cut myself. Hey?'

He started to laugh; and looked at Duncan, as if expecting Duncan to join in.

But Duncan wouldn't meet his gaze. He lay down on his bed, on his side, with his face turned to the wall. And when Fraser said, 'What's the matter with you? Pearce? What the hell's the matter?' he flung back his arm, as if to push him away.

'Shut up, will you?' he said. 'Just fucking well shut up.'

'I'll read my book,' Helen had said, when Kay was leaving. 'I'll listen to the wireless. I'll change into my lovely new pyjamas and go to bed.' And she had meant it. For almost an hour after Kay had gone, she'd stayed on the sofa reading *Frenchman's Creek*. At half-past seven she made more toast; she turned on the radio, caught the start of a play. But the play was rather dull. She listened for ten or fifteen minutes, then tried another programme. Finally she switched the radio off. The flat seemed very silent after that: it was always especially silent in the evenings and at weekends, because of Palmer's, the furniture warehouse, being so shut up and dark. The silence and the stillness sometimes got on Helen's nerves.

She sat down again with her book, but found she couldn't settle to it. She tried a magazine; her gaze slid over the words on the page and took nothing in. The idea began to rise in her that she was wasting time. It was her birthday – her birthday, in wartime. She might never have another! 'You can't expect to have a special day in wartime,' Kay had said that afternoon; but why couldn't you? How long did they have to go on, letting the war spoil everything? They had been patient, all this time. They'd lived in darkness. They'd lived without salt, without scent. They'd fed themselves little scraps of pleasure, like parings of cheese. Now she became aware of the minutes as they passed: she felt them, suddenly, for what they were, as fragments of her life, her youth, that were rushing away like so many drops of water, never to return.

I want to see Julia, she thought. And then it was exactly as if somebody was seizing her by the shoulders and whispering urgently into her face, *What are you waiting for? Come on!* She threw the magazine down, jumped up, and ran into the bathroom to use the lavatory and comb her hair and redo her make-up; and then she put on her coat and scarf, and the wool tam-o'-shanter she'd been wearing earlier that day, and went out.

The mews, of course, was perfectly dark, the

cobblestones slippery with frost; but she picked her way across it without her torch. From the various pubs on Rathbone Place she could just hear the clink of glass, the buzz of beery voices, the tipsy lilt of a mechanical piano. The sounds made her feel better. It was an ordinary Saturday night. People were out, enjoying themselves. Why shouldn't she be? She wasn't thirty yet . . . She went along Percy Street, past the blacked-out windows of the cafés and restaurants there. She crossed Tottenham Court Road, and entered the shabby streets of Bloomsbury.

The area was quiet, and she went swiftly; then her foot struck a broken kerb and she almost fell, and after that she forced herself to walk at a sensible pace, and to pick out her way, carefully, with the beam of her torch.

But her heart was racing as though she was running. She kept saying to herself, *This is crazy, Helen!* What on earth would Julia think? She probably wouldn't even be at home. Why should she be? Or she might be writing. She might have visitors. There might be somebody – a friend—

That made her slow her step again. For it hadn't occurred to her, before, that Julia might have a lover. She'd never mentioned anyone; but it would be like her, Helen thought, to keep that sort of thing a secret. Why should she mention something like that to Helen, anyway? What was there between them? They had had tea together that time, outside Marylebone Station. Then they'd wandered around that house in Bryanston Square, practically in silence. After that, they'd met up again and had drinks in a pub; and one sunny lunch-time, a few days before, they had gone into Regent's Park and sat beside the lake . . .

That was all they had done; and yet it seemed to Helen that with those slight encounters the world had been subtly transformed. She felt connected to Julia now, as if by a slender, quivering thread. She could have closed her eyes and, with a fingertip, touched the exact small point on her breast at which the thread ran delicately into her heart and tugged at it.

She had reached Russell Square Underground Station, and the streets were busier here. She got caught up, briefly, in a little knot of people who'd just come up from the platforms and were standing around rather helplessly, waiting for their eyes to grow used to the darkness.

The sight of them, like the sounds from the Rathbone Place pubs, gave her more confidence. She went on, past the garden of the Foundling Estate; hesitated only once, at the mouth of Mecklenburgh Place; and then pushed on, into the square.

It looked forbidding in the darkness, the flat Georgian houses seeming smooth as well-bred bored blank faces – until she moved, and saw the sky behind the windows, and realised that many of them had been gutted by blast and by fire. She thought she remembered which house was Julia's, though she'd only been here once before. But she was sure that Julia's house was at the end of one of the terraces. She recalled it as having a broken step, which had rocked about under her feet.

She went up the steps of the house she thought she remembered. The steps were cracked, but stayed steady. They might have been mended, she supposed.

She wasn't sure, suddenly, if this house was right. She looked for the bell to Julia's flat: there were four bells there, unmarked, unnamed. Which was the one? She had no idea, so chose one at random. She heard it ring, somewhere in the depths of the building, as if in an empty room; she knew from the sound that it wasn't the right one and, without waiting, pressed another. The ring of this one was less clear; she couldn't gauge the location of it. She thought she heard a movement on the first or second floor; but even as she heard it she said to herself, *It won't be this one, it'll be the next.* —For it was never the second thing, in tales, in spells, it was always the third . . . But the movement came again. She heard slow, soft-soled footsteps on a staircase. Then the door was opened, and Julia was there.

It took her a moment to recognise Helen, in the darkness, with only the single, shaded bulb of a torch to light her. But when she saw who it was she gripped the edge of the door and said, 'What is it? Is it Kay?'

Has Kay found out? is what Helen took her to

mean; and her heart contracted. Then she realised, horribly, that Julia thought she must have come with bad news. She said quickly, breathlessly, 'No. It's just— I wanted to see you, Julia. I just wanted to see you, that's all.'

Julia didn't answer. The torch lit her face as it must have lit Helen's, making a sort of mask of it. Her expression was impossible to read. But after a moment she opened the door wider, and moved back.

'Come in,' she said.

She led the way up a darkened staircase to the second floor. She showed Helen into a tiny hallway, then took her through a curtained doorway into a sitting-room. The light was dim, but seemed bright after the blacked-out street, and Helen felt exposed in it.

Julia stooped to pick up a pair of kicked-off shoes, a dropped tea-towel, a fallen jacket. She looked distracted, preoccupied: not at all glad, in the ordinary way of gladness, that Helen had come. Her hair was very dark, and curiously flat against her head: when she moved further into the light Helen saw with dismay that it was damp, that she must recently have washed it. Her face was pale, and quite unmade-up. She was wearing unpressed dark flannel trousers, a wide-collared shirt, and a sleeveless sweater. On her feet she had what looked like fishermen's socks, and a pair of red Moroccan slippers.

'Wait here, while I get rid of this lot,' she said,

going back out through the curtain with the jacket and the shoes.

Helen stood, nervously, helplessly, and gazed about.

The room was large, warm, untidy, not at all like Kay's neat bachelor flat; but not quite, either, what Helen had been expecting. The walls were bare, and coloured with a patchy red distemper; the carpets were an assortment of overlapping Turkish kilims and imitation rugs. The furniture was very ordinary. There was one large divan couch, covered with mismatched cushions; and a dirty pink velvet chair, with springs and strips of torn hessian showing beneath. The mantelpiece was painted marble. It had an ashtray on it, overflowing with stubs. One of these still smoked: Julia came back, picked it up and pinched it out.

Helen said, 'You don't mind, do you, that I've come?'

'Of course not.'

'I started to walk. Then I saw where I was. I remembered your house.'

'Did you?'

'Yes. I came here once, ages ago. With Kay. Do you remember? Kay was dropping something off to you – a ticket, or a book, something like that. We didn't come up, you said the place was too untidy. We stood about in the hall, downstairs . . . *Do* you remember?'

Julia frowned. Then, 'Yes,' she said slowly. 'I think I do.'

They looked at one another, and almost at once looked away, as if in embarrassment or perplexity – for it was impossible, Helen found, to imagine a time when calling on Julia with Kay would have been an ordinary thing to do; impossible to think of standing at Kay's side on a doorstep, chatting politely, thinking only how mildly awkward things were, between Julia and Kay. And again she thought, what had happened, since then? Nothing had happened, really.

But if nothing has happened, she asked herself, *why have I kept that nothing from Kay? Why the hell am I here?*

She knew why she was there. She grew afraid.

'Perhaps I should go,' she said, 'after all.'

'You've only just arrived!'

'You've been washing your hair.'

Julia frowned, as if annoyed. 'You've seen wet hair before, haven't you? Don't be idiotic. Sit down, and I'll get you a drink. I have wine! I've had it for weeks, and had no occasion for opening it. It's only Algerian, but still.'

She stooped to open a cupboard and started shifting things about inside it. Helen watched her for a second, then took a step and, nervously, looked around again. She went to a shelf of books and glanced across the titles. They were detective stories, mainly, with gaudy spines. Julia's two published novels sat amongst them: *Death By Degrees,* and *Twenty Mortal Murders.*

She looked from the books to the pictures on the

443

walls, the ornaments on the painted mantelpiece. As awkward and as anxious as she was, she wanted to absorb every little detail, for the sake of what that detail might be able to tell her about Julia.

'Your flat's charming,' she said, conventionally.

'You think so?' Julia closed the cupboard door and straightened up. She had a bottle, a corkscrew, glasses. 'It's mostly my cousin Olga's stuff, not mine.'

'Your cousin Olga's?'

'The flat's my aunt's. I'm living here to keep it from being requisitioned. One of those genteel dodges at which the upper-middle classes so excel. There's only this room and the kitchen; the kitchen serves as a bathroom, too. The loo's down the hall. Really, it's in a dreadful sort of mess. There's no glass in the windows at all: they got broken so often, Olga just gave up. Last summer I had sheets of gauze put in: it was lovely, like living in a tent. Now it's too cold for gauze, I've put in talc boards instead. It's all right at night, with the curtains drawn. But in the daytime, it does tend to get me down. Makes me feel like a tart or something.'

She was screwing the corkscrew into the bottle as she spoke and now, with a little effort, she brought out the cork. She glanced at Helen as she poured the wine, and smiled. 'Aren't you going to take your things off?'

Rather reluctantly, Helen unwound her scarf, took off her hat, and started to unfasten the buttons of her coat. Her dress was the one she'd put on that morning – the Cedric Allen one with the cream

444

lapels, which Kay admired so much. She'd kept it on, she realised now, with the idea of impressing Julia with it; but the sight of Julia herself, with her newly washed hair and crumpled trousers, her socks and slippers and colourless mouth – and, worse, the air of easy glamour with which she carried all this off – was disconcerting. She drew her arms from the coat clumsily, as if she'd never taken a coat off before in her life. Julia glanced her way again and said, 'I say, what a swell you look! What's the occasion?'

Helen hesitated. Then, 'It's my birthday,' she said.

Julia thought she was joking, and laughed. When she saw that she was serious, her expression softened. 'Helen! Why didn't you tell me? If I'd known—'

'It's nothing,' said Helen. 'Really. It's silly, how like a child the whole thing makes one feel. Everyone conspires in it. Kay gave me an orange,' she added miserably. 'She picked out *Happy Birthday* in the peel.'

Julia handed her a glass of red wine. 'I'm glad she did,' she said. 'I'm glad you feel like a child about it.'

'I wish she hadn't,' said Helen. 'I was awful, today. I was worse than a child. I was—' She couldn't finish. She made some gesture, as if to brush away the memory of her own behaviour.

'Never mind,' said Julia gently. She lifted her glass. 'Here's how. Bung-ho. Cheerio. —And all those other idiotic things people say, which always make me feel I'm about to go off on my last mission. Touch top and bottom, for luck.' They clinked glasses, twice; then drank. The wine was rough, and made them grimace.

They moved apart. Helen cleared a space for herself amongst the cushions on the divan. Julia perched on the arm of the pink velvet chair, stretching out her legs. Her legs seemed impossibly slender and long, in the flannel trousers; her hips had a fragile, vulnerable look – as if, Helen thought, you could place your two hands upon them and, with a pressing motion, make them snap. She'd picked up the ashtray, and now reached to the mantelpiece for cigarettes and matches. Her sweater rose up as she did it, and her shirt was unbuttoned at the bottom; the tails of it parted, exposing her tense, sallow stomach, her neat navel. Helen looked, then at once looked quickly away.

One of the cushions fell from the divan to the floor. Helen leant and picked it up again – and realised, as she did it, that it wasn't a cushion but a pillow; that the divan must serve, in this two-roomed flat, as Julia's bed; that every night Julia must stand here, lay down sheets and blankets, take off her clothes . . . The image was not exactly erotic, for one saw beds, pillows, night-clothes, everywhere; they'd long ago lost their charge of intimacy, of sex. Instead she found it poignant, faintly troubling. She looked again at Julia's handsome, fragile figure and thought, *What is it about Julia? Why is she always so alone?*

They were sitting in silence. Helen found she

had nothing to say. She gulped down more of her wine, then became aware of noises on the floor above: irregular steps, and creaking boards. She put back her head and looked up.

Julia looked up too. 'My neighbour's a Polish man,' she murmured. 'He's only in London by some sort of fluke. He walks about, like that, for hours. Every piece of news he gets from Warsaw, he says, is worse than the last.'

'God,' said Helen. 'This wretched war. Do you really think it's true, what everyone says? That it'll be over soon?'

'Who knows? If the Second Front kicks off, then perhaps. But I'd say we were in it for another year at least.'

'Another year. So I'll be thirty.'

'And I'll be thirty-two.'

'The worst sort of ages, don't you think? If we were twenty, we'd get over it, we'd still be almost young. And if we were forty, we'd be old enough not to mind being older still. But thirty . . . I'll have gone from youth to middle age. What will I have to look forward to? The Change of Life, I suppose. They say it's worse for childless women. Don't laugh! At least you'll have achieved something, Julia. Your books, I mean.'

Julia drew in her chin, still smiling. 'Them! They're like so many crossword puzzles. I only wrote the first one, you know, as a sort of joke. Then I discovered I was rather good at them. What that reveals about me, I can't imagine. Kay's always said that it's a queer thing to do – writing about murder, just now, while so many people are being murdered all around us.'

This was the second or third time that they had mentioned Kay's name; but they both seemed struck by it, now, in a way they hadn't been before. They sat in silence again. Julia swirled the wine in her glass, gazing fixedly into it like a fortune-teller. Without looking up, and in a different sort of voice, she said, 'I never asked you. What did Kay make of our running into each other like that, that day?'

'She was glad,' said Helen, after a second.

'And she didn't mind us meeting up again? She won't mind your coming round here, tonight?'

Helen sipped her drink and didn't answer. When Julia looked up and caught her gaze, she must have coloured or seemed guilty. Julia frowned. She said, 'You haven't told her?'

Helen shook her head.

'Why not?'

'I don't know.'

'You didn't think it worth mentioning? That's fair enough, I suppose.'

'No, Julia, it wasn't that. Don't be silly.'

Julia laughed. 'What, then? Do you mind my asking? I'm curious. But I'll shut up about it, if you'd rather. If it's something, you know, between you and Kay—'

'It's nothing like that,' said Helen quickly. 'I told you, Kay was pleased to hear we'd met up. She'd be pleased, too, to think we've gone on meeting.'

'Are you sure?'

'Of course I'm sure! She's so very fond of you; and that makes her want me to like you, too. It always has.'

'How big of her. *Do* you like me, Helen?'

'Well, naturally I do.'

'There's no naturally about it.'

'Unnaturally, then,' said Helen, making a face.

'Yet you won't tell Kay?'

Helen moved uncomfortably. She said, 'I ought to have, I know. I wish I had. It's just, sometimes, with Kay—' She stopped. 'It sounds childish, un-gracious. It's just, the way Kay is with me, taking such care of me. It makes me long, now and then, to keep things from her, even commonplace, trifling things. Just so that those things can be wholly mine.'

Her heart was fluttering as she spoke: she was afraid that Julia would hear the flutter in her voice. For even as she said all this, and meant it, she knew that it wasn't quite the truth. She was trying to make the whole thing be about some-thing else. She was playing it down, using words like *commonplace* and *childish*. She was trying to pretend that there wasn't that fine, invisible, vibrating thread telling her when Julia moved, when Julia breathed . . .

Perhaps it worked. Julia smoked her cigarette for a time, looking thoughtful, but without speaking; then she tapped ash into the ashtray and got to her feet. 'Kay wants a wife,' she said. She smiled. 'That sounds like a children's game, doesn't it?

Kay wants a wife. She always has. One must be the wife with Kay, or nothing.'

She yawned, as if bored by the idea; then went to the window and drew back the curtain. There were little chinks, Helen could see, in the grey talc boards, and she put her eye to one of these and peered out. 'Don't you hate these evenings?' she said. 'Not knowing if the Warning will sound, and so on? It's like waiting for an execution that might or might not take place.'

'Would you rather I went?' Helen asked.

'God, no! I'm glad you're here. It's much worse when one's alone, don't you think?'

'Yes, much worse. But bad in the shelters, too. Kay always wants me to go over to the one in Rathbone Place; but I can't stand it, it makes me feel trapped. I'd always rather sit and be petrified on my own, than have strangers see me being frightened.'

'Me, too,' said Julia. 'Sometimes I go out, you know. I like it better in the open space.'

'You just go strolling,' Helen asked her, 'in the black-out? Isn't it dangerous?'

Julia shrugged. 'Probably. But then everything's dangerous, just now.' She let the curtain fall and turned back into the room, and reached for her glass.

Helen felt her heart begin to flutter again. It occurred to her that she'd far rather be with Julia outside, in darkness, than in here, in the soft, exposing, intimate light. She said, 'Why don't we go out now, Julia?'

Julia looked at her. 'Now? You mean, for a walk? Would you like to?'

'Yes,' said Helen. She felt the wine inside her suddenly, and started to laugh.

Julia laughed too. Her dark eyes were shining, with excitement and mischief. She began to move more quickly, putting back her head to drink off her wine, then carelessly setting down the glass on the mantelpiece, so that it rang against the painted marble. She looked at the fire, then squatted in front of it and began to shovel ash on the coke. She did it with the cigarette clamped at the side of her mouth, and with an expression of tremendous concentration and distaste: screwing up her eyes, holding her graceful head at an awkward angle away from the rising grey cloud – like a debutante, Helen thought, on the maid's night off. Then she got up, and dusted off her knees; went back through the curtained doorway for her coat and shoes. She reappeared after a moment in a black double-breasted jacket with polished brass buttons, like a sailor's coat. She stood at the mirror, put on lipstick, powdered her face, turned up her collar. She ran her hands, critically, over her damp head, then drew a soft black corduroy cap from out of a heap of gloves and scarves: pulled it on, and tucked up her hair.

'I shall regret this, later,' she said, 'when my hair has dried at odd angles.' She caught Helen's eye. 'I don't look like Mickey, do I?'

Helen laughed, guiltily. 'Not at all like Mickey.'

'Not like a male impersonator on the stage?'

'More like an actress in a spy-film.'

Julia adjusted the angle of the cap. 'Well, so long as I don't get us arrested for espionage . . . I tell you what, let's take the rest of that wine.' There was half a bottle left. 'I shan't want it tomorrow, and we've hardly touched it.'

'That really might get us arrested.'

'Don't worry, I've a plan for that.'

She went back to the cupboard, moved things around, and brought out the night-watchman's bottle that they'd had tea from, in Bryanston Square. She pulled the cork from it, and sniffed it; then carefully filled it up with wine. There was just enough. She stoppered it up again, and put it into her jacket pocket. In her other pocket she put a torch.

'Now you look like a housebreaker,' said Helen, as she buttoned on her own coat.

'But you're forgetting,' said Julia; 'I *am* a housebreaker, by day. Now, there's just one more thing.' She opened a drawer and took out a sheaf of papers. The papers were thin, the 'flimsy' kind that Helen was issued with at work. They were covered all over with close black handwriting.

'That's not your manuscript?' asked Helen, impressed.

Julia nodded. 'It's a bore, but the bombs make me afraid for it.' She smiled. 'I suppose the wretched thing must be rather more to me than a sort of cross-word puzzle, after all. I find I have to carry it about with me wherever I go.' She rolled the papers up and stuffed them into the inside pocket of her coat. She patted the bulge they made. 'Now I feel safe.'

'But, if you get hit?'

'Then I shan't care one way or the other.' She drew on gloves. 'Are you ready?'

She led the way downstairs. As she opened the door she said, 'I hate this bit. Let's close our eyes and count, as we're supposed to' – and so they stood on the step with their faces screwed up, saying, '*One, two, three . . .*'

'When do we stop?' asked Helen.

'. . . *twelve, thirteen, fourteen, fifteen* – now!'

They opened their eyes, and blinked.

'Has that made a difference?'

'I don't think so. It's still dark as hell.'

They switched on their torches and went down the steps. Julia's face showed palely, strangely, framed by the lines of her turned-up collar and her cap. She said, 'Which way shall we go?'

'I don't know. You're the veteran at this sort of thing. You choose.'

'All right,' said Julia, suddenly deciding. She took Helen's arm. 'This way.'

They went left into Doughty Street; then left again, into the Gray's Inn Road; and then right, towards Holborn. The roads, even in the short space of time in which Helen had been at Julia's flat, had grown almost empty. There was only the occasional cab or lorry – like creeping black insects they seemed in the darkness, with gleaming, brittle-looking bodies and louvred, infernal eyes. The pavements, too, were almost clear, and Julia went quickly because of the cold. Helen could feel – as if with disturbing new senses, born of the dark – the weight and pressure of her arm and hand, the nearness of her face, her shoulder, her hip, her thigh, the roll and rhythm of her step.

At what must have been the junction with Clerkenwell Road they turned left. After a little while Julia made them turn again – right, this time. Helen looked around, suddenly confused.

'Where are we?'

'Hatton Garden, I think. Yes, it must be.'

They spoke quietly, for the street seemed deserted.

'Do you know for sure? We won't get lost?'

'How can we get lost?' asked Julia. 'We don't know where we're going. Anyway, you can't get lost in London, even in the black-out and with all the street-signs gone. If you can, you don't deserve to live here. They should make it a kind of exam.'

'If you fail, you get booted out?'

'Exactly. And then,' Julia laughed, 'you must go and live in Brighton.' They turned to the left, went down a short hill. 'Look, this must be the Farringdon Road.'

There were cabs again here, other pedestrians, a feeling of space – but a dreary feel, too, for half of the buildings that lined the street had been damaged and boarded up. Julia led Helen south, towards the river. At a warden's post in one of the arches underneath Holborn Viaduct, a man heard their voices and blew his whistle.

'Those two ladies! They must get themselves a white scarf or a paper, please!'

'All right,' called Helen meekly in reply.

But Julia murmured: 'Suppose we want to be invisible?'

They crossed Ludgate Circus and went on towards the start of the bridge. They saw people going down into the Underground with bags and blankets and pillows, and paused to watch them.

'It gives one a shock, doesn't it,' said Helen quietly, 'to see people doing this, after all this time? I hear the queues still start at four and five o'clock at some of the stations. I couldn't bear to do it, could you?'

'No, I couldn't bear it,' said Julia.

'They've got nowhere else, though. And look, it's all old ladies and men, and children.'

'It's horrible. People being made to live like moles. It's like the Dark Ages. It's worse than that. It's prehistoric.'

There was something elemental, it was true, to the heavily laden figures, as they made their uncertain way into the dimly lighted mouth of the Underground. They might have been mendicants or pedlars; refugees from some other, medieval, war – or else, from some war of the future, as imagined by H. G. Wells or a fanciful writer like that . . . Then Helen caught snatches of their conversation: *'Head over heels! How we laughed!'*; *'A pound of onions and a saddle of pork'*; *'He said, "It's got fancy teeth." I said, "It ought to have better teeth than I've got, at that price . . ."'*

She pulled at Julia's arm. 'Come on.'

'Where to?'

'The river.'

They walked to the middle of the bridge, then turned off their torches and looked out, westwards. The river ran gleamlessly beneath a starless sky, so black it might have been of treacle or of tar – or might not have been a river at all, but a channel, a gash in the earth, impossible to fathom . . . The sensation of feeling yourself supported at a height above it, by an almost-invisible bridge, was very unnerving. Helen and Julia had unlinked their arms, to lean and peer; now they moved close together again.

As Helen felt the pressure of Julia's shoulder against her own she remembered, with awful vividness, standing on the quaint little bridge on Hampstead Heath, a few hours before, with Kay. She said quietly, 'Damn.'

'What's the matter?' asked Julia. But she spoke quietly, too: as if she knew what the matter was. And when Helen didn't answer she said, 'Do you want to go back?'

'No,' said Helen, after a little hesitation. 'Do you?'

'No.'

So they were still for another moment, then started to walk again: back, at first, the way they had come; back to the bottom of Ludgate Hill. Here, without debate, they turned, and headed up towards St Paul's.

The streets grew quieter again and, once they'd passed under the railway bridge, the mood of the city seemed transformed. There was a sense – for it could not be seen, so much as felt – of exposed ground, unnatural space. The pavements were edged with fences and hoardings, but Helen found her thoughts slipping past the flimsy panels of wood to the rubble, the burnt and broken things, the uncovered girders and yawning basements and smashed brick, beyond. She and Julia walked without speaking, awed by the strangeness of the place. They stopped at the base of the cathedral steps and Helen looked up, trying to trace the outline of the huge, irregular silhouette against the dark of the sky.

'I looked at this, this afternoon,' she said, 'from Parliament Hill.' She didn't say she had also looked, anxiously, for Mecklenburgh Square; she'd forgotten it herself, for the moment. 'How it seemed to loom over London! Like a great big toad.'

'Yes,' said Julia. She seemed to shudder. 'I'm never very sure I like it here. Everyone says how grateful they are, that St Paul's hasn't been touched, but— I don't know, it seems freakish to me.'

Helen looked at her. 'You can't wish it had been bombed?'

'I'd rather it had been bombed, naturally, than a family in Croydon or Bethnal Green. Meanwhile it sits here, like – not like a toad, but like some great Union Jack, or – like Churchill, "Britain can take it", all of that – somehow making it all right that the war's still going on.'

'It *does* make it all right, though – doesn't it?' asked Helen quietly. 'In the sense, I mean, that while we've still got St Paul's— I'm not talking about Churchill, or flags. But while we've still got this and all it stands for: I mean, elegance, and reason, and – and great beauty – then the war is still worth fighting. Isn't it?'

'Is that what this war's about?' asked Julia.

'What do you think it's about?'

'I think it's about our love of savagery, rather than our love of beauty. I think the spirit that went into the building of St Paul's has shown itself to be thin: it's like gold leaf, and now it's rising, peeling away. If it couldn't keep us from the last war, and it couldn't keep us from this – from Hitler and Hitlerism, from Jew-hatred, from the bombing of women and children in cities and towns – what use is it? If we have to fight so hard to keep it – if we have to have elderly men patrolling the roofs of churches, to sweep incendiaries from them with little brushes! – how valuable can it be? How much at the centre of the human heart?'

Helen shivered – impressed, suddenly, by the awful sadness of Julia's words; and glimpsing a sort of darkness in her – a frightening, baffling darkness. She touched her arm.

'If I thought like that, Julia,' she said softly, 'I'd want to die.'

Julia was still for a moment; then moved – took a step, swept her foot, kicked gravel. 'I suppose,' she said, in a lighter voice, 'I don't think like it, really;

or I'd want to die, too. It's a thing one *can't* think, can one? Instead one concentrates one's mind' – she must have been remembering the men and women they'd seen going into the Underground with pillows – 'on the price of combs; on pork and onions. On cigarettes. Do you want one, by the way?'

They laughed, and the darkness passed. Helen drew back her hand. Julia brought out a packet from her pocket, fumbling slightly because of her gloves. She struck a match, and her face sprang startlingly into life, yellow and black. Helen bent her head to the flame, then straightened up and made to move on. The light had made her feel blind again. When Julia tugged at her arm, she let herself be led.

Then she saw where Julia was heading: east-wards, towards the ground beyond St Paul's. 'This way?' she asked, in surprise.

'Why not?' answered Julia. 'There's somewhere, now, I'd like to take you. If we keep to the road, I think we'll be all right.'

So they left the cathedral behind and started on the line of stone and broken tarmac that had once been Cannon Street, but was now more like the idea or the ghost of a road, on a landscape that might have been flat open country. Within a minute or two the sky seemed to have expanded over their heads, giving the illusion of light; as before, however, they could not see so much as sense the devastation that lay about them: they tried to peer

459

into the utter darkness of the ground, and their gazes slid about. Two or three times Helen put her hand to her eyes as if to wipe veils or cobwebs from them. They might have been walking through murky water, so absolutely strange and dense was the quality of the night here, and so freighted with violence and loss.

They kept the beams of their torches very low, following the whitened line of the kerb. Every time a car or a lorry passed they slowed their step, pressed themselves against the feeble-seeming fences that had been put there to separate pavement from rubble, and felt earth and bramble and broken stone beneath their shoes. When they spoke, they spoke in murmurs.

Julia said, 'I remember making this walk, on New Year's Day in 1941. The road was almost impassable, even on foot. I came to look at the damaged churches. I think even more have gone since then. Back there' – she nodded over her left shoulder – 'must be the remains of St Augustine's. It was bad enough when I saw it then; it was bombed again, wasn't it, right at the end of the last blitz?'

'I don't know,' said Helen.

'I think it was. And ahead of us, there – can you see?' She gestured. 'You can just make it out – that must be all that's left of St Mildred, Bread Street. That was awfully sad . . .'

She named more churches as they walked: St Mary-le-Bow, St Mary Aldermary, St James, St Michael; she seemed to be able to identify, quite clearly, the shapes of their battered towers and attenuated spires, while Helen struggled to pick them out at all. Now and then she flicked the beam of her torch across the waste-ground, to guide Helen's eye; the light caught fragments of broken glass, patches of frost, and found colour: the green and brown and silver of nettle, bracken, thistle. Once it lit up the eyes of some creature.

'Look, there!'

'Is it a cat?'

'It's a fox! Look at its red tail!'

They watched it dart, as quick and fluid as racing water; they tried to follow it with their torch-beams as it ran. Then they turned their torches off and listened, heard the rustling of leaves and the shifting of earth. But that soon became unnerving. They thought of rats, adders, vagrants. They went on, more quickly, heading away from the open ground to the shelter of the streets behind Cannon Street Station.

The buildings here were offices and banks: some had been gutted in 1940 and left unrepaired, some were still in use, but at this sort of hour on a Saturday night it was impossible to tell the exact condition of any of them; they all had an equally haunted look – more weird, in its way, than the heath-like feel of the blasted place where buildings had been lost completely.

If the streets around Ludgate Circus had been quiet, here they seemed utterly deserted. Only now and then, from deep beneath the broken pavements, came the rumbling of the Underground; as if herds of great, complaining creatures were hurling themselves through the city sewers – as, in a way, thought Helen, they were.

She gripped Julia's arm more tightly. It was always disconcerting, in a black-out, leaving the places you knew best. A particular feeling started to creep over you, a mixture of panic and dread: as if you were walking through a rifle-range with a target on your back . . . 'We must be mad, Julia,' she whispered, 'to be here!'

'It was your idea.'

'I know, but—'

'Are you frightened?'

'Yes! Anyone could come at us out of the dark.'

'But if we can't see them, they can't see us. Besides, they'd probably take us for a boy and his girl. Last week I went out in this coat and cap, and a tart in a doorway thought I was a chap and showed me her breast – flashed her torch at it. That was in Piccadilly.'

'Good God,' said Helen.

'Yes,' said Julia. 'And I can't tell you how odd a single breast looks, when lit up in the dark like that.'

She slowed her step and swung her torch. 'Here's St Clement's,' she said, 'the church from the nursery rhyme. They used to bring oranges and lemons, I suppose, to the shore of the Thames, just down there.'

Helen thought of the orange Kay had given her

that morning. But Kay and the morning felt far away, in a place like this. They were on the other side of that mad, impossible landscape.

They crossed a road. 'Where are we now?'

'This must be Eastcheap. We're nearly there.'

'Nearly where?'

'Only another church, I'm afraid. You won't be disappointed?'

'I'm thinking of the walk we must do, to get home. We'll get our throats cut.'

'How you fret!' said Julia. She made Helen walk a little further, then drew her towards a narrowish opening between two buildings. 'This is Idol Lane,' she murmured – or she might, Helen supposed, have said 'Idle Lane'. 'It's just along here.'

Helen hung back. 'It's too dark!'

'But it's just down here,' said Julia.

Her grip slid from Helen's elbow to her hand. She squeezed her fingers, and led her down a sloping path and then, a little way along it, made her stop. She swung up the beam of her torch and Helen could just make out, in the sweep of it, the shape of a tower: a high and elegant tower, with a sharp, slender spire supported by arches or buttresses – or simply blown through, perhaps, by bomb-blast, for the body of the church from which it rose seemed to be roofless, gutted, quite wrecked.

'St Dunstan-in-the-East,' said Julia quietly, looking up. 'It was rebuilt by Wren, like most of these churches, after the Great Fire of 1666. But they say that his daughter, Jane, helped him to design it. She's supposed to have gone to the top to lay the last stones, when the mason lost his nerve. And when they drew away the scaffolding, she lay down here, to show her faith that the tower wouldn't fall . . . I like to come here. I like to think of her making her way up the tower steps, with bricks and a trowel. She couldn't have been at all delicate, yet the portraits of her have made her out to be pale and slight. Shall we stay here a minute? Are you too cold?'

'No, I'm all right. Not inside the church, though.'

'No, just here. If we keep to the shadow, any sort of footpad or cutthroat could go by, and never know we were here.'

They walked cautiously around the tower, still hand in hand, guiding themselves by a set of broken railings and feeling for uneven ground. A flight of three or four shallow stone steps ran up to each of the tower doors; they made their way up to one of these doors, and sat down. The stone was icily cold. The doors, and the walls around them, were black, and threw off no light: Helen looked for Julia in her cap and dark coat and could hardly see her.

But she felt the movement of her arm, as she dipped her fingers into her pocket and brought out the night-watchman's bottle. And she heard the moist little pop of the stopper coming out of the glass neck. Julia handed the bottle over, and Helen raised it to her mouth. The rough red liquid met her lips and seemed to flare across her tongue like a flame. She swallowed, and felt easier almost at once.

'We might,' she whispered, as she handed the bottle back, 'be the only people alive in the City. Do you think there are ghosts here, Julia?'

Julia was drinking. She wiped her mouth. 'There might be the ghost of Samuel Pepys. He used to come to this church. Once he was set upon by a couple of robbers here.'

'I shouldn't like to know that,' said Helen, 'if I weren't tipsy.'

'You got tipsy rather quick.'

'I was tipsy before, I just didn't like to say. Anyway, it's my birthday and I'm allowed to be tipsy.'

'Then I ought to get tipsy, too. There's no pleasure in being tipsy on your own.'

They drank more, then sat without speaking. At last Helen, very softly, began to sing.

Oranges and lemons, say the bells of St Clement's.
Pancake and fritters say the bells of St Peter's.

'What mad sort of words they are, aren't they?' she said, interrupting herself. 'I didn't even know I'd remembered them, until now.'

> *Bull's eyes and targets, say the bells of St*
>   *Margaret's.*
> *Pokers and tongs, say the bells of St John's.*

Julia said, 'You sing nicely. I don't suppose there's a St Helen's in the song?'

'I don't think so. What would those bells say?'

'I can't imagine. Strawberries and melons?'

'Torturers and felons . . . What about St Julia?'

'I don't think there ever was a St Julia. Anyway, nothing rhymes with *Julia*. Except *peculiar*.'

'You're about the most unpeculiar person I've ever met, Julia.'

They had put back their heads against the black tower door, and turned their faces to one another, to speak softly. When Julia laughed, Helen felt the rush of breath against her own mouth: warm, wine-scented, slightly soured by tobacco.

'You don't think it's peculiar,' Julia said, 'to have brought you here, to the ruin of a church, in the middle of a black-out?'

'I think it's marvellous,' said Helen simply.

Julia answered, still laughing, 'Have some more wine.'

Helen shook her head. Her heart had risen into her throat. Too high and full, it felt, to swallow back down. 'I don't want any more,' she said softly. 'The fact is, Julia, I'm afraid to be drunk while I'm with you.'

It seemed to her that there could be no mistaking the meaning of her words: that they had penetrated some thin but resilient membrane, made a tear through which a heap of unruly passions would now come tumbling . . . But Julia laughed again, and must have turned her head, for her breath no longer came against Helen's lips; and when she spoke, she spoke musingly, distantly. She said, 'Isn't it extraordinary, though, that we know each other so little? Three weeks ago, when we had that cup of tea outside Marylebone Station – do you remember? I would never have said, then, that we'd be here now, like this . . .'

'Why did you stop me that day, Julia?' asked Helen, after a moment. 'Why did you ask me to have tea with you?'

'Why did I?' said Julia. 'Shall I tell you? I'm almost afraid to. It might make you hate me. I did it – well, out of curiosity, I suppose you'd have to call it.'

'Curiosity?'

'I wanted to – get the measure of you, something like that.' She gave an uncomfortable little laugh. 'I thought you might have guessed it.'

Helen didn't answer. She was remembering the odd, sly way in which Julia had glanced at her, when they'd been talking about Kay; she was thinking of the feeling she'd had, that Julia was testing her, weighing her up. She said slowly at last, 'I think I did guess. You wanted to see, didn't you, if you could find in me what Kay does?'

Julia moved. 'It was a lousy thing to do. I'm sorry, now.'

'It doesn't matter,' said Helen. 'Truly, it doesn't. After all—' Her feelings had faltered, just a little, but now rose again, buoyed up, by wine, by the darkness. 'After all, we're in a funny sort of situation, you and I.'

'Are we?'

'I mean, because of what happened between you and Kay—'

At once, even in the darkness, she knew that she had made a mistake. Julia stiffened. She said sharply, 'Kay told you that?'

'Yes,' said Helen, growing wary, speaking slowly. 'At least, I guessed it.'

'And you spoke with Kay about it?'

'Yes.'

'What did she say?'

'Only, that there had been a—'

'A what?'

Helen hesitated. Then, 'A misaffection, she called it,' she said.

'A misaffection?' Julia laughed. 'Christ!' She turned away again.

Helen reached for her arm. She caught hold of the sleeve of her coat instead. 'What's the matter?' she said. 'What is it? It doesn't matter, does it? It's never mattered to me, in the past. Is that what you're thinking? Or are you thinking that it's none of my business? But then, it has been my business, in a way. And since Kay was so open and honest about it with me—' She was forgetting, in her anxiety, that Kay had not really been open with her about it, at all. 'Since Kay was so open and honest about it, then shouldn't you and I be open and honest about it, too? If it's never mattered to me, why should it matter, now, to us?'

'How gallant you sound,' said Julia.

468

She said it so coldly, Helen felt afraid. 'Is it a matter for gallantry? I hope not. All I'm trying to say is, that I should hate for any of this to make a sort of – of coolness, or shadow, between us. Kay's never wanted that—'

'Oh, Kay,' said Julia. 'Kay's a great sentimentalist. Don't you think? She pretends to be so hard-boiled, but— I remember I once took her to see an Astaire and Rogers picture. She cried all the way through it. "What were you weeping at?" I asked her at the end. "The dancing," she said.'

Her manner had changed completely. She sounded almost bitter, now. 'I wasn't at all surprised,' she went on, 'when Kay met you. I wasn't surprised at the *way* she met you, I mean. It was like something from a picture in itself, wasn't it?'

'I don't know,' said Helen, confused. 'I suppose so. It didn't seem like that at the time.'

'Didn't it? Kay told me all about it – about how she found you, and so on. She put it that way, you see: that she found you. She said how frightened it made her, when she thought of how nearly you might have been lost. She described touching your face . . .'

'I remember hardly any of it,' said Helen, wretchedly. 'That's the stupid thing.'

'Kay remembers very well. But then, as I say, Kay's a sentimentalist. She remembers it as though there were a touch of fate to it, a touch of kismet.'

'There *was* a touch of kismet to it!' said Helen. 'But don't you see, how dreadfully tangled the whole thing is? If I'd never met Kay, I should never have met *you*, Julia. But Kay would never have loved me at all, if you had let her love you—'

'What?' said Julia.

'I used to be grateful to you,' Helen went on, her voice rising and starting to break. 'It seemed to me, that in not wanting Kay you had somehow given her to me. Now I've done what she did.'

'*What?*' said Julia again.

'Haven't you guessed?' said Helen. 'I've fallen in love with you, Julia, myself!'

She hadn't known, until that moment, that she'd been going to utter the words; but as soon as she said them, they became true.

Julia didn't answer. She had turned her face back to Helen's and her breath, as it had before, came fluttering, warm and bitter, against the wetness of Helen's cold lips. She sat quite still, then put out her hand and caught hold of Helen's fingers; and she gripped them hard, almost madly – as someone would clutch at a hand, or a strap of leather, blindly, in pain or grief. She said, 'Kay—'

'I know!' said Helen. 'But I simply can't help it, Julia! It makes me hate myself; but I can't help it! If you'd seen me, today. She was so kind. And all I could think of was you. I wished she was you! I wished—' She stopped. 'Oh, *God!*'

For she'd felt, very clearly, that odd little thrill or vibration that always came before the sounding of the Warning; and even before her voice had died away, the sirens started up. On and on they went, rising hectically up the scale again after every plunge towards silence; and it was impossible, even after so many years, to sit perfectly still and not mind them, not feel the urgent pull of them, the little clawing out of panic from within one's breast.

With the darkness all about, the effect was magnified. Helen put her hands across her ears and said, 'Oh, it's not fair! I can't bear them! They're like wails of grief! They're like – like the bells of London! They've got voices! *Take cover!* they're saying. *Run and hide! Here comes the chopper to chop off your head!*'

'Don't,' said Julia, touching her arm; and a moment after that, the Warning ceased. The silence, then, was almost more unnerving still. They sat very tensely, straining their ears for the sound of bombers; at last they began to make out the faint groan of engines. Crazy, it was, to think of the boys inside those funny tubes of metal, wishing you harm; to think of them having walked about, two hours before – eaten bread, drunk coffee, smoked cigarettes, shrugged on their jackets, stamped their feet against the cold . . . Then there came the first *thump-thump-thump* of anti-aircraft fire, perhaps two or three miles away.

Helen put back her head and looked up. Searchlights were on, the quality of the darkness had changed; she saw, instead of the sky, the rising wall of the tower against which she was sitting. She felt the hardness of the door against her scalp, through her hair; she imagined the stones above it

471

coming down, great pitiless blocks of masonry and mortar. She seemed to feel it swaying and lurching about, even as she peered at it.

She thought suddenly, *What am I doing here?* And then she thought, *Where's Kay?*

She scrambled to her feet.

'What is it?' asked Julia.

'I'm frightened. I don't want to stay here. I'm sorry, Julia—'

Julia drew up her legs. 'It's all right. I'm frightened, too. Help me to stand.'

She grabbed Helen's hand, braced herself against her weight, and rose. They switched on their torches and began to walk. They walked quickly, back up Idol Lane – or Idle Lane, whichever it was – to Eastcheap. Here they stopped, unsure of the safest route to take. When Julia turned to the right, Helen pulled her back.

'Wait,' she said, breathlessly. The sky, that way, was cut with the beams of searchlights. 'That's east, isn't it? That's towards the docks. Isn't it? Don't let's go that way. Let's go back the way we came.'

'Through the City? We could go into Monument Station.'

'Yes. Anywhere. I can't bear to be still, that's all, and think of things coming down—'

'Take my hand again,' said Julia. 'That's right.' Her voice was steady. Her grip was firm – not wild, as it had been before. She said, 'It was stupid of me to make you come, Helen. I ought to have thought—'

'I'm all right,' said Helen. 'I'm all right.'

They started off again, going quickly. 'We must just pass St Clement's,' said Julia, as they walked. 'St Clement's ought to be just here.' She shone her torch about, and hesitated; made Helen stop, then start again. They walked on, sometimes stumbling over broken paving-stones, sometimes groping with their feet for kerbs that weren't there; for the plunging about of the searchlights, the sudden appearance and disappearance of shadows, was disorientating. Finally they picked out the whited steps of a church.

The church, however, was not St Clement's but another. *St Edmund, King and Martyr*, its notice said.

Julia stood before it, utterly perplexed. 'We've got onto Lombard Street somehow.' She took off her cap, tugged back her hair. 'How the hell did we do that?'

'Which way is the Underground?' asked Helen.

'I'm not sure.'

Then they both gave a jump. A car had appeared, going too fast around a corner, weaving about; it went hurtling past them, then disappeared into the dark. They went on, and a moment later heard voices: men's voices, like the voices of ghosts from the blitz, floating about, echoing queerly. It was two fire-watchers, up on roofs, calling to each other across the street; one was giving a commentary on what he could see – incendiaries, he thought, on Woolwich and Bow. *'There's another packetful!'* they heard him say.

They were standing there, listening, hand in hand, when a warden came running out of the darkness and almost knocked them down.

'Where the bloody hell,' he said, panting, 'did you two spring from? Turn those torches off, and get yourselves under cover, can't you?'

Julia had pulled her fingers from Helen's the moment he'd appeared, and stepped away. She said, almost irritably, 'What does it look like we're trying to do? Where's the nearest shelter?'

The man caught her tone – or, what was more likely, Helen thought, took note of her accent – and his manner slightly changed. 'Bank Underground, miss,' he said. 'Fifty yards back there.' He jerked his thumb over his shoulder, and then ran on.

Perhaps it was the relative ordinariness of the exchange; perhaps it was the fact of seeing someone more agitated than herself; but Helen's anxiety seemed suddenly, magically, to disperse, as though drawn off by a needle. She put her arm through Julia's and they walked at quite a leisurely pace up towards what they could now easily see was a corrugated metal arch piled about with sandbags: the entrance to the station. A man and a girl went hurrying into it as they drew closer; a stout woman whose legs were sore or stiff was easing herself down the steps as quickly as she could. A schoolboy was hopping about, looking up, in great excitement, at the sky.

Julia slowed her step. 'Here it is, then,' she said, without enthusiasm.

Here's the return to company, Helen took her to mean, *to chatter and bustle and light* . . . She pulled Julia's arm. 'Wait,' she said. What were they doing? *I've fallen in love with you!* she'd cried in the darkness, fifteen minutes before. She remembered the fluttering of Julia's breath against her mouth. She remembered the feel of Julia's hand, clutching fiercely at hers. 'I don't want to go down,' she said quietly. 'I— I don't want to share you, Julia, with other people. I don't want to lose you.'

Perhaps Julia opened her mouth to answer, Helen wasn't sure. For in the next instant they were lit by a flash: a flash, like lightning, brief but unnaturally lurid, so that a thousand little details – the stitches in Julia's collar, the anchors on the buttons of her coat – seemed to spring from her body into the air, to leap into Helen's eyes and blind her. Two seconds later, the explosion came – fantastically loud, not terribly close, perhaps even as far away as Liverpool Street or Moorgate; but close enough for them to feel the shock of it, the freakish beating against them of a gust of airless wind. The schoolboy capering about the station steps gave a whoop of absolute pleasure; some adult darted out to scoop him up and carry him inside. Helen put out her hand, and Julia gripped it. They began to run – not into the station, but away from it, back down Lombard Street. They were laughing like idiots. When the next explosion came – further off, this time – they laughed more wildly, and quickened their pace.

Then, 'In here!' said Julia, tugging Helen's hand. She had seen, lit up by the second flash, a sort of baffle-wall that had been built across the entrance to an office or a bank. The space it made was deep, jute-scented, impossibly dark: she moved into it, as if passing through a curtain of ink, and drew Helen in after her.

They stood without speaking, catching their breaths; their breaths sounded louder, in that muffled space, than all the sounds of the chaos in the street. Only when they heard footsteps did they look out: they saw the warden they had spoken to, still running, but running back, in the opposite direction. He went straight past and didn't see them.

'Now we're invisible again,' whispered Julia.

They had drawn close to each other, to look out. Helen was aware, as she had been before, of the movement of Julia's breath, against her ear and cheek; she knew that all she had to do was move her head – just turn it, just tilt it, that was all – for her lips to find out Julia's in the darkness . . . But she stood quite still, unable to act; and it was Julia, in the end, who started the kiss. She put up her hand and touched Helen's face, and guided their two blind mouths together; and as the kiss, like a fire, drew, took hold, she slid her hand to the back of Helen's head and pressed her even closer.

But after a moment, she drew away. She loosened the knot of Helen's scarf, began slowly to tug at the buttons of her coat. When the coat was unfastened, she started on her own: the panels of the jacket parted, she moved forward again, and the two opened coats came together to make what seemed to Helen to be a second baffle-wall, darker even than the first. Inside it, her own and Julia's bodies felt quick, hard, astoundingly warm. They kissed again, and fitted themselves against each other, Julia's thigh coming snugly between Helen's legs, Helen's thigh sliding tightly between Julia's; and they stood hardly moving, just nudging, nudging with their hips.

At last, Helen turned her head. She said, in a whisper, 'This is what Kay wanted, isn't it? I know why she did, Julia! God! I feel like— I feel like I'm her! I want to touch you, Julia. I want to touch you, like she would—'

Julia moved back. She caught hold of Helen's hand, pulled the glove from her fingers and let it drop. She took the hand to the buttons of her trousers, opened them up, and, almost roughly, slid it inside.

'Do it, then,' she said.

When the Warning sounded at John Allen House a girl would go up and down the stairs and along the corridors, knocking on every door. 'Raiders Overhead! Raiders Overhead, girls!' After that, each boarder was supposed to make her way down to the basement, in a calm and orderly way. But the basement was like shelters everywhere: too cold, too airless and too dim; and sometimes the heartier girls of the house – the girls with whom Viv had least in common, the girls for whom this sort of life was only another kind of boarding-school – would attempt to start off games, or rounds of jolly singing. Lately, too, the various smells of the place had begun to make Viv afraid of being sick.

So for the past few weeks she'd taken to staying in her room when the sirens went, with Betty and the other girl they shared with, a girl called Anne. Betty and Anne could sleep through anything – Anne dosing herself with veramon, Betty putting an eye-mask on and sticking pink wax plugs in her ears. Only Viv would lie fretful, wincing at the blasts and the ack-ack fire; thinking of Reggie, Duncan, her father, her sister; pressing with her hands at her stomach and wondering what the hell she was going to do about the thing that was growing inside it, that must be got out.

She had tried the tablets that Felicity Withers had tried: they had given her stomach cramps and frightful diarrhoea for almost a week, but apart from that had had no effect at all. She had spent the days since then in a sort of stupor of anxiety, making endless mistakes at Portman Court; unable to smoke, unable to eat; unable to fix her mind on anything except the necessity of swallowing down the sickness that could swell inside her like a bitter black tide, for hours at a time. This morning, too, she had drawn on her skirt and, to her horror, found that the waistband wouldn't fasten; she'd had to close it with a safety-pin.

'What can I do?' she'd said to Betty; and Betty had said what she'd always said before, 'Write and tell Reggie. For God's sake, Viv, if you don't do it, I'm going to write the letter myself!'

But Viv didn't want to write, because of the Censor. And there were two more weeks before his leave came round again. She couldn't wait that long, getting fatter and sicker and more afraid. She knew she had to tell him. She knew the only way to do it was to call him up by telephone. She was lying rigidly in bed right now, nerving herself up to go downstairs and do it.

She was hoping the raid would end; but the raid, if anything, was getting worse. When, after another couple of minutes, she heard Anne muttering in her sleep, she put back the bedclothes. If the bombs came closer, Anne might wake. That would make it all harder. She must do it now, she thought, or never . . .

She got up, put on her dressing-gown and slippers, and picked up her torch.

She went out into the hall, and down one flight of stairs – going carefully, feeling her way, because the staircase was lit very badly with one blue bulb. She must have gone almost noiselessly, too: a girl coming up, with a plate in her hand, met her at the turn of the landing and nearly jumped out of her skin. 'Viv!' she hissed. 'My God! I thought you were the Ghost of Typists Past.'

'Sorry, Millie.'

'Where are you going? The basement? Rather

you than me. You'll be just in time for the second round of Boy, Girl, Flower, Animal . . . Or, did you have your eye on those cream crackers that were knocking about in the common-room? Too bad. I've bagged the lot, look, for Jacqueline Knight and Caroline Graham and me.'

Viv shook her head. 'You can have them. I'm just getting a glass of water.'

'Watch out for mice, then,' said Millie, beginning to climb the stairs. 'And remember: if anyone asks you who took those cream crackers, you never saw me. I'll do the same for you one day.'

Her voice faded. Viv waited until she'd crossed the landing, then carried on down. The staircase grew wider the lower she went; the house was an old one, built to a rather grand scale. There were great plaster roses in all the ceilings, and hooks where chandeliers had once hung. The banister rail had elegant curves and graceful finials. But though there were handsome crimson carpets in the hallways, they were all covered up with canvas, and the canvas was much damaged by high heels. The walls were painted in dispiriting gloss shades, green and cream and grey: they looked worse than ever in the dim blue light.

The lobby was a mess of women's coats and hats and umbrellas. A table spilled over with papers and unclaimed post. The fanlight, of course, had been boarded up, but the bomb-proofed glass in the door that led to the basement was gleaming turgidly. From beyond it came one girl's voice, and then others: '*Primrose . . . Pansy . . . Primula . . .*'

Viv put on her torch. The telephone was further on, in an alcove outside the common-room – horribly public, but over the years girls had unpicked the staples which attached the wire to the wall, and if you wanted to make a private call you could pull the telephone across the corridor into a cupboard, and sit, in darkness, on a gas-meter, amongst brooms and buckets and mops. Viv did this now, drawing shut the cupboard door and propping her torch on a shelf; looking rather fearfully into the cracks and corners, for fear of spiders and mice. *Think Before You Speak* said a label on the telephone.

She had the number of Reggie's unit on an old bit of paper in her dressing-gown pocket; he'd given it to her, ages ago, for emergencies, and she'd never used it. But what was this, she thought, if not an emergency? She got the number out. She picked up the receiver and dialled 0 for the Exchange, letting the dial turn slowly; muffling the clicks of it, as best she could, with a handkerchief.

The operator's voice was as bright as glass. The call, she said, would take several minutes to connect. 'Thank you,' said Viv. She sat with the telephone in her lap, nerving herself for the ring of it. Then the beam of her torch began to waver: she thought of the battery, and turned it off. She'd left the door open, just a little, and the dim blue light of the corridor showed through the crack. Apart from that, the cupboard was absolutely dark. She could just make out bursts of laughter, and groans, from the girls in the basement. There were bumps, and shivers, and trickles of dust in the walls, as bombs kept falling.

When at last the phone rang again, the noise of the bell, and the jolt of it in her lap, frightened the life out of her. She picked up the receiver with shaking hands, and almost dropped it. The glass-voiced girl said, 'Just a moment'; and there was another wait, then, and a series of clicks, as she made the connection.

A man's voice came on the line: the switchboard-operator at Reggie's camp. Viv gave him Reggie's name.

'You don't know his hut?' he asked her. She didn't. He tried a central number. The phone rang and rang . . . 'No answer, Caller,' he said.

'Please,' said Viv, 'just a minute longer. It's awfully urgent.'

'Hello?' said another voice at last. 'Is that my call to Southampton? Hello?'

'This is an incoming call, I'm afraid,' said the operator blandly.

'Blast you.'

'You're welcome.'

The phone was picked up by somebody else after that; he gave them, at least, the number of Reggie's hut. The phone rang only twice, this time, and then came a deafening burst of noise: shouting, and laughter, and music from a radio or gramophone.

A man bellowed into the phone. 'Hello?'

'Hello?' said Viv quietly.

'Hello? Who's this?'

She told him she wanted Reggie.

'Reggie? What?' he shouted.

'Who's there?' came another man's voice.

'Some girl, calling herself Reggie.'

'She's not calling herself Reggie, you oaf. It's Reggie she wants to speak to.' The receiver was taken by another hand. 'Miss, I really must apologise— Or is it Madam?'

'Please,' said Viv. She glanced out nervously, into the corridor, through the crack in the nearly closed door. She put her hand around her mouth, to muffle her voice. 'Is Reggie there?'

'Is he here? That would probably depend, if I know Reg, on who wants to know. Does he owe you money?'

'Is she sure it's Reg she wants?' said the first voice.

'My friend,' said the second, 'wants to know if you're sure it's Reg you want, and not him. He is making shapes with his hands, suggestive of what he considers must be the lovely colour of your eyes, the beautiful curl of your hair, the magnificent swell of your – voice.'

'Please,' said Viv again, 'I haven't got very long.'

'That won't bother my friend, from what I've heard.'

'Is Reggie there, or not?'

'May I say who's calling?'

'Tell him— Tell him it's his wife.'

'His lady wife? In that case, far be it from me to . . .'

The voice became a mumble, and then a distorted shout. That was followed by cheers, and a kind of scuffling sound, as the phone was passed from hand to hand. At last, Reggie's voice came on the line. He sounded breathless.

'Marilyn?' he said.

'It's not her, it's me,' said Viv, very quickly. 'Don't say my name, in case the operator's listening.'

But he said her name, anyway. 'Viv?' He sounded amazed. 'The boys told me—'

'I know. They were mucking about, and I didn't know what else to say.'

'Christ.' She heard him rubbing his bristly chin and cheeks with his hand. 'Where are you? How did you get hold of me?' He turned his mouth away. 'Woods, I swear to God, one more crack like that, and—'

'I just called the Exchange,' she said.

'What?'

'I called the Exchange.'

'Are you all right?'

'Yes. No.'

'I can't hear you. Just a minute—' He put the phone down and went off; there was more cheering, and more laughter. When he came back, he was breathless again. 'Those buggers,' he said. He had moved, or closed a door. 'Where are you? You sound like you're in the bucket at the bottom of a well.'

'I'm in a cupboard,' she whispered, 'at home. I mean, at John Allen House.'

'A cupboard?'

'Where the girls make calls. It doesn't matter. It's just— Something's happened, Reggie.'

'What? Not your bloody brother?'

'Don't call him that. No, not that. Nothing like that.'

'What, then?'

'I— It's just—' She tried to see out into the hall again; then turned her head, and spoke more quietly than ever. 'My friend hasn't come,' she said.

'Your what? Your friend?' He didn't understand. 'Which friend?'

'My *friend*.'

There was a silence. Then, 'Christ,' he said softly. 'Christ, Viv.'

'Don't say my name!'

'No. No. How much? I mean, how long?'

'About eight weeks, I think.'

'Eight weeks?' He was turning it over in his mind. 'So you mean, you must have been, already, when I saw you last—?'

'Yes, I must have been. But I didn't know.'

'And, you're absolutely sure? You couldn't just have – have missed?'

'I don't think so. I never have before.'

'But, we've been careful, haven't we? I've been careful, every fucking time. What's the point of being careful, if this happens?'

'I don't know. It's bad luck.'

485

'Bad luck? Jesus.'

He sounded disgusted. He moved the phone again; she imagined him tugging at his hair. She said, 'Don't be like that. It's been hell, for me. I've been worrying myself to death. I've tried all sorts of things. I— I took something.'

He couldn't hear her. 'What?'

She covered her mouth again, but tried to speak more clearly. 'I took something. You know . . . But it didn't work, it just made me sick.'

'Did you get the right thing?'

'I don't know. Are there different kinds of things? I got it from a chemist's. The man said it would work, but it didn't. It was awful.'

'Can't you try again?'

'I don't want to, Reggie.'

'But it might be worth just trying again.'

'It made me feel so awful.'

'But don't you just think—?'

'It'll make me sick again. Oh Reggie, I don't think I can! I don't know what to do!'

Her voice had been trembling, all this time; now, with a rush, it tightened and rose. She'd started to panic, and was almost crying.

Reggie said, 'OK. All right. Listen to me. It's all right, baby. Listen to me. This is the hell of a shock, that's all. I just need to think about it. There's a bloke here. I think his girl— I just need some time.'

She moved the receiver, and blew her nose. 'I didn't want to tell you,' she said miserably. 'I wanted to sort it out by myself. I just – I felt so awful. If my dad found out—'

'It's OK, baby.'

'It'd break his heart. It'd—'

Pip pip pip, went the line; and the operator spoke. '*One minute, Caller.*'

It was the girl who'd connected Viv right at the start; or another girl, with the same bright, glass-like voice. Viv and Reggie fell silent.

'Do you suppose she heard?' whispered Reggie at last.

'I don't know.'

'They don't listen really, do they?'

'I don't know.'

'How can they, with so many calls?'

'No. I expect they don't.'

Silence again . . . Then, 'Shit,' said Reggie, as if wearily. 'What luck. What lousy rotten luck. And I was so careful, every time!'

'I know,' said Viv.

'I'll ask this bloke, about his girl, about what she did. OK?'

Viv nodded.

'OK?'

'Yes.'

'You're not to worry any more.'

'No. I won't.'

'Promise me?'

'Yes.'

'We'll be all right. OK? Good girl.'

They stayed on the line, not speaking, until the

operator's voice came again, asking if they'd like to extend the call. Viv said they wouldn't, and the line went dead.

'Hello,' said Kay very softly, an hour or two later. She was stroking Helen's hair.

'Hello,' said Helen, opening her eyes.

'Did I wake you?'

'I'm not sure . . . What time is it?'

Kay got in beside her. 'Just past your birthday, I'm afraid. Just two o'clock.'

'Are you all right?'

'Not a scratch on me. We didn't go out. Bethnal Green and Shoreditch got it all.'

Helen took her hand and squeezed her fingers. 'I'm glad,' she said.

Kay yawned. 'I'd rather have gone out. I spent the night doing puzzles with Mickey and Hughes.' She kissed Helen's cheek, then fitted herself about her. 'You smell soapy.'

Helen stiffened. 'Do I?'

'Yes. Just like a kid. Did you have another bath? You must be clean as anything. Were you lonely?'

'No, not really.'

'I thought of sneaking back to you.'

'Did you?'

Kay smiled. 'Well, not really. It seemed an awful waste, that's all, to be there, doing nothing, while you were here.'

'Yes,' said Helen. She still held Kay's hand; now she drew Kay's arm around her – tight, as if wanting

488

comfort or warmth. Her legs were bare against Kay's; her cotton nightdress had risen, almost to her bottom. Her breasts felt loose and warm beneath Kay's arm.

Kay kissed her head, stroked back her hair. She said, in a murmur, 'I suppose you're awfully sleepy, darling?'

'I am, rather.'

'Too sleepy to kiss?'

Helen didn't answer. Kay drew free her arm. She caught hold of the collar of Helen's nightgown and, very gently, pulled it down. She put her lips to the bend of Helen's neck, moved her mouth against the hot, smooth flesh. But she became aware, as she was doing it, of the feel of the threadbare fabric in her hand. She lifted her head from her pillow and said, in surprise, 'You're not wearing your new pyjamas?'

'Hmm?' said Helen, as if from the edge of sleep.

'Your pyjamas,' said Kay softly.

'Oh,' said Helen, reaching for Kay's hand again; drawing Kay's arm about her and pulling her close. 'I forgot,' she said.

CHAPTER 5

The moon was so full and so bright that night, they didn't need their torches. Surfaces were lit up, white against black. Everything looked depthless, the fronts of houses flat as scenery on a stage, the trees like trees of papier mâché touched up with glitter and silver paint. Nobody liked it. It made you feel vulnerable, exposed. People got off the train and turned up the collars of their coats, put down their heads, darted away to darker places. A hundred yards from Cricklewood Station, the streets were silent. Only Reggie and Viv, uncertain of their route, went slowly. When Reggie took out a piece of paper to check the directions on it, Viv looked fearfully up at the sky: the paper shone in his hand as if luminous.

The house, when they found it at last, was an ordinary one; but there was a name-plate screwed to the door-frame, beneath the bell. The plate looked solid, professional – reassuring, but frightening too. Viv had her arm through Reggie's and now slightly pulled him back. He caught hold of her hand and squeezed her fingers. Her fingers felt odd, because he'd got her a gold-coloured ring, which was slightly too large and kept slipping.

'All right?' he asked her. His voice was thin. He hated doctors, hospitals, things like that. She knew he wished she had come with Betty, her sister – anyone but him.

So it was she who pressed the bell. The man – Mr Imrie – came to answer it almost at once.

'Ah yes,' he said, quite loudly, looking past them into the street. 'Come in, come in.' They stood close together in the darkness, unsure of the size of the hall, while he closed the door and re-arranged the black-out across its panels of frosted glass; then he led them into his waiting-room, where the light was bright and made them blink. The room smelt sweet: of polish, of rubber, of gas. There were pictures on the walls, showing teeth, pink gums; a case had a plaster model inside it of a single great molar, a slice removed to expose the enamel, the pulp and red nerve. The colours were livid, because of the light. Viv looked from one thing to another and felt her teeth begin to ache.

Mr Imrie was a dentist; and did this other thing on the side.

'Do sit down,' he said.

He took up a sheet of paper and clipped it to a board. He wore spectacles with heavy frames and, in order to see the page before him, he pushed them up, so that they gripped his brow like a pair of goggles on a band. He asked for Viv's name.

She'd taken off her gloves to expose the ring, and now, with a little flush of self-consciousness, gave the name that she and Reggie had agreed on: *Mrs Margaret Harrison*. He said it aloud, as he wrote it down; and then he kept saying it at the start of every question: 'And now, Mrs Harrison', 'Well, Mrs Harrison' – until the name, Viv thought, sounded so false and made-up, it might have been an actress's name, or the name of a character in a film.

The questions were simple enough at first. When they grew more personal, Mr Imrie suggested that Reggie might like to wait in the hall. Viv thought he went out pretty quickly, as if in relief. She heard the slither of his shoes on the lino as he paced up and down.

Perhaps Mr Imrie heard it too. He lowered his voice. 'The date of your last period?'

Viv gave it. He made a note of it, and seemed to frown.

'Any children?' he asked her then. 'Miscarriages? You know what a miscarriage is? Of course . . . And have you ever before been obliged to receive the, er, treatment that you've come to receive from me?'

She said 'No' to it all; but told him, after a little hesitation, about the pills, in case they made some sort of difference.

He shook his head, dismissively, as she described them. 'It's never worth bothering, if you'll take my advice,' he said, 'with that sort of thing.

Probably gave you a tummy upset, did they? Yes, I thought they would have.' He drew down his spectacles and was left with a phantom pair, marked out in lines of red, on the flesh of his brow.

He produced a case of instruments, and Viv flinched, growing frightened. He wanted only, however, to test her blood-pressure and listen to her chest; and he made her stand and loosen her skirt, and felt her stomach – felt all about it, pressing hard with his fingers and palms.

Then he straightened, and wiped his hands. 'Well,' he said gravely, 'you're a little further along than I should have liked.' He was dating it, of course, from her last period. 'I usually recommend this treatment for pregnancies of up to ten weeks, and yours is rather past that.'

The extra weeks made a difference, apparently. He went to the door and called for Reggie and explained to them both that, because of the added element of risk, he would have to charge them more than the standard fee. 'A further ten pounds, I'm afraid.'

'Ten pounds?' said Reggie, appalled.

Mr Imrie spread his hands. 'You'll understand, with the law as it is. The risk I'm running is very grave.'

'My friend said seventy-five. Seventy-five's all I've brought.'

'Seventy-five would have seen to it, a month ago. I dare say seventy-five would see to it even now, were you to go to another sort of man. I'm not that sort of man, however. I'm thinking of your wife's health. I'm thinking of my own wife. I am sorry.'

Reggie shook his head. 'This is a rum kind of way to do business,' he said bitterly, 'if you don't mind my saying so. One price one month, and another the next. What difference does it make to you, it being in there' – he nodded in the general direction of Viv's stomach – 'two or three weeks longer?'

Mr Imrie smiled, as if with tremendous patience. 'It makes a great deal of difference, I'm afraid.'

'Well, that's what you say. You'd say the same thing, I suppose, to a chap who'd come to you with a case of – of an ingrowing tooth?'

'I very well might.'

'You would, would you—?'

The argument ran on. Viv stood and said nothing, hating it all, hating Reggie, gazing at the floor. At last Mr Imrie agreed to take the extra ten pounds in the form of clothing coupons: Reggie turned his back and brought out a little stash of them, pressed them into the envelope in which he'd already put the money, and handed them over. He made a snorting noise as he did it.

'Thank you,' said Mr Imrie, with exaggerated politeness. He stowed the envelope away in a pocket of his own. 'Now, if you wouldn't mind making yourself comfortable here, just for twenty minutes or so, I'll take your wife next door.'

'Keep my coat and hat, will you?' said Viv to Reggie, coldly. He took them, and reached after her fingers.

'It'll be all right,' he said, trying to catch her eye. 'It'll be OK.'

She pulled her fingers away. A clock on the wall showed five past eight. Mr Imrie led her back across the hall and into his surgery.

She thought at first he meant to take her through this room into another. She thought he would have some quite different place set up. But he closed the door behind her and went to a counter, looking busy; and for an awful moment, then, she imagined he meant to do the operation with her sitting in his dentist's chair. Then she saw, beyond the chair, a couch, on trestle legs, covered over with a wax-paper sheet, and with a little zinc pail beside it. It looked horrible with the great steel light shining on it, and the trays of instruments all around, the queer machines, the drills, the bottles of gas. She felt the suffocated rising of tears in her chest and throat, and thought, for the first time, *I can't!*

'Now then, Mrs Harrison,' said Mr Imrie, perhaps seeing her hesitate. 'Just slip off your skirt, your shoes and underthings, and hop up onto the couch, and we'll make a start. All right? There's nothing to worry about. A very straightforward procedure indeed.'

He turned away, took off his jacket and washed his hands; began to fold back his sleeves. There was an electric fire burning, and she stood in front of it to undress; she put her clothes on a chair, and got quickly onto the crackling wax-paper before he should turn – for she felt more exposed, somehow, with only her bottom half bare, than she would have felt if she had stripped completely. It was like something a tart would do. But when she lay on the hard flat couch, she felt foolish in another way – like a fish, with gaping gills and mouth, on a fishmonger's slab.

'Let me give you a pillow,' said Mr Imrie, coming over and carefully not looking at her naked hips. 'And now, if you'd care to raise yourself?' He slid a folded towel under her bottom – moving her blouse, as he did it, a little higher up her back, and saying, 'We don't want this to spoil, do we?' She realised he was tucking it out of the way of any blood that might come; and grew frightened again. She had no idea how much blood *would* come – had only, in fact, the haziest notion of what he was about to do to her. He had not explained it; and it seemed too late, now, to ask. She didn't want to speak at all, with her lower half all exposed to his gaze like this; she was too embarrassed. She closed her eyes.

When she felt him lift and try to part her knees, she grew more self-conscious than ever. 'Lie a little less rigidly, if you can, Mrs Harrison,' he said. And then: 'Mrs Harrison? A little less rigid?' She opened her legs, and after a second felt something warm and dry come between them and begin to probe. It was his finger. He pushed firmly into her, and with his other hand pressed again at her stomach, harder than before. She gave a little gasp. He pushed and pressed on, until she couldn't help but draw her hips away. He moved back, and wiped his hands on a towel.

'You must expect, of course,' he said, in a mild and matter-of-fact kind of way, 'a certain amount of discomfort. That can't be helped, I'm afraid.'

He turned away, then brought back a sponge, or a cloth, with some sharp-smelling liquid on it, with which he began to dab at her. She lifted her head and tried to see. She could only see his face: he had put up his spectacles again, and again they looked like goggles – like a welder's goggles, or a stonemason's. On a shelf, near his head, was a toy: a bear or a rabbit in a flowered dress and a hat. She imagined him waving it before frightened boys and girls. A notice, pinned to the wall behind him, gave *Information for Patients Regarding Stoppings and Extractions*.

When he placed the mask over her mouth, it was so like an ordinary respirator – so much less unpleasant, in fact, than a regular gas-mask – that she almost didn't mind it. Then she was aware of a sensation of slipping, and made a grab at the edge of the couch, to keep herself from tumbling off it . . . It seemed to her then that she must have fallen anyway, but had inexplicably landed on her feet; for she was suddenly standing in darkness in a crowd of people, being jostled on every side. She didn't know if she was in a street, some public place like that, or where she was. A siren was sounding, but it was strange to her; it meant nothing. She didn't know the person she was with, but she clutched at their arm. 'What's that?' she asked. 'That noise? What is it?' '*Don't you know?*' the person answered. '*That's the Warning for the Bull.*' 'The Bull?' she asked. '*The German Bull,*' said the voice. At once, then, she understood that the Bull was a new and very terrifying kind of weapon. She turned, in fright; but she turned in the wrong direction, or not in the proper way. '*Here it is!*' cried the voice in terror – and she tried to turn again, but was struck in the stomach and knew she'd been caught, in the darkness, by the horn of the terrible German Bull. She put out her hands and felt the shaft of it, smooth and hard and cold; she felt the place, even, where it entered her stomach; and she knew, too, that if she were to reach around to her back she would be able to feel the tip of it jutting out there, because the horn had run right through her . . .

Then she came back to herself, and to Mr Imrie; but she could still feel the horn. She thought it had pinned her to the couch. She heard her own voice, talking nonsense, and Mr Imrie giving a chuckle.

'Bulls? Oh, no. Not in Cricklewood, my dear.'

He held a bowl to her face, and she was sick.

He gave her a handkerchief to wipe her lips with, and helped her to sit upright. The towel had gone from beneath her hips. His sleeves were rolled back down, his cuffs neatly fastened, the links in place; his brow was flushed, with a faint sheen of perspiration on it. Everything – the smells of the room, the arrangement of things – seemed subtly different to her; she had a sense of time having given a sort of lurch, while her back was turned, as if she'd been playing at Grandmother's Footsteps. On the floor there was a single shilling-sized spot of scarlet, but apart from that, nothing nasty to see. The zinc pail had been moved a little further away and covered over.

She swung her legs over the side of the couch, and the pain in her stomach and her back turned into a dragging internal ache; she became aware, too, of smaller, separate discomforts: a soreness between her legs, and a tenderness, as if she'd been kicked in the flesh of her belly. Mr Imrie said that he'd put a wad of gauze inside her, to take up the blood; and he'd left, beside her on the couch, an ordinary sanitary towel and belt. Seeing that, she grew embarrassed all over again, and tried too quickly to put on the belt and fasten the loops. He saw how she fumbled, and thought she was still dazed from the gas, and came and helped her.

When she began to dress, she realised how weak she was; she thought she could feel, too, where blood had gathered between her buttocks and was starting to grow sticky. The idea made her nervous. She asked if she could go to the lavatory, and he led her down the passage and showed her where it was. She sat, and felt for the ends of the plug of gauze, afraid of it; afraid that it might disappear inside her. When she peed, she felt stung. The ache in her womb and muscles was awful. Only a little blood showed on the toilet paper, however, and that made her realise that the moistness between her buttocks must just have been water: that Mr Imrie must have washed her, with a cloth or a sponge. She didn't like the idea. She still had the faintly frightening sense of having fallen or been plucked from time: of things having made a jump, with which she hadn't yet caught up.

'Now,' said Mr Imrie, when she went back into his surgery, 'you should anticipate a little bleeding, perhaps for a day or two. Don't be worried by that, that's perfectly normal. I should stay in bed, if I were you. Get your husband to spoil you a little . . .' He advised her to drink stout; and gave her two or three more sanitary towels, and a tub of aspirins for the pain. Then he took her back out to Reggie.

'Christ,' said Reggie, standing up, alarmed, putting out a cigarette. 'You look awful!'

She began to cry.

'There, now,' said Mr Imrie, coming in behind her. 'I've told Mrs Harrison to expect a little weakness, for twenty-four hours or so. You might telephone me, if you've any anxiety. I do ask you not to leave messages, however . . . Any fainting, of course; any serious bleeding; any vomiting, fitting, anything like that, you must call your doctor. But that's very unlikely. Very unlikely indeed. And needless to say, if a doctor were to be involved, you wouldn't feel it necessary to mention—' Again he spread his hands. 'Well, I'm sure you understand.'

Reggie looked rather wildly at him, and didn't answer. 'Are you OK?' he asked Viv.

'I think so,' she said, still crying.

'Christ,' he said, again. And then, to Mr Imrie: 'Is she supposed to look like this?'

'A little weakness, as I said. The slightly advanced nature of the pregnancy made things a shade more complicated, that's all. Just bear in mind, about the vomiting and the fits—'

Reggie swallowed. He put on his coat, and then helped Viv to put on hers. She leaned on his arm. It was ten to nine. They all went out into the hall, Mr Imrie closing the door of the waiting-room and then stepping nimbly across to close the door to the surgery. He put off the light, unlatched the front door, but only opened it a little – just enough for him to peer out into the street.

'Ah,' he said. 'The moon is still rather bright. I wonder—' He turned to Viv. 'Would you mind very much, Mrs Harrison, just holding your handkerchief across your face, like this?' He put his hand to his mouth. 'That's right. It gives the impression, you see, that you've come for some ordinary dental work; which, after all, is not uncommon . . . I'm thinking of my neighbours. The war gives people such suspicious ideas. Thank you, so much.'

He pulled the door wide, and they left him. Viv kept the handkerchief across her mouth for a minute or two, then let her hand fall. The cloth, like the piece of paper Reggie had taken from his pocket on the way, seemed almost luminous in the moonlight; but she looked at the cloudless sky now and felt too weak and sore and miserable to be frightened. She began, instead, to grow very cold. She thought she could feel the plug of gauze inside her, slipping out of its place. The edges of the sanitary towel chafed her thighs. She leant more heavily on Reggie's arm. But she wouldn't speak to him. 'All right?' he kept saying. 'OK? Good girl.' Then, when they'd gone a hundred yards or so, he broke out with, 'That shyster! Christ, what a thing to spring on us! All that stuff about the extra ten quid. He knew he'd got us over a barrel. Christ, what a bloody Jew! I ought to have stood my ground a bit harder. For two pins—'

'Shut up!' she said at last, unable to bear it.

'No, but honestly, Viv. What a racket.'

He grumbled on. At Cricklewood Broadway they waited for ten or fifteen minutes, then picked up a cab. They were going to a place Reggie had got the use of, a flat, somewhere right in the middle of town. He had the address they wanted on another piece of paper. The driver knew the street, but said that some of the roads were up; he had to take them a roundabout route. Reggie heard that, and gave a snort. Viv could feel him thinking, *That's a nice trick, as well.* The cab went slowly, and she held herself in a state of miserable tension all the way. When she thought the driver

502

wasn't looking, she opened the tub of aspirin and took three: chewing them up, swallowing and swallowing to get them down. From time to time she slipped a hand beneath herself – afraid that the gauze and the sanitary towel might not be working after all.

She didn't look at the house, when they reached it; she never knew exactly where it was – though she remembered, later, having crossed Hyde Park, and thought that it must have been in some street in Belgravia. It had a porch with pillars, she remembered that, for Reggie had to get the key to the flat they were borrowing from an old lady in the basement, and while he ran down the steps and knocked on the door she closed her eyes and leant against one of the pillars, and put her hands flat against her stomach to try and warm herself up. Her needs and wants had shrunk, condensed: she could think only of finding a place to be private and still, to be warm. She heard Reggie's voice. He was joking with the lady, in a strained kind of way: 'That's right . . . I should say so, too . . . Isn't it?' *Come on*, she thought. He reappeared, puffing, cursing, and they went inside.

The flat was up, on the highest floor. The staircase windows were uncovered, so they had to climb with only the torch to light them. She felt moisture at the top of her thighs and began to think she must be bleeding: with every step it seemed to her that she could feel the soft, hot release of a little more blood. At last she was sure that it was running down her legs, soaking her stockings, filling her shoes . . . She stood very still while Reggie fumbled with the keys in the unfamiliar locks, then stood still again as he went about from one window to another, kicking bits of furniture on his way, striking his shins, sending china rattling.

'For God's sake,' she said weakly, when something had fallen and he had stooped, swearing, to pick it up. 'Never mind this room. Do the bathroom first.'

'I would,' he said testily, 'if I knew where it was.'

'Can't you see?'

'No, I can't. Can you?'

'Put a light on; it's just for a minute.'

'We'll have Mother Hubbard coming up from her basement. We'll have a warden at the door. That's all we need.'

He had been fined a pound for showing a light, two years before; and had never forgotten it. The beam of the torch swept wildly about. She saw him move, then strike his head, hard, against the edge of a door.

'Christ!'

'Are you all right?'

'What do you think? Hell! That hurts like buggery!'

He rubbed his forehead, then went on more cautiously. When his voice came again, it was muffled. 'Here's the bedroom. The lav's meant to be off that, I think. Just a minute—' She heard a thud, as he struck his head again. There was the rattle of curtainrings, and then a click, and then another. 'Oh, to fuck!' he cried. The electricity was off. They needed shillings: he made his way back to her and sorted through his change, went through her purse; then blundered around a second time, looking for the meter.

The coins went in at last, and lights sprang on. She made her way, wincing, to the bathroom. When he saw how gingerly she was moving he came forward to help her, and she pushed him off.

'Go away,' she said. 'Go away!'

She had not bled as much as she had feared, there was only a little staining on the surface of the sanitary towel; but the tip of the gauze, which had been white before, was now the colour of rust. She felt it with her fingers: it seemed looser than it had been at first, and again she worried about it travelling about inside her, getting lost. She got a smear of blood on her hand, and stood to wash it. She looked at the bath, and imagined filling it with hot water, soaking away the pain from her hips. But the bathroom was queer and luxurious, done up with a thick, milk-coloured carpet and with tiles made to look like mother-of-pearl. It made her feel grubby; she thought of the manoeuvres it would take not to leave marks or stains. She shivered, suddenly exhausted; she lowered the lavatory lid and sat back down on it, with her elbows on her knees and her face in her hands. She still had her coat and her hat on.

She sat so long, Reggie knocked on the door to

ask if she was all right. When she let him in he glanced around with fluttering eyelids, nervously.

He helped her to walk. She had passed through the bedroom before and hardly looked at it; now she saw that, like the bathroom, it was done up outlandishly. There was a tiger-skin rug on top of a carpet, and satin cushions on the bed. It was like someone's idea of a film-star's bedroom; or as though prostitutes or playboys lived here. The whole flat was the same. The sittingroom had an electric fire built into the wall, surrounded by panels of chromium. The telephone was pearly white. There was a bar, for drinks, with bottles and glasses inside it, and on the wall were pictures of Paris: the Arc de Triomphe, the Eiffel Tower, men and women sitting gaily at pavement cafés with bottles of wine.

But everything was chill to the touch and dusty; and here and there were piles of powder: paint and plaster, that must have been shaken down in raids. The rooms smelt damp, unlived-in. Viv sat, still shivering, in the armchair closest to the fire.

'Whose flat is this?' she asked.

'It's no one's,' said Reggie, squatting beside her and fiddling with the fire's controls. 'It's a show-flat. – I think one of these elements has gone.'

'What?'

'It's just for show,' he said. 'It's just to show you what your place would be like, if you bought one. They did it all up before the war started. No one's interested now.'

'Nobody lives here?'

'People come to stay, that's all.'

'What people?'

He turned a switch, back and forth. 'Pals of Mike's, I told you. He was one of the house-agents and he's still got the key. He leaves it with the old mother downstairs. If you've got leave, and nowhere to spend it.'

She understood. 'It's for you blokes to bring girls to.'

He glanced up, laughing. 'Don't look at me like that! I don't know anything about that. But it's better than a hotel, isn't it?'

'Is it?' She wouldn't smile. 'I suppose you'd know. I suppose you bring girls here all the time.'

He laughed again. 'I wish! I've never been here before in my life.'

'That's what you say.'

'Don't be daft. You saw how I charged about, didn't you?' He rubbed his head.

She looked away, feeling desperately sorry for herself. 'It's always the same,' she said bleakly. 'It ends up nasty, every single time. Even now.'

He was still working the switch. 'Like what? What is?'

'Like this.' Her voice dissolved. The show of bitterness, the flood of self-pity, had worn her out. She began to cry again. He left the fire and rose; came to her and sat awkwardly beside her. He took her hat from her head and smoothed her hair and kissed her.

'Don't, Viv.'

'I feel so awful.'

'I know you do.'

'No, you don't. I wish I were dead.'

'Don't say that. Think how I'd feel if you were. Does it hurt?'

'Yes.'

He lowered his voice. 'Was it horrible?'

She nodded. He reached, and put his hand on her stomach. She flinched, at first. But the warmth and weight of his palm and fingers were comforting; she placed her own hands over his and held them tight. She remembered her dream about the bull, and told him.

'A bull?' he said.

'A German bull. It was sticking its horn in me. When all the time I suppose it was Mr Imrie—'

Reggie laughed. 'I knew he was a dirty old man the moment we went in. What a sod though, to hurt my girl!'

'It's not his fault.' She got out her handkerchief and blew her nose. 'It's yours.'

'Mine! I like that!' He kissed her again. 'If it wasn't for you, driving a fellow crazy . . .' He rubbed his cheek against her head. The weight of his hand on her lower belly began to feel different. He had moved his fingers. 'Oh, Viv,' he said.

Now she pushed him away. 'Get off!' She laughed, despite herself. 'It's all right for you—'

'It's hell for me.'

'The thought of— Oh!' She shuddered.

He laughed, too. 'You say that now. We'll see what you think in a week or two.'

'A week or two! You're loopy. A year or two, more like.'

'Two years? I will be loopy. Let a man hope, at least. That's more than they give you for desertion.'

She laughed again; then caught her breath and shook her head, suddenly quite unable to speak. They sat for a minute or two in silence. He moved her hair with his chin and his cheek, and now and then put his mouth to her brow. The room began gradually to warm up. The pain in her stomach and back subsided, until it felt like the deep but ordinary ache one got, every month, with the curse. But she felt utterly without strength.

In time, Reggie stood and stretched. He looked at the bar and said he fancied a drink. He went and picked out a bottle; when he opened it up and smelt it, however, he made a face: 'Coloured water!' He tried another. 'They're all the same. And, look!' There were cigarettes in a box; but they were made of pasteboard. 'What a dirty trick. We shall have to make do with this, I suppose.'

He'd brought a little bottle of brandy with him. He pulled the stopper from it, and offered it to her.

She shook her head. 'Mr Imrie said I ought to have stout.'

'I'll get you some stout later on, if you like. Have a nip of this for now, though.'

She hadn't eaten all day, because of the anaesthetic: she took a sip, and felt the liquid as she swallowed it, travelling down her throat to her empty stomach, warm as a tongue of fire. Reggie drank some too, then lit up a cigarette. She couldn't quite manage that; but the smell, at least, didn't make her sick. *I must be better*, she thought – realising it then, in that moment, for the first time. *I must be OK*. The thought spread through her like the brandy. She closed her eyes. There was only the pain, now; and that, compared to everything else, would be easy.

Reggie finished his cigarette and got up; she heard him go to the lavatory, and then he was moving about in the bedroom, drawing back the curtain, looking out into the street. The street was quiet. The whole house was quiet. There must have been empty flats, like this, on every side.

When he came back she was almost sleeping. He crouched beside her and touched her face.

'Are you warm enough, Viv? You feel cold as anything.'

'Do I? I feel all right.'

'Wouldn't you like to lie on the bed? Do you want me to take you?'

She shook her head, unable to speak. She opened her eyes, but almost at once they closed again, as if the lids were weighted down. Reggie put his hand on her forehead and drew the collar of her coat more closely around her neck. He kicked off his shoes and sat on the floor, resting his head against her knees. 'You tell me if you want anything,' he said.

They stayed like that for more than an hour. They might have been an old married couple. They had never been so much alone together before, without making love.

And then, at half-past ten or so, Viv gave a start. She made Reggie jump.

'What is it?' he said, looking up at her.

'What?' she said, confused.

'Is it hurting?'

'What?'

He got to his feet. 'You're white as a sheet. You're not going to be sick?'

She felt really odd. 'I don't know. I need the toilet again, I think.' She tried to rise.

'Let me help you.'

He walked her to the bathroom. She went more slowly even than before. Her head seemed separated from her body – as if her body were squat, dense, ungainly, her head attached to it by the merest thread. But the further she walked, the sharper the ache grew in her stomach; and that brought her back to herself. By the time she sat on the lavatory she was bent almost double with griping pains. The pains were strange: part like the pains of the curse, still; but part like a bowel pain. She thought she might have diarrhoea. She pressed with her muscles, as if to pee; there was a slithering sensation between her legs, and the splash of something striking the water. She looked in the bowl. The plug of gauze was there, quite sodden and misshapen with blood; and blood was falling from her still, thick and dark and knotted as a length of tarry rope.

She cried out for Reggie. He came at once, frightened by the sound of her voice.

'Jesus!' he said, when he saw the mess in the bowl. He stepped back, as pale as her. 'Was it like this before?'

'No.' She tried to stop it with sheets of lavatory paper. The blood slid about, got all over her hands. She'd begun to shake. Her heart was beating wildly. 'It won't stop,' she said.

'Put the thing against it.' He meant the sanitary towel.

'It just keeps coming out, I can't stop it. Oh, Reggie, I can't stop it at all!'

The more afraid she grew, the faster the blood seemed to tumble. At first it was viscous with specks and clots; soon it was ordinary blood, astonishingly red. It struck the lavatory paper in the bowl with a sound like water in a sink. It got on the seat, her legs, her fingers, everywhere.

'It shouldn't be like this, should it?' said Reggie breathlessly.

'I don't know.'

'What did Mr Imrie say? Did he say it would be like this?'

'He said I might get a bit of bleeding.'

'A bit? What's a bit? Is this a bit? This can't be a bit, this is tons.'

'Is it?'

'Isn't it?'

'I don't know.'

'Why don't you know? What's it like when it comes out normally?'

'Not like this. It's getting everywhere!'

He put his hand across his mouth. 'There must be something you can do to make it stop. You could take more aspirins.'

'Aspirins won't help, will they?'

'It's better than nothing.'

It was all they had. He fumbled about in her coat pocket, getting the tub. She couldn't touch anything with the blood on her hands. She took three more tablets, chewing them up as she had before; he gave her another sip of brandy, then drank the rest of the bottle himself. They pulled the plug of the lavatory and watched water gush into the bowl. It settled clear and pinkish at the top, dark red and syrupy at the bottom – like a clever sort of cocktail. More blood immediately began to flow from her, and to swirl and spread about.

'And you don't think,' Reggie said, nodding again to the sanitary towel, 'if you were to just put the thing against it—'

She shook her head, too panicked to speak. She pulled off sheets and sheets of paper and tried to stop herself up with them. They held for a minute or two, and she grew a little calmer; but then they fell from her, just like the gauze. Reggie tried again, with more sheets. He put his hand over hers, to hold the paper in place. But those sheets fell out too, and the blood came faster than ever.

At last, almost beside themselves, they decided that Reggie should call up Mr Imrie and get his advice. He ran into the sitting-room; she heard the little ting of the bell in the pearly white phone; but then Reggie gave a cry, a sort of yelp of frustration and despair. When he came back he was lurching about, pulling on his shoes. The telephone didn't work. Its wire ran for two or three feet and then stopped. It was like the bottles of coloured water, the pasteboard cigarettes, and just for show.

'I'll have to find a kiosk,' he said. 'Did you see one, when we came?'

The thought of him leaving her was terrifying. 'Don't go!'

'Is it still coming?' He looked between her legs, and swore. He put his hand on her shoulder. 'Listen,' he said, 'I'm going to go down to the old mother downstairs. She'll know where a phone is.'

'What will you tell her?'

'I'll just say I need a telephone.'

'Say—' Viv clutched at him. 'Say I'm losing a baby, Reggie.'

He checked himself. 'Shall I? She'll want to come up if I do. She'll want to bring a doctor.'

'Maybe we should get a doctor, shouldn't we? Mr Imrie said—'

'A doctor? Christ, Viv, I hadn't bargained on anything like that.' He took his hand from her and put it to his head, to grip at his hair. She could tell

514

from his expression that he was thinking of the money, or the fuss. She began to cry again. 'Don't cry!' he said, when he saw that; and he looked, for a moment, as if he might begin to cry himself. He said, 'A doctor will be able to tell, won't he? Won't a doctor look, and know?'

'I don't care,' she said.

'He could bring in the police, Viv. He'll want our names. He'll want to know everything about us.' His voice was strained. He stood, undecided – trying to think of another way. Then a new surge of pain rose up in her, and she gasped, and clutched at her stomach. 'All right,' he said quickly. 'All right.'

He turned and went. The flat door banged, and after that she heard nothing. Her brow and her upper lip were wet with sweat; she wiped them on her sleeve. She pulled the plug of the lavatory again, then swivelled about and reached into the basin to wash her hands, taking off the gold-coloured ring, because it was so loose. The basin looked as though it had had scarlet paint put down it: she got more sheets of lavatory paper and tried to clean it, tried to clean the seat on which she was sitting, and the rim of the bowl beneath. Then she saw a little blood on the carpet: she leaned to it, and grew dizzy; the floor of the bathroom seemed to tilt. She grabbed for the wall; left a smear of pink on one of the mother-of-pearl tiles; eased herself up and sat very still, her head in her hands. If she sat still, the blood ran less freely . . .

She longed to lie down; she remembered Mr Imrie telling her to stay in bed. But she wouldn't get up, for fear of making a mess of the milk-coloured carpet. She closed her eyes and began to count, beneath her breath. *One, two, three, four.* She ran through the numbers, over and over. *One, two, three, four. One, two, three, four—*

I'm going to die, she thought. She wanted her father, suddenly. If only her dad were here! Then she imagined him walking in and seeing all the blood . . . She started to cry again. She sat up and leant her head against the wall, weeping, but weeping so feebly her sobs were like little snorts of pain.

She was still sitting crying like this when Reggie came back. He had the old lady with him. She was wearing a nightdress and a dressing-gown, but had slipped a coat on top and had put on a hat and rubber galoshes. It was probably the outfit she kept ready for when the Warning went. She was breathing hard, from climbing all the stairs, and had no teeth in. She had got out a hankie to wipe her face. When she saw the state of Viv, however, she let the hankie fall. She came straight to her, and felt her forehead, then pulled apart her thighs to peer at the mess between them.

Then she turned back to Reggie. 'Good heavens, boy!' she said, speaking sloppily, because of her missing teeth. 'What was you thinking of, calling a doctor? A bloody ambulance is what she needs!'

'An ambulance?' said Reggie, in horror. 'Are you

sure?' He was hanging back, now that she was here.

'You heard me,' said the woman. 'Look at the colour of her! She's lost half the blood in her body. A doctor ain't going to be able to put that back in, is he?' She felt Viv's forehead again. 'Good lord . . . Go on! What you waiting for? You'll get one now, if you call before the sirens start up. Tell them to be quick. Tell them it's a matter of life and death!'

Reggie turned and ran.

'Now,' said the woman, shrugging off her coat. 'Do you think you ought to be sitting there, dear, letting it all come tumbling out of you like that?' She put her hand on Viv's shoulder. The hand was trembling. 'Don't you think you ought to lie down?'

Viv shook her head. 'I want to stay here.'

'All right, then. But let's just lift you up a bit and— That's it, you got the idea.'

The bathroom had a single towel in it – milk-coloured, like the carpet. Viv hadn't liked to use it. But the woman had plucked it from the rail at once and folded it up; she made Viv stand, and she lowered the lid of the lavatory and put the towel on it. 'You sit on that, my dear,' she said, helping Viv back down. 'That's right. And let's take these old drawers off you, too, shall we?' She stooped, and fumbled about Viv's knees; lifted up her feet. 'That's better. Not nice, is it, having your old man see you with your drawers around your ankles? I should say it ain't. There we are: when I was your age we hardly bothered with drawers at all. We had our skirts, do you see, to keep us decent. Long great skirts like you'd never believe. There. Never mind. Soon have you sorted out and looking like a queen again. Why, what handsome hair you've got, haven't you—?'

She went chatting sloppily on, lots of nonsense; she let Viv lean against her, and smoothed and patted her head with hard, blunt fingers. But Viv could tell, too, that she was frightened.

'Still coming, is it?' she'd say, from time to time, looking into the towel between Viv's legs. 'Well, young 'uns like you, you've got it to spare. That's what they say, don't they?'

Viv had closed her eyes. She was aware of the old lady's murmurs, but had begun to hold herself rigid: she was concentrating on the blood that was escaping from her – trying to slow it, to keep hold of it, to will it back into herself. Her fear rose and sank, in great dark plunging waves. For what felt like minutes at a time the blood seemed to still, and she would grow almost calm; but there would come another little gush between her legs, which sent her back into a panic. She'd be made frightened too, then, by the very galloping of her own heart, which was making the blood, she knew, run even faster.

She heard Reggie come back.

'Did you send for 'em?' called the old lady.

'Yes,' said Reggie, breathlessly. 'Yes, they're coming.'

He stood in the bathroom doorway, as pale as ash: biting his fingernails, too awed by the old lady to come in. *If only he'd come and hold my hand*, Viv thought. *If only he'd put his arm around me . . .* But all he did was meet her gaze and make a helpless sort of gesture: spread his hands, shook his head. 'I'm sorry,' he mouthed. 'I'm sorry.' He moved away. She heard him light up a cigarette. There was the rattle of curtain-hooks, and she knew he must be standing at the bedroom window, looking out.

Then the blood seeped again, and the pain inside her shut tight, like a fist around a blade; she closed her eyes and was plunged back into panic. The pain and the panic were utterly black, and time-less: it was like going under the gas at Mr Imrie's again, slipping out of the world while the world scuttled forwards . . . She felt the old lady's hard hands on her shoulders and in the small of her back, rubbing and rubbing, in little circles. She heard Reggie call out, 'Here it is!' But she couldn't imagine, at that moment, what he meant. She thought it must be something to do with the fact that he had drawn back the curtain from the window. When, after another minute or two, she opened her eyes and saw the ambulance people, in their trousers and jackets and tin hats, she supposed them an ARP man and a boy, come to complain about the black-out.

But the boy was laughing. The laugh was throaty, but light, like a girl's. He said, 'I like your tiger-skin rug. Doesn't it ever give you a scare, though, in the middle of the night? I should be afraid of it having a go at my ankles as I went by.' He examined the towel that Viv was sitting on, and his laugh faded, but his face stayed kind. The towel was utterly scarlet and sodden. He put his hand across her brow. He said to the man, quietly, 'Skin's pretty clammy.'

'I couldn't make it stop,' mumbled Viv.

The man had squatted before her. He had bared her arm and was strapping a band around it; now he quickly pumped at a rubber bladder and frowned at a dial. He touched her thigh and looked, as the boy had, at the towel beneath her bottom. She was past embarrassment. 'How long,' he asked, 'has it been coming from you like this?'

'I don't know,' she answered weakly. She thought, *Where's Reggie?* Reggie would know. 'About an hour, I think.'

The man nodded. 'You've lost an awful lot of blood by the looks of it. We'll have to take you to a hospital, as quickly as we can. All right?' He spoke calmly, comfortingly. She wanted to give herself up to his arms. He still squatted before her, putting the strap and the bladder away in his bag. He worked very swiftly. But he looked into her face again before he rose, and, 'What's your name?' he asked her gently.

'Pearce,' she answered, without thinking. 'Vivien Pearce.'

'And how far on was your baby, Mrs Pearce?'

But now she realised what she had done. She

had said Vivien Pearce, when she should have said Margaret Harrison. She started looking about for Reggie again. The man touched her knee.

'I'm sorry,' he was saying. 'It's rotten luck. But for now, we must make you better. My friend Miss Carmichael and I are going to carry you downstairs.'

She was still looking for Reggie, and couldn't concentrate on his words. She thought that when he said 'Miss Carmichael' he must mean the old lady. Then he and the boy said other things – spoke to each other, calling each other 'Kay' and 'Mickey' – and she understood, with a rush of dismay, that they were not men at all, but simply short-haired women . . . All the confidence she'd had in them, the sense of care and safety, disappeared. She began to shake. They seemed to think that she was cold, and put a blanket around her. They had brought a folding canvas chair, into which they strapped her; and they began to manoeuvre her out of the bathroom and across the tiger-skin rug, through the sitting-room, past the bar and the pictures of Paris, and down the unlit stairs. She thought she would fall, at every turning. 'I'm sorry,' she kept saying weakly. 'I'm sorry.'

They scolded her, in a playful way, for being worried.

'If you could see some of the heavy great blokes we have to haul about!' said the boyish one – Mickey – laughing. 'We're going into business, after this, as piano movers.'

The old lady went ahead of them, to tell them

about awkward steps. She held the front door open for them, and then trotted down the path to do the same with the garden gate. The ambulance was parked just beyond it, the touches of white on its dull grey paintwork lit up by the moon and making it seem to float above the inky-black surface of the street. Kay and Mickey set Viv down, and opened up the doors.

'We're going to lay you flat,' said Mickey. 'We think that'll help the bleeding. Here we go.'

They lifted her in, got her out of the chair and put her down on the bunk. She still shook as if cold, and the blood still seeped; now, too, she'd begun to labour after air, as if she'd run a race, something like that. She heard Kay speak, telling Mickey that Mickey could drive, while she stayed in the back; then the bunk tilted slightly as Kay climbed in. Viv looked up – looking for Reggie, wanting Kay to let him sit beside her and hold her hand. One of the ambulance doors was closed, and the old lady stood in the frame of the other: she was calling out, in her sloppy voice, that Viv wasn't to be frightened now; that the doctors would have her right in no time . . . She stepped back. Mickey had hold of the open door and was closing it.

Viv struggled, and sat up. She said, 'Wait. Where's Reggie?'

'Reggie?' said Kay.

'Her husband!' said the old lady. 'Lord, I clean forgot him. I saw him slip away and—'

'Reggie!' called Viv, growing frantic. There was a strap holding down her hips. She began to pluck at it. '*Reggie!*'

'Is he there?' asked Kay.

'I don't think so,' answered Mickey. 'Do you want me to go and have a look?'

Viv still struggled with the strap.

'All right,' said Kay. 'But be quick!'

Mickey went off. When she came back, a minute or two later, she was panting. She put up the brim of her tin hat and leant into the van.

'There's no one there,' she said. 'I looked all over.'

Kay nodded. 'Right, let's go. He can find her at the hospital.'

'But he was there,' said Viv breathlessly. 'You must have made a mistake— In the darkness—'

'There's no one,' Mickey said again. 'I'm sorry.'

'Now, ain't that a shame,' said the old lady, with great feeling.

Viv fell back: weaker than ever, unable to protest. She was thinking of Reggie, on the edge of tears, saying, 'A doctor will be able to tell, won't he? A doctor will want our names, he'll want to know everything about us.' She was remembering him standing in the doorway to the bathroom, shaking his head, saying, 'I'm sorry . . .'

She closed her eyes. The door was slammed and, after a moment, the ambulance started up and moved off. The engine was so loud, it felt as though she had her head against its engine. It was like being trapped in the hold of a ship. Kay's voice came, close above her face. 'All right, Mrs Pearce.' She was doing something – filling in a label, fastening it to Viv's collar. 'Be brave, Mrs Pearce—'

Viv said, wretchedly, 'Don't call me *Mrs*. He's not my husband, like the lady said. We had to make out, that's all, for Mr Imrie—'

'Never mind,' said Kay.

'We said Harrison, because that was Reggie's mother's name. You must say Harrison at the hospital. Will you? You must say I'm Mrs Harrison. Because even if they look, and can tell, it's not so bad if a married lady does it, is it?'

'Don't worry.' Kay was holding her wrist, feeling her pulse.

'They don't send for the police, do they, when it's married ladies?'

'You're getting muddled. Send for the police? Why would they do that?'

'It's against the law, isn't it?' said Viv.

She saw Kay smile. 'Being ill? Not yet.'

'Getting rid of a baby, I mean.'

The van gave a series of bumps as it ran over the broken surface of the road. Kay said, 'What?'

Viv wouldn't answer. She could feel a little more blood being shaken out of her with every jolt. She closed her eyes again.

'Vivien,' said Kay. 'What did you do?'

'We went to a man,' said Viv at last. She caught her breath. 'A dentist.'

'What did he do to you?'

'He put me to sleep. It was all right, at first. But he put a dressing inside me, and the dressing came out, and that's when it started bleeding. It was all right till then.'

Kay moved away and thumped on the wall of the cabin. 'Mickey!' The van slowed, then stopped; there was the ratcheting sound of the brake. Mickey's face appeared at the sliding glass panel above Viv's head.

'Is she OK?'

'It's not,' said Kay, 'what we thought. She's been to someone – a bloody dentist – he's mucked about with the pregnancy.'

'Oh, no,' said Mickey.

'She's bleeding, still. He might have – I don't know. He might have punctured the wall of the womb.'

'Right.' Mickey turned. 'I'll go as quick as I can.'

'Wait. Wait!' Mickey turned back. 'She's afraid of the police.'

Viv was watching their faces. She'd raised herself up again. 'There mustn't be police!' she said. 'There mustn't be police, or newspaper men. They can't tell my father!'

'Your father won't mind,' said Mickey, 'when he knows how ill you are—'

'She's not married,' said Kay.

Viv began to cry again. 'Don't tell,' she said. 'Oh, please don't tell!'

She saw Mickey looking at Kay. 'If there's been

a puncture, she might— Hell. There might be blood poisoning, mightn't there?'

'I don't know. I think so.'

'Please,' said Viv. 'Just tell them I've lost my baby.'

Mickey shook her head. 'It's too dangerous.'

'Please. Don't tell them anything. Say you found me in the street.'

'They'll know anyway,' said Mickey.

But Viv could see Kay thinking. 'They might not.'

'No,' said Mickey. 'We can't chance it. For God's sake, Kay! She might—' She looked at Viv. 'You might *die*,' she said.

'I don't care!'

'Kay,' said Mickey; and when Kay didn't answer, she turned away. The van jerked into life again and moved off, quicker than before.

Viv sank back. She couldn't feel the jolts so much, now. She felt suspended. She thought that, in losing so much blood, she must be beginning to float. She was vaguely aware of Kay adding something to the label fastened to her collar, then fumbling around with the pocket of her coat; then she felt her fingers held and squeezed. Kay had taken her hand. Her grip was sticky; Viv clutched harder, so as not to float away. She opened her eyes, and gazed into Kay's face. She gazed into it as she had never gazed into any face before; as if gazing could keep her from floating away, too.

'Just a little further, Vivien,' Kay said, over and

over, and, 'Be very brave. That's right. We're almost there.'

And in another moment, the van made a turn and came to a stop. The doors were unfastened and thrown open. Mickey climbed in, and someone else appeared behind her: a nurse, with a white cap, bright and misshapen in the light of the moon.

'You again, Langrish!' said the nurse. 'Well, and what have you brought us tonight?'

Kay looked at Mickey, but kept her fingers tight about Viv's. And when Mickey opened her mouth to speak, she spoke instead.

'Miscarriage,' she said firmly. 'Miscarriage, with complications. We think the lady, Mrs Harrison, has had a bad fall. She's lost an awful lot of blood, and is pretty confused.'

The nurse gave a nod. 'All right,' she said. She moved away, and called to a porter. 'You there! Yes, you! Fetch a trolley, and look smart about it!'

Mickey lowered her head and said nothing. She began, rather grimly, to unfasten the strap that held Viv to the bunk. 'Come on, Vivien,' Kay said, when she'd done it. 'It's all right.'

Viv still gripped her hand. 'All right? Are you sure?'

'Yes,' said Kay. 'We have to move you, that's all. But listen to me, just for a second.' She was speaking, now, in a rushed sort of whisper. She glanced over her shoulder, then touched Viv's face. 'Are you listening? Look at me . . . Your card and your ration book, Vivien. I've made a tear in the lining of your coat. You can say you lost them when you fell. All right? Do you understand me, Vivien?'

Viv did understand; but her mind had drifted to something else that seemed more important. She'd felt her hand come unstuck from Kay's, and her fingers had pins and needles in them. Their surface was sticky, but cold and bare—

'The ring,' she said. Now there seemed to be pins and needles in her lips. 'I've lost the ring. I've lost—' But she hadn't lost it, she remembered now. She'd taken it off, to wash the blood from beneath it; and she'd left it in the fancy bathroom, on the basin, beside the tap.

She looked wildly at Kay. Kay said, 'It doesn't matter, Vivien. It's not like the other things.'

'Here's the trolley coming,' said Mickey sharply.

Viv tried to rise. 'The ring,' she said, growing breathless again. 'Reggie got me a ring. We had it, so that Mr Imrie would think—'

'Hush, Vivien!' said Kay urgently. 'Vivien, hush! The ring doesn't matter.'

'I've got to go back.'

'You can't,' said Mickey. 'Bloody hell, Kay!'

'What's the trouble?' called the sister.

'I've got to go back!' said Viv, beginning to struggle. 'Just let me go back and get my ring! It's no good, without it—'

'Here's your ring!' said Kay, suddenly. 'Here's your ring. Look.'

She had drawn away from Viv and put her own hands together; she worked them as if wringing them for a second, then produced a little circle of gold. She did it so swiftly and so subtly, it was like magic.

'You had it, after all?' asked Viv, in amazement and relief; and Kay nodded: 'Yes.' She lifted Viv's hand, and slid the ring along her finger.

'It feels different.'

'That's because you're ill.'

'Is it?'

'Of course. Now, don't forget about the other things. Put your arm across my shoulders. Hold tight. Good girl.'

Viv felt herself being lifted. Soon she was moving through cold air . . . When Kay took her hand for the last time, she found that she could hardly return its pressure. She couldn't speak, even to say thank you or goodbye. She closed her eyes. They were just taking her through into the hospital lobby when the Warning went.

Helen heard the sirens from Julia's flat in Mecklenburgh Square. Almost at once there were crackles and thuds. She thought of Kay, and lifted her head.

'Where's that, do you think?'

Julia shrugged. She had got up to fetch a cigarette and was fishing about in a packet. She said, 'Maybe Kilburn? It's impossible to say. I heard a whopper come down last week and could have sworn it was the Euston Road. It turned out to be Kentish Town.' She went to the window, drew back the curtain, and put her eye to one of the little chinks in the grey talc boards. 'You should look at the moon,' she said. 'It's extraordinary tonight.'

But Helen was still listening out for the bombs. 'There's another,' she said, flinching. 'Come away from the window, will you?'

'There's no glass in it.'

'I know, but—' She stretched out her arm. 'Come back, anyway.'

Julia let the curtain fall. 'Just a minute.' She went to the fireplace, and held a spill of paper to the glowing coals in the grate, to light her cigarette. Then she straightened up, and drew in smoke – putting back her head, savouring the taste of the tobacco. She was quite naked, and stood with one hip raised: relaxed and unembarrassed in the firelight, as though at the edge of a pool of water in some lush Victorian painting of Ancient Greece.

Helen lay still, to watch her. 'You look like your name,' she said softly.

'My name?'

'Julia, Standing. I always want to put a comma in it. Hasn't anyone ever said it to you like that before? You look like your own portrait . . . Come back. You'll get cold.'

The room was too well sealed to be really chill, however. Julia put her hand to her forehead to smooth away tangled hair, then came slowly to the couch and slid back beneath the blankets. She lay bare to the waist, with her hands behind her head, sharing the cigarette with Helen, letting Helen put it between her lips and take it away when she'd drawn on it. After it was smoked, she closed her eyes. Helen studied the rise and fall of her chest and stomach as she breathed; the flutter of a pulse at the base of her throat.

There was the hollow boom of another distant explosion, a burst of gunfire, possibly the noise of planes. In the flat above Julia's the Polish man moved restlessly about: Helen could follow his passage across the floor, back and forth, by the creaks of its boards. In the room below, a wireless was playing; there was the echoey, rattling sound of somebody stirring up coke in a fireplace. The sounds were familiar to Helen now, just as the feel and sight of Julia's blankets and pillows and mismatched furniture had grown familiar. She had lain here like this perhaps six or seven times in the past three weeks. And she said to herself, as she had before: *Those people don't know that Julia and I are together here, naked in one another's arms . . .* It seemed incredible. She herself felt exposed – deliciously exposed, as if the flesh above dormant nerves had been sloughed off, peeled back.

She would never again, she thought, cross a floor, never switch on a wireless, never put a poker to the fire – never do anything at all – without thinking of the lovers who might be embracing in rooms close by.

She moved her hand to Julia's collarbone – not to the skin itself, but to a place in the air about an inch above it.

'What are you doing?' asked Julia, without opening her eyes.

'I'm divining you,' said Helen. 'I can feel the heat of you, rising up. I can feel the life of you. I can tell where your skin is pale, and where it's sallower. I can tell where it's clear and where there are freckles.'

Julia caught hold of her fingers. 'You're unhinged,' she said.

'Unhinged,' said Helen, 'by love.'

'That sounds like a book. One by Elinor Glyn or Ethel M. Dell.'

'Don't you feel a little crazy, Julia?'

Julia thought about it. 'I feel shot at by an arrow,' she said.

'Only by an arrow? I feel harpooned. Or— No, a harpoon's too brutal. I feel as if a small sort of hook had been plunged into my breast—'

'A small sort of hook?'

'A crochet hook, or something even finer.'

'A button hook?'

'A button hook, exactly.' Helen laughed. For at Julia's words a very clear image had sprung into her mind – something from her childhood, probably – a tarnished silver button hook with a slightly chipped mother-of-pearl handle. She put her hand across the place where she imagined her heart to sit. 'I feel,' she said, 'exactly as though a button hook had been plunged into my breast, and my heart were being drawn from me, fibre by fibre.'

'That sounds frightful,' said Julia. 'What a morbid girl you are.' She took Helen's fingers to her mouth and kissed them, then held them to examine their tips. 'And what little nails you have,' she said vaguely. 'Little nails, and little teeth.'

Helen grew self-conscious, though the light was so dim. 'Don't look at me,' she said, pulling her hand away.

'Why not?'

'I— I'm not worth it.'

Julia laughed. 'You mutt,' she said.

They closed their eyes, after that; and Helen, in time, must have fallen into a light sort of sleep. She was vaguely aware of Julia getting up again, putting on a dressing-gown and going down the hall to the lavatory; but she was in the midst of some absurd dream, and only came properly awake at the closing of the door, on Julia's return.

'What time is it?' she asked. She picked up Julia's alarm clock. 'God, it's quarter to one! I have to go.' She rubbed her face, then lay back down.

'Stay until one,' said Julia.

'Fifteen minutes. What's the good of that?'

'Let me come with you, then. I'll walk you to the flat.'

Helen shook her head.

'Let me,' said Julia. 'I'd rather walk than be left here, you know I would.'

She began to dress. Her clothes lay tangled on the

floor: she stooped and caught up a bra and knickers, stepped into trousers and drew on a blouse, tucking in her chin and frowning while she fastened up its buttons. She stood at the mirror and smoothed her face.

Helen lay and watched her, as she had before. It seemed extraordinary that she should be able to, incredible that Julia should offer up her own beauty like this to Helen's gaze. It was marvellous and almost frightening that, an hour before, Julia had lain in her arms, had opened her mouth, parted her legs, to Helen's lips and tongue and fingers. It seemed an impossible thing that she would, if Helen rose and went to her now, let herself be kissed . . .

Julia caught her eye, and smiled in pretend exasperation.

'Don't you get tired of looking at me?'

Helen lowered her gaze. 'I wasn't looking, really.'

'If you were a man, I'd say you ought to leave the room while I dressed. I'd want to stay a mystery to you.'

'I don't want you to be a mystery,' said Helen. 'I want to know every part of you.' Then she grew slightly sick. 'Why did you say that, Julia? You wouldn't rather a man, would you?'

Julia shook her head. She was leaning closer to the mirror, pushing out her mouth, putting lipstick on. 'It's no good for me, with men,' she said absently. She worked her lips together. 'It doesn't work for me, with men.'

'Only with women?' asked Helen.

Only with you, she wanted Julia to say. But Julia said nothing: she was tugging a comb through her hair now, looking critically at her own face. Helen turned away. She thought, *What the hell's the matter with me?* For she found she was jealous of Julia's reflection. She was jealous of Julia's clothes. She was jealous of the powder on Julia's face!

Then she thought of something else: *Is this how Kay feels, about me?*

The thought must have shown in her expression. When she turned back to Julia she saw that Julia was watching her, through the mirror. She'd stopped the comb in her hair, but her hands were still raised. She said, 'OK?'

Helen nodded; then shook her head. Julia put the comb down, came to her, and put an arm across her shoulders.

Helen closed her eyes. She said quietly, 'This is dreadfully wrong, isn't it?'

'Everything's dreadfully wrong, just now,' Julia answered, after a moment.

'But this is worse, because we might put it right.'
'Might we?'
'We might – stop. We might – go back.'
'Could you stop?'
'Perhaps,' said Helen, with an effort. 'For Kay's sake.'

'But then,' said Julia, 'the dreadfully wrong thing would still have been done. It was done, before this. It was done, almost, before we did anything at all. It was done— When was it done?'

535

Helen looked up. 'It was done the day you took me to that house in Bryanston Square,' she said. 'Or even the time before that, when you bought me tea. We stood in the sun, and you closed your eyes and I looked at your face . . . I think it was done then, Julia.'

They held each other's gaze, in silence; then moved together and kissed. Helen was still not quite used to the difference between Julia's kisses, and Kay's – to the relative strangeness of Julia's mouth, the softness of it, the dry pull of her lipstick, the tentative pressures of her tongue. But the strangeness was exciting. The kiss, being inexact, quickly became wet. They moved closer together. Julia put her fingers to Helen's bare breast – touched, then drew the fingers back; touched again, drew back again – and again – until Helen felt her flesh seem to rise, to strain after Julia's hand.

They let themselves sink back, awkwardly, on to the bunched-up blankets. Julia moved her hand between Helen's legs and, 'Christ!' she said softly. 'You're so wet. I can't— I can't feel you.'

'Put your fingers inside me!' whispered Helen. 'Push inside me, Julia!'

Julia pushed. Helen lifted her hips, to meet the movement with a movement of her own. Her breath caught. 'Do you feel me now?'

'Yes, now I feel you,' said Julia. 'I can feel you gripping me. It's amazing—'

She had what must have been her four fingers

inside Helen, up to the knuckle; but her thumb, outside, was rubbing at Helen's swollen flesh. Helen raised and lowered her hips, to keep pushing against her. The blankets were rough against her bare back, and as well as the pressure between her legs she could feel Julia's dry, trousered thigh bearing down on her own naked, damp one; she could make out separate points of discomfort – the chafing against her of the buckle of Julia's belt, the buttons on her blouse, the strap of her wrist-watch . . . She stretched out her hands behind her head, wishing with some part of herself that Julia had bound her, fastened her down: she wanted to give herself up to Julia, have Julia cover her with bruises and marks. Julia began to push almost painfully inside her, and she liked it. She was aware of herself growing rigid, as if really pulled by tightening ropes.

She lifted her head and put her mouth to Julia's again, and when she started to cry out, she cried into Julia's mouth and against her lips and cheek.

'Shush!' said Julia, even as she still pushed frantically at her. She was thinking of the people in the neighbouring flats. 'Shush, Helen! Shush!'

'I'm sorry,' said Helen breathlessly; and cried out again.

It wasn't like their leisurely love-making from before. Afterwards Helen lay shaken, chastened, as if from an argument. When she stood, she found she was trembling. She went to the mirror: she had Julia's lipstick all around her mouth, and her lips were swollen as though she'd been hit. Then she moved into the firelight and saw that her thighs and breasts were marked, as if with rashes, from the rubbing of Julia's clothes. It was what she'd wanted, while Julia was pushing at her; now the marks upset her, absurdly. She moved blindly about the room, picking things up, putting them down – feeling the gathering inside her of a sort of hysteria.

Julia had gone through to the kitchen to wash her hands and mouth. When she came back, Helen stood before her and said unsteadily, 'Look at the state of me, Julia! How the hell will I hide this from Kay?'

Julia frowned. 'What's the matter with you? Keep your voice down, can't you?'

The words were like a slap. Helen sat, and put her head in her hands.

'What have you done to me, Julia?' she said at last, still shakily. 'What have you done? I don't know myself. I used to loathe the sort of people who did the kind of thing we're doing. I used to think they must be cruel, or careless, or cowardly. But I don't want to be cruel to Kay. It seems to me I'm doing this, because I care too much! Too much, I mean, for her, and for you. Can that be true, Julia?'

Julia didn't answer. Helen looked up once, then lowered her head again. She pressed at her eyes with the heels of her hands, conscious that she mustn't let herself cry, because crying would only make more marks. 'And the worst thing is,' she went on. 'Do you know what the worst thing of all is? It's that when I'm with Kay I'm wretched, because she isn't you; and she sees that I'm wretched, and doesn't know why; and she comforts me! She comforts me, and I let her! I let her console me, for wanting you!'

She laughed. The laugh sounded horrible. She put down her hands. 'I can't keep doing it,' she said, more steadily. 'I have to tell her, Julia. But I'm afraid of it. I'm afraid of how she'll be. That it should be you, Julia! That it should be you! That she loved you, before, and now—' She shook her head and couldn't finish.

She reached to the pocket of her skirt for a hand-kerchief, and blew her nose. She felt exhausted – limp, like a doll. Julia had moved across the room to shovel ash on to the coke in the grate; but she had risen, and was standing at the mantelpiece, without having turned around. She didn't come to Helen's side, as she had before. She stood as if gazing down at the fire, brooding over the smothered coals. And when she spoke at last, her voice seemed distant.

She said, 'It wasn't like that, you know.'

Helen was blowing her nose again, and hardly heard. 'Like what?' she asked, not understanding.

'With Kay and me,' said Julia, still without turning her head. 'It wasn't the way you think it was. Kay let you imagine it, I suppose. It's awfully like her.'

'What do you mean?'

Julia hesitated. Then, 'She was never in love with me,' she said. She said it almost casually, putting down her hand to flick a piece of ash from her trouser-leg. 'I was the one. I was in love with Kay for years. She tried to love me back, but – it never took. I'm just not her type, I suppose. We're too similar; that's all it is.' She straightened up, and started picking at the paint on the mantel-piece. 'Kay wants a wife, you see. I said that once before, didn't I? She wants a wife – someone good, I mean; someone kind, untarnished. Someone to keep things in order for her, hold things in place. I could never do that. I used to tell her she wouldn't be happy until she'd found herself some nice blue-eyed girl – some girl who'd need rescuing, or fussing over, or something like that . . .' She turned her head, and met Helen's gaze at last. She said, with a sort of infinite sadness, 'That was rather a joke on me, wasn't it?'

Helen stared at her, until she blinked and looked away. She went back to picking at the mantel-piece. 'Does it matter, either way?' she asked, in the same low, casual way as before.

It mattered terribly, Helen knew. At Julia's words, something inside her had dropped, or shrunk. She felt as though she'd been tricked, made a fool of—

That was silly, for Julia hadn't tricked her. Julia hadn't lied, or anything like that. But still, Helen felt betrayed. She became aware, suddenly, of her own nakedness. She didn't want to be naked in front of Julia any more! She quickly pulled on her skirt and her blouse. She said, as she did it, 'Why didn't you tell me?'

'I don't know.'

'You knew what I thought.'

'Yes.'

'You knew it, three weeks ago!'

'It was the surprise of hearing you say it,' said Julia. 'It was thinking of Kay—You know what she's like, she's such a bloody gentleman. She's more of a gentleman than any real man I ever knew. I asked her, you see, not to tell. I never imagined—' She lifted a hand, and rubbed her eye. She went on tiredly, 'And then, I was proud. That's all it was. I was proud; and I was lonely. I was fucking lonely, if you want to know the truth.'

She blew out her breath in a rough sort of sigh; and looked back again, over her shoulder. 'Does it make a difference, what I've told you? It doesn't make any difference to me. But if you want, you know, to call the whole show off—'

'No,' said Helen. She didn't want that. And she was frightened by Julia's having raised, so casually, the possibility of their parting. For one terrible moment she saw herself completely alone – abandoned by Julia, as well as by Kay.

She put on the rest of her clothes without speaking. Julia kept her pose at the fireplace. When, at last, Helen went to her and put her arms around her, she moved into Helen's embrace with

541

something like relief. But they held each other awkwardly. Julia said, 'After all, what's changed? Nothing's changed, has it?' – and Helen shook her head and said, no, nothing had changed . . . 'I love you, Julia,' she said.

But there was that shrinking or dropping inside her, still – as if her heart, which before had seemed to yearn after Julia, to swell and expand, was drawing in its muscles, closing its valves.

She finished dressing. Julia moved around the room, putting things away. Now and then they caught each other's eye, and smiled; if they moved close to one another, they reached out their hands, automatically, and lightly touched, or drily kissed.

Outside, over London, bombs were still falling. Helen had forgotten all about them. But when Julia went back through the curtained doorway and left her alone for a moment, she moved softly to the window and looked out, through one of the cracks in the talc, at the square. She could see houses, still silvered with moonlight; and as she watched, the sky was lit by a series of lurid sparkles and flares. The booms produced by the explosions started a second later: she felt the slight vibration of them in the board against her brow.

At every one of them, she flinched. All her confidence seemed to have left her. She began to shake – as if she'd lost the habit, the trick, of being at war; as if she knew, suddenly, only menace, the certainty of danger, the sureness of harm.

*   *   *

'God!' said Fraser. 'That was close, wasn't it?'

The bombs, and the anti-aircraft fire, had woken them all up. A few men were standing at their windows, calling encouragement to the British pilots and the ack-ack guns; Giggs, as usual, was yelling at the Germans. '*This way, Fritz!*' It was a kind of pandemonium, really. Fraser had lain very rigidly for fifteen minutes, swearing at the noise; finally, unable to bear it, he'd got out of bed. He'd pulled the table across the cell and was standing on it in his socks, trying to see out of the window. Every time another blast came he flinched away from the panes of glass, sometimes covering his head; but he always moved back to them. It was better, he said, than doing nothing.

Duncan was still in his bunk. He was lying on his back, more or less comfortably, with his hands behind his head. He said, 'They sound closer than they are.'

'They don't disturb you?' asked Fraser incredulously.

'You get used to it.'

'It doesn't trouble you, that a bloody great bomb might be heading straight for you and you can't so much as duck your head?'

The cell was lit up by the moonlight, weirdly bright. Fraser's face showed clearly, but his boyish blue eyes, the blond of his hair, and the brown of the blanket across his shoulders, had lost their colours; they were all versions of silvery grey, like things in a photograph.

'They say if it's got your name on,' said Duncan, 'it'll get you wherever you are.'

Fraser snorted. 'That's the sort of thing I'd expect to hear from someone like Giggs. Except that when he says it, I really think he might imagine there's a factory somewhere on the outskirts of Berlin, stamping *Giggs, R, Wormwood Scrubs, England* into the casing.'

'All I mean,' said Duncan, 'is, if it's going to get us at all, it might as well get us here.'

Fraser put his face back to the window. 'I'd like to think I had a shot at improving my chances, that's all. – Oh, bugger!' He jumped, as another explosion sounded, rattling the glass, dislodging stones or mortar in the duct behind the heating grille in the wall. There came cries – whoops and cheers – from other cells; but someone called, too, in a high broken voice, '*Turn it off, you cunts!*' And after that, just for a moment, there was silence.

Then the ack-ack guns started up again, and more bombs fell.

Duncan looked up. 'You'll get your face blown off,' he said. 'Can you even see anything?'

'I can see the searchlights,' said Fraser. 'They're making their usual bloody muck of things. I can see the glow of fires. Christ knows where they are. For all we know, the whole damn city could be burning to the ground.' He started biting at one of his fingernails. 'My eldest brother's a warden,' he said, 'in Islington.'

'Go back to bed,' said Duncan, after another minute. 'There's nothing you can do.'

'That's what makes it so bloody! And to think of those damn twirls, down there in their shelter— What do you think they're doing right now? I bet they're playing cards and drinking whisky; and rubbing their blasted hands together in glee.'

'Mr Mundy won't be doing that,' said Duncan loyally.

Fraser laughed. 'You're right. He'll be sitting in the corner with a Christian Science tract, imagining the bombs away. Maybe I should take a tip from him. What do you say? He's persuaded you with all that nonsense, hasn't he? Is that why you're so untroubled?' He drew in his breath, and closed his eyes. When he spoke again, he spoke in a voice of unnatural calmness. '*There are no bombs. The bombs are not real. There is no war. The bombing of Portsmouth, Pisa, Cologne – that was nothing but a mass hallucination. Those people did not die, they only made a little mistake in thinking they did, it could happen to anyone. There is no war . . .*'

He opened his eyes. The night was suddenly silent again. He whispered, 'Has that done the trick?' Then he jumped about a foot, as another explosion came. 'Fuck! Not quite. Try harder, Fraser. You're not trying hard enough, damn you!' He pressed his hands to his temples and began to recite again, more softly. '*There are no bombs. There are no fires. There are no bombs. There are no fires . . .*'

At last he drew his blanket tighter across his shoulders, got down from the table and, still muttering, began to pace back and forth across the cell. With every fresh explosion, he swore and walked on faster. At last Duncan lifted his head from his pillow to say irritably, 'Stop walking about, can't you?'

'I'm sorry,' said Fraser, exaggeratedly polite, 'am I keeping you awake?' He got back on the table. 'It's this wretched moon brings them,' he said, as if to himself. 'Why can't there be clouds?' He rubbed the glass where his breath had misted it. For a minute he said nothing. Then he started up again: '*There are no bombs. There are no fires. There is no poverty and no injustice. There is no pisspot in my cell—*'

'Shut up,' said Duncan. 'You shouldn't make fun of it. It – well, it isn't fair on Mr Mundy.'

Fraser laughed outright at that. 'Mr Mundy,' he repeated. 'Not fair on Mr Mundy. What's it to you, if I make fun of old Mr Mundy?' He said this as if still to himself; but then seemed struck by the idea, and turned his head, and asked Duncan properly. 'Just what sort of a racket do you have going on with Mr Mundy, anyway?'

Duncan didn't answer. Fraser waited, then went on, 'You know what I'm talking about. Did you think I hadn't noticed? He gives you cigarettes, doesn't he? He gives you sugar for your cocoa, things like that.'

'Mr Mundy's kind,' said Duncan. 'He's the only kind twirl here, you can ask anyone.'

'But I'm asking you,' persisted Fraser. 'He doesn't give *me* cigarettes and sugar, after all.'

'He doesn't feel sorry for you, I suppose.'

'Does he feel sorry for you, then? Is that what it is?'

Duncan lifted his head. He'd begun picking at a length of wool that had come loose at the edge of his blanket. 'I expect so,' he said. 'People do, that's all. It's a thing of mine. It's always been like that, even before. Before all this, I mean.'

'You've just one of those faces,' said Fraser.

'I suppose so.'

'The fascination of your eyelashes, something like that.'

Duncan let the blanket fall. 'I can't help my eyelashes!' he said, stupidly.

Fraser laughed, and his manner changed again. 'Indeed you can't, Pearce.' He got down from the table again and sat on the chair – moving the chair so that it was close to the wall, and spreading his knees, putting back his head. 'I once knew a girl,' he began, 'with eyelashes like yours—'

'Known lots of girls, haven't you?'

'Well, I don't like to boast.'

'Don't, then.'

'I say, look here, it was you who brought the subject up! I was asking about you and Mr Mundy . . . I was wondering if it really was just for the sake of your beautiful eyelashes that he gives you such a soft time of it.'

Duncan sat up. He'd remembered the feel of Mr

Mundy's hand on his knee, and started to blush. He said hotly, 'I don't give him anything back, if that's what you mean!'

'Well, I suppose that is what I meant.'

'Is that how it works, with you and your girls?'

'Ouch. All right. I just—'

'Just what?'

Fraser hesitated again. Then, 'Just nothing,' he said. 'I was curious, that's all, about how these things go.'

'How what things go?'

'For someone like you.'

'Like me?' asked Duncan. 'What do you mean?'

Fraser moved, turned away. 'You know very well what I mean.'

'I don't.'

'You must know, at least, what gets said about you in here.'

Duncan felt himself blush harder. 'That gets said, in here, about anyone. Anyone with any kind of – of culture; who likes books, likes music. Who isn't a brute, in other words. But the fact is, it's the brutes who are worst of all at that sort of thing—'

'I know that,' said Fraser quietly. 'It isn't only that.'

'What is it, then?'

'Nothing. Something I heard, about why you're here.'

'What did you hear?'

'That you're here because— Look, forget it, it's none of my business.'

'No,' said Duncan. 'Tell me what you heard.'

Fraser smoothed back his hair. 'That you're here,' he said bluntly at last, 'because your boyfriend died, and you tried to kill yourself over it.'

Duncan lay very still, unable to answer.

'I'm sorry,' said Fraser. 'As I said, it's none of my damn business. I don't care a fig why you're here, or who you used to go around with. I think the laws about suicide are bloody, if you want to know.'

'Who told you that?' asked Duncan thickly.

'It doesn't matter. Forget it.'

'Was it Wainwright? Or Binns?'

'No.'

'Who was it, then?'

Fraser looked away. 'It was that little queer Stella, of course.'

'*Her!*' said Duncan. 'She makes me sick. They all do, all that crowd. They don't want to go to bed with girls, but they make themselves like girls. They make themselves worse than girls! They need doctors! I hate them.'

'All right,' said Fraser mildly. 'So do I.'

'You think I'm like them!'

'That's not what I said.'

'You think I used to be like them; or that Alec was—'

He stopped. He had never said Alec's name here, aloud, to anyone but Mr Mundy; and now he'd spat it out as if it were a curse.

Fraser was watching him through the gloom. 'Alec,' he said, carefully. 'Was that—Was that your boyfriend?'

'He wasn't my boyfriend!' said Duncan. Why did everybody have to think of it like that? 'He was only my friend. Don't you have friends? Doesn't everyone?'

'Of course. I'm sorry.'

'He was only my friend. If you'd grown up where I grew up, feeling like me, you'd know what that meant.'

'Yes. I expect so.'

The worst of the bombing seemed, for the moment, to have passed on. Fraser blew into his hands, worked his fingers, to get the cold out. Then he got up, reached under his pillow and brought out cigarettes. Almost shyly, he offered one to Duncan. Duncan shook his head.

But Fraser kept the cigarettes held out. 'I should like you to,' he said quietly. 'Go on. Please.'

'It'll be one less for you.'

'I don't care. Better let me light it, though.'

He put two cigarettes to his mouth, then took up the pot that he and Duncan kept their dinner-salt in, and a needle. You could make a flame, by sparking the metal against the stone: it took him a moment or two, but at last the paper caught and the tobacco started to glow. The cigarette he handed over was damp from his lips: collapsed, like a sucked-on straw. A strand or two of tobacco came loose upon Duncan's tongue.

They smoked without speaking. The cigarettes only lasted a minute. And when Fraser's was finished he opened it up, to keep what he could for the next one.

As he did it he said quietly, 'I envy you your friend, Pearce. Truly I do. I don't think I've ever cared so much for a man – or a woman either, come to that – as much as you must have cared for him. Yes, I envy you.'

'You're the only one who does, then,' said Duncan moodily. 'My own father's ashamed of me.'

'Well, so is mine of me, if it comes to that. He thinks my sort ought to be handed over to Germany, since we're all so keen on helping the Nazis along. A man ought to be a source of shame to his father, don't you think? If I ever have a son, I hope he makes my life hell. How, otherwise, will there ever be any progress?'

But Duncan wouldn't smile. 'You make a joke of things,' he said. 'It's different for people like you, for people in your world.'

'Have things really been so bad for you?'

'I dare say they wouldn't seem bad, to someone looking in from outside. My father never— He never hit me, or anything like that. It was just—' He struggled, searching for the words. 'I don't know. It was liking things you weren't supposed to like; and feeling things you weren't supposed to feel. Never being able to say the thing that people expected. And Alec felt like I did. He hated the war. His brother had died, right at the start of it, and his father kept on at him to go and fight. And it

551

was the blitz. It was nearly the end of the blitz, though we didn't know that then. It felt like – like the end of the bloody world! It was the worst time for everything. Alec and I never wanted to fight. He wanted to make a difference, to how people felt. Instead— Well—'

'Poor chap,' said Fraser feelingly, when Duncan wouldn't go on. 'He sounds all right. I'd like to have known him.'

'He *was* all right,' said Duncan. 'He was clever. Not like me. People have always said I'm clever, but that's only because I make myself talk in a certain way. But he was funny. He could never be still. He was always on to something new. He was a bit like you, I suppose; or you're like he would have been, if he'd been to a proper school, had money. He made things seem exciting. He made things – I don't know; he made them seem better than they really were. Even if afterwards, when you thought about it, you realised that some of what he'd said was silly; at the time, when you were with him, you wanted to go along with it. You felt – swept along by him.'

'I'm sorry,' said Fraser quietly. 'I can see why you— Well, why you liked him so much. How old was he?'

'He was just nineteen,' said Duncan quietly. 'He was older than me. That's why he got called up first.'

'Just nineteen. That stinks, Pearce! First his brother, and then him.' He hesitated, and lowered his voice. 'And then?'

'And then?' repeated Duncan.

'After he died? Then, you—?'

Duncan had another, violent glimpse of the scarlet kitchen in his father's house. He looked at Fraser in the moonlight, feeling his heart begin to race; wanting to tell him what had happened; longing to tell him! – but unable, finally, to say the words. He lowered his gaze and said flatly instead, 'After he died, I didn't. I meant to, and I didn't. That's all. All right?'

Fraser must not have noticed the change in his tone. He went on, 'So they put you in here! There's British justice for you, isn't it! Two lives ruined instead of one. When all you needed, I suppose—'

'Don't let's talk about it,' said Duncan.

'Not if you don't want to. Of course not. It makes me sick, that's all. If only somebody, perhaps your father, or— Shit!' He leapt from his chair. 'What the hell was that?'

A bomb had fallen, closer than ever; the blast had come so forcefully, the panes of glass in the window had been blown or sucked against their frames and one, with a sound like a pistol firing, had cracked. Duncan looked up. Fraser had darted back as far as the door and had tried to push it open. The blanket had fallen from his shoulders. 'Shit! Shit!' he said again. 'That was an oil-bomb, wasn't it? They make that whining sound, don't they?'

'I don't know,' said Duncan.

Fraser nodded. 'I've heard them come down before. That was an oil-bomb all right. – God!' Now another one had fallen. He tried the door again, then looked around, his voice rising. 'Suppose an oil-bomb hit this hall: how d'you think we'd do? We'd be roasted in our beds! Do they even have fire-watchers on the roof? I've never heard anyone talk about fire-watchers, have you? Suppose a cluster of them came down? How quickly do you think a twirl could make his way to all the landings, to open all the doors? Would they even bother to come up out of their shelter? Christ! They could at least take us down to the Firsts when the Warning goes. They could let us sleep on our mattresses in the Rec!'

His voice was high and broken as a boy's; and Duncan understood suddenly how really upset he was, and how hard he had been trying, until now, to make light of his fear. His face was white and strained and sweating. His short hair stood up: he smoothed it back with both his hands, again and again.

Then he caught Duncan's gaze; and when Duncan, embarrassed, looked away, he grew calmer. 'You think I'm funking it,' he said.

'No,' said Duncan. 'I wasn't thinking that.'

'Well, perhaps I am.' He showed his hand. He was shaking. 'Look at me!'

'What does it matter?'

'What does it matter? Christ! You've no idea! I— Shit!'

Now men were beginning to call out. They sounded afraid, like Fraser. One man was shouting for Mr Garnish. Another was thumping with something on his cell door. The windows jumped in their frames again, as another bomb fell, closer than ever . . . After that bombs fell, or seemed to fall, like rain. It was like being trapped in a dustbin while someone beat on it with a bat.

'*Giggs, you cunt!*' somebody shouted. '*This is your fucking fault! I'm going to get you, Giggs! I'm going to frigging well slaughter you!*'

But Giggs had shut up; and after a moment the shouting man shut up, too. Calling into the sound of the explosions was somehow horrible: Duncan had the sense that most of the men were in their bunks, lying tensely, silently, counting the seconds, waiting for the blasts.

Fraser was still standing, flinching, at the door. Duncan said to him, 'Get back into bed until it stops.'

'Suppose it doesn't stop? Or suppose it stops, and we stop with it?'

'It's still miles away,' said Duncan. 'The yards' – he was making it up – 'the yards make it sound worse than it is. They make the bangs bigger than they really are.'

'Do you think so?'

'Yes. Haven't you ever noticed, when a man calls out of his window, how echoey it sounds?'

Fraser nodded, fastening on to the idea. 'That's true,' he said. 'I've noticed that. That's true, you're right.' But he was still shaking; and after a minute, he rubbed his arms. He was dressed only in his pyjamas, and the cell was freezing.

'Go back to bed,' Duncan said again. And then, when Fraser didn't move, he got to his feet and climbed on to the chair, to close the curtain. He looked out of the window as he did it, and saw the yard, and the prison building opposite, lit up by the moon. A searchlight moved, as if restless or mad, about the sky, and somewhere to the east – it might have been Maida Vale, it might have been as far away as Euston – there was the faint, irregular glow of a rising fire. He brought in his gaze, to the crack in the window-pane. It was neatly done, a perfect arc; it didn't look like something made by force or violence, at all. But when he put his fingers to it he felt it give, and he knew that if he pressed at it harder, it would shatter.

He seized the black-out curtain and pulled it across, and secured it to the sill; after that the view could have been of anything, and the cell – which was plunged into an almost perfect darkness – could have been quite a different sort of room – could have been anywhere, or nowhere. Where the moonlight struck the curtain from behind, it was baffled; but here and there it leaked through weaknesses in the weave of the fabric and made brilliant little stars and spots and crescents, like spangles on the cloak of a stage magician.

He got back into bed. He heard Fraser take a couple of steps and bend to pick up his blanket.

But then he stood still, as if hesitating, still afraid . . .
At last, very quietly, he spoke.

'Let me come in with you, Pearce, will you?' he
said. 'Let me share your bunk, I mean.' And, when
Duncan didn't answer, he added simply, 'It's this
bloody war. I can't bear to lie alone.'

So Duncan put back the covers and moved in
closer to the wall, and Fraser got in beside him and
lay still. They didn't speak. But every time another
bomb fell, or a burst of anti-aircraft fire went up,
Fraser would flinch and tense – like a man in pain,
being knocked and jolted about. Soon Duncan found
himself tensing with him, not in fear, but in sympathy.

That made Fraser laugh. 'God!' he said. His teeth
were chattering. 'I'm sorry, Pearce.'

'There's nothing to be sorry for,' said Duncan.

'Now that I've started shaking, I can't seem to
stop.'

'That's how it works.'

'I'm making *you* shake.'

'It doesn't matter. You'll warm up soon, and then
you'll be all right.'

Fraser shook his head. 'It isn't just through being
cold, Pearce.'

'It doesn't matter.'

'You keep saying that. It matters terribly. Don't
you see?'

'See what?' asked Duncan.

'Don't you think I never wonder, about – about
fear? It's the very worst thing, the very worst thing
of all. I could take any amount of tribunals. I could

557

take women calling me gutless in the streets! But to think to oneself, quietly, that the tribunals and the women might be right; to have the suspicion gnawing and gnawing at one: do I truly believe this, or am I simply a – a bloody coward?' He wiped his face again, and Duncan realised that the sweat upon his cheeks was mixed with tears. 'You won't catch men like me admitting it,' he went on, less steadily. 'But we feel it, Pearce, I know we feel it . . . And meanwhile, one sees the most ordinary types of men – men like Grayson, like Wright – going cheerfully off to fight. Are they the less brave, because they're stupid? Do you think I don't wonder how I'll feel, when the war's over, knowing that I'm probably only still alive because of fellows like them? Meanwhile, here I am, and here's Watling, and Willis, and Spinks, and all the other COs in every other gaol in England. And if—' A plane buzzed loudly overhead. He grew tense again, until it passed. 'And if we're all burnt to death by an oil-bomb, will that make us brave men?'

'I think it's brave,' said Duncan, 'to do what you've done. Anyone would think it.'

Fraser wiped his nose. 'An easy kind of bravery, doing nothing at all! You're a braver man than I am, Pearce.'

'Me!'

'You did something, didn't you?'

'What do you mean?'

'You did the thing – the thing you were talking about, that brought you here.'

Duncan shuddered, turning away.

'It took a kind of courage, didn't it?' insisted Fraser. 'Christ knows, it took more courage than I've got.'

Duncan moved again. He raised his hand – as if, even in the darkness, to push away Fraser's gaze. 'You don't know anything about it,' he said roughly. 'You think— Oh!' He felt disgusted. For even now, with Fraser trembling at his side, he couldn't bring himself to tell him the simple truth. 'Don't talk about it,' he said instead. 'Shut up.'

'All right. I'm sorry.'

They were silent after that. The buzz of aeroplanes was still heavy overhead, the pounding of ack-ack fire still dreadful. But when the next explosion came it was further off, and the next was further off again, as the raiders moved on . . .

Fraser grew calmer. In another minute the All Clear went, and he gave a final quiver, passed his sleeve across his face, and then lay still. The hall was quiet. No one stood at their window to whistle or to cheer. Men who must have been lying rigid like him, or curled into balls, now lifted their heads, put out their limbs, to test the stillness of the night; and fell back exhausted.

Only the officers stirred: out they came, like beetles from underneath a stone. Duncan heard their footsteps on the cinder surface of the yard – slow, and halting, as if they were amazed to have emerged and found the prison still intact.

He knew, then, what sound would come next:

the shivering sound of the metal landings, as Mr Mundy made his round. After a moment it started up, and he lifted his head, the better to hear it. The bar of light beneath the door showed extra palely now, because the cell was so dark. He saw Mr Mundy come and slide back the guard from over the spy-hole. He knew that Fraser saw it, too. But when Fraser opened his mouth, Duncan lifted his hand and put his fingers across his lips, to keep him from speaking; and when Mr Mundy called, in his night whisper, 'All right?', Duncan didn't answer. The call came a second time, and a third, before Mr Mundy gave up and moved reluctantly away.

Duncan still had his hand across Fraser's lips. He felt Fraser's breath against his fingers, and slowly drew the hand off. They didn't speak. But Duncan was aware now, as he had not been aware before, of Fraser's body: of the heat of it, and the places – the feet, the thighs, the arms and shoulders – at which it touched Duncan's own. The bunk was narrow. Duncan had lain alone in it every night, for almost three years. He had gone about the prison, as all the men did, being occasionally jostled, occasionally struck; he had touched his fingers to Viv's across the table in the visiting-room; he had once shaken hands with the Chaplain. It ought to have been strange, to be pressed so close to another person now; but it wasn't strange. He turned his head. He said, in a whisper, 'Are you all right?' and Fraser answered,

'Yes.' 'Don't you want to go back up?' Fraser shook his head: 'Not yet . . .' It wasn't strange, at all. They moved closer together, not further apart. Duncan put up his arm and Fraser raised himself so that the arm could go beneath his head. They settled back into an embrace – as if it were nothing, as if it were easy; as if they weren't two boys, in a prison, in a city being blown and shot to bits; as if it were the most natural thing in the world.

'Why,' Mickey asked Kay, 'did you give that girl your ring?'

Kay changed smoothly up the gears. She said, 'I don't know. I felt sorry for her. It's only a ring, after all. What's a ring, in times like these?'

She tried to speak lightly; but the fact was, she was already rather regretting having given the ring up. Her hand, where it gripped the steering-wheel, felt naked and queer, unlucky.

'Maybe I'll go back to the hospital tomorrow,' she said, 'see how she's getting on.'

'Well, I hope she's still there,' said Mickey mean-ingfully.

Kay wouldn't look at her. She said, 'She wanted to chance it. It was up to her, not us.'

'She didn't know what she was saying.'

'She knew, all right. The lousy swine who made a muck of fixing her up is the one I'd like to get my hands on. Him, and the boyfriend.' She came to a junction. 'Which road do we want?'

'Not this one,' said Mickey, peering at the street, 'I think it's closed. Go on to the next.'

It was their heaviest night for weeks, because of the moon. After dropping Viv at the hospital they'd returned to Dolphin Square and had at once been sent out again. A stretch of railway line in their district had been hit; three men who'd been patching it up from the last raid had been killed, and six more injured. They took four of those casualties in one trip, then were sent to a terrace that had got its front blown off, where a family had been buried. Two women and a girl were dug out alive; a girl and a boy were discovered dead. Kay and Mickey had taken the corpses.

Now they'd been sent out again: they were heading for a street slightly to the east of Sloane Square. Kay turned a corner, and felt the tyres of the van begin to grind. The road had grit and earth and broken glass on it. She slowed to a crawl, then stopped and put down her window as a warden came over.

She saw the leisurely way he was walking. 'Too late?' she said.

The man nodded. He took them over and showed them the bodies.

'Jesus,' said Mickey.

There were two of them: a man and a woman, killed on their way back from a party. Their house, the warden said, was only fifty yards further on. The street was crescent-shaped, broken up by a slip of garden, and it was the garden that had taken the worst of the bomb. A plane tree thirty feet high had been blasted more or less into splinters; houses had lost windows and front doors and slates from their roofs, but were otherwise unmarked. The man and woman, however, had been tossed up into the air. The man had landed on the flags of a narrow area in front of the basement window of a house. The woman had fallen on to the railings on the pavement above – been caught, chest-first, on the blunt tips of the iron spikes. She was still slumped there. The warden had found a length of curtain, that was all, and covered her over. Now he drew the curtain back, for Kay and Mickey to get a better view of the body. Kay looked only once, then turned away.

The woman's coat and hat had gone, and her hair was loose about her face; the evening-gloves were smooth and unmarked, still, on her dangling arms. Her silk dress, silvered by the moon-light, was pooled about her on the pavement as though she were curtseying; but the flesh of her bare back bulged where the iron pressed at it from within.

'The last set of railings in the street,' said the warden, as he took Kay and Mickey down the area steps. 'What luck was that, eh? Left here, I think, because they were rusty. I'll be quite honest with you, I didn't want to try and move her. I could see she was dead, though. Killed at the first blow, I hope. Her husband, believe it or not, was sitting up twenty minutes ago, having a conversation with me. That's why I put in the call to you lot. But look at the state of him.'

He moved aside a piece of rubbish and they saw the man's body: he was sitting with his legs drawn up and his back to the area wall. Like the woman, he was dressed in evening gear, the neck-tie in a neat bow, still, around his collar, but the collar itself, and most of his shirt-front, stained ghastly red. Dust had settled, like a cap, on the brilliantine in his hair, but where the light of the torch played over the side of his head Kay could see his torn-up scalp, and more blood, thick and glistening as jam.

'Nice bit of muck,' said the warden, tutting, 'for the people of the house to come out to, eh, when they show their heads?' He looked Kay and Mickey over. 'Not much of a job for women, this. Got anything to wrap 'em in?'

'Only blankets.'

'Fine mess,' he said in his grumbling way, as they went back up the steps, 'they'll make of blankets.' He kicked his way along the street, and found a length of something. 'Look here, what's this? The lady's cloak, blown off her back. We could— Oh, by jiminy!'

He and Kay ducked, instinctively. But the blast was a mile or two away, somewhere to the north: not so much a bang as a muffled sort of *whump*. It was followed by a series of crashes from somewhere closer to hand: falling timbers, slithering slates, the almost musical sound of shattering glass. A couple of dogs began barking.

'What was it?' called Mickey. She had gone to the ambulance and was bringing out stretchers. 'Something going up?'

'Sounds like it,' said Kay.

'A gas-main?'

'Factory, I'll bet,' said the warden, rubbing his chin.

They looked at the sky. There were searchlights playing, thinned out by the moonlight, but making it difficult to see; but when the beams went down, the warden pointed: 'Look.' There had come, on the underside of clouds, the first reflection of some great fire. Where smoke rose up in whorls and tangles it was lit a dark, unhealthy pink.

'A grand view that'll give to Jerry, too,' said the warden.

'Where do you think it is?' Mickey asked him. 'King's Cross?'

'Could be,' he answered doubtfully. 'Could be further south than that, though. I'd say it was Bloomsbury.'

'Bloomsbury?' said Kay.

'Know the area?'

'Yes.' She narrowed her eyes, scanning the sky-line, suddenly afraid. She was looking for landmarks – spires, chimneys, something she knew. But she could see nothing – and anyway, she forgot for the moment which way she was facing, north-east or north-west; the curve of the street made things confusing. Then the searchlights went up again, and the sky became a mess of shadow and colour. She turned away, went back to the woman's body. 'Come on,' she said to Mickey.

She must have sounded odd. Mickey looked at her. 'What's the matter?'

'I don't know. Got the creeps, that's all. Christ, this is awful! Give me a hand, can you? It's no good just lifting her, there are barbs; she must be caught on them.'

By rocking the woman's body back and forth they managed to free it; but the grinding of the iron against her ribs, and the lurching about of the point of the spike beneath the skin of her back, were ghastly to feel and hear. She came away wetly. They didn't turn her over, didn't try to close her eyes, but laid her quickly on a stretcher and wrapped her around with the torn curtain that had covered her before. Her hair was fair, tangled as if from sleep – like Helen's hair, Kay thought, when Helen woke, or when she rose from a bed after making love.

'Christ,' she said again, wiping her mouth with the back of her cuff. 'This is bloody!' She moved a little way off and lit a cigarette.

But while she stood smoking it, she became anxious. She looked at the sky. The play of colour was as wild as before, the glow sometimes more intense, sometimes dimmer, as the flames producing it must have been bucking and leaping about in the breeze beneath. Again she was afraid, without quite knowing why. She threw her cigarette away after two or three puffs; the warden saw and said,

'Hey!' He picked it up and started smoking it himself.

Kay caught up the second stretcher from beside the body of the woman, and carried it down the area steps. She took a roll of bandage with her, and used it to bind up the dead man's head. Mickey came to help her, holding the head rather gingerly while Kay passed the dressing around it. Then they laid the stretcher flat, and tried to lift the body on to it. There was not much space, and the ground was cluttered, with soil thrown up from the garden, with branches and broken slates. They started to kick the rubbish aside; they began to breathe more harshly as they did it, to mutter and curse. Even so, when Kay's name was said in the street above – said urgently, but not called, or shrieked – she heard it. She heard it, and knew. She straightened up, grew still for a second; then simply stepped over the body of the man and went quickly back up the steps.

Someone was talking with the warden. She recognised him, in the darkness, by the leanness of his face, and by his glasses. It was Hughes, from the station. He'd been running. He'd taken his hat off, to come more quickly, and was pressing at his side. He saw her and said, 'Kay' – and that made it worse, for she didn't think he had ever called her Kay before; usually he called her Langrish. 'Kay—'

'What is it?' she said. 'Tell me!'

He blew out his breath. 'I've been with Cole and O'Neil, three streets away. The warden took a call, from Station 58 . . . Kay, I'm sorry. They think it was a packet of three that was aimed at Broadcasting House but went east. One was caught before it could do much damage. The other two have started fires—'

'Helen,' she said.

He caught at her arm. 'I wanted to let you know. But they couldn't say where, exactly. Kay, it might not be—'

'*Helen,*' she said again.

It was what she had dreaded, every single day of the war; and she'd told herself that, by dreading it, she'd be calm when it finally came. Now she understood that the dread had been, for her, a sort of pact: she'd imagined that if her fear was only sharp enough and unbroken, it would earn Helen's safety. But that was nonsense. She'd been afraid – and the terrible thing had happened anyway. How could she be calm? She drew her arm from Hughes's grip and covered her face; and she shook, right through. She wanted to sink to her knees, cry out. The violence of her weakness appalled her. Then she thought, *How will this help Helen?* She lowered her hands, and saw that Mickey had come, and was reaching for her, as Hughes had reached. Kay shrugged her off, beginning to move.

'I have to go there,' she said.

'Kay, don't,' said Hughes. 'I came because I didn't want you to hear from someone else. But there's nothing you can do there. It's 58's area. Leave it to them.'

'They'll funk it,' said Kay. 'They'll fuck it up! I have to get there.'

'It's too far! There's nothing you'll be able to do.'

'*Helen's there!* Don't you understand?'

'Of course I understand. That's why I came. But—'

'Kay,' said Mickey, grabbing at her arm again. 'Hughes is right. It's too far.'

'I don't care,' said Kay, almost wildly. 'I'll run. I'll—' Then she saw the ambulance. She said, more steadily, 'I'm taking the van.'

'Kay, no!'

'Kay—'

'Hey,' said the warden, who'd been looking on all this time. 'What about these bodies?'

'To hell with them,' said Kay.

She'd begun to run. Mickey and Hughes came close behind her, trying to stop her.

'Langrish,' said Hughes, growing angry. 'Don't be idiotic.'

'Get out of my way,' said Kay.

She'd gone to the back of the ambulance first, to fasten its doors. Now she went to the cabin and climbed inside. Hughes stood in the doorway, pleading with her. 'Langrish,' he said. 'For God's sake, think what you're doing!'

She felt for the key; then caught Mickey's eye, over Hughes's shoulder.

'Mickey,' she said quietly. 'Give me the key.'

Hughes turned. 'Carmichael, don't.'

'Give me the key, Mickey.'

'Carmichael—'

Mickey hesitated, looking from Kay to Hughes and back again. She took out the key, hesitated again; and then threw it. Her aim was true as a boy's. Hughes made a grab at it, but it was Kay who caught it. She fitted it into its socket and started the engine.

'Damn you!' said Hughes, striking the metal frame of the door. 'Damn you both! You'll be thrown out of the service for this! You'll be—'

Kay punched him. She punched him blindly, and caught his cheek and the edge of his glasses; and as soon as he'd fallen back she let down the handbrake and moved off. The door swung to, and she grabbed for its handle and drew it closed. Her tin hat had fallen low on her brow; she tugged at its strap and pulled it from her head, and at once felt better. She glanced in the mirror – saw Hughes sitting in the road with his hands at his face, and Mickey standing slackly, doing nothing, looking after her as she pulled away . . . She made herself drive with maddening care across the soil- and glass-strewn street; and then, when the road was smoother, she speeded up.

As she drove, she pictured Helen; she pictured her as she had last seen her, hours before: unmarked, unharmed. She saw her so clearly, she knew that she couldn't be dead or even hurt. She thought, *It can't be Rathbone Place, it must*

be some other street. It can't be! Or, if it is, then Helen will have heard the Warning and gone to the shelter. She'll have gone to the shelter, for my sake, just this once . . .

She had got on to Buckingham Palace Road, and now sped on past Victoria Station. She turned into the park, hardly slowing, so that the tyres squealed on the surface of the road and something was tilted out of its place in the back of the van, and tumbled and smashed. But ahead was that glow, irregularly pulsing, like a faltering life – dreadful, dreadful. She changed up the gears and went faster. The raid was still on, and the Mall, of course, was empty; only at Charing Cross did she meet activity: a warden and policemen attending to another incident, they heard her coming and waved her on, thinking she'd been sent to them from her station. 'Just along that way,' they called, pointing east, along the Strand. She nodded; but she didn't think, even for a moment, of stopping, of giving help. When, a little later, another man, seeing the ambulance crest on the front of her van, came lurching off the pavement, his hands at his head, his face dark with blood, she swerved around him and drove on.

Charing Cross Road was up, because a water main had been struck there three days before. She went west, to the Haymarket; drove up to Shaftesbury Avenue, and got on to Wardour Street, meaning to get to Rathbone Place like that. She found the entrance to Oxford Street blocked by trestles and ropes, and manned by policemen. She braked madly, and began to turn. A policeman came running over to her window as she was doing it.

'Where are you trying for?' he asked. She named her mews. He said at once, 'I thought your lot were there already. You can't get through this way.'

She said, 'Is it bad?'

He blinked, catching something in her voice. 'Two warehouses gone, so far as I know. Didn't you get the details from Control?'

'The furniture warehouse?' she said, ignoring his question. 'Palmer's?'

'I don't know.'

'Christ, it must be! Oh, Christ!'

She had wound the window down to talk to him; and could suddenly smell the burning. She put the van into gear, and the policeman leapt back. The engine shuddered as she reversed. She changed gear again, double-declutching as usual, but timing it badly and crashing the cogs: swearing, enraged by the clumsiness of the mechanism; almost weeping. *Don't cry, you fool!* she said to herself. She struck at her thigh, savagely, with the ball of her fist. The van swayed about. *Don't cry, don't cry . . .*

She was heading south now, but saw an unblocked road to the left, and turned sharply into it. A little way along it she was able to turn left again, into Dean Street. Here, for the first time, she saw the tips of the flames of the fire, leaping into the sky. There began to come smuts – dark, fragile webs of drifting ash – against the windscreen of the van. She pressed hard on the accelerator pedal and sped forwards; she got only a hundred yards, however, before the road was blocked again. She stuck out her head. 'Let me through!' she called to the policemen here. They made gestures with their hands: 'No chance. Go back.' She turned and, in desperation, went east again, to Soho Square. Another road-block; but a less well-manned one. She stopped the van and put on the handbrake; then got out, ran, and simply vaulted over the trestles.

'Hey!' someone called behind her. 'You, without a hat! Are you crazy?'

She thumped the flashes on her shoulder. 'Ambulance!' she shouted, panting. 'Ambulance!'

'Hey! Come back!'

But after a second, the voices faded. The wind had turned, and she found herself, suddenly, smothered in smoke. She got out her handkerchief and pressed it to her nose and mouth, but kept on running; the smoke came on in gusts, so that she passed, for a hundred feet or more, through alternate states of blindness and stinging light. Once she was caught in a shower of sparks, which singed her hair and burnt her face. A moment later she fell, and in getting to her feet lost her sense of direction: she ran forward a couple of steps, and met a wall; turned, went on, and seemed almost at once to meet another . . . Finally, something came hurtling towards her head – a piece of burning paper, she thought it was, as she dodged away. Then she saw that it was a pigeon, with blazing wings. She put out her hands and ran from it, stumbling in horror, dropping her handkerchief, drawing breath as a new wave of smoke came against her face, and starting to choke. She staggered forwards – and suddenly found herself in space and heat and chaos. She put her hands on her thighs, and coughed, and spat. Then she looked up.

She had come very close to the heart of the fire; but recognised nothing. The buildings about her that she ought to know; the running firemen; the pools of water on the ground; the snaking hoses – everything was lit with a garish, unnatural intensity, or hidden by leaping black shadows. She tried calling to a man, but he couldn't hear her over the roaring of the fire, the throbbing of the pumps. She went to somebody else, taking him by the shoulders, bellowing into his face: 'Where am I? Where the hell am I? Where's Pym's Yard?'

'Pym's Yard?' he answered, shaking her off and already moving away. 'You're in it!'

She looked down, and saw cobbles beneath her boots; gazing around again, she began to make out little familiar details. And she realised at last that the warehouse, Palmer's, must be right here, ahead of her, not quite at the centre of the blaze; and that the reason she could not make out the shape of her own building was because a side and part of the roof of Palmer's had fallen and flattened it.

The knowledge undid her. She stood, unable to act – simply gazing into the flames. Once a fireman caught hold of her arm and pushed her: 'Get out of the way, can't you?' But she took the three or four steps he made her take, and then stood slackly again. Finally someone called her by her name. It was Henry Varney, the Goodge Street warden. His face and hands were black with smoke. The sockets of his eyes were white, where he'd rubbed them. He looked like a stage minstrel.

He was gripping her by the shoulders. 'Miss Langrish!' he was saying in amazement. 'How long have you been here?'

She couldn't answer. He began to walk her away from the fire. He took off his hat and tried to put it on her head, and it was hot, like a roasting-dish. 'Come away from the flames,' he said. 'You're burnt, you're— Come back from the flames, Miss Langrish!'

'I came to get Helen,' she said to him.

He said again, 'Come back!' Then he met her gaze, and looked away. 'I'm sorry,' he said. 'The warehouse— The place went up like tinder. The shelter caught it, too.'

'The shelter, too?'

He nodded. 'God knows how many were in there.'

He had led her to the sill of a broken window; he

made her sit down, and squatted beside her, holding her hand. She said to him once, 'They're sure, Henry, about the shelter?'

'Quite sure. I'm so sorry.'

'And nobody was saved?'

'No one.'

A fireman came over. 'You ambulance people,' he said roughly to Kay, 'should have cleared out of here bloody forty minutes ago! There's nothing for you, didn't you hear?'

Henry stood up, and said something to him; the man ducked his head and moved off. 'Christ,' Kay heard him say . . .

Henry took her hand again. 'I've got to leave you, Miss Langrish. I hate to do it. Won't you go to the first-aid post? Or, is there someone – a friend – I could send for?'

She nodded to the fire. 'My friend was in there, Henry.'

He pressed her hand, and moved away; and in a second he was running, calling out . . . The fire, however, had reached its peak before Kay had arrived. Flames no longer leapt into the sky. The roar had lessened; the heat, if anything, was greater than before, but the warehouse walls burned shrunkenly in the midst of the blaze, and soon, with a final gust of sparks, they shivered and collapsed. The firemen moved from one spot to another. The water ran filthily across the cobbles, or rose as a thick acid steam. Once the ground gave a series of rumbles and thuds, which must have come from the dropping of bombs nearby; but the blast, if anything, worked on the scene as a riddling by a giant poker would have: the fire flared up brightly again for ten or fifteen minutes, then began to die. One of the engines was switched off, and its hoses reeled in. The fierce light faded, along with the clamour of the pumps. The moon had set, or been covered by cloud. Objects lost their sharp edges, their look of unrealness; little details faded back into the shadows, like so many moths folding up their wings.

No one came to Kay again, through all this time. She might have been gradually reabsorbed into the darkness, too. She sat with her hands on her thighs, simply gazing into the hot, still core of the burning building; she saw the fire change colour, from fathomless white, to yellow, to orange, and to red. The second engine was turned off and driven away. Someone called to someone else that the All Clear had gone, that the roads were opened.

She thought of roads, of movement, and could make no sense of it. She lifted her hands to her head. Her hair felt strange – it was coarse, had been singed by sparks. The skin of her face was tender where she pressed it; she dimly remembered someone telling her she was burnt.

Then Henry Varney came to her again, and touched her shoulder. She tried to look at him – tried to blink – and could hardly do it, for her eyes had been dried, been almost baked, by the heat of the fire.

'Miss Langrish,' he said – just what he'd said before; only now, his voice was gentle, and choked and queer. She watched his face, and saw tears running down his cheeks, making crooked white channels through the soot. 'Can you see?' he was saying. 'Will you look?' He'd raised his hand. She understood, at last, that he was pointing.

She turned her head, and saw two figures. They were standing a little way off, and seemed as still and as speechless as she. The dying fire lit them, picked them out of the darkness: what she noticed first was the unnatural paleness, in that filthy place, of their faces and their hands. Then one of the figures took a step, and she saw that it was Helen.

She covered her eyes. She didn't get up. Helen had to come to her and help her to her feet. And even then she wouldn't take the hand from before her face; she let Helen embrace her, awkwardly, and she laid her brow against Helen's shoulder and wept like a child into her hair. She didn't feel pleasure or relief. She felt only, still, a mixture of pain and fear so sharp, she thought it would kill her. She shuddered and shuddered, in Helen's arms; and finally raised her head.

Through the stinging film of her own tears, she saw Julia. She was hanging back, as if afraid to come any nearer; or as if she was waiting. Kay met her gaze, and shook her head, and began to weep again. 'Julia,' she said, in a kind of bafflement –

for she could understand nothing, at that moment, except that Helen had been taken, and now was returned. 'Julia. Oh, Julia! Thank God! I thought I'd lost her.'

1941

Viv was on a train, somewhere between Swindon and London – it was impossible to say where exactly, for the train kept stopping at what might or might not have been stations; and there was no point trying to see from the windows, for the blinds were down and, anyway, the station names all painted over or removed. Viv had been sitting for the last four hours with seven other people in a second-class compartment meant for six. The mood was awful. A couple of soldiers kept larking about with lighted matches, trying to set fire to each other's hair; a po-faced WAAF officer kept asking them to stop. Another woman was knitting, and the knobs of her needles were striking the thighs of the people sitting next to her. One of them – a girl in trousers – had just said, 'Do you mind? These slacks weren't cheap. Your needles are making snags in them.'

The knitting woman had drawn in her chin. 'Snags?' she was saying. 'You don't think there are rather more important things to worry about, just now?'

'No, I don't, as it happens.'

'Well, I'd like to know what sort of slacks you think you'd be able to buy if the Nazis were to invade.'

'If the Nazis invade, I don't suppose I'll care about it one way or the other. But until they do—'

'The Nazis would marry you off, all you girls like you, in no time,' said the woman. 'How should you like to have an SS man for a husband?'

The argument went on. Viv turned her head from it. In the place to her left was a younger girl, a well-to-do girl of about thirteen, gawky and earnest. She had an album filled with pictures of horses; she kept passing it across the compartment to her father, a Naval man with braid on his sleeve. 'That one's just like Cynthia's, Daddy,' she'd say as she did it. Or, 'This one's like Mabel's, he's a dear thing, isn't he? This one has exactly White Boy's head; White Boy's just a shade fuller in the flank, that's all . . .'

Her father would glance at the picture and grunt. He was filling in the blanks in a crossword puzzle in a newspaper, tapping with his pen against the page. But for the past couple of hours, too, he had been trying to catch Viv's eye. Every time she looked his way, he'd wink. If she crossed her legs, he'd let his gaze travel up and down her calves. Once he'd got out his case of cigarettes and leant across to offer her one, but the po-faced WAAF officer had stopped him and said, 'I'm afraid I'm asthmatic. If you're going to smoke, I'd appreciate it if you could do it in the corridor.' After that he'd sat back and smirked horribly at Viv, as if the WAAF had made conspirators of them.

'Look at this great brute, Daddy. He's like the fellow we saw at Colonel Webster's that time. Daddy! You're not looking!'

'For heaven's sake, Amanda,' he said irritably now, 'there are only so many ponies a father can take.'

'Fathers must be pretty silly, then, that's all I can say. Anyway, they're not ponies, they're horses.'

'Well, whatever they are I'm bored to death of them. And there, look—' Viv had got to her feet. She was going to the lavatory. 'This young lady's bored to death of them too. I shouldn't be surprised if she's so bored of them she's going to find an open window and throw herself out of it. I might very well join her. – Is there something,' he said to Viv, rising and touching her arm, 'I can help you with?'

'No, thanks,' she answered, shaking him off.

'Daddy,' his daughter cried, 'how rotten you are!'

'It would be *kinde, kirche*,' the knitting woman was saying to the trousered girl, 'and no more running about in a pair of slacks, I can tell you that—'

Viv stepped unsteadily to the door of the compartment and slid it back. She looked down the train, hesitating a little, because the corridor was crowded. A group of Canadian airmen had boarded at Swindon: they were propped against the windows or sitting on the floor, playing cards and smoking. The blue of their uniforms was

585

intense in the indigo light of the train, and the smoke from their cigarettes made them appear as if wreathed in drifting bolts of silk; they looked, in fact, for a single moment, quite beautiful and unearthly.

But when they saw Viv beginning to make her way along the narrow passage, they started into life – drawing back elaborately so that she might pass, scrambling to their feet. The bolts of silk seemed to billow, to tear and unravel, about the sharpness of their movements. There were whistles and calls: 'Whoops!' 'Look out!' 'Make way for the lady, boys!'

'Are those loaded, Mary?' said one of them, nodding to Viv's chest. Another put his arms up to steady her when the motion of the train made her sway: 'Shall we dance?'

'Want to powder your nose?' a boy asked, when she reached the end of the corridor and looked around. 'There's a place right here. My pal's been keeping it warm for you.'

She shook her head and pressed on. She'd rather not go to the lavatory at all, than go with so many men outside the door. But they grabbed at her hands, trying to pull her back. 'Don't leave us, Susie!' 'You're breaking our hearts!' They offered her beer and swigs of whisky. She shook her head again, smiling. They offered her chocolate.

'I'm watching my figure,' she said at last, pulling away. They called after her: 'So are we! It's beautiful!'

The next corridor was quieter, the one after that

quieter still: some of its lights had failed, and she passed along it almost in darkness. There were more servicemen here, but they must have started their journey sooner than the others: they didn't want to joke, they sat with their knees drawn up, their greatcoats belted, their heads lowered, trying to sleep. Viv had to pick her way around them, stepping awkwardly, reaching for holds on the walls and windows as the train shuddered and rocked.

At the end of this corridor there were another two lavatories; and the lock on one of them, she was relieved to see, was turned to *Vacant*. But when she caught hold of the doorknob and pushed, the door only moved a little way inwards and then was thrust hurriedly closed again. There was someone behind it: a soldier, in khaki; she got a glimpse of him in the mirror above the sink, turning his head. She saw the look of alarm on his face as the door was opened; she thought she'd caught him peeing, and was embarrassed. She moved back, to the junction of the carriages, and waited.

The lavatory door stayed shut for almost another minute. Then she saw the knob being slowly turned, and the door was drawn back, as if cautiously. The soldier put out his head, bit by bit, like a man expecting gunfire. When he caught her eye, he straightened up and came out properly.

'Sorry about that.'

'That's all right,' said Viv, still a little embarrassed. 'The lock's not broken, is it?'

'The lock?' He looked vague. He was glancing about from side to side, and now began to bite at one of his fingernails. His fingers, she saw, had short crisp hairs on them, dark as a monkey's. His cheeks were bluish: he needed a shave. His eyes were red at the corners and rims. As she moved past him he leant towards her and said, confidentially, 'Haven't seen the guard about, have you?'

She shook her head.

'They're like ruddy sharks.'

He took his hand from his mouth as he spoke, raised the thumb of it to suggest a fin, and moved it as a fish might move through water; then opened and closed his fingers: *Snap*. But he did it in an unexcited sort of way, still glancing about from side to side; finally biting at the nail again and frowning, and moving off. She went into the lavatory and closed the door and locked it, and more or less forgot him.

She used the toilet – stooping, rather than sitting on the stained wooden seat; swaying about again with the rocking of the train, feeling the pull of the muscles in her calves and thighs. She washed her hands, looking into the smeary mirror, going over the details of her face – thinking, as she always did, that her nose was too narrow, her lips too thin; imagining that, at twenty, she was getting old, looked tired . . . She redid her make-up and combed her hair. The single hairs and bits of fluff that got caught in the teeth of the comb she pulled out; she made a ball of them and tucked it away, neatly, in the bin under the basin.

She was just putting the comb back into her bag when someone knocked at the door. She took one last look in the mirror and called, 'All right!'

The knock came again, louder than before.

'All right! Just a sec!'

Then the handle was tried. She heard a voice, a man's voice, trying to force itself into a whisper. 'Miss! Open up, will you?'

'God!' she said to herself. She could only suppose it was one of the Canadians, larking about. Or it might, at a pinch, be the father of the horse-mad girl. But when she drew back the bolt and opened the door, a hand came around it to keep her from shutting it again; and she recognised the short black hairs on its fingers. Then came his khaki sleeve, his shoulder, his unshaven chin and blood-shot eye.

'Miss,' he said. He'd taken off his cap. 'Do me a favour, will you? The guard's on his way. I've lost my ticket and he'll give me hell—'

'I'm just coming out,' she said, 'if you'll let me.'

He shook his head. Now he was keeping her from opening the door, as well as from closing it. He said, 'I've seen this bloke and, honest to God, he's a tartar. I heard him earlier on, tearing a strip off some poor devil who had the wrong sort of warrant. If he knocks and hears my voice, he'll still want his ticket.'

'Well, what do you want me to do about it?'

'Can't you just let me in till he's gone past?'

She looked at him in amazement. 'In here, with me?'

'Just till he's gone by. And when he knocks, you can slip your ticket under the door. Please, miss. It's a thing girls do for servicemen all the time.'

'I'll bet it is. Not this girl, though.'

'Come on, I'm begging you. I'm in an awful squeeze. I've got compassionate leave, only forty-eight hours. I've spent half of that already, freezing my— Well, freezing my feet off, on Swindon station. If he throws me out I'm done for. Be a sport. It's not my fault. I had the ticket in my hand and put it down for half a minute. I think some Navy boy saw me do it—'

'A minute ago you said you'd lost it.'

He touched his hair distractedly. 'Lost it, had it pinched, what's the difference? I've been dodging up and down this train like a ruddy lunatic, in and out of lavatories all the way. All I'm looking for is someone tender-hearted to give me a bit of a break. It'll be no skin off your nose, will it? You can trust me, I swear to God. I'm not—' He stopped and drew back his head; then his face reappeared, he gave a hiss – 'Here he comes!' – and before she could do anything about it he had made a scuffling rush into the lavatory, bundling her back into it in the process. He shot the bolt and stood with his ear at the crack of the door-frame, his lower lip caught between his teeth.

Viv said, 'If you think—!'

He put his finger to his mouth: 'Shh!' He still had his ear pressed to the door-frame, and now began moving his head up and down it – like a doctor, desperately trying to find a heartbeat in the bosom of a dying man.

Then there was a smart, authoritative *tap-tap-tap!* on the door that made him jump as though he'd been shot.

'All tickets, please!'

The soldier looked at Viv and grimaced dreadfully. He went through a mad sort of pantomime, pretending to take a ticket from his pocket, stoop, and shove it under the door.

'All tickets!' the guard called again.

'This lavatory's taken!' Viv cried at last. Her voice was flustered, silly-sounding.

'I know it's taken,' came the reply from the corridor. 'I need to see your ticket please, miss.'

'Can't you see it later?'

'I need to see it now, please.'

'Just – just a minute.'

What could she do? She couldn't open the door, the guard would take one look at the soldier and think the worst. So she got out her ticket, and, 'Move over,' she hissed, flapping her hand furiously. The soldier took a step away from the door so that she could stoop and slip the ticket under it. She bent her legs self-consciously, aware of the smallness of the space they were in; aware that she was making it smaller, by stooping; feeling, in fact, her thigh pass against his knee, so that the wool of her skirt clung momentarily to the khaki of his trousers.

Her ticket lay flat in the shadow of the door for a second and then, as if through some weird agency of its own, gave a quiver and slid away. There was a moment's suspense. She stayed awkwardly squatting, and didn't look up. But at last, 'Very good, miss!' came the call. The ticket was returned, with a neat little hole punched out of it, and the guard moved on.

She stood up, stepped back, put her ticket into her bag and snapped closed its clasp.

'Happy now?'

The soldier was wiping his forehead with his sleeve. 'Miss,' he said, 'you're an angel! The sort of girl, I swear to God, who restores a fellow's faith in life. The sort of girl the songs are written for.'

'Well, you can write one now,' she said, moving forward, 'and sing it to yourself.'

'What?' He put his arm across the door. 'You can't go yet. Suppose the ticket fellow comes back? Give it another minute, at least. Look—' He put his hand to his jacket pocket and brought out a crumpled packet of Woodbines. 'Just keep me company for the length of a smoke, that's all I ask. Give him time to get down to first class. I swear to God, if you knew the journey I've had, the hoops I've had to jump through—'

'That's your look-out.'

He started to smile. 'You'll be helping the war effort. Think of it that way.'

'How many girls have you used that line on?'

'You're the first. I swear!'

'The first today, you mean.'

Now he was almost grinning. His lips parted and she saw his teeth. Rather distracting teeth, they were: very straight and very even and white, and seeming to be whiter against the stubble of his chin. They made the rest of his face good-looking, suddenly. She noticed the hazel of his eyes, the thick black lashes. His hair was dark, darker even than her own; he'd tried to flatten it down with Brylcreem but individual locks were pulling against the grease, lifting back into curls.

His uniform, however, looked as though he'd slept in it. The jacket was stained and badly fitting. The trouser legs were creased in horizontal bands like stretched-out concertinas. But he held out the packet of Woodbines, imploringly; and she pictured her own empty narrow seat in the crowded compartment: the Navy man making passes, the asthmatic WAAF, the horse-mad girl.

'All right,' she said at last. 'Give me a cigarette, just for a minute. I must want my head read, though!'

He smiled more broadly, in relief. His teeth were more distracting than ever, she thought, when seen all together like that. He lit a match for her, from a match book, and she moved forward to the flame; but then she moved back and stood guardedly, with one arm folded across herself, the wrist of it propping up the elbow of the other, and the heel of her foot pressed tight to the wall, a brace against the lurching of the train. It was hard to ignore the presence of the porcelain lavatory – over which, after all, she'd recently stooped with her bottom bared. Then again, like everyone else she'd had to get used to sharing odd spaces with strangers recently. On another train journey, two months before, a raid had started up and all the passengers had had to get down on the floor. She'd had to lie for forty minutes with her face more or less in a man's lap; he'd been awfully embarrassed . . .

This man, at least, seemed quite at his ease. He leant on the counter which held the basin and started to yawn. The yawn became a low sort of yodelling groan, and when that was finished he put his cigarette between his lips and rubbed his face – rubbed it in that vigorous, unself-conscious way in which men always handled their own faces, and girls never did.

Then the train began to slow. Viv looked anxiously at the window. 'That's not Paddington, is it?'

'Paddington!' he said. 'Christ, I wish it was!' He leant to the blind and drew it back a little and tried to look out; but it was impossible to see anything. 'God knows where we are,' he said. 'Just past Didcot, I should say. There we go.' He'd almost staggered. 'They're throwing in a fun-fair ride, for free.'

The train had run quickly for a moment, then abruptly slowed; now it was moving with a series of jolts. He and Viv bounced about like jumping beans. Viv put out her arms, looking for hand-holds. It was impossible not to smile. The soldier shook his head, too, in disbelief. 'Has it been like this all the way? Where did you get on?'

After a little show of reluctance, she told him: Taunton. She'd been to visit her sister and her baby; they'd gone down there, she said, away from the bombs. He listened, nodding.

'Taunton,' he said. 'I went there once. Nice couple of pubs as I recall. One called the Ring – ever drink there? Landlord' – he made fists of his hands – 'used to box. Little chap, but with a great squashed nose. Keeps a pair of gloves in a glass case on the counter. Boy!' He sighed and folded his arms, as the train ran more smoothly. 'What I wouldn't give to be there now! A glass of Black and White at my elbow, roaring fire in the grate . . . You haven't got any whisky on you, by any chance?'

'Whisky!' she said. 'No, I haven't.'

'All right, don't be like that about it! You'd be surprised how much liquor does get carried around in ladies' purses, in my experience. Girls like to drink it, I suppose, against the bombs. You wouldn't need that, of course, with nerves like yours.'

'Nerves like mine?'

'I saw your hand when you put your ticket away. Steady as a rock. You'd make a good spy.' He narrowed his eyes and looked her over. 'You might be a spy, come to that. A lady spy, like Mata Hari.'

She said, 'You'd better watch your step, then.'

'But for all you know,' he went on, 'I might be a spy, too. Or, not a spy, but the chap the spies are after. Isn't there always one of those? Some poor sap who's got a secret message on him, because he's accidentally put on another bloke's boots, or picked up another bloke's umbrella? And he and the girl always end up tied to a chair, with the sort of knot that looks like it was done by a bad Boy Scout.'

He laughed to himself, liking the idea – *liking the sound of his own voice*, she thought, conventionally; though the fact was, it was a nice voice, and she found she rather liked it, too. 'How would you feel,' he went on, 'about being tied to a chair with me? I'm only asking out of interest, by the way. I'm not shooting you a line, or anything like that.'

'No?'

'Oh, no. I like to get to know a girl a little, before I start shooting lines at her.'

She drew on her cigarette. 'Suppose she won't let you get to know her?'

'Oh, but there are a thousand little things a fellow can find out about a girl, just by looking at her. Take you, for example.' He nodded to her hand. 'You're not married. That means you're smart. I like smartness in a woman. Fingernails rather long, so you're not on the land or in a factory.' He dropped his gaze, and worked slowly back up. 'Legs too nice to put in trousers. Figure too good to hide you away in some back-room job. I'd say you were

596

secretary to some bigwig – Admiral of the Fleet, something like that. Am I close?'

She shook her head. 'Nowhere near. I'm a common typist, that's all.'

'A typist. Ah . . . Yes, that fits. Where have they got you? Some government racket or other?'

'Just something in London.'

'Just something in London, I see. And, what's your name? Or is that hush-hush, too?'

She hesitated, but only for a moment; then thought, *Where's the harm?* and told him. He nodded, thinking it over, looking into her face. 'Vivien,' he said at last. 'Yes, it suits you.'

'Does it?'

'It's a name for a glamour girl, isn't it? Wasn't there a Lady Vivien, or someone like that? In King Arthur's times? I used to know all those stories when I was a kid; I've forgotten them now. Anyway,' he leant forward to shake her hand, 'my name's Reggie. Reggie Nigri. – Yes, I know, I know, it's lousy. And I've been stuck with it all my life. The boys at school used to call me "Nigger"; now the fellows at camp call me "Musso". Work that one out if you can. My old grandad came over from Naples. You should see the pictures! He had a moustache out to here, a waistcoat, a handkerchief round his neck; all he needed was the monkey. He sold hokey-pokey from a cart in the street. I've got second cousins twice removed – or something like that – who are fighting, now, for the other team, in Italy. They're probably just about as keen on this ruddy war as I am . . . Have you got any brothers, Vivien?— You don't mind me calling you Vivien? I'd call you Miss Pearce, but it sounds old-fashioned in times like these. – Have you got any brothers?'

Viv nodded. 'Just one.'

'Older, or younger?'

'Younger,' she said. 'Seventeen.'

'Seventeen! I bet he loves all this, doesn't he? Can't wait to join up?'

She thought of Duncan. 'Well—'

'I would too, if I was his age. Instead— I'm nearly thirty, and look at me. Two years ago I was selling motor cars in Maida Vale, and doing very nicely. Then the war starts up and, bingo, that's the end of that. I got a bit of work with a pal of mine for a while, in the costume jewellery trade; that wasn't too bad. Now I'm stuck in a ruddy OCTU in Wales, being taught which end of a rifle the bullets are supposed to come out. I've been there four months, and I swear to God it's rained every day. It's all right for our CO; he stays in a hotel. I'm living in a hut with a tin roof on it.'

He went on like this, telling her about his duties at the camp, the hopeless squaddies he was billeted with, the hopeless pubs and hotel bars, the hopeless weather . . . He made her laugh. The boys she met, of her own age, were full of the war: they wanted to talk about types of aeroplane and ship; about Army bets and Navy quarrels. He was past all that. He was past boasting. He yawned and rubbed his eyes again, and his very tiredness seemed appealing somehow. She liked the grown-up, casual way he'd said 'when I was a kid'. She liked the way he'd said her name; that he'd thought it over and said it suited her. She liked it that he knew about King Arthur. She liked the fact, after all, that his uniform didn't fit him. She pictured him in an ordinary jacket, a shirt and tie, a vest. She looked again at his monkey-like hands and imagined the rest of him: swarthy, stocky, with swirls of hair on his chest, his shoulders, his buttocks and legs—

The handle of the door was tried and, abruptly, he fell silent. There came a knock, and a cry: 'Hey! What's taking you all this time?'

It was one of the Canadians. Reggie didn't answer for a second. Then the knock came again and he called out, 'This one's busy, chum! Try another!'

'You've been in there for half an hour!'

'Can't a bloke have a bit of time to himself?'

The airman kicked the door as he moved off. 'Fuck you!'

Reggie flushed. 'Go to hell!'

He seemed more embarrassed than angry. He caught Viv's eye, then looked away. 'Nice chap,' he muttered.

She shrugged. 'Don't worry. I hear worse than that from the girls in the typing pool.'

She'd finished her cigarette, and now dropped the end of it, covering it over with her shoe. When she looked up, she found him gazing at her. His flush had faded and his expression slightly changed. He was smiling, but had drawn together his brows as if perplexed by something.

'You know,' he said, after a moment, 'you really are the hell of a good-looking girl. It's like my luck, as well. Getting holed up with a beautiful girl, I mean, in the one establishment in town where I can't even say, politely, "Have a seat."'

That made her laugh again. He watched her face, and laughed too. 'Hey, that wasn't bad going, was it, for a bloke who's dead on his feet? You should hear me when I've had some sleep. I'm telling you, I'm a killer.' He bit his lip, and again that look of slight perplexity crossed his face. 'You're not by any chance some sort of hallucination, are you?'

She shook her head. 'Not as far as I know.'

'Well, that's what you say. Hallucinations are clever like that. For all I know, I might still be on a bench on Swindon station, fast asleep. I need some sort of a shock. I need a key dropped down my collar, or— I've got it.' He turned and ground out his cigarette in the basin, then drew back his sleeve and held out his arm. 'Give me a pinch, will you?'

'A pinch?'

'Just to prove to me that I'm awake.'

She looked at his bare wrist. There was a point where the smooth pale flesh at the base of his thumb gave way to hair; and again she thought, unwillingly but not unpleasantly, of the swarthy arms and legs

600

of him . . . She reached and gave him a nip with her fingers. Her nails got caught up in it, and he quickly drew the arm back.

'Ouch! You've been practising that! I think you are a ruddy spy!' He rubbed the spot she'd pinched, then blew on it. 'Look at that.' He showed her the mark. 'I shall turn up at home and they'll suppose I've been in a fight. I'll have to say, "It wasn't a soldier, it was a girl I got talking to in the lavatory of a train." That'll go down well, in the circumstances.'

'What circumstances?' she asked, laughing again.

He was still blowing on his wrist. 'I told you, didn't I? I've got compassionate leave.' He lifted the wrist to his mouth and sucked it. 'My wife,' he said, over the ball of his thumb, 'has just had a baby.'

She thought he was joking, and kept on smiling. When she saw that he was serious her smile grew fixed, and she blushed from her collar to her hair.

'Oh,' she said, folding her arms. She might have guessed, from the age of him, even from the manner of him, that he was married; but she hadn't thought about it. 'Oh. Is it a boy, or a girl?'

He lowered his hand. 'Little girl. We've got the boy already, so you could say, I suppose, that now we've got the set.'

She said politely, 'It's nice for you.'

He almost shrugged. 'It's nice for my wife. It keeps her happy. It won't keep us rich, I know that. But here, look. Have a look at this. Here's the first one.'

He put his hand to his pocket again and brought out a wallet; he fumbled about with the papers inside it, then drew out a photo and passed it over. It was slightly grubby, and torn at the corners; it showed a woman and a little boy, sitting together, perhaps in a garden. A bright day in summer. A tartan rug on a mown lawn. The woman was shading her eyes with her hand, her face half-hidden, her fair hair loose; the boy had tilted his head and was frowning against the light. He had some home-made toy or other in his hand, a baby's motor car or train; another home-made toy lay at his feet. Just visible in the bottom right-hand corner of the square was the shadow of the person – Reggie himself, presumably – taking the picture.

Viv passed it back. 'He's a nice-looking boy. He's dark, like you.'

'He's a good little kid. The little girl's fairer, so they tell me.' He gazed at the photo, then tucked it away. 'But what a world to bring babies into, eh? I wish my wife would do what your sister's done, and get the hell out of London. I keep thinking of the poor little buggers growing up, going to bed every night under the kitchen table and supposing it's normal.'

He buttoned up his pocket, and they stood for a time without speaking – reminded of London, the war, all of that. Viv grew conscious again, too, of the lavatory: it seemed much queerer to be standing

602

beside it in silence than when Reggie was talking and grumbling and making her laugh. But he'd gone back to biting at the skin around his finger-nail; soon he lowered his hand and folded his arms and gazed moodily at the floor. It was like the dimming-down of a light, she thought. She became aware, as if for the first time, of the roar and motion of the train, the ache in her legs and in the arches of her foot from standing rigid.

She changed her pose, made a movement, and he looked up.

'You're not going?'

'We ought to, oughtn't we? Somebody else will only try the door if we don't. Are you still thinking about the guard? Did you really lose your ticket?'

He looked away. 'I won't tell you a lie. I did have a travel warrant, but a bloke took it off me in a game of cards . . . But no, the guard can go hang himself for all I care. The truth is – well, the truth is I don't want to go out and face all those bloody airmen. They look at me as though I'm an old man. I am an old man, compared to boys like that!'

He met her gaze, and blew out his cheeks. He said, tiredly and simply, 'I'm sick of being an old man, Viv. I'm sick of this bloody war. I've been on the move since Wednesday morning; I'm going to go home now and see my wife; we'll just about have time for an argument before I'll have to turn round and come back. Her sister'll be with her; she hates my guts. Her mother doesn't think much of me either. My little boy calls me "Uncle"; he sees more of the air-raid warden than he does of me. I wouldn't be surprised if my wife does, too . . . The dog, at least, will be pleased I'm home – if the dog's still there. They were talking of having it shot, last I heard. Said the standing in line for horse-meat was getting them down.'

He rubbed his red-rimmed eyes again, and passed his hand over his chin. 'I need a bath,' he said. 'I need a shave. Next to those lumberjacks out there, I look like Charlie bloody Chaplin. But somehow—' He hesitated, then began to smile. 'Somehow I've got myself locked in a room with a glamour girl; the most gorgeous glamour girl I think I ever saw in my life. Let me enjoy it, just for a few more minutes. Don't make me open that door. I'm begging you. Look—'

His mood was lifting again already. He moved forward and gently took hold of her hand, raising her knuckles to his lips. The gesture was a corny one, yet had an edge of seriousness to it; and when she laughed, she laughed most in embarrassment, because she was over-aware of his hand around hers: the maleness of it, the niceness of it, the squareness of the palm, the tufted fingers and the short hard nails. His chin was rough as sandpaper against her knuckles, but his mouth was soft.

He watched her laugh, as he had before; and smiled with pleasure. She saw again his straight white teeth. Later she'd say to herself, *I fell in love with him teeth-first.*

When she tried to think of the wife, the son, the

baby, the home, that the train was speeding him towards, she couldn't do it. They might have been dreams to her, or ghosts; she was too young.

Tap-tap-tap, there came, outside Duncan's bedroom window. *Tap-tap-tap*. And the strange thing was, he'd got used to sirens, to gunfire and bombs; but this noise, which was so little, like the pecking of a bird, woke him up and nearly frightened the life out of him. *Tap-tap-tap* . . . He put out his hand to the bedside table and switched on his torch; his hand was shaking, so that when he moved the beam of light to the window the shadows in the folds of the curtains seemed to bulge, as if the curtains were being pushed out from behind. *Tap-tap-tap* . . . Now it sounded less like the beak of a bird and more like a claw or a fingernail. *Tap-tap-tap* . . . He thought, for a second, of running to his dad.

Then he heard his name called, hoarsely: 'Duncan! Duncan! Wake up!'

He recognised the voice; and that changed everything. He threw off the covers, clambered quickly across the bed, and pulled back the curtain. Alec was there, at the next window – the window of the parlour, where Duncan slept at weekends. He was still tapping at the glass, still calling out for Duncan to wake up. But now he saw the light of Duncan's torch: he turned, and the beam of it struck his face, making him shrink back, screw up his eyes, put up his hand. His face looked yellowish, lit like that. His hair was combed back, greased flat to his head, and the fine, sharp lines of his brow and cheeks made hollow-looking shadows. He might have been a ghoul. He waited for Duncan to lower the torch, then came to his window and gestured madly to the catch: 'Open it up!'

Duncan lifted the sash. His hands were still shaking, and the sash kept sticking as it rose, the glass rattling in the frame. He moved it slowly, afraid of the noise.

'What's the matter?' he hissed, when the window was up.

Alec tried to see past him. 'What are you doing in there? I've been knocking at the other window.'

'Viv's not back. I'm sleeping in here. How long have you been there? You woke me up. You scared me to death! What's going on?'

'I've bloody well had it, Duncan, that's what,' said Alec, his voice rising. 'I've bloody well had it!'

There was the bursting of flares in the sky behind him, and a series of crackles. Duncan looked at the sky, growing afraid. He could only think that something dreadful must have happened to Alec's family, Alec's house. He said, 'What is it? What's happened?'

'I've bloody well had it!' Alec said again.

'Stop saying that! What do you mean? What's the matter with you?'

Alec twitched, as if forcing himself to be calm. 'My papers have come,' he said at last.

Duncan grew frightened, then, in a different way. He said, 'They can't have!'

'Well, they bloody well have! I'm not going, Duncan. They're not going to make me. I mean it. I mean it, and no one believes me—'

He worked his mouth. There was the flash of another bomb, and more explosions. Duncan looked at the sky again. 'How long,' he asked, 'has the raid been on?' He must have slept right through the Warning. 'Did you come through the raid?'

'I don't care about the bloody raid!' said Alec. 'I was glad when the raid started. I was hoping I'd get hit! I've been all down Mitcham Lane, right in the middle of the road.' He leant over the sill and caught hold of Duncan's arm. His hand was freezing. 'Come out with me, too.'

'Don't be daft,' said Duncan, pulling away. He glanced at the bedroom door. He was supposed to wake his father when a raid started up. They were supposed to go down the road to the public shelter. 'I should get my dad.'

Alec plucked at his arm. 'Do it in a bit. Come out with me first. I've got something to tell you.'

'What? Tell me now.'

'Come out.'

'It's too late. It's too cold.'

Alec drew his hand back, raised it to his mouth, and started biting at his fingers. 'Let me in, then,' he said, after a second. 'Let me in, with you.'

So Duncan moved away from the window and Alec hoisted himself on to the sill, working his knees and his feet over it and dropping into the room. He did it awkwardly, as he did anything like that – landing heavily, so that the floorboards thumped, and the bottles and jars on Viv's dressing-table rattled and skidded about.

Duncan drew down the sash and fixed the curtains. When he turned on the light, he and Alec blinked. The light made everything seemed weirder. It made it feel later, even, than it was. There might have been sickness in the house . . . Duncan had a sudden vivid memory of his mother, when she was ill: his father sending out for his auntie, and then for a doctor – people coming and going, murmuring, in the middle of the night; the excitement of it, turning to disaster . . .

He started to shiver with the cold. He put on his slippers and dressing-gown. As he tied the cord, he looked at what Alec was wearing: a zip-up jacket, dark flannel trousers, and dirty canvas shoes. He saw Alec's bare white bony ankles and said, 'You haven't got any socks on!'

Alec was still blinking against the light. 'I had to get dressed really fast,' he said, sitting down on the edge of the bed. 'I've been going mad, wanting to tell you! I went to Franklin's this afternoon, looking for you, and you weren't there. Where were you?'

'To Franklin's?' Duncan frowned. 'What time did you come?'

'I don't know. About four.'

'I was taking some parcels for Mr Manning. No one said you'd been.'

'I didn't ask anyone, I just looked. I just walked in and looked around. No one stopped me.'

'Why didn't you come after tea, tonight?'

Alec looked bitter. 'Why do you think? I got into a row with my bloody father. I got—' His voice grew high again. 'He bloody well hit me, Duncan! Look! Can you see?' He turned his head and showed Duncan his face. There was a faint red mark, high on his cheekbone. But his eyes, Duncan saw now, were redder than anything. He had been crying. He saw Duncan looking, and turned away again. 'He's a bloody brute,' he said quietly, as if ashamed.

'What did you do?'

'I told them I wasn't going to go, that they couldn't make me. I wouldn't have told them about the papers at all, except that the postman made such a thing out of it when he brought them. My mother got hold of the letter first. I said, "It's got my name on it, I can do what I want with it—"'

'What's it like? What does it say?'

'I've got it, look.'

He unzipped his jacket and brought out a buff-coloured envelope. Duncan sat on the bed beside him, so that he could see. The papers were addressed to *A. J. C. Planer*; they told him that, in accordance with the National Service Acts, he was called upon for service in the Territorial Army,

609

and was required to present himself in two weeks' time to a Royal Artillery Training Regiment at Shoeburyness. There was information on how he should get there and what he should take; and a postal order for four shillings, in advance of service pay. The pages were stamped all over with dates and numbers but were creased dreadfully, as if Alec had screwed them up then flattened them out again.

Duncan looked at the creases in horror. 'What have you done to them?'

'It doesn't matter, does it?'

'I don't know. They might— They might use it against you.'

'Use it against me? You sound like my mother! You don't think I'm going to go, do you? I've told you—' Alec took the papers back and, with a gesture of disgust, he crumpled them up and threw them to the floor; then, like a spring recoiling, he pounced on them again, unscrewed them, and tore them right across – even the postal order. 'There!' he said. His face was flushed, and he was shaking.

'Crumbs,' said Duncan, his horror turning to admiration. 'You've done it now, all right!'

'I told you, didn't I?'

'You're a bloody lunatic!'

'I'd rather be a lunatic,' said Alec, tossing his head, 'than do what they want me to do. They're the lunatics. They're making lunatics of everybody else, and no one's stopping them; everyone's acting as if it's ordinary. As if it's an ordinary thing, that they make a soldier of you, give you a gun.' He got up, and agitatedly smoothed back his already greased-down hair. 'I can't stand it any more. I'm getting out of it, Duncan.'

Duncan stared at him. 'You're not going to register as a conchy?'

Alec snorted. 'I don't mean *that*. That's as bad as the other thing. Having to stand in a room and say your piece, in front of all those strangers? Why should I have to do that? What's it to anybody else, if I won't fight? Anyway,' he added, 'my bloody father would kill me.'

'What do you mean, then?'

Alec put his hand to his mouth and began to bite at his fingers again. He held Duncan's gaze. 'Can't you tell?'

He said it with a sort of suppressed excitement – as if, despite everything, he wanted to laugh. Duncan felt his heart shrink in his breast. 'You're not— You're not running away?'

Alec wouldn't answer.

'You can't run away! It's not fair! You can't do it. You haven't got anything with you. You'd need money, you'd need coupons, you'd need to buy food. Where would you go? You're not— You're not going to go to Ireland, are you?' They'd talked, before, about doing that. But they'd talked about doing it together. 'They've got ways of finding you, even in Ireland.'

'I don't care,' said Alec, suddenly furious, 'about fucking Ireland! I don't care what happens to me.

I'm not going to go, that's all. Do you know what they do to you?' He turned down the corners of his mouth. 'They do filthy things! Handling you all over, looking at you – up your arse and between your legs. A row of them, Michael Warren said: a row of old men, looking you over. It's disgusting. Old men! It's all right for them. It's all right for my father, and your father. They've had their lives; they want to take our lives from us. They had one war, and now they've made another one. They don't care that we're young. They want to make us old like them. They don't care that it's not our quarrel—'

His voice was rising. 'Stop shouting!' said Duncan.

'They want to kill us!'

'Shut up, can't you!'

Duncan was thinking of the people upstairs, and of his father. His father was deaf as a bloody post; but he had a sort of radar in him, where Alec was concerned. Alec stopped talking. He kept on biting at his fingers, and started pacing around the room. Outside, the sounds of the raid had grown worse – had drawn together into a deep, low throb. The glass in Duncan's window started, very slightly, to vibrate.

'I'm getting out of it,' said Alec again, as he paced. 'I'm getting out. I mean it.'

'You're not running away,' said Duncan firmly.

'It's just not fair.'

'Nothing's fair any more.'

'You can't. You can't leave me in Streatham, with bloody Eddie Parry, and Rodney Mills, and boys like that—'

'I'm getting out. I've had it.'

'You could— Alec!' said Duncan, suddenly excited. 'You could stay here! I could hide you here! I could bring you food and water.'

'Here?' Alec looked around, frowning. 'Where would I hide?'

'You could hide in a cupboard, somewhere like that, I don't know. You'd only have to do it while my dad was here. And then on the nights when Viv was away, you could come out. You could sleep in with me. You could do it, even while Viv was here. She wouldn't mind. She'd help us. You'd be like – like the Count of Monte Cristo!' Duncan thought about it. He thought about making up plates of food – keeping back the meat, the tea and the sugar, from his own ration. He thought about secretly sharing his bed with Alec, every single night . . .

But Alec looked doubtful. 'I don't know. It would have to be for months and months, wouldn't it? It would have to be till the end of the war. And you'll get your papers, too, next year. You'll get them sooner, if they put the age down. You might get them in July! What would we do then?'

'It's ages till July,' answered Duncan. 'Anything could happen between now and July. We'll probably get blown up by July!'

Alec shook his head again. 'We won't,' he said

613

bitterly. 'I know we won't. I wish we would! Instead, it's kids and old ladies and babies and stupid people who die – stupid people who don't mind the war. Boys who are too stupid to mind being soldiers, too stupid to see that the war's not their war but a load of government men's. It's not our war, either; we have to suffer in it, though. We have to do the things they tell us. They don't even tell us the truth! They haven't told us about Birmingham. Everybody knows that Birmingham's been practically burned to the ground. How many other towns and cities are like that? They won't tell us about the weapons Hitler's got, the rockets and gas. Horrible gas, that doesn't kill you but makes your skin come off; gas that does a thing to your brain, to make a sort of robot of you, so that Hitler can take you and turn you into a slave. He's going to put us all in camps, do you know that? He's going to make us work in mines and factories, the men all digging and working machines, the women having babies; he'll make us go to bed with women, one after the other, just to make them pregnant. And all the old men and old ladies he'll just kill. He's done it in Poland. He's probably done it in Belgium and Holland, too. They don't tell us that. It isn't fair! We never wanted to go to war. There ought to be a place for people like us. They ought to let the stupid people fight, and everybody else – everyone who cares about important things, things like the arts, things like that – they ought to be allowed to go and live somewhere on their own, and to hell with Hitler—'

He kicked at one of Duncan's shoes; then went back to walking about and biting at his hands. He bit madly, moving his hand when one patch of skin or nail was gnawed, and starting on another. His gaze grew fixed, but on nothing. His face had whitened again, and his red-rimmed eyes seemed to blaze like a lunatic's.

Duncan thought of his father again. He imagined what his father would think if he could see Alec like this. *That boy's bloody crackers*, he'd said to Duncan more than once. *That boy needs to grow up. He's a waste of bloody time. He'll put ideas in your bloody head, that boy will—*

'Stop biting your fingers like that, will you?' he said uneasily. 'You look dotty.'

'Dotty?' hissed Alec. 'I shouldn't be surprised if I go off my bloody head! I got so worked up tonight I thought I was going to be sick. I had to wait for them all to go to sleep. Then I thought there was someone in the house. I could hear men, moving about – footsteps, and whispers. I thought my father had fetched the police.'

Duncan was appalled. 'He wouldn't do that, would he?'

'He might. That's how much he hates me.'

'In the middle of the night?'

'Of course then!' said Alec impatiently. 'That's just when they do come! Don't you know that? It's when you least expect them to.'

Abruptly, they stopped talking. Duncan looked at the door – remembering his mother's illness again; feeling weird again; half-expecting to hear the sound of people creeping about in the hall . . . What he heard instead was the steady throb of aircraft, the monotonous *crump-crump* of bombs, followed by the slither of soot in the chimney-breast.

He looked back at Alec; and grew more unnerved than ever. For Alec had lowered his hands at last, and seemed suddenly unnaturally calm. He met Duncan's gaze, and made some slightly theatrical gesture – shrugged his narrow shoulders, turned his head, showed his fine, handsome profile.

'This is wasting time,' he said, as if casually.

'What is?' asked Duncan, afraid. 'What do you mean?'

'I told you, didn't I? I'd rather be dead than do what they want me to do. I'd rather die than have them put a gun in my hand and make me shoot some German boy who feels just like I do. I'm getting out. I'm going to do it, before they do it to me.'

'But, do what?' Duncan asked him, stupidly.

Alec made the theatrical gesture again – as if to say, it was nothing to him, one way or the other. 'I'm going to kill myself,' he said.

Duncan stared at him. 'You can't!'

'Why not?'

'You just can't. It's not fair. What— What will your mother think?'

Alec coloured. 'That's her hard luck, isn't it? She

shouldn't have married my oaf of a father. He'll be pleased, anyway. He wants to see me dead.'

Duncan wasn't listening. He was thinking it through and growing tearful. He said, 'But what about me?' His voice sounded strangled. 'It'll be harder on me than on any of them, you know it will! You're my best friend. You can't kill yourself and leave me here.'

'Do it too, then,' said Alec.

He said it quietly. Duncan was wiping his nose on his sleeve, and wasn't sure he'd heard him properly. He said, 'What?'

'Do it too,' said Alec again.

They looked at each other. Alec's face had flushed pinker than ever; he'd drawn back his lips, unguardedly, in a nervous smile, and his crooked teeth were showing. He moved closer to Duncan and put his hands on his shoulders, so that he was facing Duncan squarely, only the length of a curved arm away. He gripped Duncan hard, almost shook him. He looked right into his eyes and said excitedly, 'It'll show them, won't it? Think how it'll look! We can leave a letter, saying why we've done it! We'll be two young people, giving up our lives. It'll get into the papers. It'll get everywhere! It might bloody well stop the war!'

'Do you think it would?' asked Duncan, excited too, suddenly; impressed and flattered; wanting to believe it, but still afraid.

'Why wouldn't it?'

'I don't know. Young people are dying all the

time. That hasn't changed anything. Why should it be different with us?'

'You chump,' said Alec, curling his lip, drawing off his hands and moving away. 'If you can't see— If you're not up to it— If you're windy—'

'I didn't say that.'

'—I'll do it on my own.'

'I won't let you do it on your own!' said Duncan. 'I told you, you're not going to leave me.'

Alec came back. 'Help me write the letter, then,' he said, excited again. 'We can write it— Look.' He stooped and picked up one of the torn-off halves of the call-up paper. 'We can write it on the back of this. It'll be symbolic. Give me a pen, will you?'

Duncan's leather writing-case was on the floor, beside the bed. Automatically, Duncan took a step towards it; then checked himself. He went instead, as if casually, to the mantelpiece, picked up a pencil, and held it out. But Alec wouldn't take it. 'Not that,' he said. 'They'll think a bloody kid wrote it, if I use that! Let me have your fountain pen.'

Duncan blinked and looked away. 'It isn't in here.'

'You bloody liar, I know it is!'

'It's just,' said Duncan, 'if a pen's any good, you're not supposed to let other people use it.'

'You always say that! It doesn't matter now, does it?'

'I don't want you to, that's all. Use the pencil. My sister bought me that pen.'

'She'll be proud of you, then,' said Alec. 'They'll

probably put that pen in some sort of frame, after they find us! Think of it like that. Come on, Duncan.'

Duncan hesitated a little longer, then reluctantly unzipped the writing-case and drew out his pen. Alec was always badgering him for a go with this pen, and he took it from Duncan now with obvious relish: making a business of unscrewing the lid, examining the nib, testing the weight of the pen in his hand. He took the writing-case too, then sat down on the edge of the bed with the case on his knee, and he smoothed out the paper, trying to press the creases from it. When he'd got it as flat as he could, he started to write.

'*To whom it may concern . . .*' He looked at Duncan. 'Shall I put that? Or shall I put, *To Mr Winston Churchill?*'

Duncan thought it over. '*To whom it may concern* sounds better,' he said. 'And it might be to Hitler and Goering and Mussolini then, too.'

'That's true,' said Alec, liking the idea. He thought for a second, sucking at his lip, tapping with the pen against his mouth; and then wrote more. He wrote swiftly, stylishly – like Keats or like Mozart, Duncan thought – dashing the nib with little flour-ishes across the paper, pausing to frown over what he had put, then writing stylishly again . . .

When he'd finished, he passed the letter over to Duncan, and gnawed at his knuckle while Duncan read.

To whom it may concern. If you are reading this, it means that we, Alec J.C. Planer and Duncan W. Pearce, of Streatham, London, England, have succeeded in our intentions and are no more. We do not undertake this deed lightly. We know that the country we are about to enter is that 'dark, undiscovered one' from which 'no traveller returns'. But we do what we are about to do on behalf of the Youth of England, and in the name of <u>Liberty</u>, <u>Honesty</u> and <u>Truth</u>. We would rather take our own lives freely, than have them stolen from us by the <u>Pedlars of War</u>. We ask for one epitaph only, and it is this: that, like the great <u>T.E. Lawrence</u>, we 'drew the tides of men into our hands, and wrote our will across the sky in stars'.

Duncan gazed at Alec in amazement. He said, 'That's bloody wizard!'

Alec flushed. He said, as if shyly, 'D'you really think so? I thought of some of it, you know, on my way here.'

'You're a genius!'

Alec started to laugh. The laugh came out as a sort of giggle, like a girl's. 'It *is* all right, isn't it? It'll bloody well show them, anyway!' He held out his hand. 'Give it back, though, for me to sign. Then you sign it, too.'

They added their names, and then the date. Alec raised the page up and looked it over, tilting his head. 'This date,' he said, 'will become like the ones we learned in school. Isn't that a funny thought? Isn't it funny to think of kids being made to remember it, in a hundred years' time?'

'Yes,' said Duncan, vaguely. He'd thought of something else, and was only half listening. As Alec smoothed out the paper again he asked diffidently, 'Can't we put something in it for our families, too, Alec?'

Alec curled his lip. 'Our families! Of course we can't, don't be stupid.'

'I'm thinking of Viv. She'll be bloody upset by all this.'

'I told you,' said Alec, 'she'll be proud of you. They all will. Even my father will. He calls me a bloody coward. I'd like to see his face when this gets into the papers! We'll be like – like martyrs!' He grew thoughtful. 'All we need to do now is decide on how we're going to do it. I suppose we could gas ourselves.'

'Gas!' said Duncan in horror. 'That'll take too long, won't it? That'll take ages. And anyway, the gas will get out; we might end up gassing my father. He's an old sod but, you know, that wouldn't be very fair.'

'It wouldn't be sporting,' said Alec.

'It wouldn't be cricket, old chap.'

They began to laugh. They laughed so hard, they had to cover their mouths with their hands. Alec fell back on to the bed and buried his face in Duncan's pillow. He said, still laughing, 'We could poison ourselves. We could eat arsenic. Like that old tart, Madame Bovary.'

'An admirable plan, Mr Holmes,' said Duncan in a silly voice, 'but one with one substantial flaw. My father keeps no arsenic in the house.'

'No arsenic? And you call this a modern, well-appointed establishment? What about rat-poison, pray?'

'No rat-poison, either. Anyway – wouldn't poison hurt like billy-oh?'

'It's going to hurt like billy-oh, you imbecile, whatever we do. It wouldn't be a gesture if it didn't hurt.'

'Even so—'

Alec had stopped laughing. He lay thinking for a second, then sat up. 'How about,' he said seriously, 'if we drown ourselves? We'd see our life flash before our eyes. Not that I want to see mine, my life's been lousy—'

Duncan said, 'I'd see my mother again.'

'There you are. A man should see his mother before he dies. You can ask her why the hell she married your father.'

They laughed again. 'But, how could we do it?' asked Duncan at last. 'We'd have to find a canal or something.'

'No, we wouldn't. You can drown in four inches of water; I thought everybody knew that. It's a scientific fact. Don't you keep your bath filled up in this house, against fire?'

Duncan looked at him. 'Bloody hell, you're right!'

'Let's do it, D.P.!'

They got to their feet. 'Bring the letter,' said Duncan, 'and a drawing-pin. – Wait! Let me comb my hair.'

'The man wants to comb his hair,' said Alec, 'at a time like this!'

'Shut up!'

'Go ahead, Leslie Howard.'

Duncan stood at the dressing-table mirror and quickly tidied himself up. Then, as quietly as they could, he and Alec went out of the bedroom and down the hall, through the parlour and into the kitchen. The doors were open, in case of blast; Duncan closed them, very softly. He could hear his father as he did it, snoring his head off. Alec whispered, 'Your father sounds like a Messerschmitt!' And that set them off laughing, all over again.

They put the kitchen light on. The shadeless bulb was rather weak, and made the room spring into life in flat, drab colours: the stained white of the sink, the grey and yellow of the patched linoleum floor, the brown-as-gravy of the woodwork. The bath was next to the kitchen table, against the wall; Duncan's father had boxed it in with more gravy-coloured wood, years before, and made a cover for it. The cover was used as a draining-board: it had bits of crockery on it, and some of Duncan's and his father's underwear, soaking in soda in a big zinc pail. Duncan blushed when he saw this, and quickly moved the pail aside. Alec moved the crockery, piece by piece, to the kitchen table.

Then they each took an end of the bath cover and lifted it off.

The water beneath was left over from a bath that Duncan's father had taken days before. It was cloudy, and filled with little hairs – coarse, curling hairs, more shaming even than the underwear, so that Duncan took one look at them and had to turn away. He made fists of his hands. If his father had been before him now, he would have punched him. 'That swine!' he said.

'There's about enough, anyway,' said Alec dubiously. 'How will we do it, though? We can't both lie in it at once. I suppose we could hold each other's heads in?'

The thought of putting his face in that filthy water, which had sloshed round his father's feet, his private parts, his arse, made Duncan want to be sick. 'I don't want to,' he said.

'Well, I don't, much,' Alec answered. 'But look here, we can't afford to be choosy.'

'Let's make it gas, after all, and risk it.'

'Shall we?'

'Yes.'

'All right. Or— Crikey, I've got it!' Alec snapped his fingers. 'Let's hang ourselves!'

The idea was almost a relief. Duncan didn't mind what they did, now, so long as it didn't involve his father's bath-water. They put the draining-board cover back in place, then looked about, at the walls and ceiling, in search of hooks, something to tie ropes to. They decided at last that the pulley of the laundry-rack would take the weight of one of them; the other could hang himself, they thought, from the coat-hook on the back of the kitchen door.

'Have you got any rope?' asked Alec next.

'I've got this,' said Duncan, with a flash of inspiration. He meant the cord of his dressing-gown. He untied it, pulled it out of its loops, and tested the strength of it with his hands. 'I think it'll hold me.'

'That's you taken care of, then. What about me? You haven't got another, I suppose?'

'I've got plenty of belts and things like that. I've got plenty of ties.'

'A tie would do it.'

'Shall I go and get one? What kind do you want?'

Alec frowned. 'A black one, I suppose. No! The one with the blue and gold stripe. That looks like a university tie.'

'What difference does that make?'

'There might be photographs. It'll make more of an impression.'

'All right,' said Duncan reluctantly – for, as it happened, he felt about that particular tie more or less as he'd felt about his fountain pen: that it was a good one, and belonged to him; and what was the point of using one like that, when an ordinary one would do? But he wouldn't argue about it now. He went quietly back through the parlour and hall, into the bedroom, and got the tie out. He could hear his father, still snoring, and he stood for a second in the darkness, with the tie in his hand, half wanting to go in and give his father a kicking, to scream and yell into his face. *You bloody old fool! I'm going to kill myself! I'm going to go out to the kitchen and actually do it! Wake up, can't you?*

His father snored on. Duncan went softly back out to Alec. 'My old man sounds like a bloody hurricane now!' he said as he closed the kitchen door.

But Alec didn't answer. He'd put the dressing-gown cord down and was standing at the sink, half-turned away. He'd picked something up from beside the taps.

'Duncan,' he said, in a queer, low voice. 'Look at this.'

He had Duncan's father's old-fashioned razor in his hand. He'd drawn out the blade, and was gazing at it as if mesmerised – as if he had to tear his eyes away from it to look at Duncan. He said, 'I'm going to use this. That's what I'm going to do. You can hang yourself if you like. But I'm going to use this. It's better than a rope. It's quicker, and cleaner. I'm going to cut my throat.'

'Your throat?' said Duncan. He looked at Alec's slender white neck – at the cords in it, and the Adam's apple, that seemed hard, not soft like something you could slice through . . .

'It's sharp, isn't it?' Alec put his finger to the blade – then quickly drew the finger back and sucked it. 'God!' He laughed. 'It's sharp as anything. It won't hurt at all, if we do it quick enough.'

'Are you sure?'

'Of course I'm sure. It's how they kill animals, isn't it? I'm going to do it, right now. You'll have to go second. Will you mind? There might be a bit of mess, I'm afraid. The best thing will be, not to look too hard. If only we had two of them! Then we could do it at the same time . . . Look.' He gestured with the razor to the bit of paper he'd written their letter on. 'Be a good chap and pin that letter to the wall. Somewhere they'll see it.'

Duncan picked up the letter and the pin; but glanced anxiously at the razor. He said, 'Don't do it while my back's turned, will you?' He was afraid to look away . . . He gazed quickly about for a place, and ended up fixing the note to the door of a cupboard. 'Is that all right?'

Alec nodded. 'Yes, that's good.'

He'd begun to grow breathless. He was still holding the open razor as if simply madly admiring it; but now, as Duncan watched, he grasped its handle more firmly in his two hands, lifted the blade and put it tight against his throat. He put it just below the bend of his right jaw, where the skin was quivering because of the pulse.

Duncan took an involuntary step towards him. He said nervously, 'You're not going to do it straight away?'

Alec's eyelids fluttered. 'I'm going to do it in just a minute.'

'How does it feel?'

'It feels OK.'

627

'Are you scared?'

'A bit,' said Alec. 'How about you? You've gone white as a sheet! Don't faint, before it's your turn.' He changed his grip on the handle of the razor. He closed his eyes, and stood still . . . Then, with his eyes shut tight, and in a slightly different voice from before, he said, 'What will you miss, Duncan?'

Duncan bit his lip. 'I don't know. Nothing! No, I'll miss Viv . . . What about you?'

'I'll miss books,' said Alec, 'and music and art, and fine buildings', so that Duncan wished that he'd said that too, instead of his sister. 'But those things are all gone, anyway. A year from now, people will start to forget that there ever were those things.'

He opened his eyes, and swallowed, then changed his hold again. Duncan could see that his fingers were sweating; he could see the marks they left on the razor's tortoiseshell handle. He didn't want Alec to do it, now. The whole thing had raced forward too quickly. Again he almost wished that his father would wake up, come out, and stop them. What was the point of having a father, if he let you do things like this? He said – as a way of keeping Alec talking; as a way of stringing everything out – 'What do you think will happen to us, Alec, after we die?'

Alec thought about it, with the blade still close to his throat. Then, 'Nothing,' he said quietly. 'We'll just go out, like lights do. There can't be anything else. There can't be a God. A God would've stopped the war! There can't be a heaven or a hell or anything like that. *This* is hell, where we are. And if there is a place, then we'll be there together, anyway.' He held Duncan's gaze, with his blazing red-rimmed eyes. 'That would be the worst thing, wouldn't it?' he said simply. 'To be there on your own?'

Duncan nodded. 'Yes,' he said. 'Yes, that would be awful.'

Alec drew in his breath. The pulse in his neck began to beat more quickly, to almost jump against the blade. But when he spoke, he spoke as if casually, so that Duncan thought he was joking, and almost laughed. He said, 'See you then, Duncan.' And he tightened his grip and raised his elbows, as if about to swing a bat; and then he cut.

'It's this way,' the warden was saying. Kay and Mickey followed him, carefully, over the rubble.

The rubble, until very recently, had been a four-storey terraced Pimlico house. The house appeared, in the almost darkness, to have been neatly plucked from its socket. A woman had been killed outright by the blast; her body had already been removed, by another driver. But a girl was still caught by her legs in the rubble; the Rescue and Demolition workers were planning to set up a hoist to lift the beams that were pinning her. They couldn't do that, however, until they'd brought out another woman and a boy who were thought to be trapped in the basement.

'We've sent for lights,' the warden said, 'but the fellows have been digging for half an hour. One's managed to get himself pretty badly cut.'

'How long,' Kay asked, 'before they get to the basement?'

'I'd say, an hour. Maybe two.'

'And the girl who's caught?'

'Yes, take a look at her, will you? She seems all right, but that might be shock, I don't know. She's over there. One of the men is with her, keeping her spirits up.'

He showed Kay where to walk. She left Mickey to see to the man who'd got cut, and began to pick her way to the back of the site. Her steps broke glass; once a board gave way beneath her and she sank into a mess of plaster and wood almost to the thigh. The crack of the board as it snapped was a sharp one, and she heard a girl cry out at the sound.

'It's all right,' said someone, softly. Kay flipped up her torch and made out the figure of a man, squatting on the rubble twenty feet away. He had his arms on his knees, his ARP helmet pushed matily back; he saw Kay coming, and lifted his hand. 'Ambulance? We're here. Watch out for the doodah, look.' He gestured to an object in her path: pale, gleaming, oddly shaped. It took her a moment to realise that it was a lavatory. 'Been blown clean out of its moorings,' said the man, straightening up. 'Lost its seat, though.'

He reached forward to help guide Kay over the

last stretch of chaos; and as she drew nearer to him she noticed something at his feet. She took it to be a heap of curtains or bedclothes, at first; but now, as she watched, the bedclothes seemed to billow or bulge, as if inflated from beneath; and an arm and a white face showed – showed as palely, almost, as the displaced lavatory. It was the girl who was trapped. She was covered in a film of plaster, and buried to the waist by a mess of beams and bricks. She was pushing herself up by her arms, to look at Kay. Kay went to her side and squatted, as the man had.

'I say, you are in a fix.' She gave the man a nod, and he went off.

The girl put her hand on Kay's ankle. 'Please,' she said, 'can you tell me?' Her voice was gritty, and light with fear. She coughed. 'Are they coming to get me out?'

'They are,' said Kay, 'just as soon as they can. Right now, however, I have to see if you're all right. May I feel for your pulse?' She took the girl's powdery arm. The pulse was quick, but pretty strong. 'There. And now, will you mind very much if I just shine this torch into your eyes? It won't take a moment.'

She put her fingers to the girl's chin, to steady her face. The girl blinked in apprehension. The rims and corners of her eyes were pink as a rabbit's against the white of the plaster dust. Her pupils shrank from the probing of the light. She seemed young, but not as young as Kay had thought her at first; perhaps twenty-four or -five. She turned her head before the beam of the torch was lowered, and tried to peer across the site.

'What are they doing?' she asked, of the men.

'They think there might be people,' Kay told her, 'a woman and a boy, trapped in the basement of your house.'

'Madeleine and Tony?'

'Are those their names? Are they friends of yours?'

'Madeleine is Mrs Finch's daughter.'

'Mrs Finch?'

'My landlady. She—'

She didn't go on. Kay guessed that Mrs Finch was the woman who'd been killed. She began to feel the girl's arms and shoulders. 'Can you tell me,' she said as she did it, 'if you think you might be injured?'

The girl swallowed, and coughed again. 'I don't know.'

'Can you move your legs?'

'I think I could, a minute ago. I don't like to try, in case it topples the stuff and it crushes me.'

'Can you feel your feet?'

'I don't know. They're cold. It is just the cold, isn't it? What else could it be? It's not something worse, is it?'

She'd begun to shiver. She was dressed in what must have been a nightdress and dressing-gown, but the ARP man had put a blanket across her shoulders for extra warmth. Kay drew the blanket tighter, then looked around for something else. She found what might have been a bath-sheet; but it was sodden, and black with soot. She threw it away, then saw a cushion, its horsehair stuffing spilling from a gash in its velvet case. She put this against the girl's side, where she thought the sharp edges of rubble might be cutting or pressing against her.

The girl didn't notice. She was peering across the site again. She said, in an agitated way, 'What's that? Have they switched on lights? Tell them they mustn't!'

A lorry had come, bringing a single lamp and a little generator, and the R and D men had fitted them up and set them running. They'd tried to keep the lamp dim by stretching a square of tarpaulin above it; but light was leaking across the site, changing the look and the feel of things. Kay glanced about and saw quite plainly objects which, a moment before, had baffled her eye: an ironing-board with broken legs, a bucket, a little box to which someone had pasted shells . . . The lavatory lost its nacreous glamour and showed its stains. The walls of the houses rising up on either side of the heap of rubble were revealed to be not walls at all, but open rooms, with beds and chairs and tables and fireplaces in them, all intact.

'Tell them to turn off the lights!' the girl was still saying; but she was looking around, too, as Kay was – as if understanding, for the first time, the nature of the chaos in which she was trapped, perhaps seeing fragments of her old life in it. Then, 'Oh!' she said. The men had begun to hammer. She shuddered with every thud. 'What are they doing?'

'They have to work quickly,' said Kay. 'There might be gas, or water, you see, filling up the basement.'

'Gas or water?' asked the girl, as if not understanding. Then she winced, as another thud came. She must have been able to feel the blows through the rubble. She began to cry. She rubbed at her face, and the plaster grew thick with her tears. Kay touched her shoulder.

'Are you in pain?'

The girl shook her head. 'I can't tell. I don't think so. It's just – I'm so frightened.'

She put both her hands across her eyes and at last grew silent and almost still. When she took the hands away and spoke again her voice had changed, she sounded calmer, and older. 'What a coward you must think me,' she said.

Kay said gently, 'Not at all.'

The girl wiped her eyes and nose on a corner of the blanket. She made a face against the taste and the feel of the grit on her tongue. She said, 'I don't suppose you could give me a cigarette?'

'I'm afraid I can't, while there might be gas.'

'Of course not. Oh!' The men were hammering again. She held herself rigid.

Kay watched, growing rigid too, in sympathy. 'I think you must be in pain,' she said at last. 'There's a doctor coming. You must be brave just a little bit longer.'

Then they both turned their heads. Mickey was making her way towards them, her boots making boards crack, as Kay's had.

'Blimey!' she said, seeing the lavatory. Then she made out the figure of the girl. 'Blimey again! You *are* in trouble.'

'You'll forgive us,' Kay said to her, 'if we don't get up?' She turned back to the girl. 'This is my great friend, Miss Iris Carmichael. Did you ever see anything less like an iris in your life? Be nice to her, and she might let you call her Mickey.'

The girl was looking up, blinking. Mickey crouched and took her hand, squeezing her fingers. 'Not broken? Glad to hear it. How do you do?'

'Not so well just now,' said Kay, when Mickey got no answer. 'But soon to be better. But, what a rotten hostess I am!' She turned back to the girl. 'I never took the trouble to find out your name.'

The girl swallowed. She said awkwardly, 'It's Giniver.'

'Jennifer?'

The girl shook her head. 'Giniver. Helen Giniver.'

'Helen Giniver,' repeated Kay, as if trying it out. Then: 'Mrs, or Miss?'

Mickey laughed. She said softly, 'Give the girl a break.'

But, 'Miss,' said Helen, not understanding.

Kay shook her hand, as Mickey had, and introduced herself. Helen looked into her face, then turned to Mickey. 'I thought you were a boy,' she said, beginning to cough again.

'Everyone does,' answered Mickey. 'I'm used to it. Here, have some water.'

She had brought a flask. While Helen drank, Kay fished out an injury label from her jacket pocket, and filled in various details; she attached the label to Helen's collar. 'There. Just like a parcel, you see?' Then she and Mickey stood up for a moment, to watch the men at work on the demolition.

The men moved with what seemed maddening slowness: for there was something queer, Mickey said, about the way the house had fallen, and it made the job a stickier one than they'd supposed. But at last they put their hammers aside and fixed ropes to a flattened section of wall, and began to pull. The wall was raised, and stood eerily upright for a moment; then the ropes tugged it backwards and it toppled and broke, sending out a new cloud of dust.

In the patch of freshly exposed ground there seemed only more rubble and a mess of twisted pipes; but a man moved quickly forward to the pipes, took up a brick, and gave a series of taps on the lead. He held up his hand. Another man called, sharply, for silence. The little generator was switched off, and the scene grew dark again, and still. There was the drone, of course, of aeroplanes, the thudding of the guns from Hyde Park and elsewhere; but those sounds had been there, it seemed incessantly, for the past six months: you filtered them out, Kay found, as you filtered out the roaring of the blood in your own ears.

The man with the brick said something too low for Kay to catch. He gave another tap on the pipes . . . And then, very faintly, there came a cry, like the mewing of a cat, from beneath the rubble.

Kay had heard such sounds before: they were thrilling and unnerving, much more so than the sight of blasted limbs and mucked-up bodies. They made her shiver. She let out her breath. The site had grown noisy and alive again, as if in response to some small electric charge. The generator was started up, and the light switched back on. The men moved in and began to work with a new kind of purpose.

A car drew up, bumping over the broken road, a white cross gleaming from its bonnet. Mickey went to meet it. Kay hesitated, then squatted again at Helen's side.

Helen was bracing herself awkwardly against the rubble. She'd been straining to listen, too. 'Those voices,' she said, 'that was Madeleine and Tony, wasn't it? Are they all right?'

'We hope they are.'

'They will be, won't they? But how can they be? Mrs Finch—' She shook her head. 'I saw them taking her away, before you came. We'd been out in the kitchen. She wanted her glasses, that was all. I said I'd run up and get them for her. They were on the table, beside her bed. I had them, right here—' She held up her hand and looked at her palm, then gazed around, as if suddenly bewildered. 'She didn't want me to go,' she said. 'She wanted Tony to do it, she wanted Tony to go.'

Her voice had begun to shake. She looked at Kay, her eyes wide open. Then, 'Listen,' she said suddenly. 'Listen, would you mind very much if I were to hold your hand?'

'Mind?' said Kay, moved by the simplicity of the request. 'Good heavens! I would have offered it at the start; only, you know, I didn't want to seem forward.'

She took hold of Helen's fingers and began to chafe them between her own; then she raised them, and breathed on them – breathed slowly, steadily, on the knuckles and the palm.

Helen kept her gaze on her face as she did it, her eyes still wide. She said, 'You must be so brave. You and your friend. I could never be brave like that.'

'Nonsense,' said Kay, still chafing her hand. 'Is that better? It's easier to be out in the fuss, that's all, than sitting home listening to it.'

Helen's fingers were chill and dusty in her own, but the palm and the pads of the fingertips were soft, yielding. Kay pressed them harder, then let them go. 'Here's the doctor,' she said, hearing cracking boards again. And she added quietly: 'That was a secret, by the way, about its being easier to be out.'

The doctor was a brisk, handsome woman of forty-five or so. She was dressed in dungarees and a turban. 'Hello,' she said, seeing Helen, 'what have we here?'

Kay moved away while the woman squatted at Helen's side. She heard her murmur, and caught Helen's replies: 'No . . . I don't know . . . A little . . . Thank you . . .'

'Impossible to tell the extent of the trouble,' said the doctor, joining Kay again, wiping dust from her hands, 'until the legs are freed. I don't think there's any blood loss, but she seems pretty feverish, which might be from pain. I've given her a shot of morphia, take her mind off things.' She stretched, and grimaced.

Kay asked, 'Bad night?'

'You might say that. Nine dead from a shell on Victoria Street, four gone at Chelsea. One here, I gather? We were told this blasted woman and her boy would be out for us to take a look at; no time to hang about now. There's a chap with his hands blown off, apparently, over in Vauxhall.'

As she spoke, a demolition man called out that there was no more fear of gas, and automatically she reached into her pocket and brought out a packet of cigarettes. She opened it up, and held it out.

'Give me two, could you?' said Kay.

'You've a nerve.'

Kay laughed. 'The first's for me; the other's medicinal.' She lit them both from the woman's lighter, and went back to Helen. 'Hey,' she said gently, 'look what I have.'

She put a cigarette between Helen's lips, then took one of her hands and held it, simply, as before. Helen's eyes, as she narrowed them against the smoke, were darker, and her voice had changed again.

'How kind you are,' she said.

'Don't mention it.'

'I seem to be drunk. How can that be?'

'It's the morphia, I expect.'

'How nice that doctor was!'

'Yes, wasn't she?'

'Should you like to be a doctor?'

'Not much,' said Kay. 'Should you?'

'I know a boy who means to be one.'

'Yes?'

'A boy I was in love with.'

'Ah.'

'He threw me over for another girl.'

'Silly chap.'

'He's gone into the army now. You're not in love with anyone, are you?'

'No,' said Kay. 'Someone's in love with me, as it happens. A grand person, too . . . But that's another secret. I'm thinking of the morphia, you see. I'm counting on your not being able to remember any of this.'

'Why is it a secret?'

'I promised the person it would be, that's all.'

'But you won't love him back?'

Kay smiled. 'You'd think I would, wouldn't you? But, isn't it funny – we never seem to love the people we ought to, I can't think why . . .'

'Don't let go of my hand, will you?'

'Never.'

'Are you holding it? I can't feel it.'

'There! Do you feel that?'

'Yes, I feel that. Keep it like that, will you? Just like that.'

They smoked in silence, and presently Helen seemed to doze: the cigarette smouldered forgotten in her hand, so Kay took it gently from her fingers and smoked the last of it herself. The demolition work went on. From time to time the drone of planes and the thump of shells grew louder; there were spectacular flashes in the sky, green and red, and tumbling flares. Now and then Mickey came over, to sit beside Kay and to yawn. Two or three times Helen stirred, and mumbled, or spoke quite clearly: 'Are you there?' 'I can't see you.' 'Where are you?'

'I'm here,' Kay answered, every time, and squeezed her hand a little harder.

'She'll be yours for life,' said Mickey.

And then, finally, the demolition work revealed a fallen staircase, and when this was raised by a winch the woman and her son were found beneath it, almost perfectly unharmed. The boy came out first – head-first, as he must have come out of the womb; but rigid, dry, dusty, his hair an old man's. He and his mother stood quite stunned. 'Where's Mum?' Kay heard the woman say. Mickey went to them with blankets, and Kay got to her feet.

Helen felt her move, and woke, and reached for her. 'What is it?'

'Madeleine and Tony are freed.'

'Are they all right?'

'They seem to be. Can you see? Now the men will come and free you.'

Helen shook her head. 'Don't leave me. Please!'

'I have to go.'

'Please don't.'

'I must go, so the men can free you.'

'I'm afraid of it!'

'I have to drive the woman and her son to the hospital.'

'Your friend can do it, can't she?'

Kay laughed. 'Look here, do you want to get me chucked out of the service?'

She put her hand to Helen's head, to brush back the dusty hair from her brow. She did it casually enough; but the sight of Helen's anxious expression – the large, darkened eyes, above the plaster-white cheeks – made her hesitate.

'Just a second,' she said. 'You must look your best, for the R and D men.'

She ran to Mickey, and returned to Helen with the flask of water. She fished out her handkerchief, and wet it; and began, very gently, to wipe the dust from Helen's face. She started at her brow, and worked downwards. 'Just close your eyes,' she murmured. She brushed at Helen's lashes, and then at the little dints at the side of her nose, the groove above her lip, the corners of her mouth, her cheeks and chin.

'Kay!' called Mickey.

'All right! I'm coming!'

The dust fell away. The skin beneath was pink, plump, astonishingly smooth. Kay brushed a little longer, then moved her hand to the curve of Helen's jaw and cupped it with her palm – not wanting to leave her, after all; gazing at her in a sort of wonder; unable to believe that something so fresh and so unmarked could have emerged from so much chaos.

ACKNOWLEDGEMENTS

Thanks to Lennie Goodings and staff at Time Warner Book Group UK, to Julie Grau and staff at the Penguin Group, to Judith Murray and everyone at Greene & Heaton Ltd; and to the inestimable Sally O-J.

Thanks to Hirani Himona, Sarah Plescia, Alison Oram, Liz Woodcraft, Amy Rubin, Fidelis Morgan, Val Bond, Betty Saunders, Robyn Vinten, Bridget Ibbs, Ron Waters, Mary Waters, Caroline Halliday, Mary Garner, Trudie Sacker, Vicky Wharton, Betty Vaughan, Jennifer Vaughan, Pamela Pearce, Roger Haworth, and Lesley Hall; to Terry Spurr at the London Ambulance Service Museum, Christine Goode and Chani Jones at Price's Candles Ltd, Jan Pimblett and staff at the London Metropolitan Archives, staff at the Imperial War Museum Archive, staff at the City of Westminster Archives Centre, staff at Camden Local Studies and Archives Centre; and to the various people with whom, over the past four years, I've had conversations about the 1940s – especially those who've given me advice and ideas on ladies' underwear, electric light fittings, and silk pyjamas.

Thanks to Martina Cole for generously bidding to have her name appear in this novel at an Immortality Auction on behalf of the Medical Foundation for the Care of Victims of Torture; and for kindly giving me permission to use her name in abbreviated form.

I drew ideas and inspiration for *The Night Watch* from many sources, including novels and films of the 1940s, photographs, maps, diaries, letters, and modern accounts of life during and after the Second World War. The non-fiction I found most useful includes the following: Verily Anderson, *Spam Tomorrow* (London, 1956); Peter Baker, *Time Out of Life* (London, 1961); George Beardmore, *Civilians at War: Journals 1938–1946* (London, 1984); Barbara Bell, *Just Take Your Frock Off: A Lesbian Life* (Brighton, 1999); A. S. G. Butler, *Recording Ruin* (London, 1942); Gerald Fancourt Clayton, *The Wall is Strong: The Life of a Prison Governor* (London, 1958); Rupert Croft Cooke, *The Verdict of You All* (London, 1955); Diana Cooper, *Trumpets from the Steep* (London, 1960); Michael De-la-Noy, *Denton Welch: The Making of a Writer* (Harmondsworth, 1984); Mary Baker Eddy, *Science and Health: With Key to the Scriptures* (Boston, 1906); Jill Gardiner, *From the Closet to the Screen: Women at the Gateways Club, 1945–85* (London, 2003); Pete Grafton, *You, You & You!: The People Out of Step with World War II* (London, 1981); Jenny Hartley (ed.), *Hearts Undefeated: Women's Writing of the Second World War* (London, 1994);

Jenny Hartley (ed.), *Millions Like Us: British Women's Fiction of the Second World War* (London, 1997); Anthony Heckstall-Smith, *Eighteen Months* (London, 1954); Vere Hodgson, *Few Eggs and No Oranges: A Diary Showing How Unimportant People in London and Birmingham Lived Throughout the War Years 1940–1945* (London, 1999); Elizabeth Jane Howard, *Slipstream: A Memoir* (London, 2002); Audrey Johnson, *Do March in Step Girls: A Wren's Story* (Sandford, North Somerset, 1997); Edward Ancel Kimball, *Lectures and Articles on Christian Science* (Chesterton, Indiana, 1921); Henrietta Frances Lord, *Christian Science Healing* (London, 1888); Raynes Minns, *Bombers and Mash: The Domestic Front 1939–45* (London, 1980); Barbara Nixon, *Raiders Overhead* (London, 1943); Frank Norman, *Bang to Rights: An Account of Prison Life* (London, 1958); Patrick O'Hara, *I Got No Brother* (London, 1967); Frances Partridge, *A Pacifist's War* (London, 1978); Phyllis Pearsall, *Women at War* (Aldershot, 1990); Colin Perry, *Boy in the Blitz* (London, 1972); Philip Priestley, *Jail Journeys: The English Prison Experience Since 1918* (London, 1989); Barbara Pym, *A Very Private Eye: The Diaries, Letters and Notebooks of Barbara Pym*, ed. Hazel Holt and Hilary Pym (London, 1984); Angela Raby, *The Forgotten Service: Auxiliary Ambulance Station 39, Weymouth Mews* (London, 1999); Julian Maclaren Ross, *Memoirs of the Forties* (London, 1965); Dorothy Sheridan (ed.), *Wartime Women: A Mass-Observation Anthology 1937–45,*

(London, 2000); Nerina Shute, *We Mixed Our Drinks: The Story of a Generation* (London, 1945); Clifford Simmons (ed.), *The Objectors* (London, 1965); Maureen Waller, *London 1945: Life in the Debris of War* (London, 2004); Denton Welch, *The Journals of Denton Welch*, ed. Michael De-la-Noy (London, 1984); Maureen Wells, *Entertaining Eric: Letters From the Home Front 1941–44* (London, 1988); Peter Wildeblood, *Against the Law* (London, 1955); Joan Wyndham, *Love Lessons: A Wartime Diary* (London, 1985); Joan Wyndham, *Love is Blue: A Wartime Diary* (London, 1986).